The Waiting Hours is Ellie Dean's thirteenth novel in her Cliffehaven series. She lives in a tiny hamlet set deep in the heart of the South Downs in Sussex, which has been her home for many years and where she raised her three children.

To find out more visit www.ellie-dean.co.uk

ELLIE DEAN

The Waiting Hours

arrow books

1 3 5 7 9 10 8 6 4 2

Arrow Books
20 Vauxhall Bridge Road
London SW1V 2SA

Arrow Books is part of the Penguin Random House group of companies
whose addresses can be found at global.penguinrandomhouse.com

Penguin
Random House
UK

First published in Great Britain by Arrow Books in 2017

www.penguin.co.uk

A CIP catalogue record for this book is available from the British Library

ISBN 9781784758103
ISBN 9781473539792 (ebook)

Typeset in 11.5/14.5 pt Palatino by Jouve (UK), Milton Keynes
Printed and bound in Great Britain by Clays Ltd, St Ives plc

Penguin Random House is committed to a
sustainable future for our business, our readers
and our planet. This book is made from Forest
Stewardship Council® certified paper.

This book is dedicated to the American troops who lost their lives during the terrible events in Lyme Bay. And to the people of the South Hams of Devon, who gave up their homes, their farms and businesses for a year so that the rehearsals for D-Day would ensure a successful invasion into France.

A note from the author

The research into what happened at Lyme Bay and on Slapton Sands during April 1944 was complicated by the fact that so many reports were conflicting, and quite often tainted by rumour and differing points of view. I have done my best to keep to the facts, and fully accept any errors as my own.

The story of Slapton Sands is one I've wanted to write since I began the Cliffehaven series, and in order to do so I have had to go back on myself in time. In *The Waiting Hours* I've retraced some of the steps covered in *Until You Come Home*, which ended in April 1944, but from a new perspective. I hope you still love this book as much as I loved writing it.

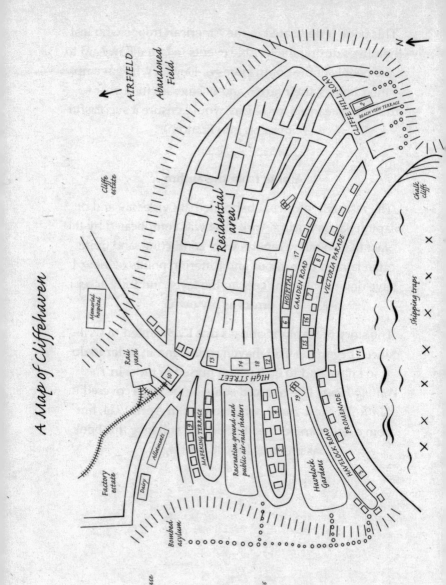

A Map of Cliffehaven

1 Café
2 Beach View Boarding House
3 Doris's House
4 Vet
5 Doctor's Surgery
6 Cliffehaven General
7 Lilac Tea rooms
8 The Anchor
9 Ruby and Ethel's House
10 Station
11 Pier
12 Home and Colonial Stores
13 Plummer Roddis
14 Town Hall
15 Fire Station
16 Uniform Factory
17 Bombed School
18 Bombed Odeon Cinema
19 Bombed Church

AIRFIELD

Abandoned Field

Cliffe estate

Memorial hospital

Rail yard

Factory estate

Dairy

Allotments

Bombed asylum

Recreation ground and public air-raid shelters

MAFEKING TERRACE

HIGH STREET

Havelock Gardens

HAVELOCK ROAD

PROMENADE

HOSPITAL

CAMDEN ROAD

VICTORIA PARADE

CLIFFE HILL ROAD

BEACH VIEW TERRACE

Residential area

Chalk cliffs

Shipping traps

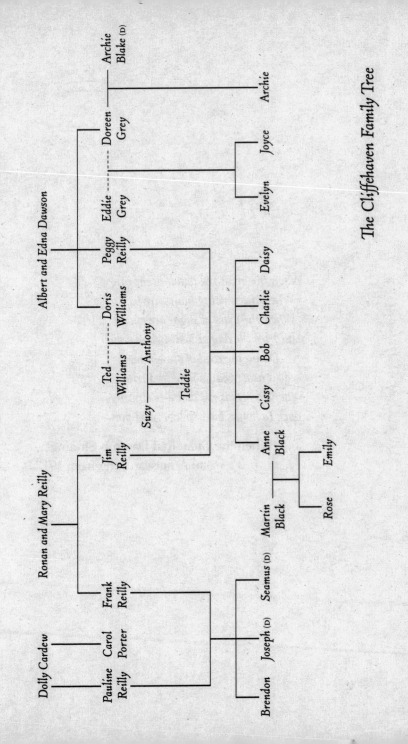

The Cliffehaven Family Tree

When the great red dawn is shining,
  When the waiting hours are past,
  When the tears of night are ended
And I see the day at last, I shall come
    Down the road of sunshine,
   To a heart that is fond and true,
When the great red dawn Is shining,
Back to home, back to love, and you.

'When the Great Red Dawn Is Shining' –
an American song from 1917

PART ONE
NOVEMBER 1943

1

Devon

The sun had barely risen over the eastern hills when Carol set out from Coombe Farm with the horse and cart. Dressed in the land-army uniform of beige sweater, shirt and khaki dungarees beneath the standard-issue gabardine mac and thick scarf, she was insulated against the cold, though she knew she must look rather ridiculous with her fair curls tucked beneath the hand-knitted tea cosy-style hat.

Carol had always liked these early hours when she made the milk delivery, especially at this time of year when the steep-sided coombs were shrouded in mist. The dew glittered on the freshly ploughed earth, and a hush lay over the scattered huddles of villages and the patchwork quilt of fields and grazing pastures. Her work as a land girl suited her perfectly, and the fact that she could go home to her cottage every night was an added bonus, for she guarded her privacy and independence fiercely.

Hector the shire had plodded patiently along the winding cobbled streets, where thick-walled thatched cottages nestled against one another like loaves on a baker's tray, and the housewives came out with their billycans to collect their milk ration and make a fuss of him. He'd negotiated the narrow lanes winding between high banks to stop by farm gates atop lonely hills and waited stoically as she'd exchanged empty churns for the heavy full ones, and then carried on with a whicker of pleasure as they'd approached Slapton village, for this was where he would head for home and a well-deserved breakfast.

Carol held the reins loosely in her gloved hands and let her thoughts wander. There was no need to guide Hector as he'd been doing this round for years, and she enjoyed these quiet moments after the earlier hectic activity in the milking shed, the silence broken only by the sound of the heavy clomp of his hooves on the stony tracks, the jingle of harness and the occasional cry of a sea bird.

Carol's dreamy mood was broken by a familiar sound and she looked out towards the distant seashore and the freshwater lake that glittered in the early sunlight behind its shingle bar. With a smile of pleasure she watched the flock of geese rising from Slapton Ley, their honking conversation echoing in the stillness as they formed a chevron and flew towards Kingsbridge estuary. It was a sight she'd seen many times before, but still it entranced her, confirming once again how very lucky she was to live in this special part of England.

With the lighter load, Hector had picked up the pace as they climbed the hill towards Slapton, the empty churns rattling against one another, the harness jangling with every thud of his hooves. Now Carol could see the ruin of the fourteenth-century tower looming over the thatched roofs of the village. The imposing remains had once been part of an ecclesiastic college and chantry before the dissolution; the cottages for the men who'd built it long since converted into the quaint and popular Tower Inn, the chantry now a rather grand private home.

As they crested the hill Carol could see that the village was coming to life. They approached the village school and she caught sight of her best friend, Betty Wellings, who was busy shepherding her small charges through the door into the single classroom. Betty was small and fair and had just celebrated her twenty-fifth birthday. Had fate been kinder, she would have liked to have joined the WAAFs, but she'd been struck down by polio as a child and now walked with a calliper and cane. Yet that couldn't overshadow her enthusiasm for life, or her pleasure in teaching the children.

Betty must have heard Hector's approach, for she looked up and waved, her beaming smile lighting up her pretty face. 'I'll see you at the weekend,' she called over the heads of the children. 'Are we still going to the pictures?'

'Two o'clock matinee,' Carol replied. 'See you about eleven, and we can have some lunch in town first.'

Hector plodded on and Betty went back to her little ones, but Carol's thoughts remained on her friend. They were looking forward to a day out in Kingsbridge, for it was rare for Carol to have a Saturday off, and Betty usually went out with her young man, Ken, whose family owned a large farm at Chillington.

Carol thought Ken was a bit of a stick-in-the-mud

and not nearly imaginative or bright enough for Betty. They'd been walking out for two years and Betty still hoped he'd pop the question, which made Carol wonder if perhaps Ken was stringing her along. If that was the case then Carol vowed to give him a good piece of her mind, for Betty didn't deserve to be treated so badly after all she'd gone through. Her years in the orphanage, the trials of recovering from polio and the struggle to attain her teaching certificate showed that Betty was not easily defeated, but Carol suspected that if Ken let her down, she'd find it hard to recover.

Hector's hooves rang on the cobbles as they entered the village, and Carol's gaze was drawn as ever towards the cemetery surrounding the church of St James the Great. She felt the familiar prick of tears and blinked them away, for they couldn't bring David back, or breathe life into the stillborn baby girl who now lay beside him in that lovingly tended plot. And yet the pain was still raw after eight months, the loss like an open wound which seemed no nearer to being healed.

The shire continued on past the steep cobbled lane where Thyme Cottage overlooked the sweeping fields of the old manor house right down to the sea. David had inherited it from his widowed father who'd died of lung disease two years before the war, and he'd set up his successful carpentry business there before the world had been thrown into turmoil and everything changed.

They'd met at a wedding in Dartmouth and, following a whirlwind romance, had been married in the centuries-old village church of St James the Great. David had carried Carol over the threshold into Thyme Cottage for what they'd hoped would be a long, happy future together, but the declaration of war had ruined that dream, and once he'd enlisted they'd had only a few snatched days of leave to share over the following years – and now he was gone.

David had been with Montgomery's Eighth Army when they'd broken through the Mareth Line in Tunisia back in March. The news of his death had come shortly after she'd written excitedly to tell him about her pregnancy. She'd known he'd received that letter, for it had been opened when it was returned to her along with the rest of his effects, but there had clearly been no time for him to write a reply. However, the shock of losing him had made her careless and clumsy, and a heavy fall down a slippery flagstone step had brought the baby into the world too soon. The only solace was that her precious little girl was with David, and that one day all three of them would be together again.

Carol took a quavering breath. David used to say he admired her strength of character and her determination to make the best of things no matter how difficult life became, and she'd certainly been put to that test. Although he was no longer here, she needed to prove to him – and herself – that his faith in her was justified; that she wouldn't weaken and let the grief overwhelm her. At times she found it almost unbearably hard, but even in her darkest moments she knew it was important to hold on to the fact that she was not the only one to have suffered tragedy. If her elder sister

Pauline could carry on with such courage, then so must she.

Fate had been so cruel to Pauline and her husband, Frank Reilly, taking two of their three sons during a U-boat attack in the Atlantic. Pauline was fifteen years older than Carol but they'd always been very close, and Carol dearly wished she could see her more often, especially during these past traumatic months. But Pauline lived down in Cliffehaven, and wartime travel restrictions made visiting almost impossible. Pauline had a great network of friends and family around her, including her sister-in-law, Peggy Reilly, who could always be relied upon in any moment of need, and although Carol had good friends in Slapton, there was nothing quite like family.

She let the reins go slack and wiped her eyes, determined not to give in to self-pity. She should be careful what she wished for, and be thankful that their mother was living far enough away from them both not to make things worse with her smothering and over-enthusiastic attempts to make up for all the years when she'd been absent.

Dorothy Cardew, or Dolly, as she preferred, was a woman possessed of a great passion for life which, unfortunately, had led her down many a wrong turning in her sixty-one years, and when things went haywire – as they often did – she'd return momentarily to her role as loving mother before leaving again. She was vivacious, glamorous, exasperating and totally unreliable, but her love for her daughters was never in doubt – which was why Carol and Pauline adored her.

But they both agreed that she would try the patience of a saint, and Carol was certain that Dolly would be ruffling a few feathers down in Bournemouth now she'd joined the Women's Institute.

Carol emerged from her thoughts as Hector drew to his usual stop outside the village pub, the Queen's Arms, where a gaggle of housewives were waiting with their tin pails. Greeting them all cheerfully, she jumped down and opened the tap on the large churn to pour the milk into the cans, stamping their ration books once they'd paid her. There were extra rations for Mrs Parnell and Mrs Rogers because they had children under five and were both expecting again.

Carol spent a few moments nattering with them and then climbed back onto the wagon and flicked the reins over the horse's back. They were her neighbours, and although she was an incomer from Dorset, they'd made her welcome and offered loving and practical support when she'd needed it most. But there was only so much sympathy to be had from friends and neighbours and she knew that the passing of time and the lack of nearby family meant she had little choice but to deal with her burden and get on with life as best she could.

The old horse snorted and broke into a trot which made the empty churns clang against one another in the wagon, the wheels rumbling over the rough ground as they headed out of the village towards the hillside hamlet of Beeson and the farm that sprawled along Tinsey Head.

Coombe dairy farm had been in the Burnley family

for over a century, and from the precipitous fields on the headland there was a magnificent panorama of the entire curving arc of Start Bay, from Start Point to Combe Point. Jack Burnley, the taciturn farmer, didn't believe in using new-fangled machinery or changing the routine his ancestors had laid down over the years, and still relied on his horses, steam traction engine and the trusty old methods of tilling, sowing and harvesting. His only concession to modernity was the huge generator which gave light and heat to the farmhouse, and ran the vast cooling vats and milking machines in the dairy.

He'd kept his prize-winning South Devon Red dairy herd despite the Ministry of Agriculture, Fisheries and Food demanding that he turn some of his grazing into fields of crops, for he'd grudgingly cleared the steepest fields for this purpose; and because his was the only dairy herd for many miles around, the officials had relented and he was now the main supplier of milk to the area.

Jack was waiting impatiently for Carol at the gate, dressed as always in wellington boots, baggy corduroy trousers and layers of ragged flannel shirts and disreputable sweaters, his filthy cap wedged firmly over his thick white hair. His face was as brown as a conker and etched with deep lines, his large hands roughened by over sixty years of being out in all weathers, but his eyes were the same bright blue as the sea on a sunny day, and on rare occasions would gleam with humour, reminding her of Pauline's father-in-law, Ron Reilly. Unfortunately this was not one of those moments.

'You be late,' he grumbled in his deep Devon burr. 'And I need there horse for pulling the tilling machine.'

Carol knew she wasn't late, but then Jack always liked to have something to moan about, so there was little point in arguing. 'Hector needs to be fed and watered and free of the shafts for a bit,' she said firmly. 'Why don't you use Harriet?'

His jaw worked as he regarded her sourly from beneath his shaggy brows, then he muttered something under his breath and slammed the gate behind her as she led Hector and the cart towards the dairy. 'Don't feed him too well or he'll think he be on holiday,' he called after her.

Carol ignored him, for she knew from having worked here for three years that under that dour exterior beat the heart of a man who really cared for his animals and begrudged them nothing. She grinned at the two land girls who came out of the dairy to help unload the empty churns. 'I see he's his usual cheerful self this morning,' she said, unhitching the wagon and giving Hector's neck a hearty pat.

There were actually three other land girls working on the farm alongside the elderly farm labourers who lived nearby. Maisie, Pru and Ida were all twenty-one, and had come from the East End of London where they'd been neighbours since childhood – until Hitler's Luftwaffe had flattened their homes, scattering their families to all four corners of the country whilst their fathers and brothers fought abroad. Having previously worked in Billingsgate fish market, they were used to dealing with bad-tempered men.

Maisie and Pru grinned back at her. 'Don't mind 'im, ducks,' said Pru. 'He can't 'elp being a misery-guts when he's married to 'er.' She tipped her head towards the field where Carol saw Jack's wife, the formidable Millicent Burnley, berating a red-faced – and clearly furious – Ida.

'What's Ida done now?' Carol asked with amused affection.

'Answered back,' muttered Pru. 'Silly cow never did learn to keep 'er gob shut, and if she don't watch it, she'll be out on 'er ear.'

'I doubt it,' said Carol. 'They need us more than we need them.'

'Yeah, but the harvest's almost over and there's only the barley seeding and mangold picking to do before winter sets in,' said Maisie. 'I do wish Ida wouldn't argue all the flaming time. It makes life very 'ard for the rest of us.'

'There'll always be the herd to look after,' Carol soothed. 'I'm sure our jobs are safe enough.'

'Stop this fiddle-faddle and get on with you'm work,' barked Jack who was hitching Hector's stable-mate, Harriet, to the high-sided wagon which would carry the harvested sugar beet. 'More trouble than you'm worth, the lot of you – yet I'm expected to house and feed ye and . . .' His grumbling faded as he stomped off to check that the enormous thatched hay-stacks dotted about the far field hadn't been damaged by the night's heavy rain.

'See what I mean?' Maisie grimaced. 'I'll 'ave a word with Ida, and that's a fact.'

With Hector rubbed down and happily munching his bag of oats, Carol grabbed a quick cuppa and then joined the other girls who were standing, arms folded, expressions blank, pretending to listen to Millicent as she once again went through the correct way to harvest the beet. This would be their third harvest and they knew the drill well enough, so there was a collective sigh of relief when she finally left them to get on with their work so she could go and bully her husband.

'Poor bloke,' muttered Ida, pulling down the hem of her thick sweater and rolling up the sleeves before digging her hands into the pockets of her dungarees. 'I reckon it's a flamin' miracle he ain't done 'er in. Any other man would've by now.' She was clearly still disgruntled from her earlier ticking-off.

Carol paused in the act of drawing a reluctant Hector away from the yard. 'But despite the pair of them, you all like it here, don't you?' she asked, concerned they might decide to throw it all in and return to London.

Ida squinted into the bright sunlight that had pierced through the heavy layer of cloud. 'Yeah, it's blindin' after the smog and noise of London where you didn't know if you was about to be bombed to bits along with 'alf the neighbourhood, or trapped down some 'orrible tube station for hours on end.' She looked appreciatively at her surroundings and gave a sigh. 'You wouldn't know there was a war on 'ere, would you?'

Pru must have seen Carol's expression falter, for she dug Ida in the ribs and shot her a furious frown. 'Gob almighty,' she hissed.

'Oh, lawks,' the girl squeaked. 'I done it again, ain't I?' She reached out a grubby hand to Carol. 'I'm sorry, mate. Me and me big mouth. It always runs off with me.'

'It's all right, Ida. I know what you meant.' Carol squeezed the girl's hand then turned away. 'Let's get on, shall we? It looks like we might have rain before the day's out, and the ground's already claggy.'

Carol's mood was sombre as she led Hector into the field and hitched him to the tilling machine so the rich red earth could be turned around the beet, making it easier to harvest. The peace of the rearing hills and plunging valleys was deceptive, for although there was little evidence of the war here, the echoes of it had touched all their lives in one way or another.

It was past seven o'clock and the long working day was finally over. The beet was already on its way to the processing factory in Kingsbridge, the stalks and leaves stored for winter fodder or crushed into compost bins as fertiliser for the barley crop that would be planted within the next few days. Having helped with the evening milking, Carol sat with the silent old farm labourers and the other girls in the farmhouse kitchen and ate the rabbit stew which was hot, filling and surprisingly delicious. Millicent might be a harridan, she thought with a wry smile, but her cooking was sublime, which was probably why Jack hadn't 'done 'er in'.

With the meal over and the old men leaving for their

homes in Beeson village, the girls helped Millicent with the clearing and washing-up as Jack sprawled in a chair by the fire contentedly smoking his pipe. 'I reckon things are about to change round here,' he said to no one in particular.

'Why's that?' asked Carol, putting the last of the clean dishes away in the dresser.

'Can't rightly say,' he muttered. 'But you'll find out soon enough.'

Carol exchanged glances with the other girls who rolled their eyes and shrugged. Jack was fond of coming out with these enigmatic pronouncements, and they usually meant nothing.

'You're not about to give us all the sack, are you?' Maisie asked with a light-heartedness that didn't quite disguise the worry in her eyes.

'Chance'd be a fine thing,' he replied moodily. 'Reckon we'm be stuck together for a good while yet with all that's going on in these parts.'

'That's enough loose talk, Jack Burnley,' snapped Millicent. 'Smoke your pipe and be still.'

Carol and the girls beat a hasty retreat into the cobbled yard, unwilling to witness what would surely be another heated exchange between Jack and his awful wife. 'What on earth were that all about?' asked Ida. 'It didn't sound like Jack's usual 'ot air.'

'Goodness only knows,' said Carol. 'No doubt we'll find out soon enough if it's anything important.'

'Why don't you come to the pub with us?' asked Pru, changing the subject. 'It can get quite lively if someone starts a sing-song – and we still have to have that last game of darts if we want to win the competition.'

'Thanks for asking, but maybe another night,' Carol replied, too tired and really not in the mood for anything more than a long hot bath and a good night's sleep.

The others wished her goodnight, then she fetched her bicycle from the lean-to beside the farmhouse, checked that her torch was in her pocket, and was soon pedalling down the hill towards home. The farm work had made her much stronger and fitter, and being out in the fresh air all day was good for her spirits after those years of working in the Dartmouth office of an elderly solicitor, but every muscle was aching after having spent hours bent over the seemingly endless lines of beet, and she was looking forward to that bath and maybe even a glass of the sherry she'd been hoarding since last Christmas.

There wasn't a glimmer of light coming from any of the windows in the village, but the pale, hooded beam of her bicycle lamp showed her the way, and she could smell woodsmoke coming from the chimneys, and could hear a heated discussion going on in the saloon bar of the Queen's Arms.

There had been rumours for days that something was afoot, but as no one knew anything for certain, Carol hadn't joined in the gossip and speculation. But perhaps Jack Burnley, who was a member of the local council, knew more than he'd let on – which would explain Millicent's admonishment about loose talk.

Carol was unsettled by it all, for she'd lived in Slapton long enough to know there was always a seed of truth in every rumour.

Cycling along, she caught sight of a large notice pinned on the board outside the village hall, which she was sure hadn't been there this morning. Curiosity got the better of her, and she got off her bike to read it. Looking furtively around, nervous of breaking blackout regulations, she dug her torch out of her pocket, switched it on and was immediately transfixed by the stark message.

IMPORTANT MEETINGS

The Area described below is to be **REQUISITIONED** urgently for military purposes, and must be cleared of its inhabitants by **20th DECEMBER 1943**. Arrangements have been made to help the people in their moves, to settle them elsewhere, and to advise and assist them in the many problems with which they will be faced.

Carol skimmed through the list of public meetings to be held over the next two days down to the final devastating paragraph.

THE AREA AFFECTED

ALL LAND AND BUILDINGS lying within the line from the sea at the east end of Blackpool Bay in Stoke Fleming parish to Bowden; thence northward along the road to the Sportsman's Arms; thence west along the Dittisham-Halwell road to the crossroads ¼ mile east of Halwell village; from this crossroad along the

Kingsbridge road to Woodleigh-Buckland crossroads. **THE VILLAGES OF FROGMORE, BEESON AND BEESANDS ARE EXCLUDED FROM THIS REQUISITION ORDER.**

Carol switched off the torch and stood immobile in the darkness, shocked by what she'd read and deeply troubled by its implications. She understood now what Jack had been hinting at earlier, and why there was currently such an altercation going on in the bar of the Queen's Arms, for deep within that requisitioned zone lay the village of Slapton and all that she held most precious.

She cycled down the hill away from the Queen's Arms and that life-changing notice, just wanting to get home to the comfort of her little cottage. Her mind was whirling with questions, for how would it be possible to evacuate every man, woman and child from the area before the twentieth – and where would they all go? She certainly didn't want to leave her precious cottage for a shared billet at Coombe Farm, but it seemed that was probably her only option.

She reached the sanctuary of Thyme Cottage and felt some of the tension ease as she closed the gate and looked at her beloved home. The cottage was white-washed, with thick, rounded walls and deeply inset diamond-paned windows which she'd crisscrossed with tape to protect them from any bomb-blast, despite the fact there had only been two air raids over the area in the past four years. Set back from the narrow lane behind a picket fence, it was central in a row of five, the front gardens uniformly planted with vegetables for the kitchen.

She wheeled her bicycle up the cinder path to the front door, which sat beside the sitting-room window and led into a narrow hall and the kitchen at the back. With two tiny bedrooms nestled beneath the eaves of sheltering thatch, it had been modernised by David, who'd used his carpentry and plumbing skills to convert the old lean-to scullery into a brick extension housing a fully equipped bathroom, which was an absolute luxury in a village where the lavatory was usually outside and baths were taken in tin tubs before the fire. There were few telephones and no electricity or gas in most of the dwellings, but the fire in the cooking range heated the boiler for water, and with kerosene lamps and candles, the cottage was cosy during the long winter nights.

She propped the bike against the wall and grabbed her gas mask from the basket. Glancing at the thickly entwined branches of the wisteria, she could picture them blossoming into purple droplets in the spring. The thought that she might not be here to see seemed unutterably sad.

Slamming the front door behind her, she pushed her way past the heavy curtain she'd hung over it to hide any light and then bent to pick up the post from the mat. Easing off her muddy boots, she padded along the dark hall in her socks to the kitchen. She'd kept the blackout curtains drawn over all the windows when she'd left the house at four this morning, but the glow of the range fire was welcoming. She plumped down on a stool and stared into the flames, and with terrible clarity, the full impact of what she'd learned this evening began to sink in.

This mass evacuation would bring about the most terrible upheaval for everyone, especially the farmers, the elderly – like her neighbour Mrs Rayner, who was in her nineties – the pregnant and the sick. For her personally it would mean leaving the home she and David had made together and – worst of all – abandoning him and their baby in the churchyard.

Carol shivered despite the warmth radiating from the fire. There had been no indication of when they might be allowed to return, but if the army was moving into the area, then what guarantee was there that there would be any homes to return to? She'd heard from Pauline and her sister-in-law, Peggy, about what happened to requisitioned land and properties; how they were used for training purposes and shot to pieces with almost careless abandon by the troops who had little respect for the deserted homes where they'd been billeted.

She couldn't bear the thought of her home being invaded; of heavy boots tramping down the lanes of this peaceful village, the rich farming lands and silent reaches of the bay scarred by tank tracks and echoing with bomb-blast and gunfire.

The images these thoughts evoked brought her slowly to her feet. There was nothing she or anyone else could do about it. There was a war on, a requisition order was to be obeyed, and no doubt the meeting on Saturday would explain more fully the reason behind it. For now she had to bathe and sleep. Regardless of everything, the cows would need milking in the morning, and she would have to face Jack and Millicent and ask them if she could move in with the other girls.

2

Cliffehaven

Peggy Reilly sat in her kitchen with her knitting lying idle in her lap and Queenie the cat curled tightly on the mat at her feet. The fire in the Kitchener range glowed warmly now the long-awaited delivery of anthracite had arrived, and the house was peaceful with Daisy finally asleep in her cot. Her little girl had been in a rotten mood all day, but then she was teething and had a cold, so Peggy understood how miserable she must be feeling – but it was a blessed relief to have her tucked up and not grizzling.

Peggy sighed and decided to give up on the knitting, for the central light bulb was so weak she couldn't see very well, and her eyes were tired after a long, busy day. She rested her head back on the old chair that needed upholstering and regarded the line of photographs on the mantelpiece. Her husband, Jim, looked down at her with that twinkle in his eyes which always set her heart racing and she smiled back at him. He looked so handsome in his army uniform, but now he'd been sent to India it was doubtful she'd see him again before this blasted war was over.

Her gaze moved on to her daughter Cissy in her

WAAF uniform before trawling along to the photograph of Anne, her eldest, with her husband Martin and their two little girls. Anne probably wouldn't come home from Somerset before peace was declared either, and she felt the usual weight of sadness settle around her heart at the thought of her granddaughters growing up far from Beach View. And then there were her young sons, Bob and Charlie, maturing rapidly down on that Somerset farm, the snapshots Anne had sent showing they were barely recognisable from the little boys she'd waved goodbye to all that time ago.

The yearning to have them all home again made her want to weep, but she knew that at least they were safe in the West Country – and that she hadn't had to bear the tragedy of losing any of them as her poor sister-in-law Pauline had done. Peggy felt ashamed of her momentary self-pity, for there were many who were far worse off than her, including Pauline's younger sister Carol, all alone down there in Devon. She really should pull herself together and stop being so feeble.

Accepting that she was merely tired after a long, fraught day, she got out of the chair and went to make a fresh pot of tea. Having queued half the morning for the quarter-pound packet of tea, she felt she'd earned the right to enjoy a decent brew for once. Waiting for the kettle to boil on the hob, she listened to the creaks and groans of the old Victorian villa and was comforted by their familiarity. This boarding house had been her home since childhood, and once her parents had retired, she and Jim had taken over and raised their own children here. Then war had been

23

declared and the visitors stopped coming to the seaside, so Peggy had gone to the billeting office and signed up to take in evacuees.

The elderly Cordelia Finch and the four girls who now lived here had become part of her family, and she regarded each and every one of them as her chicks, to be loved and watched over and kept safe within the shelter of these old walls. They filled the silence of the echoing empty rooms left by her departed children and husband, and gave her something important to focus on as she battled with rationing, endless queues and the dilemma of how to feed everyone.

She made the tea and settled once more by the fire. It was rare to have the house to herself, but all the girls were out, Cordelia was being wined and dined by her admirer Bertie Grantley-Adams, or Bertie Double-Barrelled as they called him, and her father-in-law, Ron, was at the Anchor with his dog Harvey, helping the love of his life, Rosie Braithwaite, pull pints behind the bar.

Poor old Ron, Peggy thought, sipping her tea. He'd been courting Rosie for years, but with her husband in an asylum and the laws of the day forbidding her to divorce him, their romance had reached stalemate. But her father-in-law seemed determined to hang on in there, and she admired him for that. She gave a sigh. Ron and his dog were laws unto themselves with their shaggy appearances and their wilful ways, but Beach View wouldn't be the same without them, and if nothing else, their hearts were in the right place.

Peggy finished her cup of tea, and was about to

re-read the letters and airgraphs that had come this morning when there was a knock on the scullery door and the sound of footsteps coming up the concrete steps.

The door opened and Pauline stood there with a holdall, her face pinched with the cold, her eyes red and puffy. 'I'm sorry, Peggy, but I couldn't stand being alone in that house a minute longer,' she said hoarsely. 'Would you mind if I stayed the night?'

Peggy rushed over and held her close. 'Of course I don't mind.' She touched the other woman's cold face and drew her towards the fire. 'I've just made a fresh pot, so you sit there and thaw out while I get you a cup.'

As she hunted out the china and poured the tea, she threw a surreptitious glance at her sister-in-law, who was now huddled by the fire, and her soft heart ached for her. Married to Jim's older brother, Frank, who'd also been called up, Pauline now lived alone in the fisherman's cottage down in Tamarisk Bay where Frank and Jim had been raised by their father, Ron, after their mother had died shortly after Jim had been born. Pauline was older than Peggy by only a couple of months, but this war had taken its toll on her, for her once pretty brown curls were lifeless, and there were shadows of grief beneath her hazel eyes, and in the hollows of her wan face.

Peggy could barely imagine the agony she must have gone through at the loss of Seamus and Joseph, and suspected the anguish over her remaining son's safety tormented her every time he returned to his

RNR posting in the London docks. Of course she was lonely now Frank had been called up, but despite all Peggy's best efforts to persuade her to move in with her at Beach View, Pauline had resisted. Tonight must have been very bad for her to have come all this way across the headland to seek shelter at Beach View.

'Here we are,' she said, handing Pauline the tea and sitting opposite her. She regarded her closely and noted with concern that her shabby clothes hung off her, and her nails had been bitten to the quick. Everyone had lost weight because of this war, but Pauline looked half-starved, and distressingly unkempt. 'I do worry about you, Pauline,' she murmured. 'Are you sure you're taking care of yourself and eating properly?'

Pauline squared her shoulders and sipped the hot tea. 'No one's eating properly these days,' she replied with a shrug. 'I'm fine, really, so there's no need to be worried about me.'

'I've got a bit of rabbit stew left over from tea if you'd like it,' Peggy said hopefully.

'Thanks, Peg, but I ate before I came out.'

'Well, it's lovely to see you,' said Peggy, disappointed that she couldn't do anything practical to help. 'But something must have happened to bring you out on such a raw night. Do you want to talk about it, love?'

Pauline encircled the cup with both hands as if afraid her trembling fingers might drop it. 'Brendon came down today on a twelve-hour pass, and now he's gone back to London the house seemed emptier than ever.' The cup rattled in its saucer as she placed it on the floor. 'It would have been all right if Frank was home,' she added wistfully, 'but the sound of the sea echoed through the house bringing back all the memories of my boys, and I had to get out.'

Peggy reached across and took her hand, painfully aware that whatever she said couldn't relieve Pauline's awful grief. 'Frank will be back very soon,' she murmured, giving her hand a squeeze. 'The army will chuck him out on his next birthday and then you'll have him home for Christmas and getting under your feet again.'

Pauline nodded and blinked back the ready tears. 'I'm sorry, Peggy,' she stuttered. 'I realise I'm being selfish coming here with my moans and groans. You have Jim and the rest of the family to worry about, without me going on. But with Mother gadding about in Bournemouth and Carol stuck all the way down in Devon, you and Ron are really the only family I have.'

She dredged up a smile as she returned the pressure of Peggy's hand. 'And I'm so grateful for that, Peggy. I don't know how I'd have got through these past months without you both.'

'It's what families are for, and you know you're always welcome here,' Peggy murmured. She patted her cheek, then sat back and decided to try and lighten the conversation. 'Talking of family, I haven't heard from your mother Dolly in a while. What's she up to now?'

Pauline managed a weak smile. 'Goodness only knows,' she admitted. 'Her letters are full of gossip about her friends and the endless parties and card evenings they seem to have, but she did say she'd joined

27

the WI – which actually came as quite a shock.' Her smile slowly became an impish grin. 'I mean, can you imagine my mother consorting with all those crusty old fuddy-duddies?'

'Goodness me, no,' breathed Peggy. The thought of the glamorous Dolly Cardew doing anything so mundane made her giggle. 'I'd have loved to be a fly on the wall when she waltzed into that first meeting, looking like a film star with her sharp suit, high heels and fur. I bet she's caused a real stir.'

Pauline chuckled. 'I expect she did. She wouldn't be Mother otherwise.' She finished the cup of tea and offered Peggy a cigarette from her packet of Park Drive. Once they were alight, she leaned back in the chair and Queenie took immediate advantage of her lap and jumped up to curl there contentedly.

Pauline stroked the soft black fur. 'There are times when I wish she was like other mothers, but that would have made life very dull. I do miss her, though. She brings colour and life with her, and in these dark days, that has to be a rare talent, don't you think?'

'It certainly is,' agreed Peggy, who'd always loved and admired Dolly as one of her closest confidantes – but she also knew that if Dolly was to appear in Cliffehaven she would soon drive them all demented with her restless energy and determination to always look on the bright side of things and turn everything into a lark.

She reached for the letters stacked on the kitchen table. 'I got a card from Carol today,' she said, hoping to keep Pauline cheerful. 'She seems to be coping, although I don't think she has much time to herself with all the hours she has to do at that farm.'

Pauline took the postcard and read the message. 'I was surprised she joined the Land Army,' she said. 'Carol always dressed nicely and seemed very happy working in that town office. I can't imagine her in dungarees and wellingtons, and up to her armpits in dung and mud.' She frowned, clearly unable to picture her young sister trudging around at Coombe Farm.

She handed the card back and stroked the cat. 'Still, war and loss does strange things to all of us,' she said on a sigh. 'I'm beginning to wonder if I shouldn't find more to do for the war effort. Brendon suggested I join the Women's Voluntary Service.'

'Only if you can put up with Doris and her horrible snooty friends,' said Peggy acidly. 'My sister will drive you potty in five minutes, and before you know it, you'll get all the rotten jobs and be expected to be at her beck and call at all hours – and that's no exaggeration, Pauline, it's a heartfelt warning from years of bitter personal experience.'

'I know she's a tartar and that you don't get on, but it's water off a duck's back with me,' Pauline said. 'I simply ignore her when she gets on her high horse. But I must do something more than the odd night on fire watch or helping out occasionally with the Red Cross.'

Peggy thought this was a splendid idea, for Pauline had far too much time on her hands, which wasn't a good thing when grieving. 'Well, there are comfort boxes to be packed for the troops abroad, postcards to write with Christmas greetings, and people to help with finding a new billet or things to replace what they've lost during the raids. I'll take you to the Town Hall tomorrow and introduce you to May Buller. She's an absolute whizz when it comes to organising anything, and I suspect she'll welcome you with open arms.'

Pauline nodded, her caressing hand making Queenie purr and stretch luxuriously. 'Yes, I'd like that. What with Carol doing her bit in Devon and Mother causing mayhem amongst the ladies of Bournemouth's WI, it's time I pulled myself together and mucked in.'

3

London

Dolly Cardew was enjoying her war, for like the last one, she'd again found something that enthralled and excited her, kept her on her toes and at the very heart of the action. Dolly had always had a thirst for adventure, drawn by the hint of danger in a man or a situation that caused her blood to sing and made her feel alive.

She didn't really understand this need, but justified it by citing a solitary childhood with staid parents who were bewildered not only by her rejection of the mundane routine of their lives, but by her driving ambition to break free and experience things beyond the stultifying boundaries of their middle-class world. The rigours of a boarding school where the slightest sign of a rebellious nature or imagination was frowned upon and swiftly quashed had sealed her fate, and so here she was at sixty-one, foot-loose and fancy-free, but having to live with deeply held regrets for the hurt she'd caused through her wayward-ness. For she'd left home at sixteen for the bright lights of London and had to pay the price for that rebellion – as had her daughters and parents – and the wisdom of age had made her realise how thoughtless she'd been.

Pulling the fur wrap more firmly around her neck against the bitter wind knifing across the isolated landing strip, Dolly watched the girl she'd been mentoring stride through the twilight towards the small plane which would parachute her into enemy territory. Aline wasn't her real name, and although she was regarded as one of the best and most experienced of the SOE agents, she was still very young. Yet her grip on the handle of the small cardboard suitcase was firm, her shoulders beneath the parachute pack were squared, and her head was held high.

They had said their farewells earlier, but Dolly waited as she always did on these occasions for the moment when the girl would turn before boarding the plane – they all did it, either to wave and show they weren't afraid, or to look back one last time on their old lives before having to face the dangers of their new one.

Aline stopped, glanced over her shoulder and gave Dolly a brief nod of acknowledgement before clambering onto the wing and settling into the rear cockpit.

Dolly held on to her hat and clutched her fur as the small plane motored down the isolated country runway lit by tar pots then lifted into the air. 'Godspeed, Aline,' she murmured, the words heartfelt as always, yet tinged with envy, for had she been younger she might have been on that plane and heading for occupied France tonight.

With a cluck of impatience she climbed back into her car as the men began extinguishing the fire pots. It was all very well to feel that way, but she was wise enough to realise that at her age she had other skills that could be put to good use in this war; skills honed over the years of travelling about the world and mixing with the right – and wrong – people, ultimately bringing her to London and the nondescript building in Baker Street which hid some of the most important secrets of a country at war.

She drove carefully through the blackout towards the city. Despite the devastation caused by the Luftwaffe, London still hummed with energy and the determination not to be beaten. After an hour and a half she parked the car in Baker Street and sat for a moment, relieved the long journey was over.

She regarded the stacked sandbags at the entrances to the buildings, the armed guards, and the gun emplacement at the bottom of the street where soldiers stamped their feet and rubbed their hands against the chill wind which swirled leaves and litter along the gutters. It was all far removed from the suburban tranquillity of her little house in Bournemouth where her daughters thought she'd finally settled down to enjoy peaceful old age and cause mayhem at the local WI.

Her smile was wan as she wondered how they'd react if they could see her now. But of course they'd never learn what their mother had done during both wars, and probably wouldn't have believed it if they had; to them she was a flibbertigibbet, a social butterfly with no real purpose in life but to look glamorous and have fun. Whereas, in reality, she'd worked secretly behind enemy lines during the first shout, using her illustrious contacts and her fluent French and German to glean vital information and pass it on to London. Now she prepared the men and women who were following in her footsteps, making sure their French was flawless and their clothes and possessions didn't betray their identity.

She settled back into the soft leather seat, unwound the window a fraction and lit a cigarette. There was no rush, and although chilled and stiff, she needed to relax after that hair-raising drive before she had to report in to her superior.

Having seen brave little Aline boarding that plane tonight, her thoughts drifted to her daughters, Pauline and Carol. She adored them both, but a quirk in her nature had meant she'd had to escape the tedium of the nursery and the demands of those small beings who depended upon her for something she was unable to give for any length of time. Her parents had reluctantly stepped into the breach when it had come to caring for Pauline – but when, fifteen years later, she'd made another mistake and brought a second fatherless baby home, it had been harder to persuade them to look after her. Yet they'd provided a stable, loving upbringing for her girls, and now they were gone, she missed them terribly and wished she'd told them more often how very much she loved and admired them.

Dolly fully acknowledged that she'd been a rotten, selfish mother who, despite the fact she truly adored her children, couldn't resist the siren call of the great wide world beyond hearth and home. And yet her children had forgiven her, had loved her without question, accepting her infrequent appearances with an unbridled joy she didn't deserve; and now she was miles from either of them, her heart aching for them in their grief – a grief she'd had no way of easing, and which made her own even more painful.

The loss of her darling young grandsons, Seamus and Joseph, had been a terrible blow, and she suspected Pauline would never really get over it. There was a small comfort in the fact that at least her girl had sweet Peggy Reilly nearby to keep an eye on her and provide the stability and nurture she so needed – and that Frank would soon be demobbed and could return home to her.

Dolly blew smoke out of the window. She'd always liked Pauline's Frank. He was a good, solid sort of man – much like his father, Ron – the type she herself should have married if only she'd had the sense. But of course she hadn't had anything of the sort, and had fallen for entirely the wrong sort of man – twice.

She met her own gaze in the rear-view mirror and blinked away the memory of that ill-fated, hasty wedding she'd been forced to go through shortly after her seventeenth birthday – and the aftermath when he'd left her and baby Pauline in that squalid tenement, and she'd had no choice but to return home to her parents. She'd never seen him again, and as Pauline had shown little curiosity about him, she hadn't bothered to find out where he was.

Her thoughts turned to Carol, who was alone down in Devon. At twenty-eight, she was too young to be in mourning, but proving strong enough to cope with it all if her letters were anything to go by. There was a good deal of steel in Carol despite her fair and feminine appearance, and Dolly often wondered if she'd inherited that from her, or from the man who'd fathered her.

At this unsettling thought, Dolly grabbed her handbag, gas-mask box and small holdall from the passenger seat and climbed out of the car. She mashed the remains of her cigarette beneath her high-heeled shoe before showing her identity card to the guard, then ran up the steps. The echoing hall smelled of paper, ink and dust, and the indefinable atmosphere of important work being done.

Reaching her small office on the second floor, Dolly dumped her bag and shed her coat and fur. The room was warmed by a gas fire which sputtered in the cast-iron hearth, and, silently blessing whoever had lit it in readiness for her return, she held her hands out to it and checked her appearance in the mirror.

Her face was holding up well despite the passing years, for she'd adhered strictly to the regimen of skincare she'd learned in Paris as a young woman. Her blue eyes were clear, the lashes enhanced with mascara, and her lightly powdered cheeks were attractively flushed from the cold.

She patted her honey-coloured hair, which now owed more to the hairdresser's skills with colourants than nature, and then touched the single strand of pearls at her neck which had become a sort of talisman. Dressed in her favourite light grey two-piece suit and cream silk blouse, she knew she looked good and could pass for a woman at least a decade younger. It had become a matter of pride to remain chic – it was what people expected of her – but they would never know that deep beneath that facade beat the heart of a woman who'd loved and lost and was condemned to a life alone because of her inability to see that the man she adored was not Mr Right, but Mr Very Wrong.

She noted the sparkle dim in her eyes at the thought of the one man she might have settled down with, but who'd ultimately betrayed her. She turned away. He was in the past, and she refused to allow the memory of him to overshadow the present.

She reached for the stack of letters that had been placed on her desk during her absence. She'd arranged for her private mail to be sent on from Bournemouth to the anonymous Post Office box number here in London, but because of the disruption caused to the mail deliveries by the war, and her frequent stays at Bletchley, they were often out of date and out of sequence. She noted there were two from Carol, one from Pauline and another from Peggy, plus several from various acquaintances, as well as a hastily scrawled postcard from Brendon, her only surviving grandson who was with the Royal Naval Reserve and based in London's Docklands.

Dolly flicked the card over and smiled. Brendon was thanking her for the slap-up tea she'd treated him to at the Ritz a few weeks ago, and informing her that he'd managed to get down to Cliffehaven to visit his mother for a few hours, and had met a nice girl on the train journey back to London. He hoped he'd see her again, but with things being as unpredictable as they were at the moment, it was unlikely. He signed off with a flourish and two kisses.

'Bless him,' she murmured, thinking of the dark-haired, blue-eyed, handsome little boy who'd grown into a sturdy, striking young man. The realisation that he might soon settle down and have a family of his own dampened her spirits somewhat, for it would mean she'd become a great-grandmother. 'Perish the thought,' she breathed. 'I'm certainly not ready for that.'

'Bad news?'

Dolly turned towards the elegantly dressed late-middle-aged man standing in the doorway and smiled. 'Just contemplating my mortality, Hugh, and I can't say I'm too enamoured by the thought of old age and decrepitude.'

Sir Hugh Cuthbertson closed the door behind him, kissed her cheek and then carefully adjusted the knife-edged crease in his tailored trousers as he sat down in the chair by the desk. 'You'll never grow old, Dolly,' he said affectionately, 'but I do wish you'd let me know you were back. I've been waiting in my office for over an hour.'

'Sorry, Hugh,' she said unrepentantly. 'But I've only just returned and needed to thaw out after that long drive. The heater still isn't working in that car.'

'I'll get my chap to look at it, but I can't promise anything.' His grey eyes regarded her. 'Got away all right, did she? No last-minute hitches or nerves?'

'She didn't say much on the journey and I could tell she was tense, but when I suddenly asked her a question in French she didn't bat an eyelid and replied fluently.' She reached for the decanter of whisky which she always kept on top of the filing cabinet. 'Your usual, Hugh?'

'Thank you, Dolly, yes.' He opened his silver cigarette case and offered it to her before selecting a black Sobranie, which he carefully threaded into a short ivory holder. Lighting both cigarettes, he sat back and watched her pour the drinks. 'I must say,' he murmured, 'you do look well considering that long drive. I don't know how you do it.'

'Thank you, Hugh. You always say the sweetest things.'

Dolly smiled at him as she handed him the cut crystal glass and an ashtray before settling into the other chair. She'd known Hugh for years and although he was a wily silver fox, she respected and admired him for his life's dedication to serving his country as ambassador and now behind the scenes at the Home Office. They'd met at a British Embassy party in Paris back in 1912 and although he was a confirmed bachelor there had been an instant spark between them and they'd remained close friends and confidants ever since.

'It's good to have you back, Dolly,' he said, gazing at her appreciatively. 'This place is horribly dull without you, and Robert and I miss you at our little soirées.'

'I've missed being here,' she admitted. 'There's nothing like the buzz of London to lift one's spirits, is there?' She sipped the whisky and then grinned mischievously at him. 'So, what's been happening since I've been at Bletchley? Any delicious scandal I should know about?'

'Nothing to write home about,' he replied, his expression suddenly solemn as he placed his empty glass on the desk. 'Look, Dolly, I realise you must be tired after that ghastly drive from Bletchley, but there is something I need to say before we part company this evening.'

She eyed him sharply and noted that he was looking rather uncomfortable for once, as if he was weighing his words before he spoke again. 'What is it, Hugh?' she prompted warily.

His long, pale fingers brushed at an invisible speck on his beautifully cut suit jacket. 'With this American thing about to go on down in Devon, I just wanted to reassure you that Carol will come to no harm.'

Dolly stared at him in bewilderment. 'I haven't the slightest idea what you're talking about, Hugh. What thing in Devon? And why would my Carol be in any danger?'

'Oh, my dear, I am sorry,' he said hastily. 'I thought you'd have heard about it on the jungle drums which seem to be a constant presence in this place.'

'I've been at Bletchley for the past three weeks and out of touch with everyone,' she reminded him, her hand trembling as she stubbed out the cigarette and eyed Carol's unopened letters. 'You'd better tell me what this is all about.'

He sat forward and clasped her hand. 'As you and the rest of the world know,' he said quietly, 'Roosevelt, Churchill and Stalin met last month. However, the decisions made at that conference are top secret, Dolly, so it goes no further than this room.'

She nodded, unable to speak for the fear trapped in her throat.

'The leaders agreed to launch an invasion into Europe sometime in 1944, but Eisenhower was concerned that the thousands of young Americans drafted into the army lacked experience of beachhead landings and exposure to real battle conditions under fire. To this end, thousands of raw recruits are being sent down to Slapton, and the training exercises will take place over the next six months or so.'

Dolly was bewildered. 'But why Slapton when there's Dartmoor right on the doorstep? And why should some army exercise concern Carol?'

'There are no beachheads on Dartmoor,' he replied dryly. 'And that part of the Devon coastline is very similar to the Normandy beaches where the Americans are proposing to land – but that too must be kept under your very fetching little hat.'

She gripped his fingers. 'And my daughter?'

'She and everyone else will be evacuated out of the requisitioned area. But once the exercises are over and the land is cleared of ordnance, they'll be allowed to return.' Clearly reading the doubt in her expression, he leaned closer. 'Carol will be quite safe, Dolly. I suspect she'll move to the farm where she works, which very fortunately is outside the restricted zone.'

'I know where it is,' she said hoarsely, retrieving her hand to lay it on the unopened letters. 'I visited there when I went down for that awful funeral.'

'So you'll know that although the conditions are rather basic she'll have other girls for company, which might do her some good. It can't be healthy grieving alone.'

'She wanted it that way,' said Dolly on a sigh. 'I offered to stay after the funeral, but I could see I was getting on her nerves by fussing over her. Perhaps you're right, though – the move away from that house and churchyard could do her good, even though it will be the most awful wrench.'

She looked into his eyes and saw something there that chilled her. 'There's something else, isn't there?' she managed.

'Nothing you have to worry about, Dolly, I assure you.' He rose from his chair and helped himself to another whisky.

His reply was too glib, his demeanour too evasive for her to believe him. She regarded him for a long moment, her thoughts whirling before the answer came to her in all its shocking clarity. She left her chair and put her hand on his shoulder, forcing him to look her in the eye. 'He's back in England, isn't he?'

Hugh nodded reluctantly. 'He's the only man Ike would trust to liaise with on the project, Dolly. I'm sorry, my dear. I really didn't want you to know.'

Dolly's pulse was racing. 'Is he already down there?'

Hugh swallowed the whisky in one gulp. 'He's staying at the American Embassy for the moment, but I suspect that once the groundwork is done and the exercises begin, he'll move down to Devon.'

Dolly finished her own whisky. 'Forewarned is forearmed,' she said lightly to mask the inner turmoil.

42

'Thanks for telling me, Hugh. It would have been ghastly to bump into him at some party unprepared.' She pulled on her coat, her fingers unusually clumsy.

He drew the wonderfully soft mink about her shoulders and kissed her hand. 'Don't let his presence here rattle you, Dolly,' he murmured. 'He won't be in London for very long, and once his business down in Devon is concluded, he'll be going back to America.'

Dolly kissed his cheek and swiftly turned to gather up her things and stuff the unopened letters into her handbag. Hugh might be one of her closest friends, but he didn't know all her secrets, so it was impossible for him to realise how deeply she'd been affected by this latest bombshell.

They parted on the front steps; Hugh to his well-appointed apartment in Sloane Square, and Dolly to the service flat provided by the Home Office, around the corner from the Baker Street office.

Upon gaining the austerely furnished, chilly rooms on the third floor of the Victorian villa, Dolly didn't bother to switch on the light. She dropped her bags onto the bed and walked across to the window to stare out over the rooftops towards the American Embassy.

Just knowing he was there was enough to bring it all rushing back – the passion – the heady excitement – the belief that at last she'd found the man who could satisfy and nurture all her needs – and the ultimate betrayal that had destroyed everything and forced her to spin a web of lies ever since.

4

On the Road to Devon

General Felix Addington pulled up the collar of his greatcoat and stared grimly out of the car window, barely recognising this grey, shattered London. The large staff car made its way through the devastation, driven carefully by Sergeant Herbert Cornwallis of the Royal Military Police, on loan from Whitehall.

The weather was awful, the long-forgotten damp chill of an English winter seeping into his bones despite the thick layers of clothing he'd donned before they'd left the American Embassy that Friday morning; the stench of burning rubber and decay drifting into the car even though the rain-spattered windows were tightly closed.

He'd heard the news reports and read the papers back in California, but the reality was far worse than he'd imagined. During his short stay at the embassy, he'd walked the once familiar streets of the city and couldn't begin to understand how people carried on living here amongst the rubble with so very little to brighten their lives.

He wiped the condensation from the window and watched as boys played in the bomb sites, men in bowler hats strode importantly past, and women carefully picked their way over the rubble, their knotted headscarves adding the only splash of colour to the dourness of it all. Everyone looked thin and drawn, their shabby clothes hanging off them, their shoes down at heel, but he was amazed by their cheerfulness, their smiles as they waved at the sleek black car with the Stars and Stripes pennants fluttering from the wings. It seemed that nothing could break that bulldog spirit Churchill had engendered, and Felix could only hope that the people within the requisitioned zone where he was headed felt the same way – although he had serious doubts about that, seeing as they were on the point of being swiftly evicted.

As Sergeant Cornwallis took the large staff car smoothly out of London and headed into the equally dowdy and damaged suburbs, Felix closed his eyes and rested back in the soft leather seat, wondering what the hell he'd let himself in for. He was sixty-two and had retired from the army almost twenty years ago, a three-star general with a generous pension and still fit enough to enjoy life in his California orange and lemon groves, and to go sailing with his son, who thankfully was now too old to be drafted back into active service.

This peaceful existence had been interrupted by a presidential summons to the Pentagon. Although he was grateful that his service to his country had been recognised, Felix had donned his uniform again with reluctance. Travelling to Arlington County in Virginia, he'd learned that he was needed to oversee the forthcoming invasion rehearsals and report back to the Pentagon, as well as liaise with the British forces down in Devon, and help smooth the way during the civilian evacuation.

He'd been enormously flattered by the faith they had in him, yet he'd hesitated before accepting. England held memories that were still painful even after so long, and he'd vowed never to return. But his country needed him; his president and the Supreme Allied Commander in Europe had specifically asked for him – and as a career soldier and fiercely loyal American, he'd really had no choice but to put aside his own sensibilities and accept the honour.

Felix dug his gloved hands into the deep pockets of his greatcoat and tried to retain some sort of body heat. He thought again about his short stay in London and the woman whose heart he'd broken all those years before. Dolly's smile could light up a room, and just thinking about her brought back the sound of her voice, the scent of her perfume and the softness of her skin. Like him, she would no longer be young, but knowing Dolly she would still retain that beauty and zest for life which he'd so loved and admired.

He wondered where she was and what she was doing now, for he'd gone to the mansion block where she'd been living all those years ago only to find an ugly bomb crater surrounded by the pitiful remains of the once elegant row of houses. He sincerely hoped she hadn't been killed or injured, and that she was safe somewhere, just as lively and lovely as ever – perhaps even married with children and grandchildren surrounding her. But the old crowd they'd once mixed with couldn't be traced, and in a way he was relieved. They had parted in anger and hurt, and although his circumstances had changed, he doubted very much if she'd want to see him anyway.

Impatient with his thoughts and shivering with cold, he leaned forward and slid back the glass partition between him and his driver. 'Is there any chance of getting some heat back here, Herby?'

'Sorry, General,' replied the young policeman. 'The heater's not working.'

'Like most things in this darn country,' muttered Felix, remembering the trouble he'd had trying to get the radiator working in his room at the embassy. He peered out of the window and realised the day was already closing in. 'How long is this journey gonna take?'

'About another five hours to Exeter, sir. After that, it's anyone's guess.'

'How come? Don't you know where you're going?'

'I know the way, sir,' the younger man replied stiffly, 'but the lanes are narrow and winding in the West Country, and what with cows wandering about and farm machinery getting in the way, it could take another six hours to just go the last few miles.'

'Then I suggest you put your foot down, buddy, and stop dawdling. I have a meeting to attend tomorrow.'

Herbert looked askance. 'Can't be done, sir. Not now it's getting dark. It's the blackout, you see,' he went on, his ears going pink with annoyance. 'There's a very strict speed limit, and with these shuttered headlights, it's difficult to see where I'm going. We don't want an accident, do we, sir?'

'No, I don't suppose we do,' sighed Felix in defeat, closing the window and slumping back into his seat. He'd forgotten how complicated it was to get anywhere in England, with endless villages and towns getting in the way, confusing crossroads and junctions, and not a decent highway to be had which would cut through the chaos. Now, with all the signposts taken down to deter an invading army, roads blocked by bomb craters and the detritus of shattered buildings, and no proper headlights to light their way, it was like trying to get through a maze blindfolded.

Accepting that it could well be dawn before he arrived in Slapton, he could only pray he didn't die of hypothermia before he got there.

Felix woke, stiff and cold with an aching full bladder. He realised he must have been asleep for several hours, for a grey dawn was lightening the sky and the car was slowly moving along a deep, narrow lane overshadowed by high hedgerows.

He slid back the glass. 'Where are we, Herby?'

'Just crossing from Dorset into Devon, sir,' he replied, his attention fixed to the winding lane ahead of him which only just accommodated the wide car.

'Well, Herby, I guess as you've been driving all night it's time to pull over and rest.'

'We've not far to go now, sir,' he replied through a vast yawn. 'But I'll stop at the Ploughman's Inn for breakfast and a bit of a wash and brush-up if you don't mind.'

Felix smiled at the delicate way the young Englishman had mentioned the need for a piss. An American driver would have been far more blunt and probably stopped the car close to a convenient bush so they could both relieve themselves. There was no doubt about it, he thought, the British were a different breed – and in a way he preferred that to the rather brash informality of so many of his own countrymen. You knew where you were with the English, for although they spoke quietly and weren't at all pushy, they had their own way of getting things done with a minimum of fuss and fanfare.

His thoughts turned to breakfast. A gallon of hot, strong coffee, pancakes with maple syrup, fried eggs and crisp bacon would certainly be welcome, for he hadn't eaten more than a disgusting spam sandwich since leaving London.

To take his mind off his bladder and his rumbling stomach, he continued the conversation. 'You sound as if you know the area,' he said. 'Is that why you were seconded to me?'

'Yes, sir. I was born in Blackawton, which is a village within the evacuation area. I was thirteen when my family moved north to Bude. Dad was promoted to police inspector, and a house came with the job, so we were well set up. He's gone now,' he added sadly, 'and Mum's on her own since my brother joined the navy.'

'So, you're a Devon man by birth? How do you think the people will take this eviction, Herby?'

'They won't like it,' he replied. 'Not used to change, see. Most of them probably haven't even left their villages before, so there'll be a good deal of consternation and upset.'

'But they know there's a war on,' Felix said

thoughtfully. 'Surely they understand the importance of what we'll be doing down there?'

'All they'll understand is that they've got to clear out and leave their homes, businesses and farms behind.' The younger man cleared his throat. 'If you don't mind me saying, sir,' he said hesitantly, 'I think you might find some of them will be quite hostile towards the Americans.'

'But we're here to help you win this war, dammit,' Felix spluttered.

'You and I know that, but these are country folk, sir. They'll regard the Americans as an invading army – in the same way as they would if Hitler's lot was to descend on them and take over.'

'It sounds as if I'll have my work cut out trying to liaise with them,' sighed Felix.

'I would count on it, sir,' Herbert replied dryly. 'But there will be some on your side, and of course there will already be a couple of small American units setting up down there to help with the evacuation.'

Felix stared out of the windscreen at the narrow rutted lane which appeared to have grass and moss growing along its centre. He gave another deep sigh as his belly rumbled again. 'Then let's hope they do a good breakfast at this inn,' he muttered. 'If I've got a battle ahead of me I need a full stomach.'

The younger man stifled another yawn. 'I wouldn't hold out much hope of the sort of breakfast you're probably used to back in America, sir,' he said. 'If we're lucky we might get lumpy porridge, toast and marge, and of course a pot of tea.'

As Felix had never eaten porridge or marge, he had no idea what the man was talking about, but he knew when he was beaten. He stared gloomily out at the high hedges and steep, muddy banks that closed in on both sides, understanding that rationing was tight but perplexed by the lack of farm produce in the countryside.

He slumped back in the leather seat, resigned to his discomfort. It seemed that nothing about his time in Devon was going to be plain sailing.

They arrived at the Ploughman's Inn to discover it was shut. The building leaned precariously to one side beneath a rotting thatched roof, the shuttered windows and beamed mellow brick walls telling of its great age. There was a weathered sign hanging above the door showing a man with horses and an old-fashioned plough tilling a field of dark red earth while being followed by a flock of gulls.

Felix had always been fascinated by England's historical buildings, for there was nothing so old to be found in America – but now his mind was on food. 'Wake 'em up, Herby, and tell them we need breakfast,' he ordered.

Herbert climbed out of the car, settled the red-topped cap on his head and went to hammer on the heavily studded oak door. A window opened above him and a plump, ruddy-faced woman leaned out. She was clearly unhappy at being disturbed at this unearthly hour, but Felix couldn't understand a word she was saying. Yet it appeared that Herbert was conversant in the lingo, for he gave Felix a thumbs-up, and within minutes the door was opened. The woman was dishevelled, and still in her dressing gown and slippers.

Felix apologised for disturbing her as he followed Herby into a narrow dark hallway with an uneven brick floor, roughly plastered walls and a very low ceiling. It was so dimly lit he didn't see the huge black beam crossing the ceiling and banged his head against it. He shot a wry smile at the woman. 'I guess this old place wasn't built for the likes of me,' he said ruefully.

'Come by you'm in 'ere, sir,' she said, unashamedly looking him up and down in admiration as his height and breadth filled her hallway. 'We'm do food d'rectly.'

He nodded and smiled politely even though he hadn't understood her, and followed her into what he recognised as an English saloon bar. The remembered smell of beer, tobacco and woodsmoke assailed him, and as his eyes finally adjusted to the gloom he saw there was an inglenook fireplace with benches right inside it – just as he'd seen in the old London coaching inns on his previous trip.

The woman fussed about lighting the fire, and then held a muttered exchange with Herbert before she bustled out to what Felix hoped was the kitchen to get their breakfast. 'Don't they speak English in these parts?' he asked with concern, his cold hands held towards the meagre fire smouldering in the great hearth.

'Of course we do,' protested Herbert. 'It's just the accent which makes outsiders find it difficult to understand.' He flushed and shifted his gaze. 'Sorry, sir. I didn't mean to be rude.'

Felix waved away his apology. 'I suppose I'll get to

understand it,' he said without much hope. 'But I'll probably need you to interpret for a while until I do.' He eyed the younger man keenly. 'What was it she was saying to you?'

'Her husband's in the army and she's struggling to cope with four children and this place to look after, so breakfast might be a bit delayed.'

The two men went in search of the bathroom, which turned out to be a ramshackle shed in the back garden, and on their return, Felix made himself as comfortable as possible on the hard wooden bench closest to the fire and lit a cigar.

The landlady finally returned bearing a laden tray which Felix eyed with a rapidly shrinking appetite. It seemed Herbert's predictions were right, for the breakfast consisted of bowls of grey, lumpy sludge, slices of gritty toast smeared with something that smelled of fish oil, and tea so weak the leaves were probably older than the inn. There was no sugar or milk to add flavour to what Herbert assured him was porridge, and no jam or marmalade to hide the taste of the butter substitute which bore no resemblance to anything that might have come from a dairy.

Felix thought longingly of the food provided by the American army then quickly reined himself in. America didn't share England's hardships and he had to learn British stoicism if he was to earn the respect of the people he would have to mix with from now on.

However, his good intentions fled when he was confronted by a plate of yellow gunge. 'What the hell am I supposed to do with this?' he rasped as soon as the woman left the room.

'It's dried egg,' sir,' Herbert murmured. 'It doesn't look up to much, but it's quite nice when you get used to it.'

'It strikes me I'm going to have to get used to a great many things, Herby,' Felix said ruefully, poking the rubbery mess with his fork, aware that he was being watched closely by the woman and her four children from the kitchen doorway.

When the awful meal was over Felix paid and then dug in his overcoat pocket for the small bags of candies he always carried, and handed them to the children before making a quick getaway.

Climbing back into the car he once more wrapped the greatcoat about himself and contemplated the very real possibility that if the Luftwaffe didn't get him, then the food surely would.

5

Slapton

Despite her weariness after the long days at the farm where she and the other girls had had to battle with the weather and cloying mud as they'd ploughed the field and sowed the barley, Carol had found it almost impossible to sleep. Now she was cycling back to Slapton through the sullen drizzle for the long-awaited meeting in the village hall.

Her thoughts churned as she navigated the winding country lanes from Beeson to Slapton, fretting over how she'd pack up her linen and china, and all the things she and David had accumulated – including his carpentry and plumbing tools – and then get them safely up to Coombe Farm.

Millicent Burnley had agreed she could stay with the other land girls on the farm, but of course her wages would be docked for board and lodgings, and as they were only two pounds, two shillings and sixpence for a fifty-hour week, it would leave her very short. She had no savings, and although she received a war widow's pension it didn't go far, so when Millicent had told her it would cost another thrupence a week to store her things in one of the barns, she'd balked at the idea.

But there was nowhere else to put everything. Bournemouth was too far away to cart it all there, even if her mother agreed to it, and of course Cliffehaven was out of the question, so she'd had to take it on the chin and agree to pay. Carol knew she was very fortunate to be able to stay so close to home when everyone else had to rely on friends or distant relatives to take them in – or worse, have to accept billets in strange towns far from all they knew – but that didn't make this upheaval any easier.

Ida, Pru and Maisie had been hugely helpful with making a start on clearing the accumulation of old metal and junk which had been left in the allotted part of the barn, but they were all too aware they would soon disturb the nests of rats which undoubtedly lay beneath it all. The thought of vermin gnawing at her furniture and getting into the bedding made her shudder, but to pay a storage company was beyond her means.

As there were very few telephones in the village, Carol had gone to Betty's lodgings in Blackpool Cove the previous evening to try and get through to Dolly, but there'd been no reply as usual, and since she didn't want to disturb Peggy, she'd decided to write to everyone with her new address once this meeting was over and she knew more.

With communication to anyone outside the area being so difficult, Betty was deeply worried – like many others – that work and accommodation might be impossible to secure. Carol was unable to provide any practical solution, and she felt helpless and anxious about where her friend might end up. She had even offered to speak to the Burnleys on her behalf, although she knew that Betty would never be able to cope with the farm work.

Betty had turned down the offer, assuring her she'd sort something out through the school board. This didn't really ease Carol's worries, for Betty could be sent anywhere – and like most of the people living in the area, she'd never gone more than a few miles from where she'd made her home in Blackpool Cove, and was fearful of what awaited her beyond the boundaries of the exclusion zone. As for the farmers, they were at their wits' end as to what to do about their machinery and stock and the produce in their fields.

Approaching the centre of the village, Carol could see that the small unit of Royal Engineers and Artillerymen who manned the guns down on the seafront, in the cliffs at Torcross and the hills behind the Ley had been drafted in to help with the move. They were standing about in rain-dampened groups next to their army trucks, smoking, drinking tea and passing the time of day with Constable Betts. It was clear that none of them were sure what they were supposed to be doing, for the village streets were deserted but for a skinny black cat, and no one yet seemed remotely inclined to move anywhere.

Upon reaching Thyme Cottage, Carol propped her bike against the wall and went inside to wash off the muck and mud from the cowshed and fields. Changing into clean dungarees and a sweater, she pulled on fresh socks and rubbed her bedraggled hair dry, before donning the khaki-coloured mac again and stepping outside beneath an umbrella.

She splashed through the puddles in her wellington boots to the cottage next door to help old Mrs Rayner make the journey to the hall, and found her waiting in her cluttered tiny sitting room, dressed in a rusty black coat and moth-eaten hat, staring gloomily at the meagre fire, her plump Jack Russell curled at her feet.

'Nipper doesn't want to move and neither do I,' she said by way of greeting. 'I'm ninety-one, you know, and I don't see why we have to leave.'

'I think it might be too dangerous, Mrs Rayner,' soothed Carol, stepping over the plump brown and white terrier before gently grasping the old woman's arm to help her to her feet. 'The army will most likely be using their guns, and you don't want to get shot, do you?'

'They wouldn't dare shoot me,' Mrs Rayner retorted with a glare that had had many a poor soul quaking in their boots. 'I'm Slapton born and bred, and I object strongly to being ordered out of my home.'

'Well, let's see what the bigwigs have to say about it all. We'd best hurry, though, Mrs Rayner, if you want to get a front seat at the meeting.'

Carol shielded them both beneath the umbrella as they made their slow progress up the steep hill to the village hall. Her soft heart went out to Edith, for she was very old and set in her ways, and Carol suspected that her bluff and bluster was because she was frightened by the terrible changes facing her. With no children or other relatives to take her in she would undoubtedly be billeted in an old folks' home where there'd be no room for her accumulated treasures or her beloved Nipper – and the thought of her living out what remained of her life in such circumstances made Carol wish fervently that she could do something to prevent it.

The hall wasn't very big, and the corrugated iron roof leaked in places, leaving patches of damp on the walls, the smell of which mingled with the odour of dust and decay, and the reek of muddy boots, damp dog and wet clothing. The few windows were so heavily taped that barely any light got through, and the single bulb illuminating the numerous lines of chairs was so weak it was like walking into a cave. There were faded posters stuck to the thin walls with warnings to 'put out that light . . . careless talk costs lives . . . make do and mend', which everyone knew by heart and no longer even noticed, and the old velvet curtains hanging on either side of the small stage were so moth-eaten they were in danger of simply disintegrating.

'I want that seat at the front,' Mrs Rayner insisted. 'I need to look 'em in the eye when they start throwing their weight about.'

Carol dutifully managed to nab the last three, and once Edith was settled and making her views known to anyone who would listen, she looked round and saw that Betty had just come in. She caught her eye and beckoned her over.

Betty sat down and propped her walking stick against her knee. 'It will be a horrid wrench to leave,' she confided softy. 'Yet I can't help but feel quite excited at the thought of something happening at last in this quiet backwater.' She leaned closer. 'Did you know that there're at least two American army camps being set up in and around the old RAF base?'

Carol shook her head. 'Goodness,' she breathed. 'Do you think they're the reason we're being evicted?'

Betty eased her crippled leg to a more comfortable position. 'I don't know,' she admitted. 'Everyone's being horribly tight-lipped about everything, but with all the talk of an Allied invasion into France and their sudden arrival here, it very much looks like it.'

'I'm not giving up my home to any American,' snapped Mrs Rayner, who despite her great age had nothing wrong with her hearing.

'I doubt they'll move into our houses,' soothed Betty. 'They'll be in camps – and anyway, I'm sure that who-ever is coming in will respect the fact that these are our homes.'

'Hmmph,' the old lady snorted. 'Soldiers is soldiers, and I wouldn't trust 'em an inch.'

Carol turned back to Betty. 'If we really do have to leave, will you go with the children to their new school, do you think? Or will you have to go further afield?'

Betty's smile faded. 'I haven't heard anything from the school board as yet, so I don't know. It's going to depend on where the children are sent, I suppose, and if the other school actually needs an extra teacher.'

'I'm sure they will,' said Carol firmly. 'Otherwise the classes will be overcrowded.'

'Maybe,' Betty murmured, still not convinced. Then she brightened. 'At least I'll know that Ken's all right.

He's got two uncles with a farm up Bickley way, so he'll be going there with the rest of the family.' She gave an impish grin. 'The uncles are old bachelors, so it will come as a shock to them when they all turn up with their noise.'

Carol smiled back, knowing that Ken had five much younger siblings along with a twin sister who'd recently had her second baby. 'It'll certainly liven them up,' she chuckled.

Betty nodded and looked round for Ken. Spotting him leaning against the back wall alongside his parents, siblings and the other farm workers, she smiled and waved, then turned back to Carol.

'Ken was talking about perhaps making things more formal between us after Christmas,' she confided, 'but all this has rather put the brakes on everything, and I agree with him that it would be a bit foolish to make plans when neither of us know what the future holds.'

Carol glanced back to see Ken ogling Molly Jelks, one of the Tower Inn's barmaids, and wondered if he'd seen this evacuation as a way of getting out of committing to Betty, but she kept her thoughts to herself. The noise rose around them with yet more people arriving until there was standing room only.

The vicar came in, dressed in his black suit and dog collar and looking harassed as usual, to be swiftly followed by Stanley Wilmott, the pompous church warden; the stone-deaf verger; Jack Burnley in his capacity as a local councillor; and Miss Ferris, who was in charge of the local WVS and a stalwart member of the WI.

Mildred Ferris was a sturdy spinster of late middle age with the suspicion of a moustache above her top lip, and a penchant for wearing hairy tweed suits and brogues. She lived alone in a large house on the outskirts of the village and considered herself to be of a much higher status than everyone else as she'd inherited most of the land around the village from her wealthy father. Not blessed with an ounce of humility or tact, she was very fond of the sound of her own voice when it came to meetings of any sort and, when roused, could out-bellow any sergeant major.

'I suppose you're going to stick your penn'orth in as usual,' shouted Mrs Rayner, waving her stick at her. 'You should be ashamed of yourself, Mildred Ferris. Siding with the enemy.'

Miss Ferris ignored her and stuck her nose in the air as a shout came from the back: 'Good for you, Mother Rayner. You tell 'em, my flower.'

There was a general tittering, and Carol and Betty exchanged amused glances before turning back to watch the little parade climb the three steps to the dais and sit down on the chairs that had been lined up behind a lectern borrowed from the church.

'Them be like ducks lined up at the summer fair,' drawled a woman nearby.

'Arrr. Wish I had me gun,' muttered one of the farmers.

The giggles were swallowed and children quickly hushed as Sir John Daw, the chairman of Devon County Council, marched down the narrow aisle closely followed by two strangers in uniform, who drew murmurs of speculation and admiration from just about every woman in the hall.

The younger of the two wore the red cap and khaki of the military police, and was very handsome – but the more senior man was quite something to behold. Tall and broad-shouldered, he struck an imposing figure in his superbly fitted uniform of smooth olive green and burnished brown shoes. There was a scramble of gold braid on his hat and sleeves, and three gold stars were studded across his breast pocket, which they guessed must denote his rank. That he was a serviceman of some sort was obvious from his bearing, and yet, compared to the ill-fitting utilitarian rough khaki of the British Army – or even the smart blue of the RAF – it was agreed amongst the women that he did look extremely smart and was as handsome as any film star.

'Looks like 'em Yanks have invaded,' said a sour male voice from the back.

'Thurr's pretty,' purred Molly Jelks. 'I wouldn't mind 'im invading me.'

'He'd not be the first,' snapped Mrs Rayner, turning to glare at her and the other girls giggling by her side. 'Hold your tongue, Molly Jelks, and show some decorum.'

'You'm only be jealous because you'm a dried up old biddy,' retorted Molly.

'I'll thank you both to hold your tongues,' stormed Miss Ferris from the rostrum.

'It's about time you held your'n,' the girl called back. ''Tis sick I am of the sound of it clacking away.'

Carol and Betty didn't dare look at one another as,

like the girls surrounding Molly, they tried to smother their giggles. But they earned a sharp tap on the knees from Mrs Rayner's walking stick and a ferocious glare, which only made things worse.

The vicar, Samuel Fotherington, eyed the gathering nervously, his Adam's apple bobbing above the dog collar, his pale hands clutching at the lectern. He was an ineffectual speaker and inclined to dither about everything until his more forceful church warden made the decisions. He was a devout man, but the general consensus was that he'd have been better suited to a life in a monastery, for he seemed out of his depth with real life.

Perhaps sensing that this important meeting was about to descend into chaos, he shot a glance at a glowering Stanley Wilmott and then stood tall and clapped his hands. 'Order, please, ladies and gentlemen,' he pleaded.

When there was no let-up in the noise he cleared his throat and tried again. 'Silence, please,' he called out with a note of desperation.

A begrudging silence fell and a flush of embarrassment coloured his face and shiny bald head. 'I would like you to join me in a prayer before the meeting begins,' he said without much hope.

'This bain't church, vicar, growled Mrs Rayner. 'Get on with it.'

'Your prayers bain't gonna keep us in our homes,' said someone behind them.

'And you'll not be getting no money in your plate, neither,' shouted another.

There were mumbles of protests going about the room, and demands to get the meeting going so they could all get back to work.

The vicar went an even deeper scarlet and fluttered his hands as he looked in appeal to Sir John Daw. 'I think it would be best if we just went straight to the business in hand,' he said. 'There's no telling what they'll do once roused.'

Mildred was on her feet before the man had time to respond. 'Silence,' she boomed, making everyone jump. 'I will not tell you again. How *dare* you behave in such an appalling fashion in front of our esteemed visitors?'

She glared at all of them, settling her beady eye on anyone who dared giggle or try to protest. Mulish silence fell. 'That's better,' she said, tugging forcefully on the hem of her baggy tweed jacket before turning to the chairman of the county council. 'You may proceed,' she said grandly before setting her plump behind firmly on her wooden chair.

6

Felix sat on the uncomfortable chair, his hat on his knees, his feet in the burnished brown shoes firmly wedged together on the rough platform as he looked out at the audience. He was horribly aware that all eyes were upon him as Sir John began to speak, and although he'd understood very little of the interchange between the audience and the odious Miss Ferris, it had been enough to realise that tensions were running high.

He levelled his gaze above the heads and fixed it on the roof joists which had been darkened by the rain seeping through the ill-fitted sheets of corrugated iron. He tried to concentrate on the man's rather rambling and pompous speech, but the hall was freezing and smelled of damp wool and the organic odour of cows and mud brought in on wellington boots, and he wished he hadn't left his greatcoat in the car.

As the man urged the people of Slapton to accept the order of eviction as their way of doing their bit for the war effort, Felix realised he was no longer under such scrutiny so allowed his gaze to roam over the faces.

They were a mixed bunch, he saw, for among the farm labourers, land girls and artisans were elderly men and women dressed in shabby finery, neat, bright-eyed children, and young mothers who sat listening with quiet dignity despite the very real fear in their expressions. These country folk certainly looked healthier than their London counterparts, but they shared the same exhausted expressions of having to survive the hardships of a war that had already gone on for too long. And yet there was little doubt that they were possessed of a defiant spirit, for it blazed in their eyes as some of the bolder ones shouted down the speaker and waved angry fists.

'Are we to be moved because of the Yanks?' demanded a tall, thin farmhand from the back of the hall, pointing an accusing finger at Felix. 'I seen 'em already up by Blacktor Farm making camp.'

'Arr, they'm be over Strete way too,' mumbled another.

Sir John turned to Felix. 'I think a few words of assurance from you might calm things down,' he said grimly.

Felix blinked at him in horror, for he'd not been expecting to speak today, although he had been briefed by Sir John as they'd driven into the village from the man's office. 'I doubt that,' he replied. 'They're more likely to lynch me.'

Sir John looked down his nose at him and then turned to the audience. 'And now I would like to introduce you to General Felix Addington of the United States Army who is here to liaise with the various services, and of course with you.'

'We don't need no Yank telling us what to do,' snapped the old woman in the front.

Felix desperately wanted to run his finger inside his shirt collar and to brush away the bead of sweat he could feel blossoming on his temple, but knew he mustn't show any sign of discomfort in front of these people. Remembering how he'd faced the might and terror of the German guns in the trenches of the Somme, he took a deep breath and got to his feet.

'Ladies and gentlemen,' he began to the general mutter and shifting. 'As the old soldiers in the pioneering days of America used to say to the Indian warriors, "We come in peace."'

'That was before you shot them all, and stole their land,' snapped the old woman in the front row. 'Are you going to shoot us too if we don't do as we're told?'

Felix realised he'd made a mistake in thinking these people could be easily swayed with platitudes. 'No, ma'am,' he said smoothly. 'Our bullets are for the enemy, not our allies.' He hurried on before she could say more. 'Ladies and gentlemen, the American soldiers you have seen are merely the first of many more who will be coming to Devon, and they will do all they can to help you during the evacuation. All of us are fighting the same enemy, and it is our aim to help you defeat them.'

'You took you'm time about it,' growled a man at the back. 'We be fighting this'm war long afore you bothered to turn up.'

Felix swallowed a retort and refused to rise to the bait. 'The people of this village and all the villages and farms in the exclusion zone should feel proud to be playing a very important – indeed a vital – part in winning this war, for without your sacrifice, the Allied soldiers, sailors and airmen would not have the chance to become a cohesive and daunting fighting force against the enemy across the Channel.'

'So you're preparing to invade France, then?' The question came from a bright-eyed, pretty young woman sitting next to the crone with the walking stick and belligerent attitude.

He smiled down at her, struck by her similarity to someone but deciding it could just be the poor lighting. 'I'm not at liberty to tell you much more, ma'am,' he said. 'But I assure you that when it is all over, the United States Army and the people of America will forever be in your debt, and will ensure that your property and land is returned to you as you'd left it.'

She held his gaze for a moment. 'Will that assurance include the church and the old tower?'

'Indeed it will, ma'am,' he said firmly. 'All historic buildings and places of importance will be marked as out of bounds.'

'Where we supposed to go then?' asked a man on the left side of the hall. 'And what about the crops still in my fields? It's a disgrace to leave them to rot when half the country's starving.'

'And what about my stock?' asked another from the back.

'I do understand your concerns,' said Felix, 'and I believe there will be time after this meeting for the farmers and all who work on the land to discuss them with Sir John and your local councillor.'

Felix could see that although the people before him had accepted the eviction, their worries were legion and couldn't possibly be solved by one meeting. 'There will also be notices delivered to every dwelling within the zone,' he continued. 'These will give advice on who to talk to and what to do about compensation, accommodation, transport and storage. I believe there will be additional advice for publicans and shopkeepers in these notices, and of course who you should go to concerning schooling for your children, pension assistance and postal services.'

A defeated silence filled the room and as Felix looked down at the troubled faces he understood their pain, for he would have felt the same if such a thing had been forced upon him. 'I would just like to say that I admire you all for the courage you have shown in accepting what must have come as a terrible shock. This evacuation will not be easy, but I know you will face it with the same admirable British spirit you have already shown during the long years of this war.'

He took a breath. 'I know that many of you have sons, brothers or fathers already in the services, so I'd like to remind you that the American boys coming here have also been torn from their homes and loved ones, and will have to learn to adapt not only to a new country, but to the fact that they too will soon be facing an enemy under gunfire. So please, accept them as you would want your loved ones to be accepted, for this is a fight we all share, whether on land, sea or sky – and, God willing, it will come to an end very soon, and then we can all return home.'

There was absolute silence as he sat down and then everyone was on their feet clapping and cheering. Felix was stunned and he turned to Herbert Cornwallis in bemusement.

'Well done, sir,' the younger man murmured. 'You've won them over, and they'll go quietly now, you'll see.'

'I hope so,' Felix sighed. 'There's enough trouble in the world without us fighting each other.'

Once the applause had died down the chairman and Mildred Ferris were bombarded with questions. When it was clear that they were to be told little more, the majority began to shuffle towards the door, leaving the farmers and their workers behind to discuss their plight with Jack and Sir John.

Felix leaned towards the vicar. 'Who was that girl in the front row?' he asked. 'She was sitting between an old woman and a girl wearing a brace on her leg.'

The vicar looked startled by the question. 'That's Mrs Porter,' he said stiffly. 'Recently widowed and working as a land girl up at Coombe Farm. Why do you ask?'

'She reminded me of someone, that's all,' he murmured.

'There'll be no fraternising on my watch, General,' butted in Miss Ferris. 'The women here are to be respected by you and your men and left alone.'

He looked into the pale eyes which reminded him of a marlin he'd once caught off his boat. 'I will certainly make that clear to my men, Miss Ferris, but I suspect they may be led astray by certain young women in this community – and over that I have no authority.'

The woman eyed him coldly and pillowed her sagging bosom on her folded arms. 'If you're alluding to the likes of Molly Jelks, who's no better than she should be, then there's nothing I can do,' she said with a sniff. 'But there are decent girls here, and until the area has been cleared I will make it my job to see that their honour is protected.'

'And I'm sure you'll do a sterling job, Miss Ferris.' Felix put on his hat, shook hands with the rest of the people on the stage and wended his way through the gathering of farmers out into the drizzle. 'Oh boy,' he breathed to Herbert. 'What a battleaxe.'

Herbert grinned. 'Every village has a Mildred Ferris.'

'Then it's a shame we can't enlist them into the army,' replied Felix. 'A regiment of women like that would soon have Hitler's thugs on the run.'

As they reached the car, Felix saw the fair-haired girl slowly making her way through the churchyard with the girl wearing a calliper and the old woman clutching her arm. 'Hold on there, Herby. There's someone I need to talk to.'

He ignored the man's startled look and ran through the cemetery to catch up with them at the rear gate. 'Excuse me, Mrs Porter,' he said, doffing his hat. 'But I want to apologise for not being able to answer your question fully.'

She looked up at him with wide blue eyes and he noticed she had a perfect English rose complexion, and that there was the sweetest dimple in her left cheek. He felt the hammer of his heart as she smiled, for on closer inspection it was as if the clock had been turned back and it was Dolly standing before him.

'I understand, really I do,' she replied. 'Everything's

secret these days, but I can make an educated guess about why you're here and what you're planning.'

The old woman glared up at him and tugged the girl's arm. 'Come on, Carol. I'm getting cold.'

'Would you like a lift in my car?' he asked quickly; keen to grab this opportune moment to learn more about Carol Porter.

'Goodness me, no,' she chuckled. 'We only live down by there.'

He followed her pointing finger and regarded the huddled cottages with their thatched roofs and gardens full of winter vegetables. They looked like a picture postcard even on this gloomy damp day, and the thought that soon tanks and trucks would be thundering past them made his spirits plummet. 'Then perhaps we will meet again, ma'am,' he said.

'I doubt it,' she replied solemnly. 'But I do appreciate what you said back there about the boys under your command. I think it made all of us stop and think.'

'Thank you, Mrs Porter, and if there's anything we can do to help, you have only to ask.'

'I'll remember that,' she replied before she turned away.

He watched as the old woman clasped her arm and they slowly made their way down the steep hill. The girl with the leg brace waved her goodbye and limped off out of sight, but Mrs Porter didn't turn back or glance in his direction before entering the cottage. Once the door had closed behind her, he went back to the car where Herbert was waiting for him.

Felix noted the questioning glint in the younger

man's eye and chose not to justify his actions as he climbed into the car. He'd heard somewhere that everyone had a double, but how extraordinary that he should find Dolly's here in this quiet backwater. Could they be related? Was Dolly actually living here?

'Where to, sir?'

Felix quickly gathered his thoughts. 'The American camps, Herby. I have to introduce myself to the commanding officers and make sure the set-up is going smoothly. And then I'd like to meet whoever's in charge of the local regiment manning those gun emplacements we saw coming here. After that I'd like to go to the officers' HQ and take a bath.'

'That'll be Moorcoombe Place, sir.'

Felix frowned and flicked through the wad of notes Sir John had handed him earlier, certain that he'd seen that address written down somewhere. He found it and gave a deep sigh. 'Just my bad luck, Herby. It's owned by that darn Ferris woman.'

Carol helped Mrs Rayner out of her coat, and, having settled her in her chair, stoked the fire to warm her while she put the kettle on for tea. She was puzzled by the American general, for he'd made a point of speaking to her when it really hadn't been necessary, and he'd looked at her with such intensity that it had been quite unnerving. It was as if he'd been trying to place her in the context of having met her before – which didn't make any sense at all.

Shrugging off this minor concern, she carried the tray into the warm sitting room and placed it on a low table before sitting down to wait for the tea to steep in the pot.

'That Yank's interested in you,' said Mrs Rayner sourly. 'You watch your step, Carol. Men like that can't be trusted.'

Carol chuckled. 'He's old enough to be my father, so I doubt very much if he has designs on me. Besides, I'll be leaving for Coombe Farm soon and probably won't ever see him again.'

7

Cliffehaven

Peggy steered the pushchair up the almost deserted pavement in the High Street towards the Town Hall, her chin tucked into her coat collar in an attempt to avoid the sleet blowing down the street and stinging her face.

It was halfway through November and the wet, miserable autumn was continuing into winter, which was making life drearier than ever; and with no end in sight to this awful, draining war, the shops empty of anything festive or even remotely tempting, and her family dispersed, Christmas would not be the joyful time it had once been. Yet she was determined to do her best to make it jolly, for the girls and Cordelia always looked forward to Christmas, and of course this year Daisy would be two and old enough to really enjoy it.

There was a very slight chance that Cissy and her American pilot would get leave for the day from Cliffe Aerodrome, along with Anne's husband, Martin, who was the station commander. And of course Cordelia would invite Bertie Double-Barrelled, whilst Ron would ask Rosie to join them as he did every year.

At least Frank was due to be demobbed very soon,

and although Peggy suspected he and Pauline might prefer to have a quiet day at Tamarisk Bay in the hope Brendon might get some leave, she would ask them anyway. Pauline was a bit more cheerful now she'd joined the WVS, for having other things to think about instead of dwelling on her awful loss was doing her good – and even if Brendon did get leave, there was always room for one more around the table at Beach View.

Peggy supposed she ought to invite her sister Doris, although she didn't really want to – but the thought of her alone in that big house now she and Ted were divorced, and their son and daughter-in-law were living away, made Peggy feel guilty. Doris was family, and although Peggy had been avoiding her these past months while April Wilton was awaiting the birth of her baby, Peggy knew that her sister would feel slighted if the invitation wasn't given, and would probably cause an almighty fuss.

In a way, Peggy rather hoped Doris would refuse to come even though April was now living with her Uncle Stan and his new wife Ethel at the stationmaster's cottage. Doris wouldn't be able to resist making her opinions known about unmarried girls having babies – and about the fact that Peggy had willingly taken her in and colluded in the deceit by pretending there was a fiancé fighting abroad. If Doris had had the faintest inkling that gorgeous little Paula's father had been a black GI, then there was no telling what trouble her sister might have caused.

Snobbish and prejudiced to the point of being

unbearable at times, Doris didn't possess an ounce of tolerance for those less fortunate than herself – which included Peggy, her lodgers and her family. Her attitude was baffling, for she'd set herself apart from Peggy and their younger sister Doreen, seemingly determined to turn her back on her working-class upbringing and lord it over them all now she had that fine house in Havelock Gardens and a more than generous divorce settlement from the long-suffering but very decent Ted.

Peggy heaved a sigh, wondering why she bothered with Doris at all. She only caused grief and wound her up like a clock – but family was important no matter how awful they were, and she would issue the invitation with a smile.

Peggy reached the Town Hall at last and dragged Daisy's pushchair up the stone steps to bundle her way backwards through the heavy double doors into the relative warmth of the reception area. She took off her wet headscarf, shook the rain from her coat and headed towards the nursery. A retired nanny had volunteered to look after the children whilst their mothers worked in the main room to provide comfort boxes to the troops abroad, or prepared piles of sandwiches and urns of tea to take up to the station to feed the endless number of servicemen who were now passing through.

Having relieved Daisy of her outdoor clothes, she just managed to kiss her dark curls before the child toddled off to play with her little friends. With a smile to the woman in charge, Peggy headed for the main room. She saw Pauline and hurried across to give her a hug.

'You're looking chipper today,' Peggy said, taking in the freshly washed hair, the touch of lipstick and the pretty blue woollen dress beneath the floral apron and white cardigan.

'I am feeling much better now I have other things to think about,' Pauline replied, busily packing socks, shaving soap and packets of cigarettes into one of the comfort boxes. 'And with Frank due home soon, the house won't seem so empty.'

Peggy pulled her wrap-round apron from her string bag and draped it over her sweater and skirt before tying it around her waist. 'I know it's a bit early, but I've been thinking about Christmas,' she said, beginning to pack another box. 'Would you both like to come to me and stay the night? And of course if Brendon manages to get leave, he'd be more than welcome.'

Pauline's eyes filmed with tears as she paused in her work and grasped Peggy's hand. 'Oh, Peggy, that would be lovely. Beach View is always filled with laughter and warmth, especially at Christmas, and it will help enormously to chase away the ghosts. I'll tell Frank the minute he gets home, and I'm sure he and Ron will manage to find some sort of bird for the table.'

Peggy giggled. 'Knowing Ron, he's already got an eye on something from Lord Cliffe's estate which will find its way into his poacher's coat pockets. Let's just hope he hasn't lost his touch and that new gamekeeper doesn't finally catch up with him.'

'I heard from your Sarah that with so many Yanks up there the stock of pheasants, chickens and salmon has gone down drastically. It seems the Americans have realised that the gift of a tasty dinner far out-weighs the lure of chewing gum, candy and nylons when it comes to attracting the women.' Pauline chuckled. 'Not that they need much encouragement. Those American boys are a good-looking lot, and their manners are impeccable.'

'Yes,' said Peggy fondly. 'I've been lucky enough to have a few around my table over the past couple of years, and of course Cissy is walking out with one of their airmen. I've always found them to be generous to a fault, and very pleasant company.'

They finished their boxes at the same time and quickly taped them up before starting on the next. 'I got a letter from Carol yesterday,' Pauline confided. 'I don't know what's going on in Devon, but she's moving out of her cottage and up to Coombe Farm for a while.'

'But that cottage means so much to her,' gasped Peggy. 'Why on earth is she moving out?'

Pauline shook her head, her hands still busy with the small gifts of soap, cigarettes and postcards she was putting into the box. 'She didn't give any explanation, which is very odd, simply asked me to send any mail straight to the farm for the foreseeable future. I tried to get hold of Mother to see if she'd heard anything, but the telephone just rang and rang, and someone was waiting to use the box, so I had to give up.'

'You must come to Beach View and use my telephone,' said Peggy. 'But I shouldn't worry too much. Carol is probably feeling lonely in that cottage and has decided to be with the other land girls now the weather's closing in and Christmas is looming. I understand it's a long, uphill cycle ride to the farm, so it can't be pleasant leaving and returning home in the pitch dark.'

'I suppose so,' Pauline sighed. 'But if that's the case, why not just tell me instead of being so mysterious about it?'

Peggy shrugged. 'It was probably a spur-of-the-moment thing. And no doubt once she's settled up there, she'll write and explain more fully.'

8

Devon

It was now early December, with only ten days to go before the thirty thousand acres of this South Devon corner was closed off to everyone but the military. Carol's milk round had taken twice as long as usual despite the fact that the villages, hamlets and farms were being swiftly cleared, for she'd met long convoys of overladen cars and farm vehicles carrying household furniture, machinery and their hastily harvested crops which clogged the narrow lanes; and even longer military convoys which took precedence over all other traffic, thereby forcing everyone to either reverse or risk getting bogged down in field gateways.

Carol was saddened by the fact that the quiet hours with Hector had almost come to an end, for the milk would soon be collected by truck and taken to a central delivery point each day to be distributed across the area. She was saddened too at the changes being wrought by the thousands of incoming American army and navy personnel; for where there had once been pastures and fields of crops, there were now forests of tents and wooden huts, and the ugly scars of tyre and tank tracks, the peaceful silence shattered by the unceasing roar and rumble of heavy machinery.

She sat with the reins loose in her hands as Hector took them down the hill towards the bay and the Ley. Gun emplacements manned by the Royal Artillery Regiment and Home Guard were now accompanied by American rocket launchers which made the outdated English Bofors guns look small in comparison; and up in the cliffs above Torcross there were even more anti-aircraft guns pointing towards the Channel where an enormous flotilla of landing craft was bobbing at anchor. Patrolling the bay were three Motor Torpedo Boats and two Motor Gun Boats, and it was rumoured that there were more keeping an eye on the Cherbourg side where the German E-boats were supposedly based.

Carol looked towards the small, sheltered patch of beach which had previously been left unmined so the locals could use it in the summer. She and the other girls had swum from there and enjoyed picnics on the sand, but now the fences had been torn down and it was indiscernible from the rest. There was little doubt that this upheaval was in preparation for something very big, and it could only mean that the rumours of an impending invasion into France were true.

She regarded the dark-skinned soldiers who'd caused such a stir amongst the community which had never seen their like before, but on discovering they were polite and friendly, had accepted them as they did the white GIs. They were laying down a broad apron of hardstanding along the curve of the bay to the high-water line with wide tracks leading from the beach towards the Ley.

Carol saw that a guard post and barrier were being erected at the Blackpool Cove end. She'd seen similar ones all along the boundaries of the eviction zone, and more barbed-wire fencing being put up to keep people out. Trees were being cut down and lanes filled with piles of hard core between the flattened hedgerows to make easy access for the heavy vehicles to get to the shore.

Turning her gaze towards the Ley, she noted sadly that the geese had gone along with all the other wildfowl, and ugly steel Bailey bridges now stretched across the water to the hills behind, where foxholes had been dug and guns were positioned along the skyline. It was as they'd all feared, for the arrival of the Americans *was* like an invasion.

The changes were apparent in Slapton village too, for the school had been closed, and poor Betty was still waiting to hear from the school board about a new posting and a fresh billet – but with communications even worse than before, Carol hadn't seen her friend since the meeting in the hall, and she was deeply concerned about what would happen to her.

The narrow cobbled lanes of the village seemed to permanently ring with the sound of horses, cattle and sheep being herded to one of the special markets that were now running at Kingsbridge and Totnes. With such vast numbers of stock for sale, the farmers saw the value of their beasts plummet, but could only hope that the promise of compensation was fully met and they wouldn't be out of pocket.

Now that extra petrol rations had been issued to assist in the move, the village streets had become blocked by army vehicles, cars, farm carts, tractors and trailers, as well as removal trucks which had been brought in to transport the families and their possessions out of the area. The American GIs assigned to assist in the clearance had been billeted in the old chantry, and had proved to be as helpful as General Addington had promised – the chaos and heartbreak of the locals having to leave their homes with all their possessions made a fraction easier by the GIs' cheerful willingness, and the seemingly endless provision of sweets and chewing gum for the children.

Carol waited patiently for enough room to be cleared so she could get Hector and the cart through the melee of badly parked vehicles and a herd of cattle being stoically encouraged to get a move on by two small boys wielding sticks. She watched Mildred Ferris come out of one of the cottages laden with a box of cooking utensils, which she deposited on the back seat of her car, where there was already a collection of cases and cartons.

Mildred had more than proved her mettle, for although her large mansion had been requisitioned by the Americans as officers' quarters she'd accepted the fact with good grace and moved to one of the farm cottages belonging to her estate outside the exclusion zone. Yet she could be seen each day in the village organising the ladies of the local WVS so there was always hot food and tea available, and plenty of packing cases and boxes to hand – and was proving a stalwart help in sorting out alternative accommodation, as well as schooling for the children and jobs for those who needed them. She'd even promised Carol that she'd find suitable accommodation for Mrs Rayner.

Hector stamped his hooves on the cobbles and shook his head impatiently, so Carol climbed down to give him a couple of windfall apples she'd picked up earlier from one of the abandoned orchards. He slobbered and crunched these treats and when he'd finished, he rested his great head on her shoulder and snorted heavily at all the goings-on.

The truck finally moved and Carol steered Hector past the church where the vicar was overseeing the painstaking removal of the ancient and very fragile rood screen, as well as the Jacobean cover for the font and the five bells from the tower. The ancient church would be divested of its portable treasures, but Carol shared the vicar's concerns that the ninth- and tenth-century tiles found during the restoration of 1905 might be damaged along with the intricately carved wooden pulpit and beautiful stained-glass windows. And then there was the cemetery, which was already showing signs of being trampled as the men from the Home Guard helped the GIs to pack the treasures away in a truck.

She passed the Queen's Arms, which had become a favourite watering hole for the Americans, who seemed to prefer the local cider to the English beer which they regarded as undrinkable. As Carol and Hector reached the junction where they would turn off for Coombe Farm, the butcher came out of his empty shop carrying a bag of coal and loaded it onto the open door of the boot of his car. There was already a bedstead lashed to the roof along with a rolled-up mattress and a chicken coop complete with chickens, firmly tethered with rope.

His wife emerged armed with the last of her cooking pots and joined her other three children in the car as their youngest son straddled the sack of coal. With his cheeks bulging from the sweets he'd just been given by a passing GI, he waved a cheerful goodbye to Carol before wedging himself more firmly into the boot. The butcher would be setting up another shop in Prawle, and once a final check was made to ensure they had everything, he locked the door and handed the tagged key to Constable Betts.

Carol watched in some trepidation as the overladen car began to move and the boy gripped the sides of the boot as the coal shifted beneath him, but luckily his father was driving very slowly and he seemed to be hanging on all right.

Once the sound of the car had faded she regarded the locked, empty houses and shops which had already taken on an air of abandonment, and with a heavy heart, turned Hector's head towards Coombe Farm.

Felix had hoped to be back in London by now, but following his initial written report to his superiors, he'd received a terse telephone call from the American Army HQ instructing him to stay put in Devon. His brief was to try and bring some sort of order to the chaotic preparations for the invasion rehearsals which would culminate in Operation Tiger.

He stood on the cliffs, chewing his cigar, his hands

dug deeply into his greatcoat pockets and the collar turned up against the wind that was tearing up from the sea. His gaze was fixed on the men working to finish the accommodation huts before the winter got any worse. Someone was playing big band music over the loudspeaker to keep their spirits up, and a tantalising smell of roasting meat was coming from the cookhouse. At least the priority of decent food had been dealt with, he thought grimly.

He'd swiftly come to realise he was facing a mammoth task. Operation Tiger would begin in earnest at the end of April, with a series of practice assaults over the following weeks which would mirror the planned landings on what were secretly coded Utah and Omaha beaches the other side of the Channel. Live ammunition would be fired over their heads and they would also have to deal with a bombardment from the ships as well as the guns on the hills, which would begin as they made their way towards the beachhead.

Four and a half months seemed like plenty of time to get these boys prepared, but their youthful inexperience, lack of discipline and the foul weather would eat into those months, and all he could do was hope that the newly built hospital was not called into service.

Rehearsals had yet to begin. Troops were pouring into Slapton and the surrounding area by the day, and there was still a vast amount to do to set up proper camps, for there were too few large residences in the area to provide proper billets, and the tents they'd brought were more suited to Californian weather, not the relentless downpour and blustery winds of an English winter.

Ike had been right to insist upon these training exercises, for these were inexperienced boys with absolutely no idea of what they would be facing when these rehearsals came to an end. It was all very well getting them to march in unison, dig foxholes and trenches, complete the obstacle courses and shoot their guns at static targets, but they were merely playing at being soldiers, and having watched as they'd struggled to get the LSTs – Landing Ship, Tanks – through the heavy seas and onto the beach, he could see they weren't nearly ready to face action under fire.

And then there was the issue of the Royal Naval protection of the exercise area, which apart from three MTBs and two MGBs consisted of a single corvette, and a World War I destroyer which was so slow and lumbering it would be of no use at all if pursued by the much swifter and more manoeuvrable German E-boats.

Felix had used all his diplomatic skills in trying to persuade the American admiral in charge, Don Moon, and his British counterpart, that the men needed better protection should things go wrong and the activity in the bay be spotted by the enemy. But it was to little avail. The admirals had pointed out that the guns on the ships were in full working order and would be enough, but on his pressing further, had merely given a grudging promise that the S-class destroyer, HMS *Saladin*, would be kept in readiness at Plymouth should the need arise. As this was yet another old ship well past its prime, it was hardly a comfort – but the admirals were adamant that it was all they could spare, for the more modern fleet was fully occupied in the Pacific.

Felix turned away and plodded back across the deeply rutted field to where Herbert was waiting at the barrier. He threw up a casual salute to the guards manning the barrier and climbed into the car. 'Take me back to the billet, Herby,' he said dolefully. 'I need to get warm again before I have to check on the progress in Slapton. Then I think we'll call into the Queen's Arms for a glass of their great cider.'

'A pint of beer would certainly go down well, sir,' said Herbert.

Felix shuddered. 'I don't know how you drink that stuff. It's warm and flat and sour, and nothing like the beer we have at home.'

Herbert didn't reply as he steered the car away from camp and headed for the large house nestled within the folds of sweeping parkland behind Strete. He was becoming used to the informal ways of the general, but he wasn't about to get into a debate over the local ale, which he considered to be like nectar compared to the rather cloying cider, and the light, fizzy rubbish the Americans had the nerve to call beer.

9

Slapton

With the days becoming even shorter as they approached Christmas, Carol and the other girls were, nonetheless, kept busy between the two milking sessions. They trapped rats, mucked out the stables and byres, trimmed hedges and chopped wood for the fires. The barley had been sown, the mangolds and potatoes harvested, and the bales of straw neatly stacked in the barns out of the wind and rain, but despite the few hours of daylight, there were still chickens to feed, horses to groom, harness to be kept supple with wax, and repairs to be made to some of the ancient machinery. Jack had also taken on two more working horses which would stay at the farm until their owner was permitted to return to his own place. Bluebell and Fred were now happily ensconced in the stables with Hector and Harriet, who'd perked up no end to have new companions.

All four girls were perspiring as they finished mucking out the byre and laid down fresh straw. The cattle would be kept in overnight now the weather was so bad, and as there had been rumours of animals and machinery going missing since the area had been overrun by the military, Jack had purchased a small flock of geese which roamed free in the yard and would alert him to any trespassers.

'He'll be lucky if those geese don't go missing too,' said Pru, wiping her sweaty face on her sleeve. 'I heard tell that chickens and all sorts are being nicked.'

'I don't know why,' said Ida. 'The Yanks have got trucks full of food we ain't seen for years.'

'Yeah, that's right,' said Maisie. 'They're handing out tins of 'am and pineapple chunks like sweets – probably in the hope they'll get their wicked way with us gels.'

'I don't think it's the Yanks,' said Carol. 'PC Betts told me he'd caught a truck full of our boys making off with at least a dozen chickens which they'd already strangled and begun to pluck.'

Ida shrugged. 'They're probably doing it to eke out their rotten rations. I can't say I blame 'em,' she added. 'Compared to the Yanks they get lower pay, 'orrid food and uniforms that make most of them look like sacks of spuds.'

Pru giggled. 'Never mind about the chickens, it's us what needs to watch out from now on,' she said with a wink. 'With that new camp going up just over the 'ill, the old pub will be getting very lively.'

'Lively or not, with old Mother Burnley on the constant warpath I doubt she'll let us go up there no more,' said Ida dolefully.

'Where's your sense of adventure?' asked Maisie, digging Ida sharply in the ribs with her elbow. 'She can't keep an eye on us all the time, and we can sneak out the back window and be off before she knows it.'

Carol joined in the giggles, glad of their cheerful company, and mildly surprised that she was actually looking forward to moving in with them now the village was mostly deserted. She followed them as they trooped round to the lean-to behind their billet to wash their hands before they began the evening milking.

The accommodation for the land girls was rough and ready, with an outside lav and a lean-to supplying a chipped basin and a recalcitrant boiler to heat the rusty water that came out of the taps in fits and splutters. But the small barn was kept cosy by a pot-bellied wood-stove, and there were pages torn from film magazines pinned to the thick oak beams and thin plaster walls alongside photographs of their loved ones.

Bright bedspreads and cushions added to the homely feel, along with rather mildewed rugs and overstuffed chairs. Moth-eaten velvet curtains hung over the single window which looked over the back field they'd just planted, and a collection of battered furniture provided storage for their few clothes. It might not have stood up in comparison to what Carol was used to, but the other girls assured her it was a palace compared to the rat-infested tenement hovels they'd been crammed in back in the East End.

Having finished the milking and herded the cows into the byres, Carol ate her supper of vegetable stew, wished them all goodnight and cycled towards home. It seemed darker than ever now the village was all but deserted, but she could see the gathering of army trucks and staff cars outside the Queen's Arms and could hear the raucous sing-song coming from the bar.

She steered the bike down the steep hill to her cottage, but instead of going through her own gate, headed for Mrs Rayner's front door to check she was all right. Pushing it open, she called out and found her in her sitting room with a tray of supper on her lap, which consisted of thickly sliced ham, beans from the garden and a mound of mashed potato.

'Goodness,' Carol breathed. 'Where did that ham come from?'

'That American general called in and gave it to me,' Mrs Rayner said, offering a sliver to the drooling dog.

Carol raised an eyebrow. 'Really? That was very kind of him.'

'There's tins of ham and peaches on that table for you too,' she mumbled through a mouthful. 'But then he can afford to be generous,' she added sourly. 'I've heard they've got food in those camps we haven't seen since before rationing started.'

'Still, it was thoughtful of him,' said Carol, her mouth watering at the thought of proper ham and tinned fruit even though she'd only just eaten a large portion of stew. 'But I don't understand why he should single us out for such bounty.'

The old woman shrugged. 'Probably after something,' she muttered. 'Men like that always are.'

'I'm sure not,' replied Carol gently. 'Perhaps he was just being neighbourly now the village is almost empty.'

'Well, he did ask what arrangements had been made for me and Nipper,' Mrs Rayner admitted, giving another morsel to the dog, who gulped it down instantly and begged for more.

'I still haven't heard anything from Mildred,' Carol said. 'But I promise I'll see her tomorrow and give her a reminder that time's getting very short.'

'No need for that,' the old woman said, scraping up the last of the mash with her fork. 'She came in this afternoon and told me where I'd be going.'

Carol sank onto the footstool, feeling rather bereft, for with Mrs Rayner leaving she would be the last one left in the street. 'Where's that?'

'It's a cottage up in Frogmore that's part of her family estate,' she mumbled through the mashed potato. 'The tenant farmer and his wife have agreed to make it ready for me and will look out for me and Nipper all the time I have to be there. I asked about the rent, but Mildred said it was free, so I suppose I should be grateful.'

'Goodness, how generous,' said Carol warmly. 'So when will you be moving in?'

'In three days' time. The general is organising men to pack up my things and a truck to take it all up there. Mildred said she'd give me and Nipper a lift in her car. Nipper won't like it, and neither will I – neither of us trust cars, or her driving – but you know what she's like once she gets an idea into her head, so I suppose I'll just have to shut my eyes and put up with it.'

'I shall be sorry to see you go,' said Carol, reaching for her hand. 'But it sounds as if you'll be very comfortable up there.'

'I'll be sorry to leave,' she said on a sigh, her faded

eyes taking in the clutter of her possessions and the familiarity of her surroundings. 'I just hope I'm still alive when all this nonsense is over and I get to die in my own home.'

Carol hoped so too, but said nothing as she kissed her cheek. 'I've got the day off tomorrow, so I'll come in and help you pack your private and most delicate things,' she said, 'and I might even be able to find a basket for Nipper to travel in. I'm sure I saw one somewhere up at the farm.'

Mrs Rayner's sad expression was lifted by a sweet smile. 'You're a good girl, Carol,' she said softly. 'Thanks for being a friend to an old woman who doesn't always appreciate what others do for me.'

Warmed by this unexpected sentiment, Carol kissed her again and took the tray into the kitchen. Having washed the plate and cutlery, she made sure the old woman had all she needed for the night before putting the tins of ham and fruit in her coat pocket and leaving the cottage.

Edith Rayner had proved to be a difficult woman over the years, but tonight there had been a glimmer of the soft heart which she'd shown during the first awful weeks of Carol's bereavement – and as for Mildred Ferris, she'd proved to be an absolute brick. It just went to show that you could never tell the true nature of people by merely judging them on their looks and manners – it took much more to see behind the facades they showed to the outside world.

Stepping back out into the cold and dark, Carol wheeled her bike along the cinder path and leaned it against the wall before opening her front door. She froze in the act of drawing back the heavy curtain, realising there was a glow of firelight coming from the sitting room and something was cooking in the kitchen. 'Who's there?' she called.

Dolly came flying out of the sitting room and threw her arms about her. 'Surprise, surprise!'

Carol laughed as they hugged, breathing in her familiar perfume and so delighted to see her she was almost lost for words. 'When did you get here?' she managed as they finally drew apart.

'A couple of hours ago. I hope you don't mind, but the door wasn't locked, so I made myself at home.'

'You're lucky you found me at all.' Carol had to fight back her sudden tears. 'I have to be out of here by the end of next week.'

'I got your letter with the change of address, and had to come to find out what's going on here. The local policeman told me about the evictions, which of course explains the reason why most of your furniture is missing, and I saw for myself the devastation being caused by all those Americans. What on earth is going on here?'

Carol took off her coat and scarf and toed off her filthy boots. 'You know as much as me, Mum, but it's fairly easy to guess that it has something to do with the expected invasion into France.'

Dolly regarded her daughter with some concern. 'You can't be finding this at all easy, darling,' she murmured. 'I know how much this little cottage means to you.'

Carol took a quavering breath, determined not to let her mother see how deeply affected she was at the thought of leaving. 'I've had to come to terms with the fact that I have no choice in the matter, and count myself lucky that at least I'll still be able to keep an eye on the village from the hills at the farm.' She forced a smile. 'And the other girls are lovely company, so it will probably do me good to get away from all the sad memories for a while.'

'Well, I have to say you do look well,' said Dolly, gently easing a lock of fair hair from Carol's forehead and lovingly patting her cheek. 'All this country air must be doing you good.'

Carol didn't want to spoil her mother's surprise arrival by getting tearful, so she determinedly made an effort to appear cheerful. 'You don't look too bad yourself,' she responded, taking in the tailored suit, high heels and slender legs encased in delicate nylon stockings. 'Life in Bournemouth obviously agrees with you.'

Dolly chuckled. 'It's life itself that does me good, Carol. Now come on into the sitting room and relax for a while by the fire. I didn't know if you'd eat before coming back so I've made a cauliflower cheese for our supper, and there's some lovely whisky for us to indulge in while we catch up on things.'

Carol wasn't in the least bit hungry, but as her mother rarely did anything domesticated, she didn't want to spoil the moment by telling her so. She dug into her deep coat pockets and pulled out the tins of ham and peaches. 'I'll just put these in the kitchen, then I'm all yours.'

'Goodness,' gasped Dolly. 'Where on earth did you get those?'

'They were a gift from an American general.'

'An American general?' Dolly's eyes were suddenly wary. 'Why would such a man give you tins of ham and peaches?'

Carol giggled. 'There's nothing sinister about it,' she said, carrying the tins into the kitchen. 'He gave the same to Mrs Rayner next door and she's in her nineties.'

'Well, you watch your step, Carol,' said Dolly solemnly. 'American men can be far too charming for anyone's good – especially during wartime when there's so much uncertainty about everything.'

Carol smiled at this. 'Now there speaks the voice of experience,' she teased. 'If you hadn't been bowled over by the American charms of Frederick Adams in the last shout, I wouldn't be here.'

Dolly shrugged and tried not to look flustered. 'Your father was a very attractive man – but we all make mistakes in the heat of the moment,' she said. 'I'm merely asking you not to do the same.'

'Well, Mrs Rayner's already given me that lecture, Mum – and as I have no intention of following in your footsteps, there's no need to worry.' She stowed the tins away on a shelf above the sink, checked the cauliflower cheese bubbling away in the range oven and turned back to Dolly.

'I'm well aware of their attraction,' she said mildly, 'and can quite understand why you were bowled over by my father. From his photograph I can see that

Frederick was a very handsome man – but charm, good looks and tins of ham won't get the general very far with me – if that's his intention.'

She was distracted by the sight of discarded Harrods packaging and jars of marmalade on the drainer. 'What's all this?'

Dolly looked mischievous as Carol picked up the wrapping paper and eyed her quizzically. 'I had to go to London to visit someone,' she said quickly, 'and popped into Harrods to buy you a few treats. There's butter, flour and more cheese in the larder, as well as pots of strawberry jam and marmalade.'

Carol chuckled. 'My goodness, Mum, you do get about, don't you? Bournemouth to London, and then all the way down here to Devon – how on earth did you manage with transport the way it is?'

Dolly's dimples showed as she giggled. 'A friend lent me his car along with lots of lovely petrol coupons, so I didn't have to battle my way on buses and trains.'

'You're incorrigible,' Carol said fondly. 'Please don't ever change.'

'I don't intend to,' Dolly replied, reaching for the oven gloves and drawing out the cauliflower cheese. 'Let's have supper, and then you can tell me all about this generous American who's plying you with treats from the army stores.'

'There's nothing much to tell,' said Carol. 'We've only met once to exchange a few words after he'd come to address a meeting in the village hall. General Addington is—'

Dolly's hands slipped and the boiling hot dish

thudded onto the table, spilling molten cheese over the clean tablecloth. 'Oh, how careless of me,' she cried out, dabbing ineffectually at the spillage with the oven glove.

'Leave it, Mum, or you'll burn yourself.' Carol quickly grabbed a kitchen towel and moved the heavy pot onto the stove top. She went to gather up the table-cloth to soak it in the sink when she noticed that her mother had gone quite pale and her hands were trem-bling. 'What is it, Mum? Did you get burnt?'

'No, darling,' she said distractedly. 'I'm quite all right, really, please don't fuss.'

Carol eyed her with deep concern. 'It's not like you to be so careless,' she murmured. 'The long journey down here must have tired you out.'

'Yes,' said Dolly, squaring her shoulders and dig-ging her hands into her jacket pockets. 'That's it absolutely, of course. I must be getting too old for such things.'

'I never thought I'd hear you say that,' teased Carol as she dumped the cloth into the sink and scraped off the rapidly congealing cheese sauce. 'Why don't you go and sit in the other room and relax with a whisky while I sort this out? The supper will be far too hot to eat yet, and I want to hear what you've been up to in Bournemouth.'

Dolly left the kitchen and sank into the couch by the roaring fire. Reaching for the whisky, she poured a generous tot into her glass and then downed it in one before lighting a cigarette. She'd thought Felix was still in London, which was why she'd badgered Hugh into letting her come down to see Carol before she had to move out and the rehearsals began – but the knowledge that he was already here and had made himself known to Carol was a terrible shock, and for once in her life she had no idea what to do for the best.

10

London

Frank Reilly had finally shaken off the dust of the army camp and been given his demob papers three days earlier than expected. There wasn't an inch of space to be had on the special troop train that was chugging through the early darkness, and he'd stood crammed in by soldiers and sailors in the corridor for the entire journey down from the Midlands.

He felt a little out of place in his civvies amongst all the uniforms, and all too aware of how old he must seem to his youthful travelling companions – but then he would be fifty in a matter of days, had done his bit in the last shout and completed his call-up in this one. He didn't envy the boys surrounding him, for he knew that their bright chatter and over-loud laughter was their way of hiding the fear of what they might have to face now an invasion into France was looking ever more likely.

Frank could remember how he'd felt all those years ago on a similar train that was taking him to the battlefields and trenches of France and Belgium. He'd been twenty-one, and, despite his father's warnings of what awaited him there, he'd been excited and eager to prove himself and be a hero like his father.

He grimaced as he threw the end of his cigarette out of the window, remembering how terrifying it had all been as they'd cowered in stinking trenches waiting for the order to go over the top while the enemy bombarded their lines and mustard gas drifted with the wind. Heroes were made during that time, but it was more by luck than anything else that any of them had survived in one piece to tell the tale.

Frank became aware of a general shuffling around him as the train slowed to approach the station. Emerging from his gloomy thoughts, he grabbed the cord of his kitbag more firmly and waited for the hectic exodus that would soon follow. Doors were already being opened, the more foolhardy jumping down as soon as the platform came into view, and as the train gave one final great sigh of steam and ground to a halt, he felt the pressure of those around him forcing him down the step and into the chaos of a dimly lit, busy mainline station.

He hoisted his kitbag over his shoulder and strode down the platform, his gaze trawling the faces of the people waiting at the barrier. The announcements coming over the loudspeakers were muffled and unintelligible in the babble of voices and the clank and hiss of the vast engines arriving and leaving, and as he showed his travel warrant to the ticket collector, he wondered if he'd ever find that one beloved face amongst the shifting, noisy melee.

Frank was tall and broadly built, so he was at some advantage as he stood there looking over the heads of the people dashing back and forth or standing in groups surrounded by their luggage. The majority of the men were in uniform, the clean-cut Americans standing out in their olive green against the drab khaki and dark blue. Factory women in knotted headscarves, worn overcoats and dungarees stood in groups chattering and smoking as they eyed up the men from the forces, and amongst them all were harried mothers with small children, girls in uniform, and men in bowler hats carrying tightly furled umbrellas.

'Hello, Da.'

Frank turned in delight and was swiftly swamped in an enthusiastic hug. 'I was beginning to wonder if we'd ever find one another,' he said after they'd drawn apart. He was still grinning as he drank in the sight of his much-loved boy who looked so handsome in his Royal Naval Reserve uniform. 'To be sure, Brendon, you're looking fine, so you are.'

The dark blue eyes shone with affection as he returned his father's smile. 'You're not looking so bad for an auld fella yourself,' he teased.

'Less of the old,' retorted Frank, giving him a soft punch on the arm. 'You might be as tall and broad as me, but I bet I could still get the better of you in a wrestling match.'

Brendon laughed and lightly patted his father's protruding stomach. 'You'd have to catch me first, and it looks as if you've put on a bit of winter condition, Da. The army obviously fed you too well.'

Frank quickly drew in his belly and pushed out his chest, but found he couldn't maintain the stance for very long, so let it sag over his belt again. 'Aye, you could be right,' he said woefully. 'Too much bully beef and mash, and not enough exercise being stuck in an engineering workshop every day.'

Brendon grabbed his father's kitbag and slung it easily over his shoulder. 'Come on, let's get out of here and find somewhere quiet where we can talk.'

'It would have been nice to spend more time with you, son,' said Frank as they strolled across the vast, crowded concourse. 'But we only have two hours before my train leaves for home.'

'It's longer than some people get,' replied Brendon, 'and I could only manage a four-hour pass. But I know a little café just round the corner which does a decent cup of tea and pie and chips.' He winked at his father. 'Just don't ask what's in the pie.'

They walked out of the station into a darkness eerily lit by dancing flames. Thick smoke swirled everywhere and Frank could hear emergency bells and the shouts of the firemen as they battled to put out the fires. He had witnessed too many scenes like this to get emotional any more, so he regarded the damage to the nearby buildings and the rubble piled in the street with jaded acceptance.

Brendon led the way down a narrow side street to a tiny café which had condensation running down the blacked-out windows. Pushing open the door, they were assailed by the smell of frying and fragrant steam coming from several pots boiling on a stove. The place was empty, so without conferring with Frank, Brendon ordered pies, chips and peas and a pot of tea, and then joined him at a table by the window.

'How's your mother?' Frank asked anxiously. 'She doesn't say much in her letters, but from what Peggy's written, she's still not handling things too well.'

Brendon offered his cigarettes and once they were lit, he gave a sigh. 'Mum's actually a lot better now Aunt Peg has got her volunteering for the WVS. She's also staying at Beach View for the nights after her shifts at the Town Hall, and I think having company again has really helped.' He flicked ash from his cigarette into the battered metal ashtray on the table between them. 'But she'll be glad to have you back, Da.'

'Aye, I hope so,' Frank murmured. 'But I still have to be involved with the Home Guard and Civil Defence, so there will be nights when I can't be at home with her.'

Brendon chewed his lip, his gaze avoiding his father. 'I still mourn for them, Da, just as you and Mum do, but it happened some time ago and we all have to get on with our lives. It doesn't mean we'll love or miss them less, but what sort of memorial would it be to them if we didn't make the best of what we have?'

'Aye, I agree, but Pauline's a mother, and they feel things differently to us.' He regarded his son with deep affection. 'I know she worries over you, and if she could, she'd wrap you up in cotton wool and hide you for the duration of the war.'

Brendon's smile was sad. 'I know, but there's nothing I can do about it – and at least I'm not still out in the Atlantic or in the Pacific on a minesweeper – which actually I'd prefer to being a sitting duck on London's docks.'

They fell silent as the woman brought over the

pot of tea and two plates heaped with pie, chips and mushy peas.

'Is it very bad here?' asked Frank after he'd tasted the pie and found that, although he couldn't identify the meat, it was delicious.

'Not half as bad as it was,' Brendon replied. 'Harris's bombing campaign is biting and the Germans can't build enough planes to replace the ones the RAF boys have taken down, so it's been relatively quiet just lately.'

'It's the same up north.' Frank retrieved a lump of gristle from the pie and discarded it on the side of his plate. 'This damned war has gone on for too long and everyone's sick of it – now it's all quietened down, we've become impatient to get on and finish it.'

'It will happen,' said Brendon quietly, 'and probably quite soon. You've heard the rumours, no doubt?'

'The invasion into France?' murmured Frank, aware of the woman behind the counter watching them. At his son's nod, he finished his food and pushed the plate away. 'It can't come soon enough,' he said, pouring the thick, dark tea into their cups, 'and having noticed the build-up of Allied troops all heading south, I suspect it could even be early next year.'

Brendon shrugged. 'I can't comment on that, Da. But it's a fair estimate.'

Frank eyed him sharply. 'But you won't be playing any part in it, will you?'

'I'm under orders the same as everyone in the services, Da. I do as I'm told, and go where I'm needed.' He pushed his own plate away and reached for the cup of tea. 'But I think you can safely say that, as a reserve, I won't get involved.'

'Thank God for that,' breathed Frank. 'I don't know how your mother would react if you were caught up in the fighting again.'

Brendon lit their cigarettes. 'You know, Da,' he said carefully, 'it's a terrible responsibility being the only survivor of three brothers, and I'm finding it harder than ever to go down and see Mum.' His dark blue eyes regarded Frank steadily. 'She smothers me, Da, makes me afraid to tell her anything in case she gets upset. And then I feel guilty, and return to base wishing I'd been honest with her and told her how I really felt about it all.'

'I'll have a wee word with her once I've settled in back home,' said Frank. 'You should have written and told me what you couldn't say to your mother.'

Brendon let out a deep sigh. 'I didn't want to upset you either,' he confessed. 'But Dolly understood, and she's a very good listener. For someone who pretends to be empty-headed, she's a very sensible woman.' He grinned. 'Did I tell you she took me to afternoon tea at the Ritz?'

Frank's eyes widened. 'What on earth was Dolly doing up here?'

Brendon shrugged. 'She said she'd come up to meet some friends and do some shopping.' He grinned. 'The tea was quite the best I've ever had, with proper cream cake and little cucumber and smoked salmon sandwiches in really soft white bread. The memory of it still makes my mouth water.'

'Aye, well the nobs that go to the Ritz only expect the best,' said Frank sourly. 'I'm surprised our Dolly can afford such things.'

Brendon chuckled. 'Dolly will always surprise us one way or the other,' he said. 'She's a unique woman – and I love and admire her enormously.'

Frank grinned. 'Aye, she's not like any other grandmother I've ever met, but I'm glad she's not living on our doorstep – she's got enough energy to wear anyone out.'

They continued to talk as the tea went cold in the pot and customers arrived and left, and all too soon it was time to return to the station.

Brendon reached into his thick overcoat pocket. 'I don't know if I'll be down for Christmas, so would you give these to Mum, Peggy and Grandad on the day? They're not up to much, I'm afraid; the shops don't seem to be stocking anything decent this year.'

'Aye,' Frank muttered gruffly as he took the three neatly wrapped packages and transferred them into his own coat pockets. 'I'll do that.'

They regarded one another in silence, knowing their short time together was over. Frank put his kitbag down and gathered his son into his arms, holding him close, wishing he could take him home with him. 'Look after yourself, wee boy,' he murmured. 'And don't do anything I wouldn't.'

Brendon's arms tightened about him. 'I love you, Da,' he muttered. 'And I'll do my best to come home sometime over Christmas, I promise.'

Frank could barely see through his tears as he swung

the kitbag over his shoulder and walked quickly towards the platform where his train was waiting. He turned at the barrier, waved to the tall figure standing still amid the swirl of people and then hurried to climb on board as the guard raised his flag.

The train was packed with troops and kitbags, so Frank remained in the corridor by the open window and leaned out. But Brendon could no longer be seen beyond the great swirls of steam and smoke from the engine, so he closed the window against the flying cinders and leaned against it, his emotions jumbled as the great wheels began to turn and the train slowly drew away from the station.

It had been wonderful to see his son after so long, but like Pauline he wished he could just bundle him up and keep him safe. Not that he'd ever let anyone but his father Ron know that. He stared out of the window, wondering about his return to the cottage in Tamarisk Bay, and if Pauline really was coming to terms with their awful loss. He hoped she was, for Brendon was right: the time for mourning was over and they needed to get on with the lives they'd been granted.

11

Cliffehaven

Supper was over, the dishes washed and put away by the four girls while Peggy took Daisy upstairs for her nightly bath. Fran was now getting ready to go on night shift at the hospital, Rita and Ivy were playing their gramophone records upstairs, and Sarah was on the telephone in the hall arranging to meet a friend the following night.

Ron surreptitiously looked at the clock on the mantelpiece as Cordelia turned her back on him and became engrossed in trying to tune the wireless for the evening news. The coast was clear. It was time to make his escape. He grabbed his cap from the table, clicked his fingers at Harvey who was slumped in front of the fire, and began to back away towards the cellar steps.

'And where do you think you're going?' asked Peggy, who had suddenly appeared in the kitchen doorway carrying a grizzling Daisy on her hip. 'I asked you to move the furniture in the front room so I can get it ready for Christmas, and as far as I can see, nothing's changed.'

'Well, now, Peggy,' he began, avoiding her stern gaze. ''Tis a while yet before Christmas, and I have other things to be doing.'

Peggy set Daisy on her feet and folded her arms. 'What things?'

'Ach, just things,' he said vaguely, taking a few more steps back.

'What are you up to, you old rascal?' Cordelia chipped in, eyeing him over her reading glasses. 'No good, I'll be bound.'

Ron put on his best hangdog expression and eyed them from beneath his sweeping brows. ''Tis a sad thing that an old soldier who suffers terrible from the shrapnel moving about in me back is treated with such little respect,' he muttered.

'You're an old fraud,' said Cordelia.

'Yes,' agreed Peggy. 'And we've all heard that excuse too many times to be swayed by it, so there's no point in using it yet again to get out of doing things round the house.'

'What's he trying to get out of now?' asked Rita, appearing with Sarah, Ivy and Fran in the kitchen doorway.

Ron rammed the grubby cap on his head as little Daisy clung to his legs and looked up at him in tearful reproach. 'This house has too many females in it,' he grumbled. 'A man can do nothing right, and it's making me life a misery, so it is.'

'I'll make it even more miserable if you don't go and shift that furniture,' said Peggy, the glint in her eye emphasising the threat.

Ron glanced at the clock with some urgency. 'Aye, I can believe that, but the furniture will have to wait. I've somewhere important to be and I can't be late.' With that, he picked up Daisy, dumped her into Peggy's arms and swiftly ran down the steps, Harvey at his heels.

Grabbing his ratty old poacher's coat along the way, he stomped off down the garden path and slammed the gate behind him. There were times when the responsibility for looking after all those females became too much, and he really didn't see what the fuss was about. Christmas wasn't for another couple of weeks yet, and it would only take a matter of an hour to clear the furniture and get it straight.

He cut through the back streets and along the alley-way that ran behind Gloria Stevens' pub and came out halfway up the High Street. He was late, so didn't wait for Harvey who kept stopping to water lamp posts and follow smells, but kept going up the hill until he reached the station.

'You look flustered,' said Stan, the stationmaster. 'Meeting someone off the train?'

'Aye, and it should be in by now,' said Ron, peering through the gloom along the empty track.

Stan shook his head. 'It's been delayed with a hold-up on the outskirts of London.' He placed a meaty arm round Ron's shoulders. 'Never mind, old chum, there's time for a cup of tea from the lovely WVS ladies who've been standing about with only me to talk to.'

Ron had a moment of panic as he realised the WVS tea wagon was parked at the end of the platform, but it soon ebbed, for thankfully Pauline wasn't amongst them. He bought a cup of tea, his pennies rattling in the empty tin mug on the counter, and went to sit by his old friend Stan on the bench.

'So,' he said, 'how're things at home now you've got April and baby Paula living with you?'

Stan's face lit up in a beaming smile. 'She's the most perfect baby,' he said with a soppy look in his eyes, 'and April's a perfect little mother. Ethel and I are over the moon to have them both home at last – and in time for Christmas.'

'Don't talk to me about Christmas,' Ron grumbled. 'It brings nothing but hard work and women bossing me about from morning to night.'

Stan grimaced. 'I know what you mean. Ethel's been putting up decorations and cleaning the place from top to bottom and April's fussing about what we'll eat, and how to dress the table.' He gave a sigh. 'I'm not allowed to eat anything tasty since my heart attack, because everything I like is supposed to be bad for me. Christmas won't be much fun, I can tell you that, Ron.'

'The diet's doing you good, though,' said Ron, taking in the slimmer waistline, the much looser railway uniform, and healthier colour in his face. 'And you look a lot better for it, if you don't mind me saying so.'

Stan patted his midriff which was half the size it had been before the heart attack floored him on his and Ethel's wedding day six months before. 'Aye, I feel better too. But I'll miss not having lovely plum pudding or a mince pie.'

'I doubt you'll get either with the rationing the way it is,' said Ron gloomily, filling his pipe as Harvey tried hard to persuade the adoring ladies of the WVS that he was starving and that only one of their sandwiches would keep him alive.

'But knowing how clever your Ethel is,' Ron continued, 'I expect she'll manage to find the ingredients and let you have a wee taste or two as a treat.'

'My Ethel's proved to be a very strong-minded woman,' said Stan darkly. 'If she decides I can't have something then nothing will shift her.'

'Then you'll just have to sneak something when she's not looking,' said Ron, puffing on his pipe to draw the flame through the tobacco. 'It's the only way I get enough sugar in me tea.'

'Life's difficult, isn't it?' sighed Stan.

'When women are involved it is,' agreed Ron. 'But God love 'em, I don't know what we'd do without 'em.'

'Aye, and there's the rub.' Stan folded his arms and settled more comfortably on the hard bench. 'So, Ron, who are you waiting for this evening?'

'My boy, Frank. The army let him go finally, and I promised to meet him.'

'I'm surprised Pauline's not here.'

Ron regarded the women at the end of the platform. 'He wanted to talk to me on the quiet before he got caught up in all the female hysterics,' he replied. 'Pauline's helping out at the Town Hall today and should be making her way to Beach View by now – so she'll see him soon enough.'

Their conversation was brought to an end by the sound of the steam engine huffing and puffing towards them. Stan carefully placed his stationmaster's cap on his head, picked up his lantern to guide the train safely in and got to his feet. Harvey was immediately alert and stood at Ron's side as the sound of the engine grew nearer, somehow sensing that someone important to him would soon be arriving.

The train pulled in with a great exhalation of smoke and steam, and the grubby-faced engine driver leaned out to greet them. 'Sorry we're late,' he shouted above the noise of slamming doors. 'Jerry bombed a bit of track and we had to wait for it to be repaired.'

As Stan stood chatting to the man, Ron stood back from the mad rush of troops all clamouring to get a cup of tea and a sandwich from the WVS wagon before they continued their journey, and looked anxiously for sight of his son.

It was Harvey who spotted him first and with a yelp of delight went barging through the crush on the platform to throw himself at him.

Frank dropped his kitbag and made a huge fuss of him, then, upon seeing his father, he opened his arms wide and enfolded him in an embrace. 'Thanks for coming, Da,' he said quietly.

'I nearly didn't make it,' Ron replied, emerging rather breathlessly from the all-encompassing bear hug. 'There are jobs to be done and Peggy's on the warpath.'

Frank grinned and hoisted the kitbag over his shoulder. 'Let's take our time walking back,' he said. 'It's been too long since we had a chance to really talk, and once Pauline sees me that will be gone.'

Cordelia Finch settled down with her tangled knitting in her favourite chair to listen to *It's That Man Again* on the wireless. Pauline had just come back from finishing her stint at the Town Hall and was eating the supper

Peggy had kept warm for her in the range oven, and now Fran had left for the hospital, the other three girls were sitting round the table enjoying the comedy show.

Peggy walked into the kitchen having finally got Daisy to sleep after a long, trying day, and she plumped down in the other fireside chair, glad to be off her feet for a while. The kitchen was warm and cosy with the blackout curtains tightly pulled against the night and the fire glowing, and it was lovely to have Rita, Sarah and Ivy for company when all too often they were either working or out at one of the dances that seemed to be held most nights.

She looked at them fondly. Rita was a local girl who'd come to live with her when her home had been flattened in a firebomb early on in the war. Small, dark-haired and with an elfin face, she was however a tomboy who favoured wearing trousers, boots and her World War I flying jacket and helmet, and racing about on her motorbike. Her hours at the fire station were erratic, for if there was a raid, then she was expected to attend to clear up the aftermath.

Ivy had been billeted with Doris when she'd first come down from London to work in the armaments factory, but she'd had a miserable time there, so Peggy had willingly taken her in. She and Rita were a couple of imps who seemed to find it impossible to keep their room tidy – and like Ron, always seemed to have an excuse for not doing anything about it. The two girls had become close friends, and now Ivy was stepping out with Andy who also worked at the fire station, that friendship had blossomed even more.

Sarah was a completely different kettle of fish. Brought up amongst the expats in Singapore with her sister Jane, she was well educated and very sophisticated for a girl her age. Sarah and Jane had escaped Singapore as the Japanese had poured in, and although their mother and baby brother were now safe in Australia, there had been no word of their father or Sarah's fiancé who'd been left behind.

Peggy kept half an ear on the wireless programme, but her thoughts were elsewhere. There had been ugly rumours coming out of that part of the world, and she knew that since Jane had left for some secret posting for the MOD, the worry over it all had deepened for poor Sarah, who worked in the office of the Women's Timber Corps up on Lord Cliffe's estate.

Peggy admired Sarah's steadfast loyalty to Philip, the fiancé she'd left behind, but it saddened her that the girl was being forced into a kind of limbo, unable to move on with her life. There had been an American army captain who'd caught her eye, but Delaney Hammond had turned out to be married, and Sarah had crept back into her shell after that, pinning her hopes and her future on a man who might, tragically, already be dead.

Peggy stared into the fire, thinking how cruel it was of the Japanese not to give out any information on their prisoners. At least the Germans honoured the Geneva Convention and passed on news of men they'd killed or captured – even giving the fallen a decent burial when possible. But whatever was going on in the Far East remained a mystery, and both girls had to be going through agonies from not knowing anything.

Peggy's thoughts turned to Fran, who'd left earlier to work in the theatre at the hospital. She was a lovely Irish girl, with autumnal hair, green eyes and a sweet nature – unless roused to a fiery temper, which fortunately always blew itself out quickly. She could play the violin like an angel and had managed to capture the heart of the lovely Robert, who worked for the MOD and often serenaded her quite beautifully on the saxophone.

Her gaze fell on Cordelia, who was on the point of nodding off in her chair. Cordelia Finch was a bird-like little woman who'd just celebrated her seventy-ninth birthday. She was in the habit of not turning up her hearing aid, which sometimes made conversations highly convoluted, and she and Ron were always exchanging insults and arguing about everything – but as they seemed to enjoy these exchanges, and there was no real rancour in them, everyone accepted them as part and parcel of the chaos that was Beach View.

Cordelia had become an intrinsic part of Peggy's family since she'd moved in as a lodger several years before the war. The absence of Anne, Cissy and the boys had saddened her as much as it had Peggy, for she'd become used to being surrounded by the noise and bustle of youngsters. But the arrival of little Daisy and the evacuees had brought colour and life back into the empty rooms, and Cordelia had blossomed again. She'd taken on the role of grandmother, advisor and willing accomplice in their mischief and fun, and Peggy was warmed by the love and care she brought into their home.

Not wanting to interrupt the comedy show, Peggy

waited patiently until the theme music was being played and then got to her feet. 'As Ron has done his usual disappearing act and that front room still has to be cleared, I thought I might tackle it tonight. Anyone feel like giving me a hand?'

Pauline and the three girls cheerfully agreed, and without disturbing Cordelia, who'd fallen asleep over her knitting, they donned aprons and headscarves before trooping out into the hall to take a look at what needed doing.

The large room had been used to serve breakfast to the paying guests when Peggy had been running Beach View as a boarding house – and every Christmas, birthday and special occasion had been celebrated in it until the restrictions of the war had made any kind of party too expensive and difficult to contemplate. Now it was more of a storeroom for unwanted furniture and bags and boxes of things that might be useful in the future, but had remained untouched since the previous Christmas.

Peggy noted the scratches on the parquet flooring, the dust clinging to the cornices and central plaster rose from which a single lightbulb dangled forlornly. The grand marble fireplace had been boarded up after the chimney had been damaged during a raid, and although it had been cobbled back together, it still leaked and was inclined to shed bits of soot and brick dust when the wind got up.

Peggy took a deep breath, tied the strings of her wrap-round apron more firmly about her waist and started issuing instructions. 'We need to get the boxes and bags out so we can see the wood for the trees,' she said. 'Go through them to see if there's anything remotely useful in them and if not, stuff them into the cupboard under the stairs. Those that won't fit can go up on the top landing for Ron to put in the attic.'

She regarded the furniture. 'We'll need the two tables and at least twelve chairs, so let's push them up against the wall out of the way while we clear the rest. The rug will need to be unrolled and given a good shake, and the curtains will have to come down to be washed. I can't believe how filthy they are.' She grimaced at the greasy feel of them, but as it was night, they would have to stay up for now as blackouts.

Everyone set to, and before long the room was looking much clearer. Sarah had unearthed a box filled with old Christmas decorations which they set aside for when the room had been cleaned properly, and Peggy found some of Ron's tattered shirts which were beyond mending but would make excellent dusters or cleaning cloths.

Ivy and Rita fetched brooms, dustpans, scrubbing brushes, mops, bucket and dusters, and Pauline brought in the gramophone, closely followed by Sarah, who was laden with an armful of records. With the lively music making it feel festive, they set to with a will, singing along to the popular songs as they scrubbed and mopped in unison from one end of the room to the other.

They reached the doorway and rested back on their haunches to admire their handiwork, unaware that Ron and Frank were standing in the hall watching them in amusement.

'I don't know about you lot,' said Pauline, getting

off her aching knees to stretch her legs, 'but I need a cuppa and a fag after that.'

'I've got something better than a cuppa,' said Frank.

Pauline swung round, and, with a shriek of delight, threw herself into his arms.

Peggy nodded to Ron and the others and they quietly left them to it. Homecomings were rare and very personal, and although it was wonderful to see Frank again, it was a painful reminder to Peggy that Jim and the rest of her family wouldn't be returning to Beach View until peace was declared – and with the way things were going, it could be years before she saw them again.

12

Slapton

It had proved to be an uncomfortable night for Dolly. Acutely aware of Carol sleeping next to her, she tried not to fidget or sprawl across the bed as was her custom. She was bone-weary after the long, difficult drive, but her tortured thoughts refused to let her sleep, so she lay in the profound darkness of the tiny bedroom listening to what she suspected were mice scuttling about in the thatch.

Dolly was furious with herself for reacting so carelessly to the mention of Felix's name. She'd had a lifetime of experience in keeping herself poised for any such occurrence and should not have been caught unawares. After all, she'd known Felix was due down here at some point and she should have stayed on her guard, even though her delight at seeing Carol again had made her forget about the outside world beyond the cottage. It was lucky Carol had given her an excuse for dropping that blasted bowl, otherwise she could have had a lot of explaining to do.

Dolly's immediate instinct was to get out of Slapton as quickly as possible. She'd be on tenterhooks all the time waiting to bump into Felix, and that would make for an uncomfortable visit. This village was too small and sparsely populated to be able to avoid anyone, let alone Felix, who had clearly made himself a presence in the place.

In reality, however, Dolly knew things weren't that simple, for during their cosy evening sipping whisky on the sofa, she had seen through her daughter's strong exterior to the real heart of the matter. Carol had been managing with her grief these past few months, but Dolly could tell that the notice to evacuate had knocked her for six. Being forced out of her little cottage and away from the churchyard where her precious little family now resided was breaking Carol's heart and stifling her spirit – and for Dolly to leave so suddenly would cause Carol even more upset. Dolly knew she hadn't been the most stable of mothers while Carol was growing up, but she couldn't leave her now she was facing such an upheaval.

Dolly took the sleeping Carol gently into her arms and held her close, filled with regret that she hadn't been a better mother, and aching for her inability to ease her daughter's pain. Perhaps she should persuade Carol to give up her work as a land girl and move herself and her belongings into the Bournemouth house? She instantly dismissed the idea, for there was no way she'd be able to explain her prolonged absences when she had to be in London or Bletchley.

Dolly carefully eased away from Carol, turned onto her side and nestled her face into the pillow. Then it came to her. It wouldn't take too much to persuade Hugh to provide the necessary travel warrants for

Carol to stay with either Pauline or Peggy. Peggy nearly always had a spare room, and although Frank would be back in Tamarisk Bay by Christmas, their house was quite big enough to accommodate Carol, and it might do both sisters good to have each other's company. This idea pleased her and she smiled into the darkness.

Dolly realised she must have fallen asleep at some point, for when she next opened her eyes it was to discover that Carol was already up and the aroma of toast was floating up the stairs. Dolly's stomach rumbled, for she was very hungry after eating so little the day before. She clambered out of bed and got dressed in smart slacks, blouse and sweater, and draped a silk scarf around her neck to combat the chill of the early morning.

Carol's dressing table and mirror had already gone up to the farm, so she fumbled about in her handbag and found her powder compact. Swishing the curtains open to reveal a hazy sun spreading across the ruins of what had once been miles of pristine farmland, she used the poor light to put on some powder and lipstick. No one – not even her daughters – was allowed to see her without make-up.

Dolly pulled the bedclothes straight, plumped the pillows and smoothed the counterpane, admiring the fancy iron bedstead with its brass knobs, which had once belonged to David's parents. She looked round the small room, noting that although it was almost bare, Carol had kept the framed photographs on display. She regarded the one of Carol and David, taken on their wedding day, and the snapshot of Pauline, Frank and Peggy Reilly which had clearly been taken outside Beach View – they'd been happier days, she mused, eyeing the photograph of herself standing so proudly between her daughters.

And then her gaze fell on the sepia studio shot she'd given Carol all those years ago when she'd begun to ask questions about her father. It was a shock to see it again after so long, for she hadn't realised Carol still had it. Clearly it meant something to her, and as Dolly regarded the handsome man smiling back at her, she felt a twinge of unease at the realisation that Frederick Adams was still very much a part of Carol's life.

'If only I could turn the clock back,' she murmured. 'But it's too late. What's done is done, and the sooner I get Carol away from here and down with her sister, the better it will be.'

She took a breath and smiled widely as she stepped into the kitchen and gave Carol a hug and kiss. 'Good morning, darling. I thought you'd be at work,' she said, regarding the pretty cloth on the table and the mismatched china. The jar of Harrods marmalade stood next to the pat of butter on a chipped saucer, and the teapot was an ugly brown thing sitting next to a small can of milk.

'I've got the day off, so I said I'd go round to Mrs Rayner's and help her pack her things.' Carol put toast and scrambled egg on a thick china plate. 'I'm sorry breakfast's a bit of a mishmash, but my good stuff is packed away and already at the farm.'

She sat down at the small table and once Dolly had used the freezing bathroom, they tucked into the lovely fluffy eggs and buttered toast.

'I shouldn't be too long next door,' Carol said. 'Why don't you come and meet Mrs Rayner and lend us a hand? She was lovely to me when I lost David and the baby, and although she's a bit brusque, you'll soon get used to it.'

'I'm not much good at packing – or with little old ladies,' said Dolly, 'so I'll hang about here for a bit and write a few letters. If it looks as if you'll be some time, I might take myself off for a walk.'

She finished the eggs and buttered a slice of toast to go with a smear of the marmalade. 'I've had a thought,' she said.

Carol eyed her warily. 'Oh dear, that's always dangerous. What are you planning now?'

Dolly smiled affectionately at her, well aware that Carol was familiar with the strange workings of her mind. 'While I was waiting for you to come home yesterday I read the pamphlet you've all had delivered. And I must say it was filled with comprehensive advice on just about everything this move will involve, which rather proves there's clearly been a great deal of thought put into this evacuation.'

'Yes, I know,' Carol agreed, 'and I suspect those plans have been in the making for quite a while.'

'I noted that travel warrants and haulage are restricted to certain distances,' said Dolly, her focus on the toast, 'but I happen to have a friend who could bypass all that and get you and your belongings down to Cliffehaven. I'd go with you, of course,' she added hastily, 'and spend Christmas with you and Pauline.'

Carol fidgeted with a fold in the tablecloth. 'I don't want to go to Cliffehaven,' she said evenly.

'But why not?' pressed Dolly. 'I can't bear to think of you living up there in that draughty barn and spending Christmas amongst strangers, when you could be with your family.'

'They're not strangers, Mum, they're lovely, friendly girls – and although I won't be in my own home, at least I'll be close enough to keep an eye on it from the farm.' Carol reached across the table and took Dolly's hand, her tone conciliatory. 'It's a lovely idea, but I'm not ready to leave here. Maybe next Christmas I'll feel differently.'

Dolly could see she was not to be persuaded, and so didn't press the issue. 'You go next door and get on with whatever you have to do, and I'll clear up here,' she said once they'd finished breakfast. 'Is there anything else you'd like me to do until you get back? Only I'll feel rather useless otherwise.'

Carol laughed and shook her head. 'There's only a bit of washing, but I can see to that later.' She glanced out of the window to the small strip of muddy grass at the back of the house. 'The weather doesn't look too bad, so it should be a good drying day.' She blew her mother a kiss and went into the hall for her coat and wellingtons before leaving the house.

Dolly always packed rubber gloves when she visited her daughters, for there was invariably washing-up or housework to do and she didn't want to spoil her fresh manicure. She would clear the breakfast dishes and make a start on the laundry, for anything was better than hanging about doing nothing, and it was far too cold and soggy to go walking.

Carol closed the door behind her and took a deep breath of the crisp, clean air. She could understand why her mother wanted her to go to Pauline's for the duration of this eviction, for she probably saw her as being isolated and lonely. And yet that wasn't the case at all, for unlike her mother, who craved the social whirl, she was a solitary person, and comfortable with her own company.

Brought up by ageing and very loving grandparents, she'd learned to amuse herself with toys, crafts and books as a child, and as she'd matured, those early influences had meant she didn't need to seek out lots of friends – just one or two like-minded girls who enjoyed the same things, and didn't need to be surrounded by crowds. That was not to say they were stuck-up or prudish, for they went to parties and dances and enjoyed them immensely, but they preferred playing sport or going for long rides with the local cycling and pony clubs to chasing boys and giggling in corners.

Carol shut the gate behind her and looked along the row of abandoned cottages. She knew that the time was rapidly approaching for her to leave, and the thought of moving away from David and her baby weighed heavy on her heart. But once Mrs Rayner was safely on her way, she would have no further excuse to stay, so she'd bring Hector down with the cart, collect the last of her belongings and try not to look back as she headed for Coombe Farm.

She walked up the cinder path between the rows of carrots, potatoes and cabbages and frowned as she saw the downstairs curtains were still drawn. It was most unusual, for Edith was an early riser, and she'd often heard her moving about before it was even light. She knocked on the door, then pushed it open. 'Hello? It's me – Carol,' she called out.

There was no reply. With a sense of foreboding, Carol looked into the dark sitting room. Nipper waddled down the stairs on his stubby legs to paw at her with little yelps and whines, which probably meant he needed food or to be let out. She patted him, which made him squirm, so she rubbed his fat belly and then went to open the curtains. The weak light showed that there were cold ashes in the hearth; a library book lay open on the arm of Mrs Rayner's chair, and an empty teacup sat on the floor beside it.

The foreboding grew as Nipper continued to whine agitatedly and kept heading for the stairs instead of the kitchen. Carol stood on the bottom step. 'Mrs Rayner?' she called again. 'Mrs Rayner, are you all right?'

There was still no reply, and with the dog following closely at her heels, Carol slowly went up the narrow wooden stairs to the front bedroom. Nipper was out of breath, but eagerly clawed at the door, looking up at Carol as she hesitated to open it.

She took a deep breath, then reluctantly turned the brass knob and let the door swing open.

Nipper scrambled past her before she could stop him, and began to whine and fret beside the high bed.

Carol took it all in at a glance. The curtains had been drawn back and the bright sunlight fell on the slight figure lying so still in that big brass bed. Edith Rayner lay beneath the downy quilt, her unpinned hair spilling like silver over her shoulders and across the pillow, her face turned towards the window, perhaps seeking one more glimpse of the view she'd known all her life before she went to her final sleep.

Carol scooped up a wriggling, frantic Nipper and tried to soothe him before she gently put him outside the room. Having closed the door on him, she sank into the bedside chair.

'Oh, Edith,' she murmured through her tears. 'You were quite determined not to leave, weren't you?' She touched the cold, still face lightly with her fingers and closed the eyes which now must see another horizon far beyond the hills and coombes of her beloved Slapton. 'Be at peace now,' she whispered.

Carol sat there holding Edith's lifeless hand, remembering her fierce energy, her impatience with fools and her determination to always get her own way – which she'd achieved to the very end of her long life. Edith Rayner might have been difficult to get along with, but she'd be remembered throughout this part of Devon with respect, and mourned as the last of her generation.

Carol eventually folded the old woman's hands

and drew the sheet over her face. There would be a great deal to arrange from now on, but how was it all to be paid for, and what about her cottage and belongings – and Nipper? Carol could hear him scratching at the door and making strange noises. Did he somehow understand that she'd gone? She didn't know – just as she didn't know the answers to all the questions and dilemmas that Mrs Rayner's death would raise.

She drew her coat collar to her chin, suddenly feeling the chill that seemed to settle within a house once the spirit of life had been extinguished. She blinked back her tears and reached for the little prayer book on the side table to find some solace in the lovely familiar words, but as she picked it up, she saw the envelope lying beneath it.

The writing was scrawled and difficult to read, but it was addressed to her, and Carol held it for a moment, realising the old woman had known she was leaving, and had prepared for it in the only way she knew – by having the last word.

She sat back down in the chair and carefully opened the envelope to find a single sheet of paper carefully folded over a dried four-leaf clover.

Dear Carol,

I have not always been an easy woman to befriend, but I want you to know that I've come to love and admire you for the way you have conducted yourself during these past trying months, and although Bert and I weren't blessed

with children, you have become as dear to me as any
daughter, which is why I know I can trust you to see me
buried alongside my husband, and the rest of my family. To
that end, there is money in the bedside drawer to pay for
everything.

As you know, I have no living relatives, and so I drew
up a will some time ago leaving everything to you in the
belief that you will know what to do with my few treasures.
Nipper has been my companion for many years, so please
give him a home for the time he has left. He's been a good
and faithful friend, just as you have, and if I had any
regrets, it's leaving you both behind.

Shed no tears for me, Carol. I'm ready to meet my
Maker,

Edith Rayner

Carol sat in stunned silence for a while and then
folded the letter back into the envelope with the clover
leaf, and put it carefully in her pocket. She was finding
it almost impossible to take it all in, for Edith had never
once confided her true feelings, or her intentions. Now
she was gone, and those moments they could have
shared were lost. She found a handkerchief and dried
her eyes, the enormity of all that had happened slowly
sinking in as Nipper continued to scratch frantically at
the door.

She was on the point of leaving the room when
her gaze fell on the bedside chest. If Edith had left
money in the drawer, it wouldn't be wise to leave it
there with people coming and going and a village full
of strangers. Feeling like an intruder, she opened the

drawer and drew out a fat envelope, a Post Office book and a copy of Mrs Rayner's will.

Without looking through them, she stuffed it all into the deep pocket of her overcoat. They'd need to be stowed somewhere safe until she'd recovered from the shock and could think more clearly. For now there were more important things to sort out – like finding the doctor to come and sign the death certificate, speaking to the vicar and the undertaker, and notifying Edith's solicitor of her passing. With everyone leaving the area, the local banks and post offices were closed and there were even fewer telephones, so it wouldn't be easy.

Carol placed a gentle hand on the narrow, still shoulder beneath the sheet. 'I'll look after everything,' she murmured, 'and don't worry about Nipper. I'll make sure his last years are happy ones. Sleep well, Edith.'

The tears were blinding her as she drew the curtains over the window. Then she opened the door and quickly scooped up a squirming Nipper, holding tightly to his collar as she firmly closed the door behind her and went down the stairs.

'I don't know what the Burnleys will make of you,' she muttered to the little dog, 'but if you're true to your kind, they might be glad to have you as their rat catcher.'

The silence of the house was profound, and Carol locked the front door behind her with a sense that an era was over. She took a deep breath of fresh air as she waited for Nipper to cock his leg against the garden gate, and then headed for home.

It was a bit of a surprise to find her mother swathed in an oversized apron and up to her elbows in hot water and suds as she did the laundry – but then this was turning out to be a strange day altogether. 'Leave that, Mum,' she said. 'There's something I need to tell you.'

Dolly's welcoming smile faded as she eyed the scrabbling Jack Russell on the end of a lead and tried to absorb what Carol was saying. Mindful of her expensive trousers, she warded off the dog, who was trying to climb her legs, and told it very firmly to sit and be still.

Satisfied that the dog had obeyed her, she whipped off her yellow gloves and apron and regarded Carol with concern. 'I'm very sorry to hear about her passing, but it must have been an awful shock to find her like that. How are you holding up?'

'I feel surprisingly calm,' Carol replied. 'She'd lived a long and fulfilled life and hadn't wanted to leave the only home she'd ever known. I think she decided it was her time and simply went to sleep. Not many people are granted such a peaceful death.'

'Oh, darling,' murmured Dolly, taking her into her arms. 'I'm so glad I came. I couldn't bear to think of you having to deal with all this on your own.'

Carol felt the onset of tears and hastily blinked them away as she returned her mother's embrace. 'I'm glad you're here too,' she managed through a tight throat.

'Not only because I love you, but because I've missed having you here.'

'But, darling, I did offer to stay on the last time, and you were quite definite that you needed to be on your own.'

Carol nodded and managed a watery smile. 'And I did then, Mum. But now there are more practical things to consider, and I need not only your company, but your advice.'

Dolly raised a questioning brow as Carol drew the letter, the envelope of money, the will and savings book from her pocket and put them on the table. Once she'd read the letter she folded it thoughtfully back into the envelope and gave a silent whistle.

'That's a big responsibility, Carol. It will be doubly difficult trying to sort out all her things as well as your own.'

'I know, but I still have time before the deadline if you'll stay and help me.'

'Well, of course I will. But that money must be put somewhere safe. There's more than enough there to pay for the funeral, and I'd suggest taking the rest along with the savings book and will and putting them in a safety deposit box at your solicitor's.'

'His office is in Kingsbridge,' Carol said.

'That's all right, we'll use my car. It's parked outside the Queen's Arms, so it won't take long to fetch it.' Dolly eyed Nipper, who was scratching luxuriously. 'What about him?'

'He'll have to come with us, I'm afraid.'

'Let's hope he doesn't get car sick, then,' said Dolly.

'My friend won't be at all pleased if he ruins the leather.'

Carol shrugged. 'If he's sick, I'll clear it up.'

'Right then,' said Dolly determinedly. 'I'll go and get changed into something more appropriate and then we'll speak to the vicar about the arrangements, and see if he has a working telephone so we can ring the funeral directors and the doctor before we drive into Kingsbridge to the solicitors.'

Carol had to smile, for her mother's idea of suitable attire was a tailored jacket and skirt, an astrakhan overcoat, fur wrap and high heels, with a neat little hat tilted at a jaunty angle over one eye. Feeling shabby and underdressed in her usual dungarees, sweater and overcoat, Carol tied Nipper's leash firmly to an outside bench, and followed her into the church.

The ancient building looked horribly bare now it had been stripped of everything that could be moved. There were sandbags piled around the font and the pulpit, and over the stained glass window beneath the belfry, with the less important windows boarded up securely with plywood, while the pendant lights and those on wrought-iron stands by the front pews had had their glass shades and bulbs removed.

The carved stone slab that served as an altar was naked of its cloth, crucifix and brass candlesticks, and the hassocks that once adorned the steps before it were gone, along with the oak bishop's chair and lectern.

They found Samuel Fotherington sitting alone in a pew staring disconsolately into the gloom of his church that was now lit by only a few candles. His face was long and solemn as he heard Carol's news and agreed to let them use his telephone at the rectory. The service would be conducted as soon as possible, for time was of the essence now there were so few days left before the deadline, and he was saddened that one of his last duties for his parishioners should be a funeral. He hesitantly suggested they could combine it with a special matins to bid farewell to the village, and both Carol and Dolly thought this was a splendid idea.

To Carol's relief, her mother took charge of organising the funeral directors, for they were the same people she'd dealt with when David had been brought home, and she simply couldn't face them again. She left Dolly the number for the doctor – his wife picked up any messages when he was out – and then went to check on Nipper, who was trying to chew through his entangling lead.

Carol untangled him and stopped for a moment at the graveside she'd taken such care to tend these past months to say a few words to her loved ones. Very soon she would be unable to make these visits She was walking back past the memorial to the fallen in the Great War when she heard Mildred Ferris's strident voice and remembered with a jolt that she had yet to tell her the news. Since there was as yet no sign of her mother, Carol followed the sound of that unmistakable voice and found her in the garden of the chantry, berating two very young GIs for letting the fire go out beneath the huge metal drum that was heating the only water available to the men billeted there.

'Miss Ferris,' Carol interrupted. 'Miss Ferris, there is something important I have to tell you.'

'What is it, girl? Can't you see I'm busy?'

Carol withstood the glare, determined to have her say. 'Mrs Rayner died this morning, so the cottage you so kindly readied for her can be used by someone else.'

The anger drained away on a deep sigh. 'I'm very sorry to hear that, but I'm not surprised. It was clear she was loath to move out.'

The piercing gaze shifted to the hapless GIs who were trying desperately to fan life into the fire and then settled back on Carol. 'What about her cottage? It's crammed full of things that will have to be shifted – and then of course there's Nipper.' Her gimlet eyes fell on the dog with little favour. 'I suppose he'll have to be put down, because no one will want him.'

'I'm keeping Nipper and seeing to sorting out her things,' said Carol firmly, 'but I will still need the truck and the men to get it all up to the farm, so if you could thank the general for organising them . . . ?'

Mildred Ferris nodded curtly, stuffed her hands into her sagging jacket pockets and returned to nagging the soldiers.

'And there's another thing,' Carol went on determinedly. 'Have you managed to find somewhere for Betty?'

Mildred gave a short sigh of impatience. 'Betty will

accompany some of her class to the junior school in Beeson, and Mrs Claxton at the Welcome Inn has kindly agreed to accommodate her for the duration of the evacuation.'

'Oh, that is such a relief,' breathed Carol. 'And it will mean we can still see each other. Thank you so much for arranging everything, Miss Ferris.'

13

On the Road to Kingsbridge

Dolly had finished the calls and as she reached the car, she saw Carol coming towards her with the fat dog waddling on its lead. The girl looked drawn and pale despite her smile, and Dolly realised that this latest setback had affected her more deeply than perhaps she herself was aware. Coming on top of having to move out, it was a lot to cope with, having to bear the responsibility of organising everything and taking on that dog.

It was very generous of Mrs Rayner to leave Carol her home and everything in it – and, of course, once the war was over Carol would be well set up, but it couldn't have come at a worse time, and she rather resented the old girl for turning up her toes at the most inopportune moment.

She waited for Carol to settle in the passenger seat, the tan and white dog on her lap. 'The doctor was out delivering a baby, but his wife promised he'd call in this evening,' she said. 'The funeral directors will be here first thing in the morning – it seems they're rather busy at the moment,' she added dryly.

'Thanks, Mum, for doing that. I simply couldn't face it.'

They started out for Kingsbridge and Carol told Dolly the good news about her friend Betty. 'It's a huge weight off my mind,' she confessed, 'and it means we'll be living closer together, which is a lovely thought on this very sad day.'

Dolly said nothing as she concentrated on driving along the winding lanes towards Kingsbridge, past the camps that seemed to be sprouting everywhere and getting repeatedly stuck behind farm vehicles towing wagons overloaded with household possessions, bales of hay and children clinging on for dear life to the ropes that lashed it all down.

She hated driving slowly and loathed being held up, so soon became impatient as she found herself stuck behind a slow-moving convoy of tractors, steam engines and herds of loitering cows.

'It's no good you getting het up, Mum,' said Carol. 'This is Devon and getting anywhere is always difficult.'

'I do wish you'd reconsider going to Pauline's,' Dolly replied, weaving the car back and forth in an attempt to find a way of getting past. 'Driving anywhere here is a complete nightmare.'

Carol chuckled. 'I'm happy where I am, but once I can move back home, perhaps I'll come and visit you in Bournemouth. How would that do?'

It wouldn't do at all, thought Dolly, for once the invasion had been achieved there would be even more work to do at Bletchley.

Kingsbridge was heaving with servicemen, the trains disgorging hundreds at a time, the trucks and jeeps roaring down the steep hills and rumbling over the stone bridge on their way to the different bases that had suddenly sprung up all along this southern coast.

Carol and Dolly soon managed to finish their business in town, and having grabbed a cheap but filling meal in the British Restaurant down by the river, they were soon faced with the torturous journey back to Slapton.

They had less than five miles to go when Dolly rounded a bend and had to almost stand on the brakes. An enormous crane machine faced them, leading what looked like an endless convoy of long trailers loaded with tanks and massive guns.

Dolly had had enough. She got out of the car and marched towards the driver of the leading vehicle. 'You'll have to back up and let us through,' she said, adopting the bossy tone of Mildred Ferris.

He leaned out of his cab. 'Sorry, ma'am, but the United States Army takes precedence. It's you who'll have to back up.'

Dolly folded her arms. 'And if I don't?'

The GI grinned and pointed to the arm of the crane which hung above him. 'Then we'll do it for you.'

'You wouldn't dare,' she snapped.

He just kept grinning and began to lower the enormous arm of the crane.

Dolly quickly got back into the car, furiously slammed it into reverse, lifted her foot too quickly off the accelerator and stalled the engine. 'Bugger,' she breathed, wrestling to get it started again and making it kangaroo-hop backwards as she'd forgotten she'd left it in gear.

'Mum! That's not very ladylike,' said Carol, trying hard not to laugh, while Nipper charged about in the back seat barking hysterically at everything.

'I don't feel ladylike with that great brute grinning and threatening me with his enormous machine. And will you please shut that dog up? He's not helping.'

Carol tried to calm Nipper, but he was having none of it. 'Would you like me to drive, Mum?' she offered.

'I can manage,' Dolly replied through gritted teeth as she twisted in the seat to look behind her, accelerated too hard, and promptly drove into an unforgiving drystone wall. She looked at Carol, her jaw working as she forced back even ruder swear words. 'Don't you dare laugh.'

Dolly ground the gears and pressed her foot to the accelerator. The wheels spun, there was a tortured scream of wrenched metal and the car didn't budge. 'Oh, bugger, bugger, bugger,' she spat. 'Now wha—?'

Her sentence was cut off by the realisation that while she'd been trying to move the car the Americans had firmly tied thick rope cables around it and looped them into the jaws of the hook dangling from the crane. She grabbed Carol's hand and stared, open-mouthed, as the crane gently and expertly lifted them into the air.

Nipper was going berserk; the GIs were grinning like Cheshire cats and the two women clung to each other in a confusion of emotions as the car hung in the air on a level with the laughing driver, who had the absolute cheek to salute them before he swung the car over the hedge to lower it gently into the muddy field.

'Y'all have a nice day, ladies,' came the cheerful voice from the other side of the hedge as the ropes were released from the hook. 'Someone will come to help – but as you Limeys keep telling us – there is a war on, so don't hold your breath.'

They heard the convoy rumble past, the shouts and whistles of the men and the cacophony of hooters and horns simply adding insult to injury.

'I will kill him,' snarled Dolly. Then she caught Carol's eye and they both fell about laughing while Nipper looked at them in confusion.

'Now what?' spluttered Carol. 'How the heck do we get out of here?'

'I haven't got the faintest idea,' replied Dolly, tears of laughter running down her face.

'We could be here until nightfall,' said Carol more soberly, 'and the doctor is due in a couple of hours. Perhaps we ought to get out and push it to the nearest gate? I thought I saw one just back there.'

Dolly looked out of the window in horror at the thick mud and slime on the ground that had recently accommodated a herd of cattle. 'You're wearing stout shoes. Go and check there is one before we start pushing.'

Carol returned a few minutes later to discover that her mother had taken off her expensive shoes, stockings and skirt along with her jacket, overcoat and fur wrap, and was sitting behind the wheel in her sweater, suspender belt and silk knickers. She collapsed with laughter and had to sit down until she'd recovered.

'It's not elegant, I know,' said Dolly, fighting her own giggles, 'but God help that Yank, because if I ever see him again, I will stuff that crane into a very dark and uncomfortable place.'

She warned Nipper that her clothes on the back shelf were out of bounds, and then switched on the engine. 'Let's see if we can move the car without having to push,' she muttered. 'How far's that gate?'

'About a hundred yards back. But there is a bit of a slope, so we might be able to let the car just roll down once we give it a helping hand.'

Dolly put the car in gear, took off the handbrake and carefully pressed the accelerator. The wheels turned, the tyres slithered and spun and it was soon very clear that the car was going nowhere without help.

'There's nothing for it but to push,' Dolly said crossly as she opened the door and gingerly put her bare feet into the sludge. She shuddered with horror at the feel of it seeping between her manicured toes and then braced herself for worse to come.

Nipper thought this was a great game and bundled out of the car to race round it barking in encouragement.

Carol got out the other side and once they'd moved the rope out of the way Dolly grabbed the steering wheel in one hand and the sill of the door in the other. They began to push. The wheels turned, the tyres splattering muck and mud everywhere.

They pushed harder, grimacing with the effort and

the foul stench rising from the filth that was now clinging wetly to them.

The tyres finally found purchase on tufts of grass
and the car slowly began to move towards the gate. It
reached the downward slope that ended in a water-
filled ditch and started to roll towards it, so Dolly leapt
into the car and yanked hard on the handbrake.

Carol climbed in beside her and Nipper swiftly followed. He'd clearly rolled in something foul and taken
a dip in the ditch, so when he vigorously shook himself
Dolly and Carol recoiled in horror at being splattered
even more.

'Do I look as awful as I feel?' Carol asked, touching
her mud-streaked face and looking down at her filthy
clothes and shoes.

'We both look an absolute fright, and probably stink
to high heaven,' said Dolly, avoiding the mirror as she
drove the car through the farm gate. 'I can only pray
no one sees us before we get home.'

'It will take hours to get the car clean,' Carol said
woefully.

'Perhaps I should send a bill for dry-cleaning and
car valeting to the general,' said Dolly waspishly. 'It's
about time the Americans paid for the damage they're
causing.'

They didn't speak much on the way home, for they
were both feeling wrung out, cold to the bone and worried that the doctor might already be at the cottage
waiting for them. However, they were lucky, for the
village was eerily deserted, and there was no sign of
the doctor.

149

With Nipper bundled under her arm, Carol and her mother scuttled inside and slammed the door behind them on what had been one of the strangest days of their lives.

14

Cliffehaven

'Are ye sure about this, son?' asked Ron.

'Aye,' Frank replied gruffly. 'It's the best chance we have of putting something decent on the table for Christmas.' He looked at his father and grinned as he turned up the collar of his oiled hunting coat. 'What's the matter, Da, losing your nerve?'

'Ach, it's not that,' Ron grunted. 'I just don't feel right not having Harvey with me.'

'No one takes their dog to a party,' said Frank firmly. He saw his father was about to argue and carried on, 'At least, no one but you. I hope you're wearing decent clothes under that old coat, because this is a posh officers' do, and they won't let you in otherwise.'

'To be sure I'm not addle-headed,' Ron protested, running a finger inside the stiff collar and flexing his neck. He walked beside his son along the deserted country lane lit only by the fleeting gleam of the moon that appeared occasionally from behind the scudding clouds. It would rain again before the night was out – and his best suit was hardly appropriate for a poaching foray through Lord Cliffe's estate. There would be questions enough from Peggy when he got back, but a ruined suit would cause all sorts of trouble.

'How did you wangle the invitation, Frank?'

'One of their trucks broke down over by the old ruins, and I happened to be passing and managed to fix it. We got chatting, he mentioned the party and here we are.'

Ron felt a certain amount of pride in his son, for he was certainly a chip off the old block, quick thinking and always with an eye to the main chance. They slowed as the sound of music and laughter drifted out into the quiet night, and before going round the bend to the grand entrance of Cliffe Manor, they slipped off their poachers' coats and folded them over their arms.

Frank eyed him up and down with a nod of approval, then smoothed back his own short hair and squared his shoulders. 'Ready for the fray, Da?'

'Aye, that I am, son.'

They walked on, showed their identity cards to the armed soldiers on guard, and were soon strolling down the long drive towards the Edwardian house that stood squarely and elegantly at the end. No light shone from the many windows, but they could hear the noise of the party, and see the gathering of jeeps and trucks parked to one side of the marble fountain which stood in the centre of the turning circle in front of the house.

Ron and Frank slowed and surreptitiously looked beyond the drive into the deep darkness of the surrounding forest. They both knew it well, for it was here that Ron had taught his sons all he knew about the art of poaching. However, there was now a trigger-happy gamekeeper in charge who was neither deaf nor turned a blind eye. His dog was a vicious beast he let free to roam the grounds at night while he sat in his nice warm cottage, but Ron had heard enough stories coming out of the estate to know how to deal with it.

They paused at the bottom of the broad stone steps leading up to the front door, sheltered by an ornate pair of marble pillars and portico. They exchanged knowing smiles, then opened the door, stepped through the heavy blackout curtain and into the glittering lights of an enormous chandelier and the noise and bustle of a party in full swing.

Two hours later they'd eaten their fill of the delicious food the Americans had laid on, and drunk just enough beer to enjoy themselves and still keep a clear head. Now they were camouflaged by their coats and moving stealthily through the trees, past the wooden huts that housed the office of the WTC, the clothing store and the camp kitchen, and down towards the other huts in which the girls of the Timber Corps were billeted.

All was quiet and they continued on to the pools where Lord Cliffe bred the salmon he sold to the posh restaurants and hotels in London. They crouched down in the darkest shadows beneath the trees and regarded the sturdy wire fencing surrounding the pool, and the heavy padlock and chain on the gate. They could hear the electricity humming in the wire, and Frank looked at Ron in dismay, for this was a new innovation.

Ron put a finger to his lips and winked. 'Stay here,' he whispered.

Before Frank could stop him, he ran in a crouch towards the shed at the side of the girls' billet, and with a twist of his lethal hunting knife soon opened the lock and was inside. Holding the door shut behind him, he flicked on his torch, found the right switch in the electrical box and cut the power to the fence.

Easing the door open and peering outside to make sure no one was moving about, he closed and locked it again before returning to Frank. Beckoning his son to follow him, he warily circumnavigated the lake until he was on the far side and well hidden in the thick vegetation that grew right to the water's edge. With freshly sharpened wire-cutters he sliced through the fence and slipped through with Frank swiftly following him.

The reeds were thickly massed on the muddy bank, and as the moon briefly appeared, Ron caught a glimpse of the lazing fish just below the surface. He could already feel the cold, muddy water seeping over his boots and up his trouser legs, but paid it no heed. He drew the folds of his large coat round him to protect his good clothes and, without a sound, lay flat within the reeds. Frank followed suit, the thrill of the adventure almost tangible between them as they rolled back their sleeves and then inched their hands and then their arms into the still water without creating a single ripple.

Tickling salmon was easy if you knew how and the fish were sluggish. Within minutes they both had a wriggling, gasping, silvery prize which they stunned and quickly stuffed into the deep pockets of their coats.

Father and son grinned at one another as they slithered back out of the reeds and through the fence. Christmas lunch was almost sorted. Ron twisted the fencing wire back into place so the connection would be made when the electricity was turned back on, and then they crept away, their footfalls soft and silent on the damp forest floor.

Taking a different route to the shed to avoid the main track through the trees, they approached the back of the land girls' billet. Within minutes Ron had reconnected the electricity and locked the door behind him. No one would guess at a glance that the ponds had been raided, and he could only hope that the break he'd made in the fence wouldn't be noticed so he could come back after Christmas and bag something for New Year.

They were following a narrow track through the forest which would eventually take them back to the lane, thereby avoiding the sentries at the gate, thanking their lucky stars that the keeper and his dog were nowhere to be seen. And then they heard a noise behind them, and froze.

It wasn't a man's footsteps going through the drift of fallen leaves, but the soft pad of large paws and the snuffling of a dog following a scent.

Father and son melted into the profound darkness within a high wall of wild rhododendron. Ron reached into another of his pockets and pulled out the packet of minced offal he'd collected from Alf the butcher that morning. Stealthily opening the packet he wafted it about and waited for the dog to smell it. The panting grew louder, the pad of paws on dead leaves sped up, and when he'd judged the animal was close enough, Ron threw the meat towards him.

They waited in tense silence as the dog snuffled and slobbered over the mess of meat that was heavily laced with the quick-acting knock-out drops Ron had kept hidden in his shed. He'd found the bottle amongst the litter of a bombed-out chemist some time ago, and had known immediately it would come in handy.

The dog gave a whine and, as they watched through the camouflage of thick green leaves, it swayed and then toppled over onto its side, legs twitching for a moment before it lay still.

They waited to make sure it really was comatose, and then lifted it out of sight of the forest path and into the heart of the rampant rhododendrons. No harm would come to it, and within a couple of hours it would simply wake with a thick head and return home wondering what had happened.

Ron nodded to Frank and they set off again. There was just one more place to go to complete their poaching trip – and then they could make for home.

Peggy had been extremely suspicious about Ron's behaviour the night before. He never went anywhere without Harvey – and he'd gone out dressed in his best suit, which was very unusual. She'd finally come to the conclusion that he'd probably taken Rosie out to somewhere special that didn't allow dogs, and so had gone to bed and thought no more about it.

It was almost noon by the time she'd finished her housework, so she'd quickly bundled Daisy up in her warmest clothes, strapped her into the pushchair and hurried into town to do all the things she'd been meaning to do for days, but hadn't found the time.

When the Town Hall clock struck two she'd already done the bulk of her shopping and been to the Post Office to send off her parcels and mail her Christmas cards. She could only hope that her parcel to Jim would get to him in time, for she'd taken an age choosing what to send and there was only a fortnight left before Christmas Day. She used to love shopping for Christmas, but as the war had dragged on it had become a dispiriting experience, for there was no joy in battling through the crowds only to find there was little choice in the shops, and what there was looked suspiciously like old, dowdy stock.

In the end, she'd decided that it was probably best to be practical. Jim had said in his letters that the heat and humidity was so bad in India that his clothes were rotting, so she'd made him a shirt out of a length of thin cotton she'd found on a market stall, bought two pairs of underpants, two cotton vests, a shaving brush and his favourite hair cream. She'd realised it wasn't a very exciting collection, so she'd added a roll of tobacco, cigarette papers, handmade cards from Cordelia and the girls, a scribbled drawing from Daisy and a clutch of photographs to remind him of everyone who was missing him.

She wheeled the pushchair down the High Street, stopping every now and then to chat to a friend or admire a baby in a pram before continuing on. Despite the lack of pretty lights strung across the street, the absence of the traditional dressed tree outside the council offices or any festively decorated shop windows, there was an air of suppressed excitement and expectancy in the town which was only partially due to the Christmas spirit.

The rumours of an Allied invasion into France were increasing daily, and they seemed to be borne out by the number of troops amassing in hurriedly erected camps on the hills around the town and coming through it in ever-lengthening convoys. More rocket-launching and anti-aircraft guns could now be seen about the place, and Peggy suspected her sister Doris wouldn't be at all pleased that an enormous emplacement had appeared on the hill overlooking her house, the lethal twin barrels of the mighty guns jutting out towards the Channel.

She swerved to avoid a group of drunken servicemen staggering out of the Crown and waved to Gloria Stevens, who was busy behind her bar. Dodging around clusters of people hobnobbing on the pavement or queuing outside the Home and Colonial, Peggy finally reached the bottom of the street.

She paused for a moment to catch her breath and look out to the beach, where huge coils of barbed wire fenced off the mined shingle, and men from the Artillery Regiment were stoically awaiting a chance to fire their guns. A line of concrete shipping traps was strung across the bay, and beyond that she could just make out several large warships at anchor, their grey hulls almost lost in the invisible line between steely sea and gloomy sky.

Peggy checked that Daisy was warm beneath her blankets and tightly fastened rainproof cover. She'd fallen asleep, her knitted hat askew over one eye, her mittened hands tucked beneath her chin. Peggy didn't disturb her, but adjusted her own gloves and wrapped her scarf more firmly about her neck to combat the cold, damp wind that seemed to go right through her many layers of clothing to her very core.

She didn't envy the soldiers, who must be fed up with having very little to do but stand about in all weathers, smoking and drinking tea. Jerry seemed to have given up trying to bomb them into submission, and if the distant booms and cracks of gunfire were anything to go by, all the action appeared to be on the other side of the Channel – but like the soldiers, she was fed up with all this hanging about. It was time to bring the sense of being in limbo to an end and get on with actually winning this blasted war.

She set off again, crossing to Havelock Gardens, which had once been a leafy oasis of lush lawns, rose-beds and quiet, contemplative corners beneath wooden arbours supporting sweet-smelling jasmine and trailing roses. The benches and arbours were still there, but the iron railing fences had been torn out to be melted and used in the production of planes and tanks, the lawns and rose-beds had been replaced by an allotment, and in the depths of this bitter winter, the trees were bare, their skeletons stark against the leaden sky.

Peggy hurried down Havelock Road until she

reached the large detached house near the end of the cul-de-sac where Doris lived. Noting that the gravel drive had been raked and the flowerbeds weeded and dug over, Peggy wondered if Doris had stirred her stumps enough to do it herself, or had got one of her unfortunate evacuees to turn their hand to gardening. She had a suspicion it was probably the latter.

Wheeling the pram over the shingle to the freshly painted front door, she grasped the polished brass knocker, rapped it twice and then stood back to wait, rather hoping that her sister was out and she could just pop the note through the letterbox.

The door opened a fraction and Doris peered out warily as if she was expecting to find a platoon of Nazi soldiers on her doorstep. 'Oh, it's you, Margaret,' she said with an obvious lack of enthusiasm. 'I've had the distinct impression that you've been avoiding me.'

'I can't imagine where you got that idea,' said Peggy. 'I thought it was the other way round. But perhaps if you remembered to call me Peggy instead of Margaret, I might make more effort to stay in touch.'

'It's the name you were christened with,' said Doris in her carefully modulated voice. 'I really cannot understand why you demean yourself by allowing everyone to call you Peggy. What do you want? I'm busy.'

'I'm not stopping,' said Peggy briskly, frustrated that her visit had already got off to a prickly start, and wanting to nip it in the bud. 'I just wanted to ask if you'd like to come to us for Christmas Day.'

The door remained almost closed, and all Peggy could see of Doris was an eye and one side of her face.

'That's kind of you,' Doris said stiffly, 'but if I do come it would only be for an hour or so. I'm awaiting an invitation to lunch at Chalk Hill House with Lord and Lady Chumley, the mayor, his wife, and the Lord Lieutenant of the county.'

'Goodness,' breathed Peggy. Despite herself, she couldn't help being impressed. 'That sounds a posh do. Beach View and the family certainly can't compete with that lot.'

'Quite,' said Doris, not budging an inch from behind the door. 'But I will do my best to call in with the season's greetings.'

'I'm sure everyone will be most grateful,' said Peggy dryly, stung by her sister's response to her well-meant invitation. She shivered as a particularly cold blast of wind came up from the sea. 'How are you getting to grips with having those enormous guns bearing down on you?'

Doris grimaced and maintained her grasp on the barely open door. 'Ghastly things,' she said with a sniff. 'They're fine all the while they're quiet, but they fired them the other night and the whole house shook in the most alarming manner. I thought we'd been hit by a bomb and the roof was about to cave in.'

'How awful for you,' said Peggy absent-mindedly, the bitter cold distracting her from Doris's petty complaint. 'Well, it's getting dark and I must get home to start on the tea.'

'Goodbye then,' said Doris, and promptly closed the door.

Peggy pulled a rude face at the door, grabbed the

handle of the pushchair and stomped back down the driveway. Doris could stuff her posh lunch right up her jumper along with the turkey they were no doubt going to be served up at Chalk Hill blooming House. Beach View might be shabby, the meal very much make-do, but at least there would be genuine people round her table – people who actually cared for one another and who shared the true spirit of Christmas.

The walk home didn't take very long. Peggy was so cross with Doris she was almost running, and upon reaching Beach View, she closed the door firmly behind her, glad to be home.

Daisy woke up and started grizzling as Peggy carried her up the stone steps to the warm, cosy kitchen. Ron was skinning rabbits by the sink, Harvey and Queenie were sprawled in front of the fire, and Cordelia was writing letters at the table. 'Put the kettle on, Ron,' she said. 'I'm frozen to the bone.'

'Aye, you look it, wee girl,' he replied, checking there was enough water in the kettle. 'Where on earth have you been?'

'She doesn't need beans, Ron,' said Cordelia, looking up from her writing pad. 'She needs a hot cup of tea.'

Ron and Peggy exchanged knowing glances. Cordelia hadn't remembered to turn up her hearing aid. 'I posted the parcels to Jim and Anne,' Peggy told him as she plumped down in the fireside chair and began to divest a wriggling, defiant Daisy of her hat, coat and mittens. 'Then I did a bit of shopping before making the mistake of going to see Doris to ask her to Christmas lunch.'

Ron's brows lowered and his blue eyes narrowed. 'Ach, Peggy, why do you do it? That sister of yours doesn't deserve the kindness you show her.'

'Then you'll be delighted to hear she's expecting a better offer, so won't be coming.'

Ron handed her the cup of tea and gathered Daisy up into his arms to stop her from pestering her mother. 'Oh, aye? Have the King and Queen sent a summons from Buckingham Palace?'

Peggy chuckled. 'Hardly, but in my sister's eyes a summons from Lady Chump-Chop is probably just as eagerly awaited.'

Ron raised an eyebrow as Peggy went on to tell him who was expected at this illustrious gathering. 'Well now, that's all very interesting,' he said, swinging Daisy onto his shoulders. 'But you say Doris is only hoping to be invited and hasn't yet received her invitation?'

Peggy thought back on their conversation and nodded.

Ron chortled and gently removed Daisy's tiny hands from over his eyes as she clung to his head. 'Then I wouldn't mind betting she does turn up here to make our lives a misery, because I happen to know those invitations went out over a fortnight ago.'

Peggy looked up at him in astonishment. 'How on earth . . . ?'

He tapped his nose and winked. 'I know a great many things,' he said mysteriously. 'And I tell you straight, Peggy, she's not on the guest list.'

Peggy felt a pang of distress for her sister's lost hopes, and a dart of concern that a thwarted Doris could end up spoiling everyone's Christmas. 'Stop messing about, Ron, and tell me how you know this for a fact,' she said firmly.

Ron winced as Daisy's tiny fingers clutched a clump of his hair. 'A pal of mine's wife organises fancy parties for those with more money than sense, and the Chumley woman called her in to help. She gave her a copy of the guest list to sort out the seating plan, and my pal showed it to me.'

He swung Daisy from his shoulders to the floor and encouraged her to play with her box of wooden bricks. 'I must say, the old trout certainly knows how to throw a party,' he muttered. 'They're not only having a turkey, but all the trimmings, with smoked salmon to start and plum pudding to finish.'

'Then I hope it chokes them,' retorted Peggy. 'How *dare* that woman raise Doris's hopes by telling her all about it and then not inviting her? I've a good mind to go to Chalk Hill and give her a punch on that snooty nose.'

'I have no doubt of it, Peggy, girl,' he replied with a twinkle in his eyes, 'but I'm thinking it's too cold and dark to be going all that way, and you haven't even started on tea yet.'

'Oh, lawks,' Peggy sighed, rubbing her face with her hands. 'What should I do, Ron? I can't bear the thought of Doris waiting and hoping every time the postman calls – and of course when the penny finally drops she'll be furious and hurt, and having boasted about it to me and probably everyone else, she'll be impossible and make everyone else's Christmas utterly miserable.'

'If we're lucky,' said Cordelia, who'd switched on her hearing aid during the discussion, 'she might stay at home and sulk – too ashamed of her bragging to face us all.'

'My sister has no truck with humility,' said Peggy evenly. 'She's more likely to arrive here full of herself, saying she's turned down the invitation so she can spread her largesse to her poor relations.'

Cordelia blew out her cheeks. 'I certainly wouldn't put it past her.'

Peggy couldn't help but feel sorry for Doris, even though most of her woes were self-inflicted. 'Well, I can only hope that if she does turn up, she'll bring a tin of ham or something to eke out the meal – because at the moment all we can look forward to is a promised chicken from Alf the butcher, vegetables from the garden and a plum pudding without fruit or brandy – or anything else remotely tasty or festive.'

'Ach, Peggy girl, you've no need to fret. Whatever you cook will be delicious, and it's the company that really counts. As for Doris . . .' Ron shrugged. 'We'll just have to grin and bear her, and have a good time regardless of what mood she's in.'

He turned back to finish gutting and skinning the rabbits, which would go in a pie the following day. He bit down on a smile as he washed the meat and placed it in a bowl beneath a strip of muslin in the larder. It would be lovely to surprise Peggy and the others with his special gifts, but it would be a while before he could reveal what they were, for Chalky White was smoking the salmon up at his place in the hills, and the three pheasants hanging in Frank's outhouse would only just be ripe enough to cook on the day.

Ron lit his pipe and sat down, his thoughts running through all the preparations that were being kept secret from his beloved daughter-in-law. Pauline was making a chestnut stuffing and cranberry jelly; Alf had been persuaded to add a few extra sausages and bacon scraps to Peggy's order in return for some of the salmon; the girls were secretly making special fancy crackers for the table, and Rosie had managed to get hold of a bottle of brandy, and enough ingredients to make a few mince pies. They would have a feast regardless of the war, the absence of most of the family – and the unwelcome presence of Doris.

15

Slapton

By the time the doctor had arrived Carol and Dolly were clean and dressed in fresh clothes, Nipper bathed and rubbed dry with a scrap of towel. Carol had escorted him next door and waited downstairs while he went up to examine Edith and provide the death certificate for the undertakers who would turn up early the following morning.

Dolly had stood beside her as the plain wooden coffin was loaded onto the back of the undertaker's black limousine, and Carol's tears were not only for the old woman who'd become an intrinsic part of her life, but for the memories that solemn departure had evoked. It was harder still to sort through Edith's possessions, for Rosemary Cottage didn't feel the same without her sitting in her chair by the fire, and Carol felt like an intruder.

It took most of that week, but Edith's cottage was finally cleared. Dolly was very businesslike, and having donned a headscarf, wrap-round apron and rubber gloves, she'd got to work sorting and sifting through several generations of clutter and memorabilia. She sent Carol off to get extra boxes from Mildred Ferris, and by the time she'd returned with them, Dolly had gone through the cottage like a whirlwind and set aside the valuable ornaments, framed paintings and watercolour portraits, along with the good linen, a family bible and several leather-bound books which she suspected might be worth something to a collector.

Dolly offered to take the valuable bits to Bournemouth and store them in her spare room. It wouldn't do them any good to be in a barn at Coombe Farm through the winter. There wasn't much else worth saving; the curtains and rugs were moth-eaten and threadbare, the china mostly chipped and mismatched, although some clothes would do for the Salvation Army. Carol felt awful about throwing so much away. Edith's possessions were all that was left of the old woman who'd spent her entire life in this little village and it just didn't feel right.

On moving day four cheerful young American soldiers arrived with a large army truck and loaded the heavy furniture, bags, suitcases and boxes into the back. Dolly and Carol swept the hearth and stuffed paper up the chimney to prevent any falls of soot, and boarded up the windows with sheets of plywood donated by the Americans. Dolly sat squashed between the men in the cab, armed with a large flagon of cider for the girls, and they headed up to Coombe Farm leaving Carol to lock up.

Carol slowly walked through the empty rooms which still seemed to be imbued with Edith's spirit, remembering how she'd been so determined to spend her final days here. She'd been feisty and abruptly scathing at times, but during those terrible first weeks of Carol's bereavement, she'd been the first to offer solace, coming each day with a small tureen of soup or stew, and sitting with her until she was satisfied Carol had eaten properly.

'Come on, Nipper,' she murmured. 'It's time to leave.' With the little dog tugging at the lead, Carol locked the front door and walked down the path to Constable Betts, who was waiting solemnly by the gate to take charge of the tagged keys.

He nodded his thanks, touched the rim of his helmet and walked away, the experiences of the last few weeks too emotional for trivial exchanges.

Carol looked back at Rosemary Cottage which, like the rest in the row, had already taken on an aura of abandonment, and then headed for home, knowing that within days she would be handing over her own keys and turning her back on Thyme Cottage with little idea of when she'd be allowed to return to it.

The thought took her up the hill and along the narrow, steep path which led to the back of the churchyard.

The day of Edith's funeral was a dreary one, with a leaden sky promising more rain, and a wind that tore up from the heaving sea to cut like a knife through the thickest of clothing. And yet the weather hadn't deterred the villagers. They'd arrived throughout the morning in cars and vans, on horseback, tractors and carts, and even on foot to pay their respects to a woman they'd known all their lives, and take this last chance to be amongst the community from which they'd gained such strength. They stood huddled against the wind, their voices a low murmur as they lined the narrow village street that led to the church.

Dolly held Carol's hand as they waited with the vicar for the funeral cortege. She knew the girl was struggling to cope, not only with the passing of Mrs Rayner, but with having to face another funeral before her own departure from her beloved cottage, and Dolly was extremely relieved that she could be with her at such a fraught time.

However, Dolly was also finding things difficult. She'd been on tenterhooks during the past week, certain that Felix would turn up to offer his condolences to Carol – but as the days had gone on with still no sign of him, she'd made a few discreet enquiries and learned that he was busy in Dartmouth. It was a huge relief, and yet Dolly knew she must remain on her guard until she left Slapton for, like the proverbial bad penny, he was sure to appear sooner or later and she had to be prepared for that moment.

The American soldiers who were billeted in the chantry had lined up in front of the picturesque cottages in Church Lane alongside the men of the Home Guard, the off-duty Artillery officers and the small local police force. As the crowd fell silent and the shining black horse-drawn hearse came into view, they stood to attention and saluted.

Dolly felt Carol tense, and tightened her grip on her hand as the coffin was hoisted onto the shoulders of six burly farmers, the single wreath of intertwined holly and ivy placed carefully on top.

The vicar began to recite the words of the funeral ritual and slowly led the way down the path to the church where he would hold a short service before the interment.

Dolly looked surreptitiously around and saw several American officers in the crowd of people already taking their seats inside the church, but thankfully none that she recognised. Hopefully, Felix was still occupied in Dartmouth.

She was not a churchgoer – enforced attendance as a child had put her off religion – but she did enjoy the pomp and ceremony of a special service, and the grandeur of an ancient church or cathedral which seemed imbued with the scent of incense and the peaceful worship of many generations.

She was sorry to see that St James's had been denuded of all its finery, for it was a stark reminder that a war was raging not so very far away. The interior was gloomy now the windows had been boarded over, the only light coming from dozens of flickering candles. There was no cloth on the carved stone altar, just a simple wooden cross and a spray of dark green holly, the red berries lustrous in the candlelight.

Carol tugged at Dolly's arm. 'There's Betty,' she whispered, 'and look, she's kept us a place.'

Dolly smiled at the pretty girl she'd got to know over the years Carol had been living here, and as the two girls hugged and began to speak in whispers, she glanced down the pew and froze. Felix was at the other end, handsome in his uniform despite the silver hair and lines around his eyes and mouth, the greatcoat not quite concealing the broad shoulders and strong torso she remembered so very well.

Their eyes met, and in that single, shocking moment she knew she'd been foolish to ever believe she could withstand the impact of seeing him again, or pretend that she no longer loved him, for those eyes drew her – the memory of his lips on her skin sent a thrill of yearning through her and all she wanted to do was walk into the shelter of his arms and be held to his heart.

'Mum? Mum, are you all right?'

It took all her strength to tear her gaze away, and in a daze, she looked into her daughter's worried face. 'I'm fine,' she said, and quickly sat down before her legs failed her.

'Are you sure?' whispered Carol. 'Only you've gone very pale.'

'I'm just cold,' she hissed back. 'Do stop fussing, Carol, and concentrate on the service.'

Carol didn't seem convinced, but she turned back to listen to Samuel Fotherington, who was talking quite animatedly as he welcomed the large gathering and asked them to join him in a prayer of thanksgiving for the long life of the departed Edith Rayner.

The shy, awkward man seemed to have gained in self-confidence since deciding to join a closed order, Dolly thought distractedly, all too aware that Felix was leaning forward and trying to catch her eye again.

She lowered her head and covered her eyes as the congregation joined in to recite the Lord's Prayer, but instead of those familiar words she'd learned at her mother's knee, she silently begged for the strength to resist Felix, and to be released from the riot of emotions that were assailing her. His presence seemed to fill the church, binding them together with gossamer threads even though there were at least six other people between them – but even as she willed herself to ignore him, she knew there would be no escape.

The congregation stood to sing 'We Plough the Fields and Scatter' without the aid of an organ or even a choir, which made it very halting and ragged. Dolly concentrated hard on the words that had been hastily printed on sheets of repulped and rather coarse paper, but they danced before her as a persistent little voice in her head ordered her to look round – to seek him out again for just one more glance.

She managed to resist all the way through 'Abide with Me' and 'All Things Bright and Beautiful', and then Carol nudged her, and as she turned her head to see what she wanted, she caught Felix watching her in puzzlement. She blinked and looked away.

'What is it?' she murmured beneath the sound of over a hundred people getting to their feet.

'You're acting very strangely, Mum. Are you sure you're all right?'

Dolly patted her cheek. 'I always get restless in church,' she said softly, 'probably because I fully expect to be hit by a bolt of lightning for daring to be in one.'

Carol smiled uncertainly, but further conversation was halted by the vicar leading the cortege down the aisle towards the door.

Dolly saw her chance. 'I'm going home to let Nipper out,' she muttered to Carol. 'I'll see you at the wake.'

Before Carol could reply Dolly had quickly filtered into the crush of people shuffling behind the cortege and managed to ease her way through until she was once more out in the bitter wind. Carol was clearly puzzled by her behaviour, but it was too late to worry about that now, and it was imperative she got away before Felix emerged from the church.

As the cortege arrived at the graveside Dolly darted round the corner and hurried along the side of the church to the back gate, and quickly ran down the steep, narrow path until she'd reached Carol's lane. She realised that should anyone be watching, she must make a strange sight in her fur coat, fancy hat and high heels, stumbling over the blasted cobbles in danger of breaking an ankle, but this was not the time to care what others thought.

She ran up the cinder path, through the front door and slammed it behind her. Leaning against it she took a while to catch her breath, for it had been a long time since she'd had to run anywhere. Once she felt slightly calmer, she slipped off her coat and gloves and walked to the kitchen door to let a scrabbling, whining Nipper free.

Wary of him damaging her good stockings, she sent him out into the tiny back garden and distractedly watched through the window as he trotted about and watered the hedge. With her arms folded tightly about her waist, she wondered what the heck had happened to her usual ice-cool reasoning. It was Felix, of course, who'd stirred up her emotions and made her act before thinking, but then he'd always managed to do that.

'You're a fool, Dolly Cardew,' she muttered crossly. 'A stupid, empty-headed fool to run away in a panic like that, when you should have just faced him and got it over with.'

Nipper scampered back indoors and Dolly quickly wiped the mud from his paws before going into the sitting room to stir up the fire with some vigour and try to regain her composure. The rotund little dog followed her in and tried to join her on the couch, but she very firmly told him to sit by the fire and behave.

Dolly lit a cigarette and stared into the red heart of the fire. She'd acted foolishly and no doubt Carol would question her, but there were more pressing things to worry about, for this moment of respite would be fleeting, and she knew, with every fibre of her being, that before too long he would come looking for her. Yet she wasn't ready to face him – couldn't think how to play it – or what to say. But she knew one thing for certain; she had to damned well pull herself together and use the experience of a lifetime to end this once and for all.

She puffed furiously on the cigarette, wondering how she'd found the courage to calmly face moments of great danger during the last war – and yet, at the sight of that particular pair of blue eyes, she'd lost all composure and had become as helpless and addle-headed as a lovesick schoolgirl. Eyeing the bottle of whisky she was tempted to have a drink, but rejected the idea almost immediately, for it wouldn't help and she needed to keep a clear head.

The click of the latch on the garden gate sounded

loud in the silence, and as she tensed, Nipper scrambled to his feet and started to bark. She hushed him, hoping it might only be Carol and Betty, but he ran to the door and continued barking as he jumped up and down.

Dolly grabbed him as she heard footsteps on the cinder path followed swiftly by the rap of the knocker. He was here. She was momentarily tempted to hide in the kitchen until he gave up and went away. Yet she knew he'd only come back, and that was the last thing she wanted, so she carried a squirming Nipper into the sitting room and closed the door on him.

Running her hands nervously down her pencil-slim skirt, she touched the pearls at her neck, quickly donned her fur coat, and took a deep breath before opening the door.

He was much taller than she remembered, and she had to look up at him even though she was wearing very high heels. 'Hello, Felix,' she managed.

He took off his hat and tucked it under his arm as his gaze devoured her. 'I can't believe it's really you,' he breathed.

'Fate works in mysterious ways,' she replied with much greater calm than she'd expected. 'You look well. Life has clearly been very good to you.'

'You haven't changed at all,' he said in admiration. 'My goodness, Dolly, the years have hardly touched you.'

She didn't respond to his flattery but stood in the doorway barring entry to the cottage as the dog continued to bark from the other room. 'Is the funeral over already?' she asked, needing to keep this conversation on an impersonal level.

'I guess so,' he replied with a frown. 'I slipped away as soon as I realised you weren't there, and suspected you might have come here to Carol's cottage. Why did you leave so suddenly, Dolly?'

'The dog needed to be let out.' She fastened her fur coat. 'I was actually about to leave for the wake.'

He looked down at her solemnly, the intensity of his gaze piercing to her very soul. 'I'd hate to think you were running away from me, Dolly, because I mean you no harm.'

'Don't flatter yourself,' she retorted, fumbling to pull on her leather gloves. 'I'm afraid of no one – least of all you, Felix.'

His reaction was unexpected, for he threw back his head and roared with laughter. 'Oh, Dolly, my fierce, darling little Dolly – you haven't changed at all – and thank God for it.'

'You can thank whomsoever you please,' she said stiffly. 'But fierce or not, I'm not *your* Dolly.'

He reached out his hand and brushed her cheek with his fingers. 'And I'm real sorry about that,' he murmured. 'There's not a day I haven't regretted treating you so badly – not a day when I haven't wondered where you were and what you were doing – and if you'd found someone who could give you what I was unable to.'

The touch of his hand was like electricity and it coursed through her, making her insides melt. She gathered her senses and firmly removed his hand from her face. 'Life has been very good to me since you ended things between us, Felix,' she said coolly. 'So I suppose I should be grateful to you for opening my eyes to your true character. It was a harsh lesson, but once I knew you to be a liar and a cheat, it served me well.'

'All that was a long time ago, Dolly, and I've said I was sorry.'

She saw the sadness and regret in him and hardened her resolve. 'Too little and far too late,' she said briskly.

His eyes clouded. 'You hate me, don't you?'

Her heart cried out to him that she loved him beyond reason, but she refused to listen to it. 'I don't care enough to hate you, Felix.'

'I'm sorry to hear that, Dolly,' he said on a sigh, 'but I guess it's what I deserve. I just hoped that, since fate has brought us together again, we might be able to put the past behind us and be friends.'

Dolly's pulse raced as she saw the yearning in his eyes. She wanted to touch him, to feel his arms about her, his lips against hers – wanted to be his lover, not just his friend. But even friendship was dangerous when so many emotions were involved. She avoided his gaze and made a sterling effort to remain calm.

'I shall be leaving here in a couple of days, so I doubt we'll meet again,' she said evenly. 'But thank you for coming to apologise – I realise it couldn't have been easy.'

'It was the easiest thing in the world,' he said sadly, 'because it was heartfelt.'

Dolly almost made the fatal mistake of touching the

pearl necklace he'd given her all those years ago, but managed to divert the gesture into pulling up her coat collar. Unable to resist firing one last barb, she looked at him squarely. 'I hope the rehearsals go well, Felix, and that it won't be too long before you can return to your wife and son.'

She saw the flicker in his eyes and knew she'd hit home, but as she made to close the door on him, she discovered there was a large, shining brown brogue in the way. 'We've finished here, Felix,' she said coldly. 'Please remove your foot.'

'Not until I've had my say,' he said determinedly. 'My wife has passed away, and I came here offering an olive branch. I can't blame you for throwing it back in my face, but although I'm guilty of a great many things, I want you to know that I never lied about loving you.'

Dolly took a trembling breath and resisted reaching out to him, reminding herself that although his love might have been true, he hadn't been honest about anything else. 'I'm glad to know you didn't lie about that, Felix, but you made promises you knew you couldn't keep, led me to believe that we'd always be together – and then went back to the wife and child you'd conveniently not mentioned during the months we were together.'

'It had to be, Dolly. You know the reason why.'

She saw the pain in his eyes and steeled herself against it – angry with him now, the old hurts rising once again to remind her of how badly it had all ended.

'I know what you told me at the time, and I accepted it as the truth because it was clear you wanted to end things between us – and I still retained enough pride not to question you – but that didn't make what happened any less painful.'

'I'm so sorry, Dolly,' he murmured. 'If I could have changed things—'

'But you couldn't,' she interrupted, 'and now too many years have passed for either of us to harbour regrets over a doomed love affair which should never have begun.'

His demeanour was one of defeat and sadness as he slowly took his foot from the threshold. 'I still have great feelings for you, Dolly. Is there nothing I can do or say to atone for the hurt I've caused?'

Dolly was about to tell him no, when she realised there was something – and although it was risky, it just might ensure what the Americans called 'closure' on the whole disastrous business. 'There is one thing you could do – although I wouldn't call it atonement, but more of a kindness.'

'Anything,' he said eagerly. 'I'll do anything you ask of me.'

He was like a little boy, she thought with affection. A little boy desperate to find favour after behaving badly, and if it had been at all possible, she would have hugged him, forgiven him and told him how profoundly this meeting had affected her – and how he had not been the only one to keep secrets and tell lies.

But she remained stiffly in the doorway, her expression giving away nothing of her thoughts. 'I want you to promise you'll never mention our previous relationship to anyone – especially Carol. She doesn't need to know anything about my youthful indiscretions. In fact it's probably best if you stay away from her just in case you let something slip.'

She forced a fleeting smile. 'I remember too well how easily you can get carried away in the heat of the moment and say all sorts of things you didn't mean to say.'

He reddened and shrugged in embarrassment. 'I guess that's about right, Dolly. I never did learn to curb my tongue when I get enthusiastic about something.'

That was one of your most endearing attractions, she thought sadly, along with your smile and the way you used to look at me as if you could see the moon and the stars in my eyes.

He looked at her intently as if he could read her thoughts, and then blinked and cleared his throat. 'I'm guessing Carol Porter's your daughter,' he said, and carried on before Dolly could reply, 'I'm glad you found someone to make you happy, and give you what I couldn't. But it came as quite a shock to see Carol at that meeting. She looks so like you, I thought time had stood still.'

Carol's pulse was racing, her heart hammering against her ribs with such ferocity she was certain he must be able to hear it. 'Do I have your promise, Felix?' she pressed.

He gazed down at her as if needing to imprint her face in his memory before they were again torn apart by bad timing and circumstance. 'Dolly, if that is all I can do to make you believe how sorry I am, then you have my solemn promise not to breathe a word to anyone.'

'Thank you, Felix.' She stepped back into the hall,

her hand clutching the edge of the door in readiness to close it.

He settled his hat on his head, and his eyes were suspiciously bright as he gazed down at her. 'Goodbye, sweet, sweet girl,' he said softly. 'I'll never forget you.'

She could feel the storm of emotions gathering strength within her as he turned and strode away. And when he didn't look back or falter before he disappeared from view, that storm became a maelstrom she could no longer control.

Closing the door, she all but collapsed on the stairs, trembling, not from the bitter cold of this winter day, but from the rending of her heart as the tears fell unheeded down her face.

16

Carol had not joined Betty and the others as they'd left the graveside for the wake in the Queen's Arms, but told Betty she'd catch up with her later to hear all about her new posting and billet. She was still concerned about her mother, and needed to check that she was all right.

Dolly had clearly been disturbed by something in the church, and she hadn't been at all convinced by her explanation. It was true she'd never felt comfortable with religion, and that Nipper probably did need letting out – but the way she'd darted off so determinedly had looked suspiciously like a bid for escape, and Carol was intrigued and worried about what could have been behind it.

She'd rounded the corner and was about to go down the hill to her cottage when she saw General Addington standing on her doorstep in what looked like a serious exchange with her mother.

She frowned and her footsteps faltered. Why would he be visiting when he must have seen both of them in the church and assumed they would be going on to the wake where he could have said what he needed without this subterfuge? The thought that he must have followed Dolly home was a bit unnerving, but her mother was perfectly capable of handling awkward situations.

Carol could see, even from here, how stiff and defensive her mother was as she faced him, and as the general reached out to caress Dolly's cheek, Carol knew beyond doubt that they weren't the strangers Dolly had led her to believe they were.

She moved silently into the deep shadows of a doorway, unable to tear her gaze from the intimate moment being played out on her doorstep. She saw her mother firmly push his hand away and there was a short exchange between them before she tried to close the door only to find it blocked by his foot.

Carol wished she was nearer so she could hear what was being said, but she could see by the set of his shoulders and the way he constantly tried to reach out to Dolly that the American was not in charge of the situation despite his foot being in the door – and that her mother was rigidly keeping him at a distance.

Carol shivered from a particularly cold blast of wind, and huddled deeper into the doorway of the abandoned house, intrigued and confused by the scene before her. And yet the incident with the cauliflower cheese could now be explained. Dolly was rarely careless with anything, but at the mention of his name she'd dropped the bowl and turned quite pale, unusually in a dither.

Carol realised that it also explained why the general had deliberately sought her out after the meeting, and the intensity in his gaze which had unsettled her. It must have come as a shock to him, she realised, for she looked very like her mother, and he must have thought he'd seen a ghost of the woman he'd once known. Was the general an old flame? He was about the right age and type of man her mother fell for, and Dolly had a legion of past admirers scattered all over the world, so it was entirely feasible.

Carol could sense the intimacy between them as he removed his foot from the door and the conversation continued, but she could also sense the tension, and guessed that perhaps their affair hadn't ended well – and for all his persuasion and charm, Dolly wanted nothing more to do with him.

Carol bit her lip, uneasy now at her prying. Whatever was between them was none of her business, and she should leave them to it before they caught her snooping, which would be mortifying. She darted out of the doorway, then slipped through the shadows of the overhanging trees by the graveyard wall and eased round the corner of the pub.

A quick glance told her she'd only just been in time, for the general was now walking disconsolately back up the hill, her mother standing in the doorway watching him until he went into the churchyard and out of sight.

Carol ignored the children who were playing amongst the jeeps and army trucks, and was deaf to the raucous noise going on inside as she leaned against the pub's wall. She would say nothing to Dolly, she decided, but it would be interesting to see if she mentioned his visit.

Dolly was reticent about her past – especially when it

came to the men she'd fallen for – and over the years, Carol and Pauline had become frustrated by her lack of willingness to talk about either of their fathers and answer their questions. They knew only that Pauline's had deserted her and Dolly, and Carol's had been killed in an accident before she'd been born. They'd had to accept that it didn't really matter who they were, for those men had played no part in their lives – and yet, deep down, it niggled, for this lack of knowledge had left a void, which every now and again needed to be filled.

Felix walked blindly up the hill, determined not to look back for one last sight of Dolly, even though he could sense her watching him. But when he rounded the corner and slowly made his way up the winding path to the back of the now deserted churchyard, he paused and gazed down to the thatched roofs where a single column of smoke rose from the chimney to be swiftly erased by the wind – just as his hopes for reconciliation had been dashed.

He pulled out a large handkerchief from his pocket to wipe his eyes, then shrugged deeper into his coat collar and tried to find solace in the fact that despite her cool reaction and cutting barbs, the exchange had been painful for both of them. He'd seen it, raw, in her eyes and in the flutter of her fingers as she'd almost touched the string of pearls he'd given her so many years before.

The fact that she still wore them heartened him – and the anguish in her face told him she did still care – but his hopes for forgiveness had been shattered when she'd made it clear that although fate had brought them together again it was too late even for friendship.

Felix had believed that the years he'd spent in the army and the experiences he'd had during the Great War had cured him of sentimentality, but he'd been wrong. The agony of losing her for a second time weighed heavily in his heart, the bitter tears a testament to his regret for having hurt her so badly she couldn't forgive him.

He took a shallow, shuddering breath and went to sit on a lichen-stained stone bench set beneath the trees. He was supposed to be attending the wake, and Herby would be wondering where he'd got to. But he needed time to absorb what had just happened – needed the tranquillity of this country graveyard to help restore his strength of purpose so he could face the many responsibilities he had without being distracted by Dolly.

Felix had no idea how long he'd been sitting there when the sound of hurrying footsteps snatched him from his thoughts. He recognised the sound and knew who it was, so remained in the lengthening shadows beneath the trees and watched her as she walked purposefully up the lane on the other side of the low stone wall.

He noted sadly that she seemed unaffected by their encounter, and appeared to be eager to join the others at the Queen's Arms. Dolly had always enjoyed a good party, he remembered, as he took in the mink coat, the high heels and fetching little veiled hat – all of which were far too chic for this country hamlet – but which were the very essence of the woman he knew he would always love.

Felix waited until she was out of sight and he could no longer hear her high heels clicking on the paving stones. He stood and eased his stiff shoulders beneath the heavy greatcoat, realising that the day was closing in, the wind was strengthening, and there was the electricity of an impending storm in the atmosphere which didn't bode well for the equipment on the shore.

With a growing sense of urgency, he strode through the graveyard and approached the chantry where he found several GIs lounging about smoking and drinking cider. They rapidly hid the drink and cigarettes, stood shakily to attention and executed sloppy salutes.

'You go and find my driver and tell him I'm here,' he ordered the steadier of the group. 'The rest of you sober up and get down to the shore. There are boats and equipment to be hauled above the high-water mark before this storm breaks.'

They scuttled off and Felix waited impatiently for Herby, glad to have something important to occupy his mind instead of raking over the past.

17

Cliffehaven

The main room of the Town Hall had been decorated with every bit of bunting, strand of worn tinsel and long, colourful and rather battered paper chains that could be found in the big box the women had unearthed from the back of a storage cupboard. It was barely mid-morning but the vast space was humming with activity as the wireless blared out Christmas carols to sing along to, and the children in the makeshift nursery got over-excited and rather fractious. Christmas was only seven days away, and at last, it really felt festive.

At the centre of the room were lines of trestle tables where women were frantically packing the very last of the Christmas boxes to be posted to the service personnel in Europe, and to one side of the room more women were sorting through the many generous donations of gifts and toys to be distributed amongst those most in need of some cheer in the town. The canteen was providing welcome cups of tea and fish paste sandwiches, and at a long table by the door nimble-fingered men and women were cutting out the pictures on old greeting cards to make gift tags and tree decorations.

Peggy and a far more relaxed Pauline were sorting

through the huge pile of donated toys, most of which had clearly been well loved by their former small owners. Peggy found a toy car that was less battered than some, checked her long list and decided little Billy Watson should have it. He was only five, but he'd already been moved twice from unsuitable billets and his poor mother was at her wits' end to provide a decent Christmas for her three little ones while her husband was on a battleship somewhere in the Pacific.

She spied a baby doll for his sister and a pea-shooter for his older brother. 'I doubt Amy will thank me for giving him this,' she said on a sigh, 'but he's too old for toy cars and teddies.'

'I found a lovely embroidered sweater I put aside for Amy,' said Pauline, 'so that should make up for it.' She stopped to take a sip of tea. 'It's sad to realise there are so many dispossessed, needy families in the town. When I think how it was before the war . . .'

'It was still a struggle for some, even then,' said Peggy, wrapping the gifts in old newspaper and adding a hand-made tag, 'but at least the community hasn't lost its sense of charity. I can't believe how much stuff we've been given this year.'

'The special Christmas party should go with a swing,' said Pauline happily. 'Has Ron tried on that Father Christmas suit yet?'

Peggy nodded. 'He tries to make out he's grumpy about it, but I have a suspicion he's really looking forward to being the centre of attention. He's marvellous with small children, and I heard him practising his ho ho hos the other night.'

'Bless him,' sighed Pauline. 'He must be missing his grandchildren, but at least he has Daisy to spoil.'

'Daisy is in danger of getting too precocious with so much attention lavished on her,' said Peggy briskly, 'and of course he misses the others. We all do.'

Pauline must have heard the wistfulness in Peggy's voice, for she squeezed her hand in sympathy before they continued sorting, choosing and wrapping as the carols rang out from the wireless and the chatter around them rose in volume.

'By the way,' said Pauline some time later, 'have you heard anything from Doris about Christmas Day?'

'Not a peep,' said Peggy. 'I do worry about her, you know. She must have been dreadfully hurt when it was clear there would be no invitation to that stuck-up lunch, and I don't like the thought of her shutting herself away to lick her wounds.'

'I wouldn't have thought that was at all like Doris,' retorted Pauline, who'd never got on with her. 'She's more likely to brazen it out and cause misery on everyone else's Christmas in revenge. Don't waste your pity on her, Peggy, she really doesn't deserve it.'

Peggy knew she was right, but despite everything, Doris was her sister, and she felt disloyal at not having warned her that Lady Chump-Chop had absolutely no intention of sending her an invitation. And yet that would only have caused a terrible row, with Doris accusing her of jealousy and spite even though her warning would have been given out of love. It was terribly sad that her sister was so blinkered and unapproachable when it came to her so-called 'friends', and the knowledge that Doris must be a very unhappy woman right now didn't sit easily with her – almost tempting her to call in and comfort her even though she knew Doris would only send her off with a flea in her ear.

Pauline broke into her troubled thoughts by changing the topic. 'I got letters from Mum and Carol yesterday. I'm relieved Mum went down to be with her. She must be finding it very hard to leave that cottage – and I still don't really understand why it's necessary. Neither of them explained anything in much detail, only that the army has requisitioned the entire area.'

Glad to have something other than Doris to think about, Peggy said, 'It must be something to do with the invasion rumours. I got letters too, and the lack of any real information must be because whatever the army is up to, it's all very hush-hush.'

Pauline paused and eased her back. 'I do worry about little Carol,' she murmured. 'She's had such a tough year and having to move out must be the last straw. And it doesn't help being so close to Christmas. You'd have thought the powers that be would have organised things better, and at least left it until the New Year.'

'Winning the war has to come first, no matter how inconvenient it is to everyone,' said Peggy sadly. 'Poor Carol. It's rotten luck, and I can't begin to imagine how she must be feeling about moving out tomorrow.'

'I wish she'd come to me instead of that farm. I don't like the sound of Jack and his wife at all, and she should be home with her family, not stuck in a draughty billet that sounds from her letters to be little better than a barn.'

'Dolly did say she'd suggested it,' said Peggy, 'and even offered to take her back to Bournemouth, but Carol seems determined to stay as close as possible to the village, and I can't say I blame her.'

Pauline gave a deep sigh. 'I can understand why she doesn't want to go far from David and the baby – I'd feel the same if I had a memorial to my boys that I could visit.'

Peggy heard the quaver in her voice and quickly put her arm about her shoulders in a hug of deeply felt, silent empathy. Seamus and Joseph had not come home to be buried in a peaceful graveyard, but they would be remembered, and when this war was finally over, their names would be carved into the stone of yet another war memorial to the fallen.

She looked up as the door opened and gave a gasp as the tall, handsome figure in the dark uniform of the RNR surveyed the room. 'Pauline,' she squeaked excitedly, 'look who's here.'

Pauline turned and gave a little cry of delight as Brendon strode towards her and then gathered her into his arms, lifting her off the floor so he could kiss her cheek.

'Hello, Mum,' he said, still holding her aloft. 'It's good to see you looking so well.'

'Oh, Brendon. Why didn't you tell me you were coming? I would have stayed at home and cooked a meal and—'

'Now, Mum, there's no need to make a fuss.' He

grinned and carefully set her back on her feet. 'It's why I wanted it to be a surprise.'

Pauline hugged him, the top of her head barely reaching above his midriff. 'It's a wonderful surprise – the best ever,' she murmured. She looked up at him, her hand lovingly cupping his cheek. 'You look tired,' she said fretfully, 'and you seem to have lost weight. Aren't the navy feeding you properly?'

He chuckled. 'The navy feeds me very well, Mum, it's all the exercise that's keeping me trim. As for being tired . . . To be sure we're all tired of this war dragging on with no end in sight.'

Pauline frowned but nodded her acceptance. 'Does your father know you're here?'

He shook his head. 'I came straight from the train hoping to find you first.' His dark blue eyes met Peggy's and he reached out to bring her into the embrace. 'And how's my favourite auntie?' he asked after kissing her. 'Still keeping busy, I see,' he teased.

'I'm all the better for seeing you,' she replied, holding back happy tears. 'And staying busy keeps me out of mischief – unlike your grandad, who's still up to all his old tricks.'

'I'm glad he hasn't changed,' said Brendon affectionately. 'Life would be very dull without his shenanigans.'

Peggy asked the question that had so far been avoided. 'How long can you stay, Brendon? Are you home for Christmas?'

His smile faded. 'I'm sorry, but I only have a day pass. All leave has been cancelled for the foreseeable future.'

'Oh, Brendon, no,' moaned Pauline. 'And I was so looking forward to having you home for once.'

'It can't be helped, Mum,' he said gently. 'But don't let's spoil the time we do have together by being downcast. How about a slap-up lunch at the British Restaurant once I've tracked down Dad?'

'That would be lovely,' Pauline said raggedly as she tried to swallow her disappointment and be brave. 'But I think he went out with your grandfather, so they could be anywhere.'

'Ron said he was taking some of the boys out with the Home Guard for rifle practice,' said Peggy, 'so I suspect they'll be up by the ruined farmhouse and barn.'

Brendon glanced up at the large clock on the wall above the door. 'It shouldn't take me long to get up there, and the walk will do me good after sitting in that train for half the morning.'

'But you've only just arrived, and we've hardly had time to catch our breath,' protested Pauline. 'And what if they aren't there? Half your day's leave will be wasted and—'

He put his large hands on her shoulders to still her anxiety as he looked lovingly into her eyes. 'If I don't find them straight off, I'll come back,' he promised. He bent to kiss both women, and before they could delay him any further, hurried from the hall.

Pauline scrabbled in her apron pocket for a handkerchief to dry her tears. 'I must look an absolute fright,' she rasped. 'Why on earth can't I stop being so weepy and needy every time I get to see him?'

Peggy hugged her. 'Because you love him,' she said quietly, 'and that's nothing to be ashamed of, Pauline, just try not to overdo it.' She became more brisk. 'Let's get out of these aprons and headscarves and find some lipstick and powder. I'm betting all three will be back before we know it, and then we'll have the double treat of being with Brendon as well as enjoying a lunch out.'

Brendon strode up the High Street, glad to be back in the familiar surroundings where he'd grown up, but saddened by the changes war had wrought. He noted the bomb craters and piles of rubble that had once been shops and the cinema where his Uncle Jim had worked as a projectionist, and the lack of the Christmas lights which used to be strung across the street and in the branches of the town's traditional tree.

He remembered that, as little boys, he and his brothers had always loved to come with their parents to look in awe at the wonderfully decorated tree outside the council offices, the magic of Christmas still powerful in his innocent belief that the jolly, fat, bearded man in the red suit would come on his sleigh laden with presents while he was asleep. What he wouldn't give now for a return to that innocence when the world felt safe and his family was whole, unscarred by the ugliness and horror of war, and unaware of what fate had in store for them.

He firmly banished the memories that had been darkened by the events of the last few years, and walked faster, past the Crown which had just opened and was heaving with servicemen and factory girls, and then down a narrow side street which would lead to a track across the hills. He was eager to see Ron and his father again, for this would be the last time he could come home for several months, and he wanted a quiet word with them whilst they had no women around.

He'd almost reached the brow of the hill when he saw the gathering of old men and boys walking towards him armed with World War I rifles. The practice must be over, but he couldn't see his father or Ron amongst them, so he kept on going.

It was Harvey who spotted him first and came galloping towards him, ears flapping and tongue lolling, to fling himself against him. 'Whoa there, boy,' he chuckled, making a fuss of him and trying to ward him off at the same time. 'You're all muddy and these are my best number twos.'

Harvey didn't care about uniforms; he was just delighted to see Brendon, and did his best to climb into his arms so he could lick his face.

'Will ye be getting down, ye heathen beast,' roared Ron, emerging from behind a thick entanglement of gorse and brambles armed with two snared rabbits, to grab the dog's collar. 'Now,' he said firmly, 'you will sit down and behave.'

Harvey slumped to the ground in defeat, his eyes liquid and beseeching, his tail twitching in supplication.

'Poor old boy,' said Brendon, feeling sorry for the dog as he squirmed on his side, edging ever closer until his nose rested on Brendon's shoe.

'Ach, you don't want to be encouraging him,' said Ron, putting the rabbits in his coat pocket. ''Tis a fine act and one he's perfected over the years.' He eyed the muddy paw-prints on Brendon's uniform. 'And to be sure he's made a mess, but I'm afeared I'll only make it worse if I hug you,' he said, glancing down at his filthy poaching coat.

Brendon threw his arms about his grandfather and held him close. 'To hell with that,' he said, kissing him soundly on both bristled cheeks. 'It can be sponged off.'

'Brendon!'

He turned and was immediately swamped in his father's arms, and the three big men stood there tightly embraced, slapping backs, kissing cheeks and revelling in the fact they were together again as Harvey circled them and barked joyously.

'Mum and Peggy are waiting for us at the Town Hall and I promised them I wouldn't be long,' Brendon said rather breathlessly emerging from the bear hugs. 'It's so good to see you both again. I've really missed you.'

'Aye, we've missed you too, wee boy,' rumbled Ron, his eyes suspiciously bright beneath the shaggy brows. 'But why aren't they waiting at Beach View?'

'I'm taking everyone to lunch at the British Restaurant as a treat.'

Frank's great hand clamped hard on his shoulder. 'Then lead on, son. I could do with a decent bite to eat after gallivanting all over these hills since the crack of dawn.'

'So could I,' said Ron, 'but I'll have to stop off home to get rid of the rabbits and ferrets.' He shot them both an impish grin. 'I'm thinking they'll not be welcome in their fine restaurant.'

Brendon stilled them as they made to leave. 'There's something I want to tell you before we go back into town.'

'Oh, aye?' said Ron warily.

'I don't like the sound of that,' said Frank with a frown. 'It's not bad news, is it?'

'That depends on how you view it,' said Brendon, stroking an adoring Harvey's silken ears. 'This is my last leave for a few months. I'm being posted out of London.'

They stared at him in horror and it was Frank who broke the stunned silence. 'Where are you going?' he asked hoarsely.

'I can't tell you, Da, I'm sorry.'

'Will you see action?' Frank demanded.

'Not in the sense you mean,' he replied carefully.

'What other sense is there?' said Ron. 'You either are, or aren't. So which is it?'

'Grandad, I'd trust you and Da with most secrets – but this time it really is highly classified and I'd be risking prison. I'm sorry.'

'Then you'd've been better to say nothing,' Ron grumbled.

Brendon put his hand on his beloved grandfather's broad shoulder. 'You would have questioned why I couldn't come home, even for a few hours like today, and I thought you should know and be prepared when Mum and Peggy start fretting.'

'Aye, it's best to keep such a thing from the women,' said Ron, clenching the stem of his unlit pipe between his teeth. 'They only get to imagining all sorts and worry themselves to a frazzle.'

'Especially your poor wee mother,' said Frank. 'She's borne enough these past years without the added worry of you being posted to God knows where.'

'That's why I'm not telling either of them,' Brendon replied. 'But I wanted you to know.' He looked at his watch. 'We'd better get back before they send out a search party,' he said with a lightness he didn't really feel.

As they slowly made their way down the hill he wondered if perhaps he shouldn't have told them about his posting, for it had only added to their responsibilities and their worries. And yet he'd wanted them to know, for it was the first time since he'd been released from his duties aboard the minesweeper in the Atlantic that he'd felt he would be doing something important towards the war effort. Sitting on a rusting old warship keeping the guns prepared for attacks that rarely came, and occasionally manoeuvring MTBs and MGBs to their new assignments, was hardly exciting – and he was looking forward to going to sea again.

Ron came to a sudden halt, his gaze piercing as he regarded Brendon. 'There are things going on in the West Country,' he said. 'You wouldn't be playing any part in that, would you?'

Despite his surprise, Brendon managed to return his grandad's gaze steadily. 'I have no idea what you're talking about.'

'Aye, maybe not,' said Ron. 'But should you ever be down that way, watch your back, wee boy. The Americans might have the cash, dash and flash, but they've yet to learn what war is really all about, and are inclined to get gung-ho.'

'I'll bear that in mind.'

Brendon dug his hands into his coat pockets and carried on walking as Ron headed towards Beach View to unload his pockets of rabbits and ferrets. His grandfather was an amazing man with a real nose for secrets. How the heck he'd cottoned on to what was happening in Slapton, he had no idea, but he'd certainly hit the nail on the head this time. Brendon's ship, HMS *Saladin*, would be leaving tomorrow for Plymouth, and within hours of arriving, he would take up his post as an officer on the British corvette, HMS *Azalea*, to join the rehearsals for the Allied landings into France.

The three-course lunch at the British Restaurant cost nine-pence and served only things that weren't rationed. But the portions were generous, and the cooking was of a high standard despite the faded oil-cloth on the rickety tables, the mismatched chairs, the elderly and rather dithery waitress, and the cheap cutlery which bent out of shape at the slightest pressure.

With Harvey out of sight under the table, and Daisy in a high chair, they caught up on their news as they ploughed their way through the rich mushroom soup, a delicious vegetable curry served with mashed potato, and an apple crumble with a spoonful of custard. When the very last morsel had been devoured, they sat back and lit cigarettes as Peggy poured out the tea and Harvey mopped up the few bits that Daisy had dropped on the floor.

Peggy quietly drank her tea and smoked her cigarette as the talk turned to Anne and her husband, Station Commander Martin Black, and the boys up at Cliffe Aerodrome where young Cissy was stationed, and then to Carol down in Devon, Dolly in Bournemouth, and Jim out in India. Letters had gone back and forth between them all, but it was good to catch up on the things their own letters hadn't included.

Everyone was surprised to hear that Brendon had met Dolly in London for tea at the Ritz, for they didn't think she had connections there now she'd moved to Bournemouth. But then Dolly never had done what was expected of her, and her life was a bit of a mystery to all of them.

Peggy slowly became aware of how Pauline clutched at Brendon's arm as if terrified he'd disappear and not come back. It was little wonder he didn't come down very often, she thought. Pauline smothered him, and it must make him feel very awkward at times – rather like Doris with her son Anthony. She'd smothered him too, but the moment he'd married Suzie, he'd made his escape to another town in the Midlands, and didn't encourage her visits. Peggy was reminded of the old adage of a son being a son until he got him a wife, and hoped it didn't hold true with Brendon, for Pauline's sake.

As the hands of the clock relentlessly marked the time, they all realised that this lovely day would soon be over and they'd have to say goodbye to him again. Brendon paid the bill, refusing to let his father or grandfather chip in, and once Daisy was firmly tethered into the pushchair, they slowly walked up the High Street towards the station, Pauline clinging even more tightly to his arm as Harvey trotted alongside him.

Stan was there, pocket watch in hand as his wife Ethel pulled levers and rang bells up in the signal box. He'd known Brendon since he was a baby, and he grasped his hand and pumped it hard. 'Glad to see you, boy, even if it was only for a minute or two. Now you look after yourself, and come back as soon as you've got those Jerries on the run, you hear?'

'I'll do my best, Uncle Stan,' he replied as the signal clattered down to warn them the train was on its way.

'When *will* you be home again?' asked a tearful Pauline.

'Next year,' he replied, taking her into his arms and giving her a hug. 'Please don't cry, Mum. You have such a lovely smile, and that's what I want to take with me.'

She hastily pulled herself together and stood back as Frank and Ron wrapped him in their embrace, murmuring things in his ear that neither she nor Peggy could catch.

Peggy eyed the men and wondered what was going on. There was something between them, she'd felt it all through the afternoon. Yet she said nothing as she hugged her sturdy, handsome nephew and wished him a safe journey and a swift return.

Brendon squatted down to say goodbye to Daisy as the train pulled into the station with a sigh of steam and a screech of iron wheels, and then made a fuss of Harvey before kissing everyone again and gently disentangling himself from Pauline's clutches.

'I'll be back before you know it,' he said cheerfully.

Frank wrapped his arm around Pauline and they stood in a miserable huddle as their son walked down the platform and stepped onto the train, slamming the door behind him. He opened the window and leaned out, and they all plastered on smiles and waved, but he was soon lost in the billowing smoke as the train slowly pulled away and chugged out of sight.

Peggy caught the look between Ron and Frank, but said nothing. She'd tackle Ron once they were alone – although from past experience Ron had proved to be as tight-lipped as a clam with things he didn't think she needed to know – but tackle him she would.

18

Slapton

It was Carol's last day in Slapton. The village was eerily silent as the wind sifted the leaves along the deserted lanes and ruffled the grass in the cemetery. Thirty thousand acres of land had been cleared of not only stock and crops, but over three thousand men, women and children in less than five weeks – a task no one had believed could be achieved so swiftly or efficiently.

Now the water, gas and electricity had been turned off, and the information centre was closed down. There were so few people to help move out, the soldiers billeted in the chantry had gone on manoeuvres with their fellow troops, leaving Constable Betts, Mildred Ferris, and only a couple of artillery men on duty.

There had been no sign of General Addington since the day of the funeral, and when Carol had casually mentioned his absence in the hope it might lead Dolly into a conversation about him, she'd been disappointed. Dolly had merely shrugged and continued packing up the last few boxes in tight-lipped silence.

His name never came up again, and it was clear that Dolly had no intention of revealing anything, which only served to intrigue Carol more. General Addington seemed very approachable; perhaps she would get a chance to talk to him again, to find out just what had gone on between him and her mother. For Dolly might be a consummate actress, but she couldn't hide the shadows of something painful in her eyes, despite her bright smiles and bustling determination to clean the house from top to bottom. Carol was certain that she'd been deeply affected by their meeting.

However, in the short time she'd had following the funeral, Carol had other, more important things on her mind, and as the sun had struggled to rise through the lowering clouds of her final day in Slapton, she'd come to the churchyard to contemplate all that had happened in the past year.

Walking through the grass, which was still damp from the previous night's rain, she passed the stack of sandbags protecting the stained-glass window in the belfry and was about to head towards the plot by the war memorial when she saw the vicar pinning something inside the notice-board box to one side of the church door.

'Good afternoon, Mrs Porter,' he said shyly. 'I see you've taken charge of Nipper. Friendly little chap, isn't he?'

Nipper put his front paws against Samuel's knees and yapped in excitement as the vicar made a fuss of him.

'I never really wanted a dog,' Carol confessed, 'but he's proving to be very good company.' She eyed the sheet of paper which was flapping in the wind. 'What's that all about, Vicar?'

He smoothed the paper flat and firmly tacked the

final two corners down before closing the glazed door and locking it. 'The Bishop of Exeter has ordered these to be put up outside all the churches within the exclusion area.' He stood back and regarded it with a sigh. 'I do pray they heed the message, but I fear that their minds are on other things.'

He looked at her dolefully. 'I'll see you again, I hope, Mrs Porter, when all of this wretched business is over,' he said, and raised his hat to her before hurrying away.

Nipper got up on his hind legs at the end of the lead in an attempt to follow the vicar, but Carol tugged him back and ordered him to sit while she read the message.

TO OUR ALLIES FROM THE USA

This church has stood here for several hundred years. Around it has grown a community which has lived in these houses and tilled the fields ever since there was a church.

This church, this churchyard in which their loved ones lie at rest, these homes, these fields are as dear to those who have left them as are the homes and graves and fields which you, our allies, have left behind you.

They hope to return one day, as you hope to return to yours, to find them waiting to welcome them home. They entrust them to your care meanwhile and pray that God's blessing rest upon us all.

Charles, Bishop of Exeter

To Carol, it seemed to encapsulate the essence of how everyone was feeling to be forced out of their homes in the fear that all they treasured might come to harm, and she turned away, almost blinded by tears at the thought. She would sit for a while with David and their baby and try not to think about having to leave them behind.

She had no flowers to put in the stone urn beneath the marble cherub on her baby's grave, and the grass was too wet to sit on, so she stood with her hand caressing the headstones as she told them why she had to leave and promised to return as soon as possible. It was silly talking to them, she realised, for if they were keeping watch on her they would know what was happening – and yet it brought her a modicum of comfort to voice her thoughts.

She was looking at the fresh mound of earth in Edith Rayner's family plot, noting that the holly and ivy wreath was already looking weathered, when she heard the sound of an engine and the slam of a car door, swiftly followed by the familiar halting footsteps of her friend Betty. She rushed to greet her with a hug.

'I had to come and see how you're coping today,' said Betty, 'and thought I might find you here.' Her sweet face was full of concern.

'Bless you, Betty, but I'm holding up much better than I thought I would,' Carol confessed. 'Mum's been an absolute brick, and now the cottage is empty, I feel quite ready to leave.' She took her friend's arm and they moved out of the wind into the lee of the sandbags by the church wall. 'And how are you managing out at Beeson?'

Betty dug her gloved hands into her coat pockets and

dipped her chin into the thick scarf she'd wound round her neck. 'The headmistress is a bit of a bossy dragon, and with all the extra children crammed into those two tiny classrooms it will soon get quite chaotic.'

She smiled. 'But Mrs Claxton at the Welcome Inn is lovely – a really homely sort who's done her best to make me feel welcome.'

'I'm glad you're settled,' said Carol, squeezing her hand. 'I was getting very worried that you'd end up miles away in some horrid billet with no job.'

Betty grimaced and tried to make light of the anxious weeks she'd been through until Mildred Ferris had come up trumps. 'I was beginning to wonder where I'd end up after being turned down for so many positions,' she admitted. 'It's my stupid leg, you see. They take one look at this blessed brace and see a cripple – not an experienced primary teacher.'

'Oh, Betty, that's awfully unfair. You're such a good teacher. What fools they were not to snap you up when you've worked so hard and proved yourself. Thank goodness you had Mildred on your side.'

'She's been a Godsend, and I count myself very lucky, even though Ken's been a bit half-hearted about it all and isn't too happy that I've been billeted in a pub.' She gave a wan smile. 'He doesn't approve of women in pubs unless they're like Molly Jelks.'

'Then he's being very short-sighted,' said Carol firmly. 'He should be glad you've got a decent billet and another post so close to Slapton.'

Betty nodded, her expression wistful. 'I had rather hoped he'd pop the question when he saw the situation I was in.' She gave a sigh. 'But if we'd got married I'd have had to give up work altogether, because he doesn't approve of working wives – even though he knows how much I love my job.'

'It seems to me that Ken has very strong opinions about most things without much thought for your feelings,' said Carol dryly. 'Perhaps it'll be good to have some time away from each other so you can see things more clearly, and decide what you really want to do in the future.'

'He does seem rather preoccupied with settling in at his uncle's farm at the moment,' Betty admitted, 'and with me moving further away and starting the new post straight after Christmas there hasn't been much chance of seeing one another.' She looked evenly at Carol. 'I know you've never really thought much of Ken, and although he's a bit old-fashioned and inclined to want to take over, he's a good man at heart.'

'I'm sure he is,' Carol soothed, although her friend had hit the nail on the head about Ken's dubious ideas of working wives, seeing as how his mother and married sister put in as many hours as the men on the farm. 'And the post in Beeson will only be temporary until we can all come back home to Slapton and then, if you still feel the same way about each other, you can take up where you left off.'

'I suppose so,' Betty murmured, 'but what if absence doesn't make the heart grow fonder and Ken decides he doesn't want me after all?'

Carol held her close. 'Oh, Betty, whatever the outcome, you're strong enough to pull through. Ken isn't the only man in the world, and you're pretty and talented and great company, and any man would be proud to walk out with you. But if you and Ken are meant to be together it will happen.'

'Do you really think so?'

There was so much hope in her expression that Carol dismissed any thought she might have had that Ken was behaving badly towards this lovely girl and didn't deserve her. 'Of course I do. Now, forget about Ken, and tell me how you're settling in over at Beeson.'

Betty became animated. 'It's quite a large building with two classrooms, an assembly hall, cloakroom and a big playground. The children are all ages, and I'll be in charge of the youngest ones now that Miss Fortescue has joined the ATA. Miss Jones is Welsh, and has an unfortunate bossy manner when it comes to ordering me about, but she's a good teacher and is very hot on discipline.'

She giggled. 'The children call her "the stick insect", which is very appropriate, because she is terribly thin and lanky, and wears dowdy brown dresses which look as if she'd bought them back in the twenties – which is a shame, because they make her look very old, even though she's barely out of her thirties.'

She hurried on breathlessly. 'My billet is on the top floor of the inn, which is a bit of a struggle with all those stairs – but it's such a lovely cosy room, with the bathroom right next door, so I'm happy to darn well struggle. You must promise to come and visit very soon, Carol, so you can see it for yourself.'

'I'll come as soon as I can, I promise,' Carol breathed.

'Oh, Betty, I'm so glad you'll still be close by. It would have been awful not seeing you for months on end.'

'I feel the same way,' she replied, returning the pressure on Carol's fingers, her eyes bright with unshed tears. 'You're the only person I can really talk to, and I feel so lucky to have you for a friend – my very best friend.'

'You'll set me off crying in a minute, you soppy thing,' said Carol, nudging her gently with her shoulder. She blinked back her own tears as they embraced. 'Thank you for coming today, and for being the best friend any girl could have.'

They drew apart and smiled at one another before they began to walk back to Betty's little car which she'd been permitted to keep because of her crippled leg.

'We'll get to see one another often,' said Betty, 'and I managed quite well today, even with the endless convoys and blocked roads, so I'm sure it'll be a lot easier with us being so close from now on.' She giggled. 'At least I didn't end up being hoisted over a hedge into a field, like some I could mention.'

Carol chuckled. 'Yes, that was quite an experience, and one I definitely don't want to repeat – but the sight of my mother bare-legged in her knickers and up to her ankles in mud is one that I'll never forget.'

'She's quite a character, your mother. And certainly unlike any other I've met. I'm glad she managed to be with you through all this.' Betty paused as they reached the gate and regarded the deserted lane, the boarded-up cottages and weed-filled alleyway that led to the abandoned Tower Inn.

'Strange, isn't it?' she murmured. 'Even the birds seem to have deserted the place.'

Carol looked up at the top of the ruined tower where there had always been jackdaws roosting, and suddenly realised Betty was right. The birds had gone, and there was no birdsong but for the faint mewling of the gulls down on the shore. 'It all makes it seem so final, doesn't it?' she murmured sadly.

Betty nodded, and gave a last glance down Church Lane towards the chantry. 'I'd better get going before the rain sets in,' she said reluctantly.

'I'm sorry I can't even offer you a cup of tea before you go, but—'

'That's all right, Carol,' she interrupted. 'I didn't come for tea, but to see you.'

They hugged fiercely, then Betty clambered into the little black Austen and slammed the door. She wound down the window and leaned out. 'I'd wish you a happy Christmas, but it doesn't seem appropriate, so here's to 1944 in the hope it will be a much better year.'

'I'd drink to that if I could. Drive carefully, Betty, and I'll see you very soon.'

With a nod, a smile and a clashing of gears, Betty drove the little car down the hill and was soon out of sight. When silence was restored, Carol took one final look back at the church and cemetery, and then with a heavy heart made her way home for the last time.

The short row of cottages nestled against one another beneath their thatched roofs, the front gardens stripped of vegetables, the windows either heavily taped or boarded up. There was no smoke rising from the chimneys, and not a sound broke the profound silence. It felt to Carol as if the whole village had died, for it had taken on that same aura that had imbued Rosemary Cottage when Edith Rayner had passed away.

As she approached Thyme Cottage the front door opened and Dolly bustled out, accompanied by Nipper and carrying a large screwdriver. 'What on earth are you going to do with that?' Carol called.

'I'm removing all the brass,' said Dolly, attacking the dolphin-shaped knocker vigorously. 'These empty cottages are an open invitation to the light-fingered.'

'I doubt they'd bother with a bit of brass,' said Carol, bending to grab the dog's collar to stop him from digging in the empty vegetable plot.

'You'd be surprised. Brass can fetch a bob or two at a scrap metal dealer's.'

Carol chuckled. 'How on earth would you know that?'

Dolly grinned back at her and winked. 'You'd be surprised at what I've learnt over the years.' She finally managed to undo the screws and went back inside, her heels clattering on the bare floorboards and echoing through the empty rooms. She placed the knocker in a box with all the brass door knobs, and chucked the screwdriver in after it before closing the box and adding it to the stack by the door.

'How long before Ida's due to arrive?' she asked, reaching for her coat.

'She should be here in about half an hour.'

'Then I'll take Nipper for a bit of a walk while you say goodbye to the cottage,' said Dolly, clipping the leash to his collar.

'There's really no need, Mum.'

'Well, I don't agree,' she said, giving her a soft kiss. 'You need peace and quiet to say *au revoir*. I'll see you in about fifteen minutes.'

As the front door closed behind her, Carol felt the silence of the cottage settle around her, and with it came the memories – sweet memories of those precious times with David. She wandered from room to room, seeing David carry her over the threshold on their wedding day; remembering how they'd snuggled on the couch by the fire during the long winter evenings, planning all the things they wanted to do to the cottage to make it their own, and how he'd always woken her in the mornings with a kiss and a cup of tea.

Carol eventually returned to the hall and realised that now the house was empty the memories – although poignant – no longer hurt. She could look back with fondness, feeling blessed that, although their time together had been short, it had been full of love, warmth and togetherness. 'And that's what I'll take with me,' she murmured into the silence.

There was a scratch of a key in the door and Dolly came in with Nipper, her expression anxious. 'I haven't been too long, have I? Only Nipper refused to come when I called him and I had to chase him halfway through the village.'

Carol smiled at her and ruffled the dog's ears. 'Edith said he was stone deaf, but I think he just chooses not to hear. The next time the vet calls at the farm I'll get him to check him over.'

Dolly took off her gloves and cupped Carol's cheek. 'Are you all right?'

'I'm fine, really, so please don't worry about me.'

Dolly regarded her thoughtfully. 'You certainly seem to be more positive.'

Carol nodded. 'When I was going round the cottage I realised I've been clinging to all the sad memories, when I should have been concentrating on the happy ones – and there are many more of those which I will cherish. David wouldn't have wanted me to live in mourning, shut away in here with only regrets for company, but until now I haven't had the will to accept that. This move is the spur I need to make a fresh start – to look more clearly at my life and learn to enjoy it again.'

'Those are brave words, my darling, and I'm very proud of you and the strength you've shown these past weeks.'

Carol hugged her. 'I must have inherited that strength from you,' she murmured against the soft powdered cheek.

Dolly giggled. 'I don't know that I can take all the credit when your grandparents were the ones who raised you. They were the strong ones, Carol – I just pretended I was.'

Carol regarded her mother with interest. 'Surely it wasn't always a charade?'

Dolly shrugged. 'Not always, but it was my defence against a world that saw only a woman who'd made too many mistakes, caused a scandal, and then abandoned her children. It wasn't easy to live with the knowledge that I was guilty of all that and more – and

I'm sorry I couldn't be the mother you both really needed.'

Carol took her hands as she looked into those regretful eyes. 'We both knew you loved us,' she said softly, 'so there's nothing to forgive you for. You did what you had to do and Granny and Grandpa were utterly wonderful to us, so please don't harbour any regrets for what might have been.' She smiled. 'Besides, who needs a mother tied to the kitchen when we had glamorous, exciting you? We were far better off the way we were, and I think both of us have turned out all right, don't you?'

'Wonderfully well,' said Dolly gruffly, squeezing her fingers.

The moment was broken by the sound of hooves in the lane, and as Nipper ran round in circles barking, Carol embraced her mother. 'I love you, Mum. Don't ever change.'

'I love you too,' said Dolly with a break in her voice. 'Write often and I'll try to get back down very soon.'

They drew apart and Carol took charge of the leash to stop Nipper escaping as Dolly opened the door.

Ida stood by Hector, who gave a snort of pleasure at seeing Carol again before rolling his eyes at Nipper, who was straining to reach him. 'Who's this then?' asked Ida cheerfully as she bent to fuss over the dog.

'This is Nipper, and he's coming with me to the farm.'

Ida raised a brow. 'Jack's all right with that, is 'e?'

'He'll have to be,' said Carol firmly, lifting the dog onto the cart and tethering his lead firmly to the seat.

'Well, I don't fancy yer chances,' muttered Ida. 'Old Ma Burnley don't like dogs.'

'Then I'll have to find some way to change her mind,' said Carol, patting Hector's neck to reassure him that Nipper was quite harmless despite all the noise he was making.

Ida helped carry the dismantled bed and small couch from the house, and when the last box had been placed carefully on the wagon and lashed down with rope, Carol locked the front door. She felt quite calm as she handed the key to Constable Betts, who'd appeared as if by magic at the gate.

'Good luck, Mrs Porter,' he said tipping the edge of his helmet with his finger before strolling back up the hill.

Carol was thankful Nipper had finally shut up and was settled with his nose on his paws keeping an eye on Hector, who was now munching an apple. She turned to Dolly and embraced her. 'Drive carefully, Mum,' she said earnestly, 'and write as soon as you can.'

Dolly gave her a hug and a kiss, said goodbye to Ida, and then turned quickly away to climb into the car. She settled behind the wheel, checked her appearance in the rear-view mirror, turned the ignition key, and with a wave of her hand, drove up the hill at some speed, making the tyres screech as she disappeared around the corner.

'Blimey,' breathed Ida. 'Your mum's quite something, ain't she? But she don't 'alf drive fast.'

Carol laughed. 'She does everything at that rate, and

yes, she is certainly unique.' She climbed up next to Ida, drew Nipper onto her lap and looked over Hector's head as they set off. The sun had come through the clouds at last, and she'd taken the first steps into what she hoped was a more optimistic future, so she wouldn't look back.

19

Coombe Farm

Nipper had been very good on the journey up to the farm, sitting on Carol's knees, his ears pricked, nose twitching at all the different smells coming from the fields, but now and again he'd give a soft whine and look up at Carol as if needing reassurance.

'He's a sharp little thing, ain't he? said Ida, rolling a thin cigarette as the horse plodded along. 'Reminds me of me grandad's Patch. He was brown and white too, and the best ratter in Bow.' She chuckled. 'He were also the best thief, and 'e'd come 'ome quite often with a string of sausages or a pork chop. The butcher weren't best pleased, but he never managed to catch 'im – went like a bleedin' rocket, did Patch.'

'I doubt Nipper can go like a rocket with his fat belly and stubby legs,' laughed Carol. 'And I hope he doesn't share a talent for theft. It'll be hard enough persuading Millicent to let me keep him, but if he turns to stealing, it will cause no end of trouble.'

Ida grinned as she ruffled the dog's ears. 'He'll be fine, won't ya, mate?'

Nipper gave a sharp bark and licked her hand as if to reassure her that indeed he would.

Hector plodded up the last steep incline and Carol left Nipper with Ida as she jumped down to open the gate. She'd no sooner opened it than Ida let out a shout of warning and she was just in time to see Nipper tumble off the cart and hurtle away, scattering geese along the way to the byres where he scrabbled and squeezed his girth through the gap at the bottom of the weathered door.

'Bugger,' hissed Ida, bringing Hector to a halt in the yard. 'Sorry, Carol, but he were like greased lightning and I couldn't keep 'old of 'im.'

'We'd better find him before the Burnleys do,' said Carol, quickly closing the gate and running after him, the geese now honking and flapping their wings in panic.

She'd almost reached the byre when there was an almighty kerfuffle from behind the door and Jack Burnley chose that moment to come out of the barn.

'What be going on 'ere?' he growled, his voice almost drowned by the honking geese. He glared at the two girls from beneath his lowered brows, and then was distracted by the sharp squeals and ferocious growling and scrabbling coming from within the large byre.

'I can explain,' said Carol hurriedly and then stared in horror as Jack reached for his shotgun.

'You'm can explain later,' he rumbled. 'There be murder goin' on in my byre, and I aim to stop the beast what's causing it.' He strode purposefully across the yard.

Carol grasped his arm. 'You mustn't shoot,' she said desperately. 'It's only Nipper hunting rats.'

He came to an abrupt halt and stared down at her. 'Who or what be Nipper?'

'He's a Jack Russell – and he's mine,' she said firmly.

'I'll see about that,' he muttered, once more heading towards the terrible screams and growls.

'What's all this noise?' demanded Millicent, emerging from the kitchen doorway swathed in a white apron, her furious gaze falling immediately on her husband's gun. 'Has a fox got in the henhouse again?'

'Carol brought a blasted dog home and it's causing a ruckus in the byre,' he yelled at her.

'Shoot it, then. Don't want no dogs round 'ere.' She advanced on Carol, Ida and Jack with a determined expression on her face as Pru and Maisie came running from the milking shed to see what all the fuss was about.

Carol hung on to Jack's arm, desperately trying to stop him. 'Please, Mr Burnley, don't shoot him. He's a lovely dog and is only doing what comes naturally.'

He shrugged off her clutching hand and opened the byre door. The squealing and growling had strengthened in pitch, and in the deep gloom of the interior, there was only a blur of movement.

Ida took advantage of Jack's moment of stunned disbelief, grabbed the gun and quickly pocketed the shells before he had time to react. 'You'd be daft to shoot 'im,' she said. 'Look what he's managed to do in a few minutes when it would 'ave taken us hours.'

They all crowded in the doorway and as Ida switched on the light there was a general gasp. Whether it was of horror or admiration, it was hard to say – but what they were witnessing was more than murder; it was wholesale slaughter.

Nipper had an enormous rat by the neck and was shaking it furiously, a vicious growl coming from deep within his throat – and strewn across the floor was an entire nest of savaged and very dead vermin.

'Bloody hell,' muttered Ida. 'Grandad's Patch was good, but not this good.' She looked up at a stunned Jack and Millicent and grinned. 'You got yerself a champion there – and I reckon you'll be glad I stopped you from shooting 'im.'

'I detest dogs,' said Millicent with a grimace.

'I detest rats more,' snapped Jack, 'so hush, woman, and be still. We're keeping it.'

Millicent went puce, but for once held her tongue and stomped back into the farmhouse, slamming the door behind her.

'Blimey, Jack, you done it now,' muttered Maisie. 'Yer in for a right ticking-off, and no mistake.'

'You'm mind yer own business,' he rumbled, 'and get back to cleaning thar dairy.'

The girls scattered but Carol stayed where she was, terrified that Jack might still carry out his threat, and certainly not brave enough to go into the byre and grab the little dog, who continued to ferociously shake the squealing rat dangling from his mouth. She dithered by Jack, who leaned on the sturdy doorpost watching the last rat being despatched.

He gave a grunt of approval as the dog shook himself and pawed at his bloodstained muzzle. 'What be'm name again?' he muttered.

'Nipper,' said Carol as the little dog sat looking at her, bloody but unbowed and extremely pleased with himself.

'How you'm got 'im then? Didn't have no dog afore.'

'I inherited him from Mrs Rayner.'

'Oh, aye, I recall thar old biddy – tongue on her like acid when she taught school, and she didn't change until she were in 'er box.' Jack reached down and grasped Nipper by the scruff, and held him up to the light so he could have a proper look at him. 'You'm be a fine rat-catcher, Nipper – and not a scratch on ye, neither. Reckon there's a bob or two to be made out of you'm.'

'What do you mean?' Carol's voice was high with anxiety.

'Thar places down yonder will be running with vermin afore ye knows it,' he replied, 'and I reckons there's many a farmer would spend good silver to 'ave this fine feller sort 'em out.'

'But he's my dog,' Carol protested. 'What if I don't want to hire him out?'

'You bain't got much choice, girly,' he replied with a sly gleam in his eyes. 'Think on it as payment for his board and lodgings.'

'But I don't want him to turn vicious,' said Carol. 'He was a nice, friendly little dog before he got here, and I want him to stay that way.'

'He'm be a Jack Russell,' muttered Jack, cradling the dog and ruffling his blood-spattered ears. 'Born in 'em, it is – shame to waste such a talent.'

Carol could see that Nipper had come to no harm,

and if it meant there'd be no more threats to shoot or get rid of him, then she would have to compromise. She folded her arms and regarded Jack Burnley evenly. 'If you're so determined to hire him out, then I'll decide when and how often. And I want half what he earns. A dog that size doesn't eat much and takes up very little space – and I happen to know what old Keeper Bentley used to charge when he was the village rat-catcher.'

'Not as daft as ye look, are ye?' he muttered, the blue eyes warmed with humour. He dumped Nipper in her arms and stuck out his hand. 'This be between thee and me, all right?' he muttered. 'The missus don't need to know.'

She shook his hand. 'If that's how you want it, Jack, but she's not stupid, and will soon . . .' She giggled. 'I was about to say she'd soon smell a rat.'

He smiled. 'Aye, but we'll keep her guessing for a while, eh?' His smile broadened into a grin and his eyes twinkled. 'It's good to have ye back, Carol.'

She put the bloodstained Nipper back on the ground and held tightly to the leash. 'It's good to be back,' she said, rather surprised by how true that statement was.

20

Cliffehaven

It was Christmas Eve and the children's party had been a huge success, bolstered by the Americans providing wonderful food as well as music, and Ron playing his part of Father Christmas with great enthusiasm, Harvey at his side as always, his collar decorated with tinsel.

An overtired Daisy had been put to bed immediately they'd got home, and now Cordelia and the girls had banished Peggy from the dining room where, to the sound of dance music coming from the gramophone, they were putting up the decorations, setting the table and dressing the tree Ron had brought home that morning.

The air of excitement was almost tangible, for Cissy and Randy, her American flyer, had promised to do their best to come with Anne's husband Martin and three of his RAF colleagues, including Rita's young airman, Matthew Champion. Ivy's fireman, Andy, would drop in at teatime after spending the day with his Aunt Gloria, who owned the Crown; Fran's Robert was expected to arrive before lunch; and Rosie had sent over a crate of beer, a large tin of ham, a wonderfully iced cake, mince pies and a bottle of whisky with strict instructions to keep all of them away from Ron's thieving hands until the following day.

There had been no word from Doris, which both annoyed and worried Peggy, but whether she came or not, the spirit of Christmas filled the house despite the absence of half the family. Dear little Sarah was proving to be very stoic in the light of her separation from her family, especially since her younger sister Jane had been refused leave to come home from her highly secretive posting with the MOD.

Peggy understood how tough these occasions must be for the girl and had silently vowed to ensure that Sarah had a marvellous day, knowing that the other girls were of the same mind. Bless them, she thought. They're such lovely caring young things; all separated one way or another from their families, but still aware of poor Sarah's needs.

She gave a pleasurable sigh as she settled in the fireside chair and listened to the laughter and music coming from the other room. She was positively brimming with anticipation, for not only did she have two gorgeous smoked salmon and two birds to put on the table alongside the chicken and tin of ham tomorrow, but there were parcels from Anne and Jim, and a host of lovely letters and cards which she'd managed to read twice already.

'I'm not going to ask where the birds and fish came from,' she said to Ron, who was busy plucking the pheasants under the watchful gaze of Queenie, 'but of course I can guess. I suppose you took Frank with you?'

'Aye, of course I did,' he muttered.

'I don't know how you managed it with the place so heavily guarded and fenced off, but you'll push your luck once too often,' she warned. 'And Pauline has enough to deal with without worrying over Frank getting arrested.'

'Ach, Pauline's always fretting over something and nothing,' he replied. 'Frank's been poaching since he was in short trousers. He knows what he's doing.' He looked over his shoulder and winked at her. 'Why don't you just relax and tell me what was in all those letters you got today?'

'With the post getting so delayed their news isn't really that recent,' she replied, 'but it's better than no news at all. Anne says that she, Sally and the little ones are really looking forward to the Christmas party the Americans are putting on in the next village, and that Sally's Aunt Violet still has a few proper plum puddings she'd made at the start of the war, which will be perfect to finish off the lunch of roast chicken.' She sighed. 'I wish I'd thought to make puddings before everything either disappeared from the shops or was rationed.'

'You had rather more to worry about than plum puddings,' Ron muttered.

Peggy had a sharp memory of seeing Anne, her grandchild and two young sons leaving on that train to Somerset after the bombing got so bad it was no longer safe for them in Cliffehaven. They were difficult times, but at least now she could miss them without really worrying about them down on that lovely farm.

She returned to her letters. 'My sister Doreen writes that baby Archie is in danger of becoming very spoilt by his adoring older sisters, and as he slept right through their school carol concert she managed to see both girls sing their solos and enjoy the afternoon – although having slept for so long, he then kept her awake half the night.'

She held up the small black-and-white photographs which had accompanied the letter. 'Bonny little thing, isn't he?' she said delightedly.

'Aye. He reminds me of Frank when he was a wain,' replied Ron with pride. 'The biggest, bonniest wee lad you've ever seen.'

'He certainly hasn't become any smaller,' said Peggy with a chuckle. 'And neither has Brendon. The pair of them can fill a room just on their own.'

She looked wistfully at all the photographs that had arrived with the letters that morning. Her sons Bob and Charlie were no longer little boys, her granddaughters Rose and Emily no longer babies – and even Jim looked different.

She held up the snapshot to the weak light, noting how his black hair had been cut brutally short by the army barber; his skin had been darkened by the Indian sun and his broad torso seemed more toned. He was such a handsome man and she adored him – but it was awful to think of him being so very far from home when he should be here amongst his family.

'Now, Peggy,' rumbled Ron, 'I can see what you're thinking, and it will do no good, wee girl. They'll all come home when they can, and until then we must carry on in the belief that this war will soon be over, and it might be the last Christmas we have to spend apart.'

'I hope you're right,' she sighed, unfolding the thin sheets of airmail paper and regarding Jim's scrawled handwriting. 'And it does sound as if things are really on the move out in India.'

Ron put the birds on a plate in the larder, covered them with a tea towel and firmly closed the door so the animals couldn't get to them. 'Oh, aye? What does he say?'

'Jim and the rest of the men in his unit had some leave which seemed to drag a bit because there was very little to do but watch films or go swimming or drinking. He was quite glad to be on the move again. But that soon proved to be a long and uncomfortable journey by train, where he had to sleep on a hard bench with only one blanket to ward off the freezing night and was given very little food.'

Peggy bit her lip. 'Poor Jim,' she said. 'He does so love his food, but it's obvious the army aren't feeding him properly. He says he felt half-starved by the time they got off the train – and then there was no time to stop and eat because they had to catch a boat. After that they were ordered onto another overcrowded train where the only food on offer for the entire day was bully beef, tinned herring and dry biscuits.'

'It certainly doesn't sound much of a feast,' Ron

muttered. 'Did he give any clues as to where he was going on this long journey?'

Peggy shook her head. 'I have no idea, but he says that he arrived close to midnight and got to camp only to find it was so full he and his men had to sleep out in the open.'

'With so many troops on the move it's hardly surprising,' muttered Ron, handing her a cup of tea before plumping down in a chair by the table. 'I know Jim will be well out of any action, but perhaps they're preparing to beat back the Japs once and for all – just as we are with Jerry.'

'You could be right,' said Peggy, skimming through to the end of the letter. 'Because Jim says that after almost freezing to death that night he and Ernie had another long journey in a truck to their actual base, where the workshops were to be set up well back from the front lines.' She blinked back her tears. 'Poor lamb, he must be worn out by it all after leading such a quiet life here.'

'He looks well enough on it,' said Ron, regarding the photograph. 'Did he say if he'd received our parcel?'

Peggy nodded. 'It was waiting for him when he arrived at camp, and he said it was a smasher. He thanked everyone for their presents, hopes I like what he's sent me, and wished us all a happy Christmas.'

She gave a little sigh before continuing. 'He says he wishes he was at home with us, but by the sound of it he and his army friends will be celebrating quite well. He's looking forward to a slap-up dinner which will be followed by a darts match against the officers and a

231

show put on by the boys in the Royal Engineers' entertainment corps – whatever that is.'

'It's a bunch of men who don't mind dressing up and making fools of themselves because ENSA hasn't managed to send the dancing girls and singers out,' Ron told her. 'But I've heard they do a terrific job, and if they can bring a bit of light relief to the troops, then that's all to the good.'

'I do feel easier knowing he's not involved in any actual fighting, and that he has a proper billet, good food and company for Christmas,' Peggy admitted. 'I couldn't bear it otherwise.'

'Aye, to be sure it's a comfort to us all,' replied Ron, thinking of his own letter from Jim which thankfully Peggy didn't know about, and was written in a very different vein.

He pulled on his coat and old cap. 'I promised Rosie I'd help behind the bar. She's expecting a busy night, so I don't know when I'll be back.'

'I'll see you in the morning, then,' said Peggy, still immersed in the letter.

Ron went down the cellar steps with Harvey and closed the back door behind them. He took a few moments to light his pipe and then made his way down the garden, through the gate and along the alleyway between the houses. But instead of turning into Camden Road towards the Anchor, he went down the hill to the seafront.

He left Harvey to his own devices amid the rubble of what had once been the Grand Hotel, and went to sit on a stone bench. Looking up, he could see no stars despite the bitterly cold air, for the clouds had thickened during the day, promising more rain. Staring out towards the faint red glow on the other side of the Channel, he could hear the muffled thuds and crumps of yet another bombardment by the RAF and their allies. The war seemed more distant now Jerry had all but stopped the air raids on England, but for Jim on the front line of a very different kind of war to the one they'd fought back in 1916, it must feel horribly real.

Ron dug his hand in his coat pocket and felt the letter he'd managed to retrieve before Peggy spotted it. He'd recently made a point of always being first to collect the post, for Jim had begun to reveal to him what his life was really like out in the jungles of India, and Peggy didn't need to know the raw truth of his situation, for it would only cause her pain and a lot more worry.

He clenched the stem of his pipe between his teeth and hunched up his coat collar against the biting chill coming off the sea, but there was no protection against the icy dread that was settling in his heart.

Jim's letter had been written over a number of days as he'd been sent from one place to another, and it described more fully the long, torturous journey to get to his camp – freezing cold, hungry and crammed in like sardines throughout the night, and sweltering in the unforgiving heat during the day with no decent facilities to wash or relieve themselves. He'd been unable to say exactly where they were heading because of the strict censorship, but he'd said enough for Ron to guess that his new camp must be reasonably close to the front lines – if not out of India altogether – for the Japs were over-running Burma and Siam, and the whole of that part of the world was in turmoil.

Jim had told him he was now fully armed with a Sten gun and pistol, which he kept at his side day and night because the Japs were swarming in, in ever increasing numbers, and had managed to cross a particular river, which had seen them break through the front line. They were now expected to make a large-scale attack which could come at any moment, and there had been an almighty flap on during which everyone was evacuated from the forward area.

Allied reinforcements and ammunition kept pouring into the camp, and everyone was standing to, waiting and preparing for the expected incursion and news of what had happened to one of their sections that had already come under fire. As yet more troops and guns had continued to roll through the camp, everyone had been on high alert, for the Japs were known to suddenly appear out of the jungle and ambush the unsuspecting Allies with extreme brutality.

Once things had settled down, Jim and his section had been flown out to yet another camp which, by the sound of it, was in a deep jungle valley, which meant that men, ammunition, supplies and machinery had to be flown in. It had been a hell of a journey, flying over the jungle in the torpid heat, constantly being fired upon by the Japs from beneath the jungle canopy.

Jim had tried to make light of the terrifying experience, for their transport plane had been hit, and it was a definite case of 'pass the brown trousers' for a while before the American pilot managed to get them down in one piece. Repairing the plane so it could fly out again had been his team's first job – and Jim had praised the pilot's bravery, for the man flew the same perilous route almost every day to deliver men and supplies to this remote outpost.

On their arrival at the new camp, they discovered not the usual collection of huts, but tented dugouts surrounded by booby traps and wires, and hundreds of men who were exhausted by the constant need to stay alert – even during snatched moments of sleep. It was here they'd been ordered to make a new workshop so the many damaged and broken-down vehicles could be repaired.

Jim said every man was well armed, and as he and his fellow engineers dug inspection pits in temperatures that went off the scale, they were on tenterhooks in case the Japs came bursting out of the jungle. They'd laid more booby traps and wire around everything, but there was no guarantee they would keep the yellow perils out, for they were determined, cunning and fearless almost to the point of suicidal – which made them extremely dangerous.

Having spent broiling days trying to repair army trucks and freezing nights attempting to sleep in the dugouts whilst keeping his gun to hand and an ear out for marauding Japs, he was looking forward to returning to HQ, where there were proper beds and baths and a chance to actually relax. He was hoping to get back there for Christmas, but all he could think about was home and family, and if he would live long enough to see them all again.

Ron closed his eyes as he sent a silent prayer to whichever god might be listening to keep an eye on his boy as well as Brendon and Martin and all the other boys who were risking their lives – and to bring them safely home.

21

Burma

It was Christmas morning, although it didn't feel at all like it to Jim Reilly, who had his rifle cocked and ready at his side, the pistol tucked into his belt, safety catch off, whilst he drove the American army jeep at speed along the barely discernible jungle track.

Despite the debilitating heat and humidity, and the very real danger they were all in, Jim was actually enjoying himself. The jeep was a new toy that had been airlifted in by the Yanks and was a joy to handle, with its four-wheel drive, high and low gear ratio and the capability to negotiate tree roots, rivers and large rocks. He roared with laughter as the suspension sent him and his three heavily armed passengers at least a foot in the air every time it bounced and rocked its way between the trees.

Major General Orde Wingate's 77 Brigade had been in Burma since February 1943 – although the families of the men were not aware of that because of the high security surrounding their long-range-penetration mission, in which Japanese communications were cut, railroads and bridges blown up, road convoys ambushed and isolated Jap posts attacked. The badge they proudly wore on their sleeves and caps depicted a lion-headed dragon – what the Burmese called a *chinthe* – which in the Buddhist religion was the only living thing permitted to use force to guard their sacred Buddhist pagodas. Through mispronunciation, the word *chinthe* had been changed to *chindit* and taken on by the brigade.

The Japs had reacted to the incursion and finally trapped the force in the great bend of the Shweli River. It had been a terrible defeat, forcing the remnants of the brigade to work their way back to India in parties of all sizes, from single men to whole columns. Refusing to be bowed by this failure, and with Churchill's wholehearted support, Wingate had regrouped, and re-recruited, and Jim and his mate Ernie had become part of the hugely increased new penetration force in October. They were now at least fifty miles into enemy territory, which was why all four men were heavily armed and fully alert for the slightest evidence of the Japs as they headed further and further into the jungle to retrieve a broken-down army truck.

The heat was stifling in the deep valley, the steamy damp of the jungle emitting a stinking miasma as monkeys screeched and chattered in the trees, and the sweat made their salt-encrusted uniforms stick unpleasantly to their skin. Jim had been hoping they could have caught the plane out to HQ for a proper slap-up Christmas dinner and a chance to swim and relax, but despite all his efforts to blag their way onto the plane, there'd been no spare seats due to his blasted CO changing his mind, and this last-minute emergency call-out had put paid to all his carefully laid plans.

'What I wouldn't give for a nice cold English winter,' he said, swinging the jeep around tree roots and forcing it through the tangled undergrowth, the springs complaining as it landed with a thump after a particularly hairy bounce which made them all cling on tight.

'I'd prefer a cold beer,' said Ernie, 'so step on it, Jim, so we can get back to camp before the others drink the place dry.'

'To be sure I'm going as fast as I can,' he replied, 'but if we break the axle in this lot we could be stuck out here for days – and I certainly don't fancy walking back.'

He glanced across at his pal, Ernie, who was looking with disfavour at their surroundings through the sights of his Thompson sub-machine gun. They'd been friends since schooldays, and it had been quite by chance that they'd been called up at the same time and were sent to the same training barracks. They'd managed to stick together through thick and thin, bellyache and bouts of malaria – and because they were both gifted with an eye to the main chance, they had, until recently, had a fairly cushy number.

And then Wingate had brought their regiment into his vast and, some would say, unwieldy force – to be trained hard in jungle warfare. The weeks of carrying heavy backpacks along narrow tracks, up and down mountains and over rushing rivers in the almost unbearable heat had toughened Jim, made him strong, stripped him of the excess weight he'd gained back home, and given him a sense of pride in what he was doing and in the men who suffered alongside him. They were a lean, mean fighting machine, and with Wingate as their leader, he had no doubt that the Japs would soon be routed.

He thought of the letters he'd written to Peggy and his father, which had necessarily given very little real detail of where he was and what he was doing, but he wondered how his Peggy would react when she finally learned that he'd parachuted out of planes, slept wrapped in a single blanket beneath the great canopy of the jungle, and marched for hours carrying kit, gun and rations, the water canister dangling from his belt untouched until his throat cracked and his tongue felt like a wad of leather in his mouth. It was all a far cry from the cushy life of a projectionist in a small seaside town, who was regarded as a bit of a 'jack-the-lad' who could lay his hands on most things for a price.

His thoughts were broken by Ernie's grumpy voice. 'Remind me who thought it would be a lark to see some action,' he said. 'I was quite happy and settled in India with servants and baths and decent food.'

Jim grinned. 'Ach, to be sure, Ernie, the pay's much better now we've got promotion, and you said you wanted to see the world.'

Ernie grimaced. 'Not this bit of it I didn't,' he grumbled.

'Aye, well, there's not much we can do about it, me old son. We're in the army, and that's where we'll stay until this shout's over, so stop moaning and make the best of it.'

Ernie fidgeted in the seat and adjusted his khaki shorts which had ridden up. 'Bloody leather seats,' he moaned. 'Burn your backside and make you sweat even more. We should have liberated some of the upholstery from those abandoned cars at the dump. I can't believe the Burmese just left them all smashed up like that when the Japs invaded.'

'Yeah, it was a shame, but logical. They didn't want the Japs using them. I was hoping to find something we could fix up so we could swank about, but life's full of disappointments, so we'll have to lump it.'

Jim concentrated hard as he took the jeep down a steep slope and carefully steered it across a swiftly flowing stream. 'I wonder if there are wild pigs out here,' he mused. 'A bit of tasty pork and crackling would go down a treat.'

'I expect they wouldn't mind some of that back home,' said Ernie, rolling a cigarette with one hand as he kept his Thompson steady with the other. 'I don't know about your Peggy, but my Maureen wrote from her mum's in Guildford that she'd be lucky to get hold of a chicken this year, what with the rationing getting even stricter, and the price of everything soaring.'

'I wouldn't mind betting me father's sorting some-thing special out,' said Jim, changing down a gear and pressing his foot on the accelerator to send the jeep roaring up the steep bank. 'You know what he's like, Ern. Never could resist a bit of poaching around Christmastime.'

They continued through the steamy jungle in silence, Jim's thoughts returning to his darling Peggy and the oasis of home that was Beach View. The time difference meant it was barely four in the morning there, so she'd still be in bed and asleep, the house decorated and prepared for Christmas Day, and little Daisy perhaps dreaming of Santa. Peggy's last letter had said she was expecting quite a crowd, and that Daisy was getting very excited now she was old enough to really enjoy Christmas and the hullabaloo that went with it.

He felt a deep pang of sorrow as he thought of his youngest. She'd turned two at the beginning of December – another birthday he'd missed – along with all the other special occasions. His two boys were shooting up like weeds down in Somerset, his grand-daughters were growing up without him and his two older girls, Anne and Cissy, had become independent young women who were earning their own money and managing very well on their own.

It was a sobering thought to realise the younger ones would be strangers to him once this blasted war was over – and although he longed to be home with them all, he was rather dreading the return, for nothing would ever be the same again. He glanced at Ernie and over his shoulder to Big Bert, who sat grim-faced next to young Alfie in the back seat. Both men shared his concern, for although Bert didn't have kids and was an experienced career soldier, his wife was having far too good a time at home with all those Yanks pouring into London, and Jim knew it worried the man. As for Ernie, his Maureen was working in a munitions factory in Bradford, earning a good wage and clearly relishing her independence now their two kids had been evacuated to Wales.

The crack of rifle-fire made him start and he almost lost control of the steering wheel.

'Japs at two o'clock,' shouted Big Bert, leaning his brawny bulk out of the jeep, and sending off a volley of machine-gun fire into the jungle.

More shots zinged past the jeep and Ernie and the lads in the back were returning fire. As the echoes rang through the jungle and birds took flight, Jim put his foot down and sent the jeep careering away from where the snipers were hiding. The bastards were known to sit up in the trees for days waiting for someone to shoot, and Jim had no plans to die that day.

The sweat was streaming down his face and stinging his eyes as several bullets hit the side of the jeep and twanged and zipped far too close to his ear. He took a zig-zag path through the trees as his mates kept shooting and lobbed off several grenades.

The enemy return-fire rocked the jeep and Jim had to cling on to the steering wheel as the vehicle swayed and lurched and bounced over the rough terrain, and they were showered with the debris from the blasts. Batting away bits of tree and clods of moss, he got the windscreen wipers to clear away the mud and muck so he could see where he was going, and only just reacted in time to avoid driving straight into the trunk of a giant teak tree.

'Got 'em,' said Ernie with grim satisfaction as the shooting stopped and the jungle returned to the usual sounds of monkeys' calls and the harsh cries of the brightly coloured birds.

Jim gritted his teeth, his knuckles showing white as he continued to grip the steering wheel and kept his foot on the accelerator. 'Keep your eyes peeled,' he muttered. 'There could be more, and we've a way to go yet.'

Ernie nodded and turned round to Big Bert and young Alfie. 'Everybody all right?'

'Yeah – and a Happy Christmas to you too, mate,' came Alfie's laconic reply, followed by his usual boyish grin. The young recruit had joined them a week before, and Big Bert had taken him under his wing.

Jim smiled as the tension eased somewhat. He hated the heat, the humidity and this bloody jungle, but his mates were a good bunch, and he'd do his very best to get them all safely back to camp for the dubious pleasure of bully beef and tinned peas for their Christmas dinner – but at least the beer would be plentiful, and after that little skirmish, he could certainly drink his share.

It was almost noon, the hottest part of the day, when they finally reached the abandoned truck, which had come under fire and rolled down the steep bank of a swiftly flowing river to land on its roof. The injured men had been rescued by a nearby Allied patrol and brought back to camp the day before.

Jim brought the jeep to a halt a fair distance away and as the engine ticked and cooled, they sat sweltering in the heat to survey the scene, all too aware that it could be highly dangerous. The Japs were notorious for turning abandoned vehicles into booby traps, or lying in wait within the darkness of the jungle to pick them off.

The jungle noises were almost lost in the rush of the water as it raced around boulders and tumbled down natural weirs formed by ridges of stone, and the profound, eerie shadows beneath the thick canopy of trees and vines made it impossible to spot anyone who might be hiding in there.

'We can't sit here all day,' said Alfie, making to jump out of the jeep.

'Watch what you're doing,' Big Bert warned sharply. 'Remember your training and tread carefully.'

Jim hoisted a large loop of sturdy towing-rope over his shoulder, checked his pistol before shoving it back into the waistband of his khaki shorts, and grabbed his toolbox. 'All of you keep your eyes peeled. If they are in there, they'll've heard us coming some time ago and be waiting for us.'

They cocked their guns, eased the cartridge bandoliers over their shoulders and slowly moved away from the jeep, treading stealthily as they covered all four points, eyes open for tripwires and booby traps – or the slightest of movement within the jungle.

Jim's nerves were stretched almost to breaking point as they neared the truck, and he could feel the tension building in the others as they warily slid down the bank into the cool, swirling shallows that threatened to knock them off balance, their heavy boots inching for steady purchase on the gravelled riverbed.

The truck was an American Chevrolet, and although

the Japs had clearly emptied it of the supplies the men had fetched from the USAAF air-drop that had gone wide of the mark, it was an unwieldy, heavy vehicle to tow at the best of times. The fact it had turned turtle wouldn't make their job any easier, for the river was buffeting it, making it heavier still with all the water rushing through it.

Jim forced his way through the shallows into deeper water, his pistol cocked and poised in his free hand as he approached the truck. At first glance he could see that the distributor and fan belt were smashed and the main axle had been sheared off when it had hit the large boulder poking up from the bank.

'I can't do anything to it here,' he said quietly. 'We're going to have to tow it out.'

There was a general groan as the others kept watch, but Jim ignored it and went to hitch the heavy steel towing hook into the solid ring beneath the front bumper. As he bent to peer through the swirling froth of water for sight of the ring, he saw something that made his heart skip a beat before it began to race.

'Okay, lads, back off,' he warned sharply. 'And watch where you put your feet. It's been rigged to blow, and there's a tripwire somewhere under the water.'

They backed off, each booted foot carefully seeking purchase on the rough, slippery riverbed as they kept their guns aimed into the jungle and their eyes peeled for the invisible wire lying in wait beneath the foaming water.

Jim and Ernie had almost reached the bank when

the explosion knocked them from their feet, the force of it punching them in the back and sending them flying into oblivion.

Jim had no idea how long he'd been out, but when he opened his eyes, he had to blink several times before they came back into focus. His ears were ringing, his nose and mouth were plugged with foul mud and his whole body felt bruised – but as he snorted and spat out the mud and his senses slowly returned he saw the fiercely burning truck and realised what had happened. His first thought was for the others.

'Everyone all right?' he asked urgently.

Ernie sat up, rubbed his head and grimaced as he hawked mud from his nose and mouth. 'My head hurts,' he groaned. 'What the hell happened?'

Before Jim could reply there was a ragged cry from Big Bert. 'Over here. Alfie's down.'

They scrambled to their feet, no longer wary of snipers or ambush, but focused solely on their youngest comrade. One glance was enough for Jim to know that Alfie had left them, for he was lying like a ragdoll in the big man's brawny arms, his neck at a strange angle, a shard of heavy metal embedded in what was left of his head. He was only just eighteen – a mere two years older than Jim's Bob – but for Alfie, the war was over.

There was a lump in Jim's throat, and his heart ached for the tragic waste of a young life. He fought to contain his emotions and not think about his own son who might yet be called up if this bloody war continued.

They were all silent as Bert carried the boy tenderly back to the jeep, where he continued to cradle him in his strong brown arms until they'd reached camp, his craggy face streaked unashamedly with tears.

22

Coombe Farm

'That was a terrific lunch, Mrs Burnley,' said Betty, pushing away her empty pudding bowl. 'Thank you so much for inviting me today.'

Millicent Burnley was flushed from the heat of the range and rather too many glasses of home-made parsnip wine. 'Thar be reet,' she said, leaning back in her chair to give a sliver of meat to Nipper. 'Can't have you on you'm own Christmas Day.'

Carol smothered a smile and finished the delicious apple crumble which had been flavoured with cloves and served with thick cream straight from the dairy. Millicent had laid on a terrific lunch, with a large roasted goose, plenty of vegetables and beautiful roasted potatoes that were golden and crisp on the outside and fluffy inside. And it seemed that she'd taken to Betty, and had accepted that Nipper wasn't so bad after all – but perhaps that was just the effect of the parsnip wine and normality would resume tomorrow.

All the girls were sated, and as Millicent and Jack slumped in their fireside chairs with a much trimmer and fitter Nipper at their feet, they cleared away the dishes and discussed what they'd do for the rest of the day. It was too cold and wet to go for a walk; the pub and nearest cinema were shut, and the beach down at Beeson was off limits.

'Why don't we play charades?' suggested Carol.

'Yeah, good idea,' said Ida. 'How about you, Mr and Mrs Burnley? Fancy a bit of a lark?'

'I'm too full to move,' said Millicent, 'and by the look of him yonder, reckon he'll be asleep afore too long. Best if you'm play your games in your billet.'

They fetched their coats, gloves and hats with great reluctance, for their billet would be cold and the fire had probably gone out by now. Carol whistled to Nipper, who decided deafness was the best way of keeping his place by the fire, so she tucked him under her arm and carried him outside where a bitter wind blew sharp sleet.

They traipsed across the yard as Nipper went off to cock his leg, and entered the accommodation barn to discover there was the merest hint of flame coming from the last log in the burner. Quickly adding more wood and coaxing the flames into life, they lit the lanterns and stood round the stove in their overcoats and woolly hats warming their hands and faces.

Maisie drew the thick curtain over the window while Ida and Pru began to move the chairs closer to the fire. 'It'll soon warm up in 'ere,' said Maisie. 'At least we got enough places to sit with Carol's couch and chair, and there's blankets for our knees.'

'Blimey, you remind me of me gran, sitting by the fire with a rug. By this time on Christmas Day we used to be out at the pub 'aving a right old knees-up – not sitting about like oldens.' Ida grinned. 'You'll be offering us cups of cocoa in a minute.'

'I wish,' snorted Pru. 'The last of the cocoa went the other day.'

Betty dug about in her large handbag. 'I think this calls for something stronger than cocoa,' she said, triumphantly drawing out a small bottle of whisky.

'Where did you get that?' asked Carol as the other girls whistled and clapped in delight.

'Mrs Claxton gave it to me for Christmas, and as I'm not much of a drinker I thought you'd like it.'

'Good for you,' said Ida, hunting out clean glasses. 'Get it open, gel.'

The whisky went down very easily, and Betty was about to replenish the glasses for a second time when they heard the roar and burble of what could only have been a motorbike engine. Pru, Ida and Maisie rushed to the door in the hope it might be one of the American boys they'd befriended come to join the party.

Carol joined them at the door, still in her hat and coat, while Nipper barked and danced about on his hind legs in excitement. It was hard to make out who it was in the gloom, for he was clad from head to foot in waterproofs – but he was tall and broad and definitely male as he swung his leg over the motorbike engine and stood looking about in confusion.

'Over 'ere, mate,' called Ida, opening the door a fraction more so the light from the lanterns spilled out over the cobbles.

'I'm looking for Carol Porter,' he said as he drew nearer.

Carol recognised that voice and gave a little cry of pleasure. 'Brendon! Is that really you?'

'It certainly is,' he replied, pushing back the deep hood of his waterproofs and grinning down at her as the little dog ran in circles yapping about his ankles. 'And this must be Nipper that Dolly told me about.'

Carol pulled him into the barn as the other girls shut the door and retreated towards the warm glow of the fire to watch and wonder who this handsome stranger was to Carol. 'What a lovely surprise,' she breathed. 'But where the heck did you spring from?'

He was still smiling as he peeled off his dripping oilskins to reveal his RNR uniform. 'I was in the neighbourhood. I hope you don't mind me calling like this, but being Christmas, and with both of us far from home, I thought it would be nice to catch up.'

Carol hugged him fiercely. 'It's wonderful to see you after so long,' she said in delight. 'But what are you doing down here?'

'I'm taking part in what's going on down in the bay,' he replied, slicking back his dark hair and adjusting his cap, 'but that's about all I can tell you, Carol, sorry.'

'You must be frozen stiff after being on that motorbike. Come and get warm and meet the others, who are no doubt wondering who the heck you are. We've opened a bottle of whisky and were about to play charades, but you'll make a far more interesting diversion.

There are four girls here who will be only too delighted to have your company for the afternoon – and,' she added, 'they're all single.'

He chuckled and placed his large hand on her shoulder as he glanced across the room to the wide-eyed girls watching him by the stove. 'Lead on, Carol. I'm up for a game of charades, as long as you'll all join me in a tot of rum to chase away the cold.'

She eyed the bottle he'd pulled from his oilskins pocket and giggled. 'We're already a bit tiddly from home-made parsnip wine and whisky, but I'm sure that'll go down a treat.'

'Too right it will,' said Ida with a flirtatious smile. 'I'm Ida, and this is Pru, Maisie and Betty. Pleased to meet yer, I'm sure,' she simpered, batting her eyelashes.

Carol laughed. 'Behave, Ida, and stop teasing him. Brendon's my nephew, and not daft enough to fall for all your old flannel.'

'Your nephew?' Ida giggled. 'You sure about that, Carol? He ain't young enough.'

'My sister's fifteen years older than me,' she replied, 'and I can assure you, he is my nephew.'

Brendon took in the barn at a glance, noting the way they'd made it homely and cosy with colourful blankets and pictures on the wall, the chairs drawn close to the roaring fire, and the curtain blocking out the foul weather.

He shook hands with all four girls, feeling rather outnumbered and faintly ridiculous beneath their avid scrutiny, but when he took Betty's hand and was captured by a pair of laughing, cornflower-blue eyes it took all his will to let her hand go.

'Is Betty short for Elizabeth?' he managed, taking in her flawless complexion and the golden gleam of her hair.

'No, it isn't. I've always just been plain Betty.' She stuck out her leg and tapped the ugly calliper which was attached to a specially made boot. 'Betty Big Boot was what the other children called me when I was little,' she said without rancour. 'Rather appropriate, don't you think?'

'Children can be very cruel,' he replied, 'and if you don't mind me saying so, you're not plain at all, but really rather lovely.'

As Betty went scarlet the other girls hooted with mirth. 'Blimey, Betty, looks like you've got an admirer.'

'Don't be daft,' she blustered. 'I've already got a chap, and I'm sure Brendon was just being polite.'

'Actually,' he said, having cleared his throat, 'I was being very honest. You're a lovely-looking girl, and I'm not surprised you've got a chap. I hope he realises how lucky he is.'

Carol butted in before things got more awkward for poor Betty. 'You're as full of the blarney as the rest of the men in the family, Brendon Reilly, so shut up and get that bottle open. Then you can tell me what you've been up to since your last letter.'

He grinned bashfully, shot an apologetic look at Betty, and opened the rum. Once they'd made a toast to absent family and settled down by the fire, Brendon told them about his short leave home, and the letters he'd received from everyone, whilst surreptitiously watching Betty's expressive face.

She must have contracted infantile polio, he mused, but my goodness there's fire in her – I can see it in her eyes and her smile – and there's a determination not to allow her crippled leg to define her.

'So,' he said, leaning back in the comfortable chair and feeling the warmth of the fire and the strong rum beginning to thaw him out from the long ride on that motorbike. 'Who's going first in this game of charades?'

'Me,' said Ida. 'But only after we've 'ad another drop of that there rum, and you've told us what's going on down there.'

He filled the glasses, and Ida raised hers in a toast. 'Here's to 1944 and the end of the war.'

'Amen to that,' said Brendon. He downed the tot and replenished everyone's glass. 'As to what I'm doing here, I can't tell you. But I'm sure you're all bright enough to guess.'

'They're firing a lot of guns and getting seasick in the boats as well as blowing things up,' said Maisie, 'so they must be getting ready for this rumoured landing in France.'

'I wish they'd just get on with it,' sighed Pru. 'I'm fed up with all this hanging about.'

'Oh, come on, Pru,' protested Ida. 'The place is swarming with thousands of Yanks – it's not exactly a hardship.'

'Have you been able to get into Slapton?' Carol asked Brendon.

He nodded and patted her hand reassuringly. 'It looks just fine. I even found your cottage, and everything is just as Dolly told me in her letter. The army isn't living in the villages but out in the camps, and when the shooting really gets going it'll be well away from anywhere that might cause damage.'

'That is a relief,' she said on a sigh, lifting Nipper onto her lap.

The bottle of rum went the rounds again and they began to play charades, but as the level went down in the bottle, the game became quite raucous, and before they knew it, the time had come for Brendon to return to his billet and for the cows to be brought in – although quite how they'd manage the milking they had no idea.

They made Brendon promise to come again very soon, and clustered rather tipsily in the doorway of the barn to enthusiastically wave him goodbye. As the sound of the roaring motorbike faded, Carol put her arm round Betty's shoulders and steered her back inside.

'You'd better bunk in with me tonight,' she said. 'There's no way I'm going to let you drive back now you've had so much to drink.'

Betty sank onto the double bed Carol had brought up from her cottage. She grinned up at her, her eyes barely focusing. 'I'm not used to it,' she said, hiccupping, 'but I've decided I rather like rum. Brendon's nice too, isn't he?' she added dreamily.

Carol smiled. 'Yes, he is,' she said softly, drawing the thick eiderdown over her sleepy friend. 'And I rather think he likes the look of you, too.'

'That's nice,' she muttered before falling asleep with a soft smile on her lips.

23

Cliffehaven

Doris had not put in an appearance; nor had she answered Peggy's telephone calls. Although Peggy had initially worried about her being alone on such a day, she'd become cross at her lack of communication and decent manners and had decided to let her stew until after Christmas. There would be words between them, that was for certain, but this was neither the time nor the place to air her grievances and tell her sister exactly what she thought of her.

Thanks to Ron and Frank's exploits, dinner had been a triumph and Peggy was now flushed with pleasure and a little too much sherry as she sat at the large table littered with the debris of the delicious feast, and the remains of the hand-made crackers, empty bottles and crumpled napkins. The shabby dining room looked lovely with paper chains strung across the ceiling, the tree all glittery with tinsel and baubles, the old and rather tattered fairy on the top leaning to one side as if she too had imbibed rather too well.

Peggy smiled at the sight of Harvey and Rosie's Monty curled at her feet beneath the table, sated from being surreptitiously fed by all and sundry and too full to bother to move, even when Queenie insinuated herself between them.

She gave a deep sigh of contentment. It had been a wonderful day despite the absence of Jim, Anne and the children, for Anne had telephoned earlier from Somerset and she'd got to speak to her boys and grandchildren as well as Sally and her Aunt Vi. Sally's husband, John Hicks, had managed to take a couple of hours off duty to call in before noon, delighted to have been able to speak to her and their little son Harry before he had to return to the fire station with a packet of smoked salmon sandwiches, a cracker and a pair of knitted socks.

The house was once again ringing with laughter and music as the girls danced with the young men, Ron canoodled with Rosie, and a rather tiddly Cordelia flirted and twittered with Bertie Double-Barrelled and asked for more sherry. Daisy had become over-excited by it all, and Peggy had put her to bed for a short nap, certain that all the noise wouldn't disturb her, for she was used to squadrons of planes flying overhead from Cliffe Aerodrome night after night, and slept through it all.

Peggy lovingly caressed the beautiful silk scarf Jim had sent her all the way from India, along with a pair of gold bangles which jingled delicately every time she moved her hand. There had been silver bracelets for Cissy and Pauline, carved sandalwood boxes for each of the girls, a lovely brooch for Cordelia, a carved wooden doll for Daisy, and silk ties for Frank and Ron. Her own parcel now seemed dull and dreary after receiving such exotic presents, and Peggy could only hope that Jim would appreciate how very hard it was to find anything decent in war-torn Cliffehaven.

She set aside her worries and watched the fun as Cordelia demanded to be taught the jitterbug by Cissy's young American flyer, who'd brought a tin of real coffee and packs of cigarettes and nylons to show his appreciation for the invitation. Anne's Martin, and his two closest friends, Wing Commanders Freddy Pargeter and Roger Makepeace, had returned earlier this morning with Rita's young Matthew Champion from a night raid over Germany, and had managed to snatch some sleep before arriving in time for dinner at two o'clock. The older pilots' spirits were high after having talked to their wives, Charlotte and Kitty, who were based down near Southampton delivering planes with the ATS – and they too had raided the mess and brought wine, cigarettes and gin.

As Cordelia became rather giddy and out of breath she was steered to a comfortable chair by Bertie, where she promptly fell asleep, the home-made paper crown slipping rakishly over one eye. Peggy regarded her with deep affection, for Cordelia always loved a party, but had yet to learn that too much sherry meant she missed most of the fun.

'It's been a lovely day, Mum,' said Cissy, plumping down beside her. 'But we'll have to leave soon. Randy has to get back to Biggin Hill and I'm on duty tonight.'

Peggy cupped her daughter's sweet face with her hand, noting how drawn she looked despite the flawless make-up, neat WAAF uniform and carefully arranged fair hair which had been coiled back into lustrous victory rolls. 'I'm just glad you could come at all,' she said above the noise. 'We don't see nearly enough of you.'

Cissy bit her lip. 'I know, and I would come home more often if I could, but with raids going on day and night, leave isn't really on the cards.'

She watched Rita dancing with Matthew, the pair of them oblivious to everyone but each other. 'We've lost so many of our boys,' she said quietly, 'but it's been marvellous for us to have this break from it all.' She put her arm around Peggy and held her close. 'Thanks, Mum, for being you, and for everything you've done to make today special.'

Peggy blinked away her tears and held her daughter fiercely, warmed by her words, but afraid for all these youngsters who'd had to grow up too quickly to defend their country and snatch the smallest of moments to find release from the stress they were all under. If providing a joyful Christmas lessened the strain of this endless war, then at least she was doing something useful – and they all knew they'd be welcome at any time, should it be for a shoulder to cry on, motherly advice, or simply a cup of tea and a chance to relax away from their duties.

'Bless you, Cissy,' she said, kissing her cheek. 'It's no bother, and I'd do it all again tomorrow if it didn't encourage your grandfather and Frank to go on another poaching trip.' She looked across at Frank and Pauline, who were rather unsteadily slow-dancing to

Bing Crosby, while Ron was attempting to do a foxtrot and treading on Rosie's daintily shod feet.

Cissy chuckled. 'Neither of them need much encouragement, Mum – you should know that by now.'

'I'd better wake Daisy, or she won't sleep tonight,' said Peggy, getting to her feet. 'You won't leave just yet, will you?' At Cissy's promise to stay for another half-hour, she hurried into the hall just as there was a knock on the front door.

Wondering who it could be, since most people came straight into the house from the basement, she opened the door and saw her sister, resplendent in a fancy hat and mink coat, her arms laden with beautifully wrapped gifts.

'I decided to call in on my way back from the luncheon,' she said in her poshest voice as she stepped into the hall and dumped the packages on the nearby chair. 'I won't stay long, because I'm rather tired after such a splendid afternoon.'

Peggy folded her arms. 'Doris, you're always welcome here, but it would have been nice if you'd telephoned to tell me you were coming.'

'I didn't think I needed to,' she said, unfastening the luxurious mink coat. 'I'd already said I might pop in if it was convenient.'

Peggy didn't want a row, but she could feel her impatience rising. 'How very gracious of you,' she said flatly. 'I'm sure everyone will feel honoured by your grand presence.'

Doris eyed her coolly. 'Sarcasm doesn't suit you, Margaret, and it's hardly fitting for the occasion.'

'Neither is lying,' said Peggy, 'but as I refuse to let you spoil what has been a wonderful day, we'll discuss that some other time.'

'I don't know what you mean,' said Doris airily, slipping off her coat to reveal a beautifully tailored dress and jacket of cream shantung silk, a triple string of pearls and a diamond brooch.

Peggy realised in horror that her sister was going to carry on the charade of having been to that snooty lunch, but it would soon lead to trouble if she went on about it to the others, who knew the truth. Ron had had a lot to drink, and as he disliked Doris intensely, would no doubt let her rattle on until she'd dug a huge hole for herself before letting her fall into it.

She grasped Doris's arm as she was about to head for the noisy dining room. 'Listen, Doris, we know you weren't invited to that do, so I'd keep quiet about it if I were you.'

Doris went pale beneath the immaculate make-up, and Peggy could see she was silently debating whether to bluff it out, or come clean. 'How?' she managed finally.

'It doesn't matter how, just be aware that they do. Everyone will be delighted to see you,' she said, crossing her fingers behind her back at the fib, 'and although I know you must be feeling horribly hurt by the disgusting way you've been treated by that woman, we're your family – and I can promise you that we're all on your side.'

A kaleidoscope of emotions swept over Doris's face and in her eyes before they hardened into resolve. 'You should have warned me before this,' she said coldly. 'Just how long have you known?'

'A couple of weeks,' admitted Peggy. 'And I would have said something if I'd thought you might believe me and not take it the wrong way.' She wrung her hands. 'I'm sorry, Doris, really I am, and if I'd known you'd brazen it out, I would have told you – but you didn't ring or call in, and I thought you'd decided to stay at home and ignore my calls this morning.'

'Your silence speaks volumes for your so-called family loyalty,' snapped Doris.

'I've said I'm sorry,' said Peggy fretfully. 'And I did try to ring, honestly.'

'It's not good enough,' Doris retorted, fastening her coat. 'But then I shouldn't be surprised at your lack of thought or decency. You've always been unbearably smug, Margaret, and so wrapped up in the rag-tag of what you laughingly call "family" it's hardly surprising that you couldn't care less about my situation.'

'That's not fair,' gasped Peggy. 'Of course I worry about you.'

'Tell it to the marines,' Doris said, her careful diction slipping in her fury. 'You haven't given me a thought while you play happy families and bang on about how wonderful everyone is, and how they regularly send letters and photographs and little parcels.' She took a breath to steady herself. 'Whereas I'm forced to share my home with two common evacuees, and have an absent husband, son and grandson who, it seems, couldn't care less where I spend Christmas.'

Peggy was shocked by her outburst and deeply hurt

at the realisation Doris was jealous – jealous of the warmth and love at Beach View, and the close ties of her family, even though most of them were far away. 'Oh, Doris,' she gasped, 'you've got it all wrong – so very, very wrong.'

Doris rebuffed her attempts to embrace her. 'Don't let me keep you from your dubious celebrations,' she said bitterly. 'I'm sorry I interrupted.'

'What's going on out here?' slurred Ron from the dining room doorway. He caught sight of Doris and grimaced. 'Oh, I might have known it was you causing upset.' He swayed towards her and grabbed her arm. 'Come and stick that snooty nose of yours in a glass or three of gin. They'll loosen your corsets and put a smile on that frosty face.'

She slapped his hand away. 'I'll thank you not to touch me, you disgusting old man,' she snapped. 'I'm leaving.'

'Aye, 't'would probably be best,' he rumbled, glaring at her from beneath his wayward brows. 'Just mind you don't fall off that high horse along the way.'

'Don't take any notice of Ron,' begged Peggy. 'He's had too much to drink. Please stay, Doris. I hate the thought of you being all alone.'

Doris ignored them both and opened the front door. She slammed it behind her without another word, and moments later they heard the car engine start up followed by a screech of tyres as she drove away at speed.

'Good riddance to bad rubbish,' slurred Ron, leaning against the newel post to steady himself. 'Come on, Peggy, girl, don't let her upset you.'

'But I am upset, don't you see?' she replied through her tears, plumping down on the stairs. 'She thinks I'm smug and selfish and don't care about her – and she has a point. I should have warned her we knew about that blasted lunch.'

Ron's heavy hand fell on her shoulder and gave it a squeeze. 'What's done is done, Peggy, and however you'd gone about things she'd have found fault.' He fumbled in his trouser pocket and pulled out a crumpled and none-too-clean handkerchief. 'Dry your eyes, me darlin', and know that you're loved and treasured by all of us.'

Peggy found her own clean handkerchief and mopped up the tears. 'I know I am,' she replied raggedly. She looked up at him as he swayed on his feet and breathed alcoholic fumes all over her. 'But am I really guilty of being smug and self-centred, Ron?'

He pulled her to her feet and flung his arms about her. 'You're the kindest, biggest-hearted woman I know,' he said against the top of her head. 'Take no notice of your sister.'

Peggy drew back from the embrace before Ron lost his balance and had them both in a heap on the floor. 'I think you'd better sit down before you fall down,' she said, giving him a watery smile.

'Aye, I'm thinking the same,' he muttered, staggering back into the dining room to collapse into a chair.

Peggy glanced at the packages Doris had left behind and didn't have the heart to share them out. It wouldn't feel right after that exchange, and whatever Doris had wrapped in that pretty paper had probably not been purchased with love and care, but with the sole purpose of showing how well off she was.

She stood in the doorway of the shabby dining room which had been so lovingly decorated, her heart full of love for all the people in it. And because she knew they loved her back, she felt truly blessed.

But her sister's accusation had cut her to the quick, the diatribe revealing the deep-seated jealousy Doris had been harbouring despite the fact she had all the material things Peggy could only dream about. How sad it was that Doris couldn't see a way to change her life around – to stop being snobbish and cutting, and to find it in her heart to forgive her husband's lapse, and her son's choice of wife. If only she could open her mind to what really mattered, and just accept that no one was perfect, she'd have her own family around her and not be alone on this special day.

Peggy vowed then and there that she would do her very best to heal the breach between them. It would be an uphill struggle, and Doris wouldn't thank her for it, but if she didn't at least try to make her see how good life could be if only she stopped to think what she was doing, she'd be failing her.

24

London

Dolly had returned from Bletchley on Christmas Eve, having waited with Marie-Claire Rousseau at the isolated landing strip to wish her good luck and Godspeed before she was parachuted back into France. Dolly had worked with her before – in fact she'd been the one to interview her when she'd come to London back in 1940 on the strong recommendation of a mutual friend – and because she reminded her of herself at that age, had taken her under her wing. Their relationship had blossomed over the years despite the fact they rarely saw one another, and Dolly fretted every time she flew out.

And yet the young girl who'd come to her so full of hatred and thirsting for revenge against the Nazis who'd murdered her family back in Poland was now a cool, organised and very experienced undercover agent – and if she felt any fear, she didn't show it. Yet Dolly knew the SOE had lost too many operatives, and that their life expectancy was cruelly short. Marie-Claire must surely now be on borrowed time.

Dolly hadn't slept well even though she was very tired. With her thoughts in a tangle over her daughters, the situation in Slapton and Marie-Claire, it really didn't feel much like Christmas and she was in no mood to attend the grand luncheon at the American Embassy. But Hugh had insisted it was important to mingle and make new contacts, and as he'd promised Felix would still be busy down in Devon, she'd really had no choice.

She sat at her dressing table, the gloomy light from the grey sky above London barely penetrating the heavily taped window. 'The show must go on,' she sighed, noting the fine lines around her eyes and mouth that spoke of her weariness. And then she straightened her back and lifted her chin to meet her gaze in the mirror. 'Buck up, Dolly,' she said sternly. 'If they want a show, then you must give them one. You can sleep tomorrow.'

Having poured a glass of champagne and taken a reviving slug, she spent the next hour getting ready, her thoughts continuously returning to her encounter with Felix. Because of Carol, he clearly thought she'd married again and was content – and as long as he kept his promise to stay away from Carol, he'd never discover the truth. Yet the hurt remained that she'd been so cold with him, and if only things had been different she might have . . .

She impatiently set aside this thought and continued to prepare for the day, determined to make the best of things. She was dressed and ready when she heard the sound of a car horn. Looking out of the window down into the street, she saw Hugh waving to her from the pavement. She waved back and took one last assessing look at herself in the cheval mirror.

The pale green silk dress followed her curves to perfection, and was short enough to show off her slim legs and ankles which were encased in nylon stockings – a gift from an admirer she'd discarded the moment she'd returned from Slapton. Pearls gleamed at her throat and in her ears, and the darling little hat she'd found in Harrods sat coquettishly at an angle, the delicate netting over her eyes giving them a hint of mystery – as well as hiding those annoying tell-tale lines.

Dolly grinned at her reflection, finished a second glass of champagne without smudging her lipstick, and slipped on her high-heeled shoes and mink coat. Gathering up handbag and gloves, she checked she had her cigarette case, lipstick and handkerchief, and went down to meet a rather impatient Hugh.

'You're frightfully late, darling,' he murmured, kissing the air by her cheek to avoid knocking her hat. 'But as usual the wait was worth it. You look quite magnificent.'

'Thank you,' she replied, taking in the bespoke grey suit, the dazzling white shirt and silk tie. 'You don't look too bad yourself. New suit?'

He nodded and ushered her into the car, then got behind the steering wheel. 'There's a little something for you in the glove compartment,' he said, carefully easing the Rolls-Royce away from the apartment block and proceeding along the road at a snail's pace which always made Dolly want to grab the wheel and take over.

'Oh, Hugh, you shouldn't have,' she said, eagerly undoing the wrapping and giving a little cry of pleasure at the sight of an exquisite bottle of her favourite

French perfume. She dabbed some on her neck and wrists and then leaned across to kiss his fragrant, smooth cheek. 'I love it, but now I feel very guilty, because I haven't got you anything.'

'You've been busy doing other, far more important things,' he replied as they slowly approached the embassy. 'And I don't expect anything from you but undivided loyalty and a lifetime of absolute devotion,' he added with a teasing wink.

'Silly boy,' she giggled, tapping his knee. 'I'll go to Jermyn Street and buy you a silk cravat,' she said firmly. 'One that will go with that gorgeous velvet smoking jacket you wear for evenings at home.'

Conversation was halted by the heavily armed guards at the gate who asked to see their invitations and identity cards before they let them through into the vast parking area at the back of the grand building. Hugh took his time to reverse the Rolls into a space, and then hurried round to open the door for Dolly and hand her out.

'They've invited half of London,' she said, regarding the number of embassy and military cars and the long line of private limousines now arriving. She looked up at Hugh. 'Are you absolutely positive Felix is down in Devon?'

'That's what I was told,' he replied, checking his appearance in the wing mirror. He looked at her quizzically. 'Would it really matter if he wasn't? After all, your affair ended years ago – and you're usually very relaxed about bumping into past amours.'

'Felix is different,' she replied. She saw his eyes

brighten and tugged his arm. 'Curiosity killed the cat, Hugh. I'm saying no more. Now do get a move on, it's freezing out here.'

They greeted their hosts and, having left her fur with the cloakroom attendant, Dolly joined Hugh again and followed the other guests into the reception salon. It was dazzling with light from four vast chandeliers, which was reflected in the gold ormolu around the many mirrors and in the cut crystal of the champagne glasses. Stewards dressed in white jackets and black trousers were on hand to see that no one went thirsty, and although there was a string quartet playing somewhere close by, they could barely be heard above the loud laughter and chatter of at least a hundred people.

Dolly loved occasions like this – loved the noise, the crush, the different scents of perfumes, colognes and expensive cigars, and the chance to see what the latest fashions were, who was talking to whom, and eavesdropping on delicious snippets of scandal. She took a sip of the icy champagne and looked up at the enormous, over-dressed tree which was simply smothered in fairy lights, tinsel and glass baubles.

'The Americans don't do subtle, do they?'

Hugh chuckled. 'It's Christmas and there's nothing subtle about tinsel and paper chains, so stop being catty and come and mingle.'

Dolly took his arm and they drifted from group to group, reacquainting themselves with old friends and making new ones. The diplomats were here in great numbers, as were Members of Parliament, the Home and Foreign Offices and the higher echelons of all the

Allied forces. Dolly wasn't all that surprised to see them, for having moved in such circles for most of her adult life, she knew that such men always took time out for a party. But she also knew that a lot of them would be burning the midnight oil after everyone else was in bed, for with the Allied landings in France now arranged for late spring, the war was rapidly moving towards what everyone hoped would be the end.

By the time luncheon was announced everyone was a little tipsy, and as the mass of people slowly moved towards the vast banqueting hall, Dolly realised she needed to go to the powder room to freshen up. 'I'll meet you in there,' she murmured to Hugh, before hurrying away.

She emerged from the luxuriously appointed ladies' room having checked her make-up and dabbed some more perfume on her wrists and behind her ears. Feeling the buzz of champagne and eager now for her lunch, she headed for the crowd still filtering into the banqueting hall.

A hand encircled her slim arm and she looked up with a smile, expecting to see Hugh. The smile fell away instantly to be replaced by a stab of shock as she found herself staring into those all-too-familiar blue eyes.

'What are you doing here?' she rasped. 'You're supposed to be in Devon.'

Felix's grip tightened on her arm. 'We need to talk, Dolly.'

A frisson of fear shot through her. 'Let go of my arm, or I shall make a fuss,' she hissed.

'Not here you won't,' he replied, knowing her too well. 'I'll let go once you've heard what I have to say.'

'We've both said more than enough,' she said, her pulse racing as he drew her out of the crush and towards an open door which she soon discovered led into a small sitting room. 'What is it you want from me, Felix?' she asked as he closed the door behind him.

She took a step back when he advanced on her with that old familiar look in his eyes. Warding him off with her hands, she kept going back until she found herself wedged against a heavy desk. 'Don't do this, Felix. Please.'

He was standing too close. She could detect the scent of his shaving cream, and was all too aware of his dangerous masculinity as he towered over her and trapped her with his penetrating gaze. Her heart was hammering and she could barely breathe, a part of her longing for him to sweep her into his arms and kiss her senseless, and yet the little voice of reason warning where it would inevitably lead.

His gaze was hungry, but he made no move towards her. 'I have to be back in Devon by nightfall,' he said, his voice deep and roughened by his emotions. 'So this won't take long.'

She looked up at him, the yearning for him drenched by a cold wash of dread as his expression became serious. Was he about to unmask her for the liar she'd been forced to become? Like a rabbit caught in the glare of a poacher's lantern, she stared up at him as he explained why he'd come and what he wanted from her – and because of her fear, she barely managed to absorb what he was saying. And yet, when his words finally sank in they were far more shocking than anything she could have expected.

A short while later a devastated Dolly watched him close the door quietly behind him and then almost fell into a chair as her legs refused to support her. Closing her eyes, their exchange rang in her head, the memory of his kiss and his expressive face haunting her until she could no longer bear it.

She fought with all her might to overcome the storm of emotions that swept through her, and eventually emerged from the room intent upon making her escape. But Hugh had come looking for her, and she had to force a smile and pretend that her world hadn't just been shattered into a million pieces.

PART TWO
JANUARY 1944

25

Cliffehaven

It was barely mid-morning when Peggy finished hanging out the washing, her hands reddened and painful from boiling hot water, the strong carbolic soap Ron had managed to get hold of on the black market, and a bitter wind which carried the threat of yet another bleak day. The new year was a mere few days old, but the appalling weather had continued since October, with little sign of improving – and like this seemingly endless war, the winter was going on for too long.

She eyed the bedlinen which was flapping and snapping in the knifing wind, knowing that by the time she returned from the dreaded meeting with her sister, they'd be as stiff as boards and still damp, which meant she'd have to hang them on the suspended drier in the scullery where they'd drip disconsolately on her clean floor and lose that lovely fresh outdoor smell. Fed up with it all, she hoisted the empty basket onto her hip, closed the back door on the horrid day and trudged upstairs to the kitchen.

'At least it's lovely and warm in here,' she said to Cordelia, who was busy mashing some boiled parsnips in a bowl while Daisy tried to persuade a most reluctant Queenie that she really *did* want to sit in the small wooden trolley.

Peggy rescued the cat, then noticed that Cordelia was wearing fingerless gloves. 'I hope the bitter cold isn't affecting your arthritis too badly, Cordelia.'

'Arthritis is merely another penalty of old age,' said Cordelia with a soft smile. 'When you get to my age most things hurt, and you just have to learn to get used to it.' She eyed Peggy fondly. 'Why don't you have a cuppa and a cigarette before you go out again? I know you're dreading facing Doris, and it will do you good to relax a bit before you go into battle.'

Peggy blew out her cheeks and reached for the ever-present teapot. 'I'm hoping it won't be a battle,' she said pouring out the weak brew into a cup, 'but I suspect it probably will be. Doris isn't the easiest person to deal with, and she doesn't like any form of criticism or what she thinks of as poking my nose into her business. But she really does need someone to put her right, otherwise she'll lose what family she still has. And love her or loathe her, she doesn't deserve that.'

'I disagree,' said Cordelia, adding a few drops of banana essence to the mashed parsnips and vigorously stirring them in. 'Ted left her because she'd become impossible to live with. Anthony took that MOD posting after he married Suzie because she'd tried to take over his life for years and was showing distinct signs of interfering in his marriage – and to be honest, Peggy, she's hardly been the most loyal and loving sister to you or Doreen.'

Peggy chuckled, cradling the warm cup in her cold

hands. 'That was succinctly put, Cordelia. Perhaps you should go and talk to her instead of me,' she teased.

Cordelia pulled a face. 'No, thank you,' she said flatly. 'I don't have the patience, and would only end up hitting her over the head with something.'

Peggy laughed at the thought of the tiny, birdlike woman attacking the robust Doris. 'Better not, then.' She watched Cordelia spreading the parsnip mess onto a thin slice of wheatmeal bread. 'What on earth are you doing, Cordy?'

'Making banana spread for Daisy,' she replied, cutting the bread into soldiers. 'She loves it – although I find it's a rather strange concoction and a bit too sweet for my liking.'

Peggy broke off the end of one bread finger and popped it in her mouth, finding to her surprise that it wasn't bad at all considering very few things had sugar in them these days, and anything sweet was a real treat. 'I'm not surprised she likes it, but where on earth did you get the idea?'

'It was a recipe I found in one of those government leaflets in the library.' Cordelia tied a bib around Daisy's neck and drews her onto her lap. 'It's amazing what one can do with a bottle of essence. I'm thinking of trying her out with chocolate or strawberry if Ron manages to get me some more bottles from his pal.'

Daisy clapped her hands and eagerly grabbed the finger of bread, squashing it in her small fist before shoving it into her mouth and munching it happily. 'Narnar,' she shouted, spluttering bread and spread everywhere. 'Gan Gan made narnar. Yum yum.'

'Don't talk with your mouth full, darling,' reproved Cordelia mildly, removing bits of bread and goo from her wrap-round apron. 'It's very bad manners, and you've made Gan Gan's pinny all dirty.'

Peggy watched the two of them smile at one another, her heart warmed by their closeness, and the joy Cordelia had found in Daisy. She finished the weak tea, threw the stub of her cigarette into the fire and reached for her coat and hat.

'I'd better get going before I change my mind,' she said reluctantly. 'Are you sure you can manage Daisy on your own?'

'Oh yes,' replied Cordelia, feeding the little girl with another finger of bread. 'We'll get along just fine, won't we?' She lovingly patted the child's chubby cheek and earned a delighted giggle.

'Ron should be back very soon, but if there is a problem, you can always ring me at Doris's.' She pulled on her overcoat, which had become shabby over the years but was still the warmest thing she possessed, and crammed on her felt hat, anchoring it with two hatpins against the strong wind she knew she'd soon encounter. Drawing on her gloves, she hooked her rather tatty fur collar about her neck, ignoring the stink of mothballs emanating from it, and picked up her handbag.

Avoiding the sticky mess on Daisy's face, she kissed her dark curls before kissing Cordelia's soft cheek. 'Wish me luck,' she murmured.

'I certainly do,' said Cordelia, her expression concerned. 'Just remember that you're loved and valued, Peggy, and if things turn nasty come back home to us, safe in the knowledge that you did your best, but some battles can never be won.'

Peggy nodded, then hurried downstairs and out the back door. Tucking her chin into her fur collar against the bitter cold, she walked briskly along Camden Road. As she passed the fire station, she saw Rita doing something to the engine of a fire truck and gave her a wave, then hurried across the High Street into Havelock Road.

The cul-de-sac was deserted. The large houses set behind the hedges and high walls had taken on an air of abandonment now most of the residents had decamped to safer parts of the country, and the leafless trees that lined the road were stark against the lowering sky. The only sounds she could hear were the crashing waves on the shore and the plaintive mewl of the seagulls. Spring was clearly a long way off, and these weeks of waiting for something to happen were beginning to get everyone down.

Peggy's footsteps faltered as she approached Doris's house. She'd telephoned earlier to ensure her sister was at home, but her response had been less than enthusiastic – no doubt fully aware of why Peggy had asked to come over. But the die had been cast, and there really was no turning back now. She took a deep breath, counted to ten and strode purposefully towards the front door.

Doris must have been looking out for her, because she opened the door before Peggy could knock, and silently stood back to let her in.

The warmth was delicious after the freezing walk, and Peggy followed her sister into the drawing room where there was a roaring fire in the grate. 'Oh, what bliss,' she breathed, holding her hands out to it. 'It's bitter out there.'

'I've made coffee,' said Doris, settling onto the expensively upholstered couch and adjusting the tray of Georgian silver coffee-ware on the low table before her.

'Bless you. I could certainly do with it.'

Peggy unfastened her coat and removed the fur as she perched on the very edge of the couch, almost afraid to dent the military row of plump cushions along the back. Doris was very fussy about her furnishings, and it wouldn't do to upset her right at the start. She breathed in the delicious aroma of real coffee as Doris poured it into small cups and managed to resist remarking upon how lucky Doris was to have such a luxury when most people had to put up with Camp Coffee essence from a bottle – or, more often, go without.

Doris lit a cigarette without offering one to Peggy and smoothed her tweed skirt over her knees, the diamond engagement ring flashing on her finger. 'I know why you've come,' she said finally. 'And if you're expecting me to apologise for what I said, then you'll be disappointed.'

Peggy finished the cup of coffee before replying so she could choose her words carefully. 'I'm here to apologise to you,' she said, putting down the delicate china on the low table and slipping off her coat now she'd thawed out. 'I should have made sure you were warned, and reassured you that, no matter what, you'd be welcome at Beach View. It was thoughtless of me, and I've been fretting over it ever since.'

Doris tapped her cigarette against the crystal ash-tray, her expression unreadable. 'I accept your apology,' she said stiffly. 'In hindsight, I suppose I can understand your good intentions – you're not naturally unkind.' She regarded Peggy coolly. 'But it doesn't lessen the hurt you caused, or the embarrassment of knowing you were all sniggering behind my back.'

Peggy opened her mouth to reject her accusation, but Doris forestalled her. 'Don't bother denying it,' she snapped. 'I know what that rabble at Beach View are like, and they wouldn't be able to resist the slightest chance to belittle me.'

Peggy knew this was the moment where things could turn nasty, so she pulled out her own packet of Park Drive, stalling for time. Once her cigarette was lit, she chose her response carefully. 'You've got it wrong, Doris, and I'm surprised you should think that of them.'

'They don't like me, and the feeling is mutual,' said Doris flatly. 'Not that I spend any time worrying about it. Their opinions count for nothing in the scheme of things.'

'That's a shame,' said Peggy. 'They're good-hearted, genuine people who, given the chance, would welcome you with open arms and defend you to the last. But you seem determined to keep all of us at arm's length. Why is that, Doris? What have we done to earn such scorn?'

Doris took a breath. 'I doubt very much if you really want to hear the truth,' she said.

'Oh, but I do,' Peggy replied firmly. 'Let's get everything out in the open for once, because I'm sick of dancing around you, and want to know what you're really thinking and feeling.' Her pulse sped up as she regarded her sister evenly. 'But be prepared to hear what I have to say in return, Doris.'

She looked fleetingly wary, then lifted her chin and held Peggy's gaze. 'Our parents did the best they could to raise us decently, and I shall always be grateful for that. But they had few ambitions for us three girls and I always knew I was meant for better things than to work in a typing pool or run a third-rate boarding house.'

Peggy felt a stab of anger at this, but remained silent as Doris paused to finish her cup of coffee.

'Being the eldest, I always felt left out of things. You and Doreen were very close, and I knew I wasn't as pretty or clever as you both were, but I made the best of what I had, determined to escape – a bit like Dolly, I suppose.'

Doris was nothing like the vivacious and loveable Dolly, but Peggy kept that thought to herself.

'As you know, I went to secretarial college and found an office job in London where I began to plan my next move. I took elocution lessons and learned social skills so I could join the right clubs and societies and mix with the right sort of people where I'd find a suitable husband who could provide what I wanted.'

She flicked a glance at Peggy. 'It might sound cold-blooded to you, but that's how it was. Doreen did quite well until she met that wastrel of a husband, and then brought shame on us all by having that illegitimate baby. As for you ... You've squandered every opportunity to make something of yourself, and even seem to take some sort of smug satisfaction in the fact.'

She drew breath before hurrying on. 'I can do the sums, Margaret, and know you and Jim had to get married, and because of that you've been dragged down to his level. You encourage his disgusting father by letting him live with you, and then fill the house with common chits like Ivy and Rita. There's no sense of pride in you – no ambition to do more than be a skivvy for the rest of your life – and as for having another baby at your age . . .' She grimaced. 'Well, that says it all, really.'

Peggy had heard most of this before, but each word was a blow that still hurt, and it took all her will-power not to lash back. 'We're all different, Doris,' she replied quietly, stubbing out her cigarette with some vigour. 'And although we've chosen different paths, Doreen and I are content with how our lives have turned out.'

She regarded her sister sadly. 'But for all your ambi-tion, you're back here in Cliffehaven, and clearly not at all fulfilled. What happened in London to make you so bitter, Doris?'

Doris's hand wasn't steady as she replenished the cups from the silver coffee pot. 'I'm not at all bitter,' she replied, her gaze fixed firmly on the task. 'I'm on many of the most important committees in the town, have a lovely home, a wardrobe full of beautiful clothes and a generous allowance which provides me with the best of everything.'

Peggy attempted to touch her hand, but Doris

moved it out of reach. 'Yes, you have all the material things, Doris, but they don't make up for the love and companionship of a family,' she said softly.

'Of course not,' Doris retorted. 'But Anthony has a wife and child to care for, and he can't help it if the MOD sent him to the other end of the country. And I certainly don't need Ted hanging about now we're divorced. He's betrayed me once too often for me ever to forgive him.'

Peggy saw the sheen of tears in her sister's eyes before they were quickly blinked away. Doris was suffering, and Peggy's soft heart ached to give her comfort. The things she'd meant to say this morning were instantly dismissed, for her sister needed love and understanding, not harsh words.

'But you aren't alone, Doris. Daisy, Cissy and I are part of your family, and I came here to try and mend things between us,' she said. 'I've thought and thought how best to go about it, because I really don't want to lose you, but if we can't get to the nub of things, the air will never be cleared.'

She leaned towards her. 'You need to confide in me, Doris, because I can sense all that pent-up anger, frustration and hurt inside you which, I suspect, has very little to do with me or the people living at Beach View – and until you let it out, you'll never find peace.'

Doris glanced at her before lighting another cigarette. 'Oh, you'd love that, wouldn't you?' she sneered. 'What a story you'd have to tell to the others. I can just hear you all laughing – especially Ronan.'

'I'm not that cruel,' said Peggy firmly. 'You should

know me well enough by now that anything you told me in confidence I would take to the grave.' She tamped down on her impatience. 'Talk to me, Doris, for heaven's sake, or I swear I'll shake it out of you.'

Doris's mouth twitched. 'I don't doubt it,' she murmured. 'You always were fiery.'

Peggy grinned. 'We had some humdingers when we were kids, didn't we? Do you remember when we fought over the doll's pram, and I pushed you so hard you fell and cut your knee on the back step?'

Doris nodded, her fingers straying to the hem of her tweed skirt. 'I still have the scar, although it's faded now.'

'But there are other scars that haven't healed, aren't there?' Peggy asked softly. 'Why don't you tell me about them?'

Doris ditched the cigarette in the ashtray, got to her feet and walked to the enormous bay window which overlooked the garden and beyond to the expanse of grey sea which rolled and broke in white foam against the deserted promenade.

Peggy watched as she stood in silence, her arms wrapped about her waist, her shoulders tense, and knew she was struggling to break the habit of a lifetime and reveal her innermost thoughts and feelings.

'When I was eighteen, I met a man at a private weekend house party,' she began hesitantly. 'His name was Robert, and he was heir to a banking dynasty.' She kept her back to Peggy, and tightened her arms about her waist before she continued.

'He was handsome and very popular amongst the

London set I'd managed to fall in with, and when he made it clear he was keen on me, I thought all my dreams had come true.' She paused and gave a sigh. 'I was hopelessly in love with him, you see, and didn't think he'd even noticed me amongst all the glamorous debutantes that always surrounded him.'

Afraid of breaking the spell, Peggy resisted the urge to embrace Doris as she struggled to continue what was clearly a very painful story.

'Robert was very attentive, and for the first time in my life I felt truly cherished – almost serene in my happiness – and although he was enormously hard to resist, I sensed that if I slept with him as he wanted, it would change things between us, and he'd lose respect for me.' Her voice was unsteady as she went on. 'And I wanted to wait until our wedding day – to be able to walk down the aisle in white knowing I'd be pure for him. More fool me,' she rasped, continuing to stare out of the window.

Peggy had a nasty idea where this was going, but said nothing as she watched her sister battle to continue.

'We'd been seeing each other for about six months when we were both invited to another house party.' Doris's voice faltered and her whole body stiffened. 'I was hurrying down the draughty corridor to the bathroom when I overheard a conversation between two of the girls through an open bedroom door. Hearing my name, I stopped to eavesdrop.'

She turned to Peggy, her face drawn, her eyes bright with unshed tears. 'It's always been said that the eavesdropper hears no good of themselves – and what I learned that evening was extremely nasty.' She took a shuddering breath, rapidly blinked back her tears and rushed on.

'Robert and his friends had been laughing at me behind my back – calling me a parvenu – a jumped-up typist with ideas above her station who actually had the nerve to think she could snare one of the most eligible bachelors in London. They'd made bets on how quickly he could seduce me.'

As Peggy gasped in horror, Doris lifted her chin in defiance. 'It seemed I'd held out far longer than they'd expected, and everyone thought it was a huge joke. But Robert was getting bored with me and the game, and in danger of losing a hefty wager if nothing happened over that weekend.' Her voice faltered. 'So he'd set things up that evening to have his way with me while the others listened at the bedroom door.'

The tears were determinedly held back as she rushed to conclude her tale. 'I felt sick with shock; hurt and humiliated to the point where I just wanted to curl up and die. Luckily for me, everyone was getting dressed for dinner, so I packed my bag, slipped out through a back door and ran all the way down the drive to the village bus stop. It was raining, but I hardly noticed as I waited there in the dark and cold for what felt like hours.'

'Oh, Doris,' said a distressed Peggy, leaping to her feet and taking her in her arms. 'How cruel they were. I can't begin to imagine how agonising it must have been for you.'

Doris clung to her. 'Yes, it was cruel,' she replied

some moments later, drawing gently back from the embrace. 'And the pain was almost intolerable. But it taught me a valuable lesson.'

Peggy lovingly tucked a strand of hair back from her sister's face as Doris dabbed at her eyes with a scrap of handkerchief. 'And what was that?'

'I'd aimed too high – allowed myself to believe in a fantasy – and been too naïve to realise that of course I didn't really fit into their world.'

It was a great pity Doris hadn't learnt the lesson well enough to avoid women like the jumped-up Lady Chumley and her snobbish clique, thought Peggy, giving her another swift hug. 'The real toffs are a different breed,' she murmured. 'You have to be born into it to understand the unwritten rules and mores which identify them as belonging.'

Doris nodded. 'I know that now, but back then I was a silly girl with her heart on her sleeve and stars in her eyes.' She gave a deprecating shrug. 'It's no wonder they used me for sport.'

Peggy understood better now why Doris was so afraid of ridicule, and saw even the most gentle of teasing as an insult. She vowed to have a quiet word with Ron when she got back, for he made no bones about the fact he regarded Doris as a ridiculous woman, and never missed a chance to tweak her tail.

Peggy took her hand and led her back to the couch, waiting for her to finish the cigarette until she spoke again. 'Was that why you came back to Cliffehaven?' she prompted gently.

Doris nodded. 'I got a job in the council offices and

found a flat in Camden Road, unable to face the rest of you by returning home to Beach View. I needed time and privacy to recover – and I could only do that by cutting myself off from everyone.'

'But we'd guessed something bad must have happened in London to bring you back here, and Mum and Dad were at their wits' end to understand why you preferred to live in a flat instead of coming home.' Peggy took her hand. 'None of us would have judged you, and I can't bear the thought of you suffering alone like that when there was love and support just around the corner.'

'I was too ashamed,' Doris admitted. 'And as time went on and everyone accepted I wasn't going to explain things, it seemed simpler to draw a line under it all and pretend none of it had happened.'

'But it still rankles, doesn't it?' asked Peggy.

'Not as much as it did,' she replied, 'but there are still times when I feel that humiliation wash over me, and have to steel myself against it.' She shot Peggy a wan smile. 'It has helped to talk about it at last – and I do feel as if a burden has been lifted. So thank you for that, Peggy.'

Peggy gently squeezed her hand, warmed by her sister's words and the use of her pet name. 'I'm glad to have been a help, even though it was clearly painful for you to dredge it all up again. But did you never talk to Ted about it?'

Doris shook her head. 'When I met Edward, I wanted to make a fresh start without the past overshadowing it.' She mangled the handkerchief between her fingers.

'Edward was hardly the greatest catch – he was only a counter assistant at the Home and Colonial back then – but he was handsome, good company and very ambitious, with a surprising acumen for playing the stock market.'

She gave a little sigh. 'I can't honestly say I was madly in love with him, but we had a lot in common, and I liked him very much – probably because I didn't have to hide who I was or where I'd come from and felt comfortable with him.'

Peggy thought of the abiding passion she still felt for her Jim and experienced a pang of sorrow that her sister had settled for less. 'I'm sorry to hear you didn't love him, Doris,' she murmured.

'He was my best friend and I was very fond of him. I believed he loved well enough for both of us,' said Doris. 'Until I found out about the affair he'd had with that tart on the fish counter,' she added sourly.

Her chin went up and her expression hardened. 'And before you say anything, I tried my hardest to forgive and forget – even went to his flat and begged him to come home so we could try again. But everything I said fell on deaf ears – and now I know the depths of his most recent betrayal, I'm glad it's over.'

Peggy frowned. 'Why? What's he done now?'

Doris took a deep breath as if to steady her emotions. 'When baby Teddy was born, I couldn't wait to see him and offered to go up there to help. But Anthony said Susan wanted to get used to things before having visitors, so of course I did as he asked and waited for his telephone call. Then I discovered Edward had stayed with them for a whole week just after she'd brought the baby home.'

Her mouth became a thin line, her eyes glittering now with anger. 'As if that wasn't enough, he then went up there for Christmas. There was no such invitation for me,' she said bitterly. 'Not a word was said by any of them – not even my own son – and you can have absolutely no idea of how hurt and betrayed I felt.'

'Oh, yes I can,' said Peggy stoutly. 'If my family had done that to me I would want to shrivel up and die.'

'None of your lot would dream of treating you so badly,' said Doris. 'For all their faults, they are loyal, and I hope you fully appreciate how very lucky you are in that respect.'

'I certainly do. But how did you find out Ted had been up there?'

'I received a card from Susan's parents saying how sorry they were I'd missed the celebrations, but delighted that Edward had managed to find the time to be with them. They enclosed a snapshot of Edward holding the baby.'

'I'd have killed Jim if he'd done that to me,' hissed Peggy.

'The thought did cross my mind,' Doris replied dryly. 'But I still have some dignity left, and managed to restrain myself from punching him on the nose when he turned up, all smiles, to deliver a box of groceries. I confronted him with what I knew and he told me that I had been expected to join them, and that he'd have happily driven me up there so we could spend Christmas together. But as I'd already keenly accepted the invitation to Lady Chumley's, he and Anthony agreed that since it was such a grand occasion, they didn't think it would be fair to make me choose one over the other when it was clear I would be reluctant to turn down such an honour.'

'Oh, dear heavens,' sighed Peggy.

'It's my own fault,' said Doris flatly. 'I shouldn't have told anyone about that blasted invitation until I had it in my hand. Now I have to pay the price and try to make the best of things.'

'And you will, Doris,' soothed Peggy. 'You're a Dawson girl, and we Dawsons are a tough bunch, who never give up without a fight.'

Doris sank back into the cushions and reached for her gold cigarette case but left it unopened on her lap as the tears trembled on her eyelashes again. 'I've fought hard all my life to make something of myself – to prove my worth – and I'm tired, Peggy – tired of it all.'

Peggy was finding it hard to adapt to this previously unseen side of her sister, for Doris had never been vulnerable. 'Life isn't easy for any of us,' she murmured. 'We all have dreams, Doris, – even me – but there does come a time when we have to accept they're not meant to be, and come back down to earth.'

Doris dipped her chin and dabbed her eyes. 'At least you have the love and support of your family even if they are scattered,' she said with a sniff. 'Is it too much to ask the same from mine?'

Peggy didn't know how to answer, for Doris had alienated her family with her overbearing ways, and would have to have a radical personality change for her family to trust her again. She played for time by pouring the last of the now tepid coffee into the cups.

'I've learned over the years that if you love without boundaries, give of yourself without expecting anything in return, and keep silent when words will only do harm, those gifts will be returned to you threefold. Our loved ones are our mirror images, and we see in them what is in our own hearts.'

Doris stared at her. 'Good grief,' she said gruffly. 'You sound as if you're spouting from some trashy romance novel.'

Stung by her words, but determined not to show it, Peggy took her hand. 'It may have come out that way, and I admit it was a bit airy-fairy, but I was simply trying to make you see that love, trust and an open heart have to be given before they can be earned – and I'm sorry, Doris, but cutting remarks like that will not endear you to anyone.'

She held Doris's hand tightly and regarded her evenly. 'I know you don't mean to be unkind, but sometimes you say things without stopping to think how hurtful or hectoring they might be. We're none of us perfect, Doris – not even you – and it's time you came to terms with that and tried to fit into the real world.'

Doris glowered and made to pull away, but Peggy maintained her grip, determined to make her listen. 'You were given a harsh lesson all those years ago, but over time you seem to have forgotten it. Trying to be something you're not only leads to disappointment – even humiliation – and yet you still ride roughshod over my sensibilities, and persist in currying favour with that Chumley woman and her cronies.'

She noted the storm gathering in Doris's expression and hurried on. 'Lady Chumley was born above her father's shop in the High Street, and got lucky when her dubious husband was knighted for making a fortune out of manufacturing and selling guns and ammunition during the first shout.'

Doris was about to protest, but Peggy talked on, determined to make her point. 'She's not the grand lady she'd like us to believe she is; neither is she your friend. Look how she and the others snubbed you when you were going through that painful scandal and divorce – and how they gossiped and sniggered behind your back as you ran about after them doing all the hard work for their charities. It's a repeat of what happened to you back in London, and that missing invitation was a clear message, Doris. I hope you still have enough pride to walk away from the lot of them.'

Doris finally reclaimed her hand, but her fingers shook as she opened the cigarette case. 'You don't mince your words, do you?' she muttered.

'I prefer to speak plainly so there are no misunderstandings,' said Peggy. 'I'm sorry if that upsets you, but I needed to say what I've felt for a long time. That woman is no more than a jumped-up snob who enjoys playing the grand lady and lording it over everyone. She's not a role model. She's poison. And I've hated seeing her treat you so badly when you really don't deserve it.'

Doris blew a stream of smoke to the ceiling and managed a weak smile. 'Thanks, Peggy. I do appreciate all you've said, and of course I've known for a while what she's really like – I just didn't want to believe I'd been foolish enough to make the same mistake again.'

She fell silent for a moment. 'But how do I put things right with Anthony? Now he's tied to that Susan I've lost him, and I so wanted to be a part of my grandson's life.'

Peggy swallowed a swift retort, for she'd come to love Suzy when she'd lived with her as an evacuee, and Doris's attitude to her made Peggy cross. 'You haven't really lost him,' she said with more calm than she felt. 'He'll always be your son. But he has a wife and baby now, and his focus has to be on them.'

Peggy abandoned the cold, bitter coffee and sighed. 'I've yet to go through all that with my boys, but the time will come. I'm sure I'll like the girls they choose, and will do my very best to make them feel part of the family – but I'll still have to step back and watch from the sidelines until they ask for help or advice.'

She smiled fondly as she thought of Anne. 'It's different with daughters, thank goodness. They still need their mothers, and as they have children of their own, the relationship strengthens between them even if they are far from home.'

'I would have liked a daughter,' said Doris wistfully. 'But after Anthony was born, it wasn't possible to have another baby – not like you, who managed to get pregnant at the drop of a hat.'

Peggy bit her lip to hide her smile, for it was the

drop of Jim's trousers – not his hat – that had caused all the babies. 'Then why don't you think of Suzie as a daughter instead of someone who stole your son? She's a lovely, sweet girl, and I'm sure she'd leap at the chance to be friends.'

'I don't know,' murmured Doris. 'She wasn't what I wanted for Anthony, and although she comes from a good family and is pleasant enough, she rubs me up the wrong way.'

Peggy chuckled at the memory of Suzy's fury and frustration over Doris's overbearing interference during the wedding preparations. 'I suspect you both got on each other's nerves during those weeks before the wedding, but it's a stressful time for everyone, and allowances must be made.'

She patted Doris's arm. 'I think it would be nice if you wrote to Suzy, without mentioning Christmas, Ted's earlier visit, or offering any advice, but to ask how she's coping. She's probably feeling a bit isolated now she can't go back to her nursing, and is stuck at home all day with a baby in a town full of strangers.'

Doris gave this idea some thought before answering. 'I suppose if I'm not to lose my grandson completely I'll have to make the effort,' she said. 'But it won't be easy.'

That didn't sound too hopeful to Peggy, but at least it was a tentative beginning. 'The more you try the easier it will get,' she said. 'A smile or a kind word goes a long way, and Suzy will appreciate your letter, you'll see.'

Doris didn't look totally convinced. 'I can only hope

you're right,' she muttered. She looked across at Peggy who was reaching for her coat. 'Thank you for listening to my woes. I know they'll go no further.'

Peggy stood and fastened her shabby coat before wrapping the scruffy bit of moth-eaten fur around her neck, both of which elicited a horrified glare from her sister, which she chose to ignore. 'I've already promised, Doris,' she reminded her. 'And in return, I'd be grateful if you could treat my family with a kinder eye and softer tongue from now on. Some of your observations can be very hurtful, you know.'

Doris nodded. 'I'll do my best to remember that.'

They walked along the hall to the front door. 'I hope this has cleared the air between us,' Peggy said fervently. 'You're my sister and I love you. Please don't let's fall out again.'

'We seem to have got into the habit of doing that, haven't we?' sighed Doris. 'I'd be glad of a truce, to be honest.'

Peggy flung her arms round her and gave her a hug. 'A truce it is,' she said delightedly. 'Now I must run. I've left Daisy with Cordelia and Ron for far too long, and I dread to think what the state of my kitchen might be.'

The kitchen was a shambles with the wireless turned up to full volume, toys littering the floor and the contents of Cordelia's knitting bag strewn across the table and high chair. Daisy's face was smeared with parsnip goo and coal dust from where she'd explored the depths of the scuttle; Ron looked as if he'd been pulled through a hedge backwards, and Cordelia was jigging

26

Coombe Farm

It was halfway through January and Carol and the other girls had spent the last few hours in the freezing cold wind and driving rain helping Jack Burnley tether down the giant haystacks which had been damaged by the harsh weather. She'd lost all feeling in her hands and toes and was soaked to the skin despite her raincoat and wellingtons, but the long day was not yet over, for there was still the milking to do and the yard to be hosed down and swept clean.

The four girls trudged miserably across the muddy field towards the farmhouse as Nipper darted back and forth to retrieve the stick Jack Burnley was throwing for him. 'I dunno where that dog gets so much energy,' said Maisie. 'He's been on the go all day.'

Carol smiled despite her discomfort as she watched the little terrier bound back eagerly with the stick, dropping it at Jack's feet and bouncing about in anticipation of going to fetch it again. 'He's leaner and fitter and acting half his age,' she replied. 'Poor old Mrs Rayner wouldn't recognise him now.'

'Old Ma Burnley seems to 'ave taken to 'im as much

as Jack,' muttered Ida. 'I wish she were 'alf as nice to us as she is to 'im.'

'Yeah,' grumbled Maisie. 'I saw her giving 'im some scraps this morning, and I can't remember the last time we had bacon.'

They'd just reached the cobbled yard when there was a volley of gunfire swiftly followed by a series of dull booms which resounded through the valleys and along the hills. 'They're blowing things up again,' said Pru. 'I wonder what it was this time.'

'I wish we 'ad some decent binoculars so we could 'ave a proper butcher's at what's going on down there,' said Ida. 'Those old ones of Jack's are worse than useless.'

'It's at times like these that we need Grandad Ron,' said Carol wistfully. 'He'd know where to put his hands on some.'

'We wouldn't see much even if we did have them,' said Maisie. 'The bay's shrouded in thick cloud and the teeming rain's as good as a curtain.'

'I'm amazed they don't shoot each other,' said Carol fretfully as yet more shells were fired and the gunfire increased. 'I hope Brendon isn't stuck in the middle of it all.'

'I expect he's out on the water, nursemaiding all them seasick Yanks.' Ida grimaced, hosing the thick mud from her wellingtons. 'I 'eard tell from the boys in the pub the other night that they come off them tank transport carriers as green as peas.'

'What's more worrying is the fact that most of them can't swim,' said Carol, stamping her feet to try and get warm as she waited her turn at the hosepipe. 'Brendon said he was going to speak to his CO about giving them all lessons, but doesn't hold out much hope with the sea being so rough and cold.'

Carol finally got her boots clean and hurried into their billet to strip off her sodden coat and hat and warm herself at the woodstove. Nipper was already stretched out in front of it, steaming quite happily.

As she held out her hands and slowly thawed, her thoughts turned longingly to her cosy little cottage. She couldn't help but fret over the quantity of tanks and heavy machinery rumbling along those very narrow lanes – and the amount of shellfire and mortars that were now being exploded every day. It would be naïve to think the village might escape damage, especially as the troops handling the vehicles and weapons seemed to be mostly inexperienced and frighteningly gung-ho.

Ida gave her a nudge. 'Oy, you'll never guess who's become a regular visitor to the pub.'

Carol saw the gleam of eagerness in her eyes and knew she was bursting with gossip, so played along. 'Churchill? Eisenhower?' she teased.

'Nah, don't be daft. It's that American general and 'is driver, Herbert.'

Carol was immediately alert, for she hadn't seen the general since the day of the funeral, and was still very curious to know more about his relationship with her mother. 'Really? What on earth are they doing over this way?'

Ida shrugged. 'I dunno, do I?' she said, impatient to

get on with her story. 'Probably got some business at the American camp on the other side of the hill. The general's ever so nice, and bought us a round of beers the last time. He asked how we was managing with the weather and all, and if we ever got back to London for a visit.'

She chuckled. 'I told 'im there was fat chance of that,'cos we ain't got a plane on tap like some. And he laughed and said he was lucky the RAF provided him with one or he'd never get his job done proper. Then he joined in with a sing-song for a bit before he left.'

Carol grabbed a towel and began rubbing her hair to hide her disappointment at having missed him from the sharp-eyed Ida. 'It sounds as if you had a good chat,' she said. 'I wish I'd been there to join in the fun.'

'I expect 'e'll turn up again,' said Ida dismissively. 'But even if he don't, Herbert will. Nice bloke is Herbert,' she said dreamily. 'Lovely manners, and ever so 'andsome.'

'Oh, lawks, here she goes again,' said Pru, rolling her eyes. 'Is no bloke safe from you, Ida Baker?'

'Only the ugly ones,' she giggled. 'A gel's gotta make hay while the sun shines, Pru.'

'As long as you don't end up rolling in it with some bloke you've only known for five minutes,' retorted Maisie rather primly. 'I saw the way you was looking at Herbert, cosying up to 'im and batting yer lashes.'

Ida tossed back her damp hair. 'Yer only jealous,' she replied airily. 'If I was on top form, I'd've gone for the general – and got 'im too.'

'She's lost 'er marbles,' said Pru to no one in particular. 'A bloke like that's way out of 'er league. Besides, he's old and probably married with half a dozen kids and grandkids back in America.'

'He might be out of my league,' admitted Ida, 'but I do know he ain't married, and that he's got a big fruit farm right close to Hollywood and the beach in California, so some gel could get very lucky.'

'How on earth do you know all that?' asked Carol.

'Herbert told me.'

'Then he should learn to keep his mouth shut,' Carol said. 'He has no business discussing his senior officer with anyone.'

'Yeah, well, it were only in passing,' Ida muttered before brightening again. 'But I been thinking . . .'

'Watch out everyone, Ida's plotting,' said Pru. 'And we all know that can only lead to trouble for someone.'

'Well, I gotta 'ave something to do to make life interesting, ain't I?' protested Ida. 'And that general's widowed, good-looking for an old bloke and obviously as fit as a butcher's dog.' Her gaze fell on Carol. 'He were asking after you,' she said, 'and I reckon that if you play yer cards right, gel, you could be sunning yerself on a California beach once this flaming war's over.'

Carol burst out laughing. 'Oh, Ida, you're priceless. Where on earth do you get these mad ideas?'

'They ain't mad,' said Ida stoutly. 'You're quite posh, and would be a bit of a looker if you bothered with yer 'air and such – and let's face it, Carol, the pair of you are free and single and it's about time you got out into the world again.'

'Ida,' snapped Maisie. 'That's going too far.'

'Yeah, watch yer gob, or I'll shut it for yer.' Pru glared and balled her fists.

Ida folded her arms and glared back. 'Well, I'm sorry, but it 'ad to be said. It's been almost a year now, and she should be out there 'aving some fun instead of moping about 'ere writing flaming letters every night.'

Carol could see trouble was brewing and quickly cut in before things escalated into the usual hair-pulling tussle. 'I can understand why you feel like that, Ida, and I'm grateful you care, but there won't be any romance between me and the general. I'm sorry to disappoint you, but even if I *was* ready to step out with someone, it wouldn't be with one of my mother's old friends. Besides,' she added firmly, 'he's simply not my type.'

Ida looked crestfallen for an instant and then she grinned. 'So, what is your type, Carol? Maybe I can find someone else for you.'

Carol's gaze drifted to the photographs she'd placed by her bed. 'My type of man is tall and brown-haired, with gentle eyes and clever hands. He possesses a wicked sense of humour, boundless energy, and the capacity to love and cherish me without trying to clip my wings.'

She regarded their puzzled faces with a smile. 'David was my type – and as I'll probably never find another like him, you'd be wasting your time.' She laughed at their cynical expressions. 'I was lucky enough to find my one true love, and if I end up as an old withered spinster surrounded by cats, then that would be fine.'

Nipper barked at the mention of cats and got to his feet as the girls shuffled about and looked awkward.

Carol was still chuckling as she ruffled the dog's ears. 'Let's stop all this nonsense and get on with the milking. I'm meeting Betty and Brendon at eight, and will need a wash and change of clothing before I feel even halfway decent.'

'Are those two an item?' asked Maisie as they trudged back out to the field to get the cows in. ''Cos I seen 'im in Beeson most nights since Christmas.'

'I suspect they might be, but I don't think Betty realises it yet.'

'Well, I'd choose Brendon over that Ken any day,' said Pru. 'He's a right stick-in-the mud and a misery-guts to boot.'

'He's not very imaginative, I grant you,' admitted Carol, 'and since Betty's moved to Beeson, she's hardly seen him – which isn't a bad thing. Betty was in a rut down in Slapton, and she needed to get away from Ken so she could think about what she really wants from life.'

'She's a lovely gel,' murmured Pru. 'It's a shame about that there leg, but she don't let it get in the way, do she?'

'Only when it comes to thinking that Ken might be her only chance of marriage and having a family – and I'm rather hoping that Brendon will help her to see that she's worth far more than a dreary, small-minded farmer who's been stringing her along for two years.'

27

Felix Addington ducked his head beneath the dark oak beam as he led the way down the step into the bar at the Welcome Inn. He and Herbert were greeted by the mixed aromas of beer, cider, old fires and tobacco smoke, and the beaming smiles of the farm labourers at the bar, who raised their tankards in welcome.

A quick glance told him there were a few British red-caps and gunners in one corner, while a dozen or so GIs from the nearby camp were in another and clearly enjoying the company of some robust land girls. Having returned their salutes, he told them to relax and forget the formalities until they were back on duty.

'I'll have a tankard of your cider, Mrs Claxton,' he said, acknowledging the other drinkers who were lean-ing on the bar and eyeing him expectantly. 'Another round for these gentlemen – and a pint of beer for Sergeant Cornwallis.'

He waited for the drinks to be poured by the plump, ruddy-faced landlady, and trawled the gathering of chat-tering girls for sight of Carol Porter. He'd made a concerted effort to come in here ever since he'd returned from London because he was intrigued by Dolly's daughter, and curious as to why Dolly had been so adamant he should say nothing of their past relationship. Dark suspicions were forming, and he wanted to talk to the girl to see if there was any weight to them. But so far she'd proven elusive, and he'd usually only stayed for a single pint before leaving. It looked as if she was absent again tonight but, he reasoned, it was still quite early, and the other girls from the farm hadn't yet arrived, so there was still a chance she might come.

Once the drinks were paid for, he took a sip of the lovely golden cider and looked round for somewhere to sit. 'Go and enjoy yourself, Herby,' he said. 'I can see some of your colleagues over on the far side by the fireplace.'

'Will you be staying long, sir?' the younger man asked, clearly still puzzled as to why Felix had taken to coming all this way every night, but too steeped in British reserve to ask for an explanation.

'I'm not sure,' Felix replied. 'But I'll give you fair warning so you can finish your beer before we leave.'

He watched the younger man weave his way through the throng and then caught sight of an empty chair tucked away by the window. Quickly sitting down, he returned the nods of greeting from the farmers at the table next to him before they continued their rather heated argument about government quotas, the price of beef cattle, and the effects of the bombing and rifle-fire which was making the animals nervous.

Felix sipped the cider and listened in without commenting while he watched the shifting, noisy crowd around him. He knew better than to throw his money around, join in arguments or brag about how everything was bigger and better in America, for like every other American serviceman stationed in Great Britain, he'd received the booklet issued by the War and Navy Department in Washington to guide the new arrivals through the pitfalls and misunderstandings they might encounter in this strange but rather wonderful little country.

Felix had found it quite an amusing read, but then he'd been here before and had learnt the hard way that although English was supposed to be a common language between the two countries, there was much confusion on either side when a familiar word could mean something entirely different over here, and might even cause offence.

He tuned out of the nearby argument, his thoughts drifting as they so often did to Dolly. He'd gone to London on Christmas Eve to have a serious discussion with the committee in charge of the operations in Slapton about the inadequacy of basic training for the men down here. He'd been horrified to discover that most of them couldn't swim, got seasick at the mere sight of heaving waves, and were vague about the correct way to wear a life jacket.

The meeting had become extremely heated and he'd left the office, frustrated and angry that his efforts had come to nothing. To his mind, the men in charge were pompous old fossils who thought they knew best – much like the commanders in the first shout – and didn't want to hear about what they considered to be very minor concerns. But the lack of those very basic skills could cause needless deaths, and Felix was at his wits' end to know what to do about it.

The weather was against them, making swimming lessons impossible in the high seas, and the nearest public baths were in Plymouth. And although he'd had assurances from those in charge of the many camps that their men would be taught how to wear their life jackets, Felix wasn't totally convinced they would. It seemed that all the focus was on getting men and machinery across the Channel, and the small details that might save lives had been forgotten.

He'd gone for a long walk down by the Thames to try and cool off, and was on a circuitous route back to the American Embassy when he'd caught sight of Dolly getting out of a car in Baker Street. He'd been so surprised to see her in London that he'd watched, bemused, as she'd shown her identity card and hurried past the guard into the austere grey building.

There was nothing to show what sort of work went on there, but Felix knew, and his curiosity sharpened. Dolly was clearly involved somehow in the secret side of the war effort – in what capacity, he couldn't begin to guess, but admittance to that anonymous building was available only to those with the highest level of security.

He'd hung about for a while, until he realised he was being regarded suspiciously by the patrolling policeman. About to go on his way, he saw Dolly emerge from the building in deep conversation with Sir Hugh Cuthbertson, the former British ambassador in Paris, and now the head of MI5.

Not wanting to rouse further suspicion in the policeman, or risk being seen by Dolly, he'd hurried away to the embassy. Seeing her again had reinforced the urgent need to speak to her that had been growing since he'd discovered that Dolly had not married again, despite having had a second daughter. Now, if fate lent a helping hand, there was a real possibility that he might get that chance to try again. A quick look through the guest list for the gala Christmas luncheon the next day confirmed she'd be attending, and instead of returning to Slapton, he'd spent a restless evening thinking about how he could get her alone, and what he would say to her.

To his bewilderment and hurt, their exchange had solved nothing – and yet he'd been so sure that he'd read her correctly and knew what was truly in her heart. It was with profound sadness that he'd walked away – closing the door between them, the finality of the click of the catch reverberating in his head still.

'Hello, General Addington. How nice to see you again.'

He snapped from his thoughts and shot to his feet, stunned by how very much she looked like her mother. 'Good evening, Mrs Porter,' he said, shaking her hand. 'It's a pleasure to bump into you.'

'This is my friend Betty, and my nephew, Lieutenant Brendon Reilly of the RNR,' said Carol. 'I believe you've already met the others,' she added as the three land girls eagerly crowded round.

'Indeed I have,' he replied, smiling at them. He shook Betty's hand, remembering her from the day of the meeting, and gave a salute to Lieutenant Reilly, who had to be about the same age as Carol, which was puzzling.

Brendon grinned at him. 'People always wonder,' he said, as if reading Felix's thoughts. 'But having such a young aunt has its benefits,' he continued, his gaze drifting to the bright-eyed Betty who was patting the lively little terrier that Carol had brought with her.

Carol chuckled. 'Our family is a little out of the ordinary, General,' she said lightly, 'but this is neither the time nor place to go into its complexities.'

Felix thought it was the perfect time, but not wanting to show his hand too soon, changed the subject. 'Can I get you all a drink?'

'My round, sir,' said the young naval man firmly.

Felix didn't argue and offered his seat to Betty just as the farmers at the next table got up to leave. 'I guess we're all in luck,' he said cheerfully, making way for Carol and deliberately taking the seat next to her as Pru went to help Brendon, and Ida and Maisie swiftly cleared away the dirty glasses and overflowing ashtray.

'The girls told me you've been coming in since Christmas, General Addington,' said Carol, her eyes sparkling with humour as she made the little dog sit beneath the table. 'It's a bit out of your way, isn't it?'

'Well, Mrs Porter, I have to confess it is a bit. But I love your old English pubs, and this one seems to have a happy atmosphere.'

'I suppose it does,' she replied, looking round. 'I don't come into the bar very much, but usually go upstairs to visit Betty now she's billeted here.' She gave him a cheeky grin which made her dimple flash. 'I was brought up with the strict warning that decent women didn't frequent pubs, so I don't really feel that comfortable in one.'

Felix was surprised to hear this, for Dolly loved nothing better than to sit in a cosy corner of an old alehouse with a chilled glass of wine to hand while a fire glowed in an inglenook. 'Times have changed,' he said. 'It's the wars that gave women more freedom, and I guess that can only be for the good.' He smiled back at her, resisting the host of questions that were clamouring to be asked.

Their conversation was interrupted by the drinks arriving, and the three land girls dashing off, having spotted Herby and his friends.

Felix noticed Brendon hesitate before sitting down opposite him, and could see that he wanted to say something but wasn't quite sure how to go about it. 'Is something bothering you, Lieutenant?' he asked.

Brendon took a sip of his dark beer and then looked at him squarely. 'I hope you don't mind me asking, sir,' he said tentatively. 'But you're the chief liaison officer, aren't you?'

Felix smiled. 'For my sins,' he replied.

'Well, sir, I know this isn't really the right place to discuss such things, but I would like a chance to talk to you about certain concerns I have.'

Felix leaned towards him. 'If you have a problem, then surely your CO is the one to approach?'

'I tried that, and he wasn't much help,' said Brendon flatly. He took another sip of beer and carefully placed the glass back onto the table. 'I heard you share my worries, sir, and if that's true, then I think we should do something about them.'

Felix understood immediately what the young man was talking about and felt a sense of relief that he wasn't alone in his concerns. 'We can't talk now,' he said, digging into his pocket for his card and sliding it across the table. 'Come and see me tomorrow evening at that address.'

The relief on the younger man's face was telling as he tucked the card into his own pocket. 'Thank you, sir. I'm off duty from sundown. Would that be convenient?'

Felix nodded. 'I'll get the cooks to rustle up something so we can eat while we talk.'

Brendon looked pleased at that, no doubt relieved he wouldn't be served the bully beef and over-boiled cabbage Felix knew formed the staple diet of the British servicemen. As the young man turned to the girl at his side, Felix saw the look of love on his face which was reflected in Betty's eyes, and felt a pang of sorrow for their lost youth, and the dreams that could be shattered in an instant by this war.

'I'm glad you and Brendon have met,' said Carol. 'He's been at his wits' end just lately, and it will be a relief to talk to someone who actually might listen.'

'So you know what all that was about?'

Carol bit her lip. 'Not really,' she confessed. 'Brendon doesn't have a loose tongue, but he did mention his worries to me in passing.'

Felix could see she felt awkward at having said

anything that might get her nephew into trouble, so closed off the conversation by drinking his cider and taking in his surroundings.

Brendon and Betty were now in a private huddle on the other side of the table, the noise was rising, and someone had started to play the battered old piano.

'They'll start singing soon,' Carol said. 'Then you won't be able to hear yourself think.'

'I like a good singalong,' he replied.

Carol laughed. 'Not this one you won't, General. Most of them are tone deaf.'

'Before they get going, I'd like it if we could be on less formal terms,' he said. 'My name is Felix.'

The dimple appeared again. 'And mine's Carol. I look forward to getting to know you better, Felix.'

'Likewise,' he replied. They clinked glasses to seal the agreement, just as a few tuneless voices began to murder 'Danny Boy'.

Felix winced. 'Oh, boy. I see what you mean. They must be a different crowd to last night – those guys were at least in tune.'

Carol was about to reply when the pub erupted into another, jollier song, accompanied by stamping feet, the piano, a banjo and the beat of hands on the bar. She smiled back at him and gave a helpless shrug before joining in with gusto.

Felix realised in frustration that further conversation would be impossible now, but he'd warmed to this quiet English girl who was less sophisticated and worldly-wise than her mother, but nevertheless showed signs of possessing her steel. It would be most interesting to get to know her better, for he suspected there was far more to learn about Carol Porter – and perhaps, through her, he'd unravel the mystery that was Dolly.

Carol was aware of him watching her, and wondered if her name had come up in that clearly distressing exchange between him and Dolly. She'd seen the shock in his eyes at their first encounter, so knew that her similarity to her mother had not gone unnoticed – and yet he'd said nothing about knowing Dolly even when she'd mentioned the thing about pubs and decent girls, hoping he'd react and open up.

It was all very odd, but since he seemed as keen as she was to further this fledgling friendship, there would be other opportunities to learn more about him. She sipped the cool cider, enjoying its sweetness as the singing carried on and Brendon and Betty shared shy smiles and brief moments of eye contact. It was a good thing Ken was living several miles away, she thought, and therefore unlikely to suddenly appear, for if he could see Betty now, there would be ructions.

She gave a little sigh of pleasure at this burgeoning romance, and although it had echoes of how she and David had been, it didn't sadden her. She'd meant what she'd said to Ida earlier, for David had been all she'd ever needed, and even though he was gone, he'd left only happy memories to keep her company.

The singing came to a halt while glasses were recharged and dry throats eased. 'Do they have pubs like this in America?' she asked Felix.

'Only bars,' he replied, 'and they're mostly pretty roughneck kinda places no real lady would dare to go in. But we do have cocktail lounges, country clubs and discreet drinking clubs.'

'Everything looks very glamorous on the films,' said Carol. 'Are the houses really that big?'

He chuckled. 'Hollywood is a dream world where everything is made bigger and far more glamorous than any real American can hope for. I wouldn't set too much store by what you see in the movies.'

She felt the blush heat her face. 'I see,' she murmured, feeling gauche.

His very blue eyes twinkled as he continued to smile. 'We all need some fantasy to take us out of this dark, cruel world, and Hollywood gives us the chance to escape once in a while – so although it's brash and gaudy, and nothing like real life, it's doing a darn good job, wouldn't you say?'

She nodded and shot him a shy smile. 'Betty and I love the musicals the best. They're so gay we sing all the way home in the car. It's probably the most frightful racket, but we don't care.'

Felix grinned. 'My late wife enjoyed them too, whereas I prefer the westerns.' He gave a deprecating shrug. 'I saw Gary Cooper in *The Virginian* and was hooked from then on.' He shifted in his chair so he could regard her more closely. 'Would you consider letting me take you to the movies, Carol?'

She blinked in surprise. 'Well, I don't know,' she said hesitantly.

'It wouldn't be a date or anything,' he said hastily.

'I'm a bit long in the tooth for dates, and of course the invitation includes Betty.'

She giggled. 'That would be very nice. But don't you have other, more pressing things to do than sloping off to the pictures?'

'Well, yes,' he admitted. 'But I'm free most evenings unless there's some problem I have to deal with.'

She regarded him thoughtfully and then nodded and smiled. 'We'd both be delighted,' she said.

'That's great. And after the movie, perhaps we could all have dinner. I know a cute little bistro in Kingsbridge that somehow manages to serve the best roast lamb I ever tasted.'

Carol was about to reply when the singing started up again, so she merely nodded. He was as Ida had said, charming, handsome and delightfully boyish despite the silver hair and rather attractive lines on his face that crinkled at the corners of his eyes when he smiled. But as attractive as he was, the spark between them was not sensual, but of friendship and shared interest in the link they had with Dolly. What her mother would say about this new alliance Carol couldn't tell, but just to be on the safe side, she wouldn't mention it in her future letters.

28

Cliffehaven

'I admit that it's a rather shocking thing to say,' shouted Peggy above the thunder of enemy bombers passing overhead, 'but it really does feel quite exciting now something is happening again after those long months of nothing.'

'I know what you mean,' replied Rita, who'd earlier managed to snatch a couple of hours with her young man Matthew Champion before he flew out on yet another night mission over Germany. She huddled into her World War I fleece-lined flying jacket and buried her gloved hands in her pockets. 'It's been much too quiet – almost lulling us into believing that Jerry has simply packed up and gone home.'

'That's because our boys have shot down all their planes and bombed their aircraft factories,' Ron put in. He was rocking Daisy in his arms in an attempt to get her back to sleep. 'Still, it's not over yet, by a long chalk. You mark my words.'

'Well, they found planes from somewhere,' said Peggy as the sound of the enemy bombers made the damp metal walls of the Anderson shelter reverberate. 'And it's quite like old times with all the sirens going off throughout the day and night. This is the third alert today, so they obviously mean business.'

'They're retaliating for our raids on Berlin,' said Ron solemnly. 'And what with the Russians advancing into Poland, the relief of the nine-hundred-day siege in Leningrad and the Allied advances into Italy, to be sure we have Hitler on the run. And he knows that the best form of defence is attack.'

Rita shivered and pulled her woolly hat more firmly over her ears. 'I just hope my Matthew comes through. I hate the thought of him going out night after night on those raids – especially when he's so exhausted he can barely stay awake long enough to eat a decent meal.'

'You're not alone in worrying, love,' sighed Peggy. 'We all have concerns for all the brave boys who're risking their lives for us.' She pulled little Rita into her embrace until the curly dark head nestled into her neck and she felt her begin to relax. 'At least your dad is safe and not mixed up in the fighting,' she murmured. 'How is he, by the way?'

'He's trying to get some long enough leave to come for a visit, but with all the talk of an Allied invasion into France, and the renewed enemy raids, I'm not too hopeful.'

Silence fell in the dank Anderson shelter, the only light coming from a row of candles flickering in saucers. There was no oil or wicks in the shops for the lamps which still hung from the roof, and no kerosene for the heater either; consequently, they were all wrapped up like Eskimos, yet the chill seemed to still seep into their bones. There had been a debate as to whether they should just risk staying indoors, but as it soon became clear that this would be a prolonged enemy raid, they'd reluctantly braved the bitter early February night for the dubious pleasures of the odorous shelter.

Peggy continued to hold Rita as Ron tried to persuade Daisy it really was time for her to go back to sleep, and Harvey snoozed beneath the bench, with Queenie curled up against his belly. Cordelia was gently snoring amid her phalanx of stabilising pillows in the deckchair that had been wedged into the corner. Cordelia was lucky, Peggy thought wearily, for once her hearing aid was switched off she could fall asleep like a baby, undisturbed by even the loudest noise.

Weary to the core from a succession of sleepless nights, Peggy gave a vast yawn. It was almost four in the morning, and the all-clear couldn't come soon enough, for she had a busy day ahead, and Doris had promised to come for a cup of tea that afternoon.

'I hope you've remembered that Doris is coming over today,' she said to Ron.

'It'd be hard to forget,' he muttered with a glower.

'Please be nice to her,' she begged. 'This truce between us is barely a month old and still very fragile. I really don't want anything to spoil it.'

Ron nodded with reluctance. 'To be sure I'll be on me best behaviour,' he promised, 'but I'm wondering how long it will be before she reverts to her old self. Leopards don't change their spots, and that old cat has sharp claws.'

'Oh, Ron,' she sighed fretfully. 'She's making such

an effort; surely you're a big enough man to let bygones be bygones.'

'Aye, well, we'll see how things go,' he replied.

Peggy had to accept that things would always be difficult between Ron and her sister. She let her thoughts drift to the pile of laundry awaiting her in the scullery, the need to wash the hall floor and tidy the kitchen before Doris arrived – and the rather alarming damp patch she'd watched spread across the bathroom ceiling and behind the shelves under the kitchen sink.

'I'll need you to go up into the attic today,' she said to Ron once he'd settled sleeping Daisy in her cocoon of blankets. 'That damp patch is getting worse, and I live in dread of the ceiling coming down on me while I'm in the bath.'

'Ach, there's no need to fuss, Peggy girl,' he drawled. 'All the jobs around the house will be done eventually – but with Jerry on the attack again, it will most likely be a pointless exercise.'

'If that ceiling caves in it will be twice as expensive to fix it,' she replied firmly. 'I want you up there today to see what's going on. And while you're at it, you need to look under the kitchen sink. I think there's a leaking pipe.'

'Ach, to be sure me moving shrapnel's the very divil today,' he groaned, rubbing his hand over his lower back to emphasise the point. ''Tis the cold and damp in this shelter that doesn't agree with me. But I'll do me best, Peggy. Honest I will.'

'I've heard that before,' she retorted dryly. 'But if you don't do something soon the whole house will collapse about our ears.'

'You are a one for the exaggeration, aren't you?' he said with a twinkle in his eyes.

'And you're a one for procrastination,' she fired back. 'If you don't sort things out, then I'll have to get a man in who will.'

'Oh, aye?' He raised his shaggy brows. 'And how are you expecting to find such a man, let alone the money to pay him?'

'I'll find a way,' she said defiantly, even though she had no idea how.

'Well, good luck to you, wee girl,' he said through a vast yawn. 'But why pay someone when you have me to look after things?'

'Because you don't, do you?' she retorted in exasperation. 'You're always too busy helping Rosie at the pub, going on some daft manoeuvres with Dad's Army, or sneaking off with Frank to do mischief.' She folded her arms, furious with him, but too tired to carry on arguing when she knew she'd never win.

'To be sure, Peggy, there's a war on. Every man is needed to do his bit, and I can't be at your beck and call all the time.' With that, he closed his eyes and was snoring on his next breath.

Peggy could have hit him, but she simply didn't have the energy.

The all-clear finally went at five o'clock, and after Rita had carried in the air-raid box, pillows and blankets, she scampered off to the fire station to see if she was needed. With Daisy still asleep over her shoulder, Peggy hurried indoors and tucked her into her cot without removing the layers of clothes she was wrapped in. Hopefully she would sleep for another hour or two, and not wake in a foul mood after so many disturbed nights.

Looking down at her little girl's sweet face, she softly kissed her cheek before taking off her own woolly hat and gloves, and trudging back to the kitchen in her overcoat to stoke the range fire back into life so she could boil the kettle for tea.

Ron appeared with Harvey and Queenie at his heels and a clearly out-of-sorts Cordelia cradled in his sturdy arms.

'Put me down and stop showing off,' the old woman said crossly, fumbling to adjust the volume on her hearing aid. 'I'm perfectly capable of walking.'

Ron grinned down at her as he gently deposited her in the chair by the range. 'To be sure it's easier and quicker to carry you,' he said, his eyes twinkling with mischief. 'We'd both freeze to death at the rate you hobble along.'

'What did you say?' she demanded, still fumbling with her hearing aid. 'Do stop muttering, Ron. It's most impolite.'

Ron just chuckled, and turned his attention to feeding the animals.

Peggy made the pot of tea and began to heat the large saucepan of porridge. The other girls would be home soon, starving hungry, cold and tired after yet another long night, and the porridge and tea would warm and comfort them before they had to go out again to work. She had no doubt the three of them would have found shelter during the raid, for the hotel hosting last night's dance had a vast basement shelter – so at least that was one worry less.

Setting the pot of tea on the table and hunting out cups, she had to step around Ron who was fussing over the animals' feeding bowls. 'While you're by the sink you can have a look at that leak,' she said, more in hope than expectation.

Ron blew out his cheeks and rather grumpily pulled back the curtain that hid the shelves stacked with cleaning materials, and peered briefly into the gloom. 'To be sure I can't see a thing,' he muttered.

Peggy swiftly handed him the torch from the air-raid box on the drainer. 'That should help,' she said firmly.

He gave a deep sigh, clutched at his back and groaned as he went onto his knees to inspect the state of things beneath the sink. Grumbling under his breath, he flashed the torch back and forth, stuck a finger under the U-bend, poked at the shelving and the wall behind the pipes and then muttered even more crossly.

'Well?' Peggy folded her arms as his torso emerged from beneath the sink and he made a great show of how stiff and sore his back was.

'Aye, there's a leak,' he replied, reaching for his cup of tea. 'I'll fix it later.'

Peggy eyed him sternly. 'That better mean later today – not later in the week, or later this month or this year,' she said.

'Well, I have a few wee things to do first, but I'll

tackle it soon enough, so don't be fretting that pretty head of yours.' He gulped down the piping-hot tea and edged towards the door. 'I'll be back before you know it,' he said, and promptly disappeared down the steps and out of the house, Harvey chasing after him.

'There are times when I could kill that man,' hissed Peggy, venting her fury on stirring the porridge with unnecessary vigour.

'You'd have to join the queue,' said Cordelia, taking the wooden spoon from her and pressing her into a chair. 'And if he doesn't sort things out, then I'm sure we can all chip in to pay a proper plumber. Ron might think he knows it all, but he's a bit of a bodger, and pipes and leaks need to be handled professionally.'

Peggy's frustration and weariness brought tears to her eyes. 'That's very kind of you, Cordelia, but house repairs aren't your responsibility. I'll sort something out, never you mind.'

Cordelia shifted the pan of porridge away from the heat and sat down next to Peggy. 'I know you're struggling, dear,' she said softly. 'But you really must learn to let others help you. You can't do it all on your own.'

Peggy gently enfolded the gnarled hand in her own and shot her a watery smile. 'Thank you, Cordy, that's very sweet of you. But with more money coming through from Jim, I'm sure there'll be enough to get the more urgent repairs done.'

She kissed Cordelia's cheek, and quickly left the table to see to the porridge before she made a fool of herself by bursting into tears. It seemed just lately that she was always on the brink of tears – but then it was hardly surprising with all the worry and the sleepless nights she'd had to endure.

Doris arrived promptly at Beach View armed with a bright smile and a large box. She placed the box on the hall chair while they tentatively hugged, and then began to unfasten her beautiful fur coat.

'I hope you like what I've brought you,' she said, handing the box to a curious Peggy. 'They aren't new, I'm afraid, but they're in good condition, with plenty of wear in them if you look after them properly.'

Peggy was always pleased with her sister's cast-offs, for they were usually beautifully made and lasted far longer than the cheap things she cobbled together or bought from a market stall. And yet today she was reluctant to open the box, for she wasn't sure if it was a peace offering, or her sister's way of showing how well off she was to discard her expensive things so easily.

It was as if Doris had read her mind, for she smiled and patted Peggy's hand. 'It's by way of a peace offering,' she said with unusual shyness. 'I have so many lovely things, and I noticed the other day ... Well, you'll see what I mean when you open the box.'

'You don't need to give me anything, Doris,' protested Peggy.

'I know that. But I wanted to, so please don't make a fuss.'

Peggy untied the string, eased the lid off the big box and gasped. 'But this is far too generous, Doris,' she managed as she touched the soft mink collar and felt the expensive texture of the navy blue overcoat that nestled within the tissue paper. 'As wonderful as they are, they're much too posh for me, and I'd be afraid to wear them in case I spoiled them.'

'Don't be silly, Peggy,' said Doris bossily. 'A coat is a coat, a fur a fur, and in this freezing weather it's being practical.' She shook out the coat and held it up. 'Come along now, put it on and see how it fits.'

Feeling a bit like a child at Christmas, Peggy slipped her arms into the sleeves and felt the weight of the good woollen fabric settle around her, and the slither of the silk lining. It was a little long, and perhaps a size too big, but a bit of tailoring would see to that.

She stood still as Doris fastened the three big buttons down the front and then wrapped the mink round her neck. Feeling the downy softness of the light brown fur caressing her jaw, she couldn't resist tracing her fingers through it. 'Oh, Doris,' she breathed, 'it's lovely – so lovely, but really, you shouldn't have.'

'I have three overcoats and two full-length minks,' she said firmly, 'and having seen the state of your coat and that ratty collar you will persist in wearing, I knew I had to do something.' She squeezed Peggy's hand. 'I just want you to be warm and cosy, Peggy, and to share in the better things that I'm so fortunate to have.'

Peggy was close to tears as she hugged Doris. 'Thank you, thank you. I will treasure them always,' she breathed.

Doris gently disentangled herself from the embrace, her face flushed, her eyes suspiciously bright. 'Enough of all this nonsense,' she said briskly to hide her emotional state. 'I'm gasping for a cuppa, and I've got lots to tell you.'

'It'll have to be in the kitchen, I'm afraid,' said a flustered Peggy who was still finding it hard to get used to this new, sweet Doris.

'That's fine by me,' she replied. 'I'll go and put the kettle on while you take a look at yourself in your bedroom mirror.' She grinned quite girlishly. 'I think you'll be surprised at how well those suit you.'

Rather bewildered, Peggy watched her sister stride into her kitchen, heard her greeting Cordelia pleasantly and making a fuss of Daisy. 'Well, well,' she muttered, going into her bedroom. 'Who'd have thought it?'

Standing in front of the wardrobe-door mirror, she took in the image of this smart and rather glamorous Peggy. If she could get Fran to wash and set her hair, and do her nails, she'd look like a film star. She tried on the dark navy pumps Doris had given her the previous year, and perched her blue felt hat rakishly over one eye before turning to the photograph of Jim which she had on her bedside cabinet.

'So, what do you think of the new me, Jim?' she breathed.

He looked back at her, his roguish smile touching his lips and dancing in his very dark blue eyes, and she could almost hear him chuckling – telling her in that deep, lilting voice that she was lovely and he loved her – but preferred her naked beside him in their bed.

She blushed at the thought and carefully hung up the coat and placed the fur back into the box amid the tissue paper. Her poor old coat hung beside it looking very forlorn, but she would still use it for everyday and keep the new one for best, she decided. Though where on earth she could wear such finery she had no idea.

Doris and Cordelia were chatting quite pleasantly, and Daisy was leaning against Doris's knee, gazing in awe at her sparkling diamond ring. The kettle had boiled and Doris had laid out cups and saucers, found the milk and sugar and provided a packet of biscuits.

'Rich Tea,' she explained. 'I told Edward I was coming over to see you, and he gave them to me so we could have a little treat. He sends his regards, by the way – along with a packet of tea.'

Peggy smiled and sat down while Doris poured the dark brew into the cups, Daisy continued to be awed by the diamond, and Cordelia simply looked confused. She too was clearly finding it hard to accept this new, animated, friendly Doris, and wasn't at all sure she could believe what she was seeing.

'So, what news of everyone?' asked Peggy after taking a sip of the delicious tea.

'As you know, I've been writing to Susan on a regular basis, and I must say her letters are very amusing, as well as being well written. I do believe that girl has hidden depths.'

Peggy was well aware of Suzie's talents and remained silent, just glad that Doris had followed her advice and made the effort to be friends.

Doris was flushed with pleasure. 'She's invited me to go and stay with them over Easter. Her parents will be away, so I'll have the little family all to myself. Anthony has decorated the spare bedroom especially, and Susan found some lovely material for curtains and a counterpane. She sent me a snippet to show me before she made them, and I have to say, her taste is impeccable.'

It always was, thought Peggy. 'How lovely,' she murmured before Doris rattled on about the photographs they'd sent of baby Teddy, and how Susan was planning to show her around the village, and take her to the nearby town to shop. There would be walks in parks, the feeding of ducks, an introduction to the other young mothers she'd come to know, and perhaps even a trip to the theatre if she could get tickets and organise a baby-sitter.

'It sounds as if she's making a real effort,' said Peggy in delight. 'I'm so glad for you, Doris.'

'So am I,' she replied, tickling Daisy under the chin and making the diamond sparkle for her in the sunlight that was streaming through the window. 'Thank you for the advice, Peggy. I really am very grateful.'

Peggy had not raised the thorny subject of Lady Chumley and her horrid clique over the previous weeks, and she'd noticed that Doris avoided it too. There was hope yet that her sister had finally seen the error of her ways and had come down to earth.

The visit was over too soon for Peggy, but Doris never stayed for more than an hour, perhaps afraid of outstaying her welcome – or bumping into Ron.

'I'll treat you and Daisy to lunch at the British Restaurant next week,' she said as she stood on the doorstep. 'It will give you a chance to wear your new coat.'

Peggy hugged her fiercely. 'It's so lovely having you back in my life,' she murmured.

Doris returned the hug and kissed Daisy who was straddling Peggy's hip. 'I've missed you too,' she replied. 'Now, I really must go. I've got things to do at home.'

Peggy stood on the doorstep with Daisy and watched her sister drive away, feeling contented and at peace until she remembered that she'd seen neither hide nor hair of Ron since this morning.

Her emotions were mixed as she closed the front door, for although she was grateful for his absence during Doris's visit – she was still not fully convinced the pair of them could behave decently to one another when in the same room – she was utterly furious with him for not getting on with the jobs he'd promised to start today.

'Your grandad is in for a right earful when he does finally put in an appearance,' she muttered to Daisy, who responded with a giggle. 'He's tried my patience once too often, and although you might think it funny, it's no laughing matter.'

29

London

Dolly had been so rattled by that distressing encounter with Felix that she'd been finding it hard to concentrate on anything for more than a matter of minutes. As more than a month had passed since that day and there'd been no improvement in her distraction, she realised she was letting the side down by not giving her all to the men and women who relied on her. Upon waking this morning, she'd decided she had to go and see Hugh to demand some leave before she made a mistake that might jeopardise someone's life.

'With so much going on at the moment, it's not really the right time,' he said, lighting her cigarette and returning to his side of the desk. 'But it is clear that something has been bothering you lately. Do you want to talk about it?'

Dolly shook her head. 'It's personal,' she said quietly.

Hugh's grey eyes regarded her with undisguised curiosity. 'You're not usually so reticent. This wouldn't have something to do with whatever happened on Christmas Day, would it?'

Startled that he'd been so astute, she couldn't quite meet his gaze. 'I don't know what you're talking about.

I'm simply tired and distracted, and need some time to catch my breath and see my daughter.'

Hugh continued to watch her through the smoke of his Sobranie. 'How long have we been friends, Dolly?' he asked softly.

'Since we were both in Paris,' she replied. 'Why, what's that got to do with anything?'

He left the cigarette to burn in the ashtray and steepled his fingers beneath his chin. 'Dolly, you may be a consummate actress, but I know you too well. Something happened that day at the embassy, and whatever it was has affected you deeply. Will you at least do me the honour of being honest with me?'

'I'm sorry, Hugh, but I really can't talk about it.' She met his gaze finally. 'And you're right, something did happen – which is why I'm asking you to let me have some time away so I can recover.'

His tone sharpened. 'He didn't hurt you, did he?'

She blinked back at him, unable to answer.

'I saw Felix coming out of that room, Dolly,' he said. 'And he looked very angry. When you emerged a while later making a great show of being your usual gay self, I could tell you were actually in a state of shock.'

It was almost a relief to discover he'd known all the time – but she wasn't prepared to entirely share her troubles with him. 'We had a very unpleasant row,' she admitted, 'and yes, I was in a bit of a state. But Felix is not the sort of man to raise his hand to a woman, so I was in no danger.'

She regarded him evenly. 'What happened between

us was all my fault. Now I need a bit of time to get over it. Will you grant me leave, so I can do that?'

His expression told her that he'd accepted she'd reveal no more, and knowing him as she did, he would capitulate. 'I can't give you very long,' he said on a sigh. 'Things are happening in France and it will soon be all hands on deck.'

He shuffled a few papers about on his desk. 'It's impossible to grant you enough time to go all the way to Devon – which I suspect is not really on your agenda – but Cliffehaven is doable as long as you leave me a contact telephone number should there be a flap on.'

Hugh was right, for she'd had no intentions of going to Devon – not with Felix down there. It was Pauline she wanted to see – and Peggy Reilly. 'How long can I have?'

'Three days.' He rested his hands on the leather-topped desk. 'And that is not negotiable, Dolly. I want you back here, clear-headed, by Monday morning.'

Dolly got to her feet, eager to be on the move. 'Thank you, darling Hugh.' She lightly kissed his fragrant cheek before dimpling at him and regarding him through her lashes. 'And do you think I could possibly borrow a car from the pool?'

He rolled his eyes in exaggerated impatience, then signed a chit and handed it to her. '*Please* promise not to drive it as if you're on a race track,' he said wearily. 'And *do* try to bring it back in one piece.'

She grabbed the chit before he could change his mind and stuffed it into her handbag. 'You're an absolute brick. And because you've been so very kind, I'll try to bring you back a stick of rock,' she said, scribbling down Peggy's telephone number on his jotter.

He gave a delicate shudder. 'I'd rather you didn't.'

Dolly smiled, waggled goodbye with her fingers and hurried off to get packed and on her way. She was feeling much better already. Once she was clear of the chaos in London, the journey to Cliffehaven should take less than a couple of hours if she could wangle one of the more powerful cars from the dear little chap who was in charge of the car pool, and who made no secret of the fact he was rather smitten with her.

Dolly had nipped out to shop in Bond Street once she'd packed, and now there were two baskets of goodies on the back seat of the car. She'd made quite good time despite the fact that the only car in the pool had been the small black Austin with the recalcitrant heater. The chap in charge had been most apologetic – almost fawning in his eagerness to repair the heater – but she'd been in too much of a hurry to hang about waiting for him to tinker about under the bonnet, and had given him five bob as a tip to cheer him up.

This February day had been dreary since dawn, yet as she approached the coast it seemed to be brightening. She could see that the sun was still out, and it was almost spring-like. Unable to resist the view before her, she stopped the car in a layby on the brow of the hill and climbed out.

The wind was chill but not blustery, the sun sparkled on the water that was only slightly ruffled, and the white cliffs gleamed beneath the acres of wild grasses and gorse. Dolly took a deep, reviving breath of the salty air which reminded her of childhood, and the hours she'd spent alone on the beach just a bit further along the coast – hunting for crabs in rock pools, climbing the chalk cliffs in search of gulls' eggs, and digging for lugworms which she sold to the local fishermen for a few pennies so she could buy ice cream or sweets.

And then, as she'd grown older, there were the school holidays in which she'd taken long bike rides across the lonely hills, with a sandwich and a bottle of pop in the wicker basket to keep her going as she wandered through the forests and waded in the icy streams to follow the eels.

Her gaze drifted over the town that nestled within the sheltering arms of the cliffs and sprawled up into the hills. Cliffehaven had been a favourite haunt during those years, and every time she returned, it was an affirmation of her ties to this little seaside town. For it was here that she'd first met Ronan Reilly – a gangling but sturdy youth who'd slowly become a strong, handsome man with a sharp, enquiring mind and a courage that never wavered. She was eleven when they'd met, and the instant rapport between them lasted to this day – and it was rather wonderful that his son had married her daughter, for it seemed fate was determined to keep them in each other's lives.

There had never been anything between her and Ronan but friendship, for he'd understood and shared her need to escape the strictures of their lives, to stretch her wings, walk her own path, and absorb everything and anything. Over the ensuing years he'd taught her how to catch eels, to trap rabbits with net purses, and look after ferrets, and on one heady day he'd managed to persuade his father to let her go with them on the family fishing boat.

Dolly smiled at the memory, for she'd loved the wildness of the sea and the way the boat creaked and swayed beneath her feet – loved the shoals of silvery fish that came slithering from the nets as they were hauled in, and the sharp snap and crack of the sails as they'd tacked for home. Sailing had become a passion after that, and she'd haunted the marinas hoping she would be taken on as crew so she could learn how to handle her own boat when she could afford to buy one.

Dolly shivered. Those memories evoked others – of sailing with Felix, spending long, lazy days of that wonderful summer in the south of France on deserted beaches soaking up the sun and making love beneath the stars during the sultry, velvet nights. If only . . . But there was no going back – not now – not ever. And she had only herself to blame for that.

Impatient with her thoughts, she climbed back into the little car, lit a cigarette and sped down the hill into Cliffehaven. She needed to see Peggy before she went to Tamarisk Bay, for once Pauline knew she was here there would be too many awkward questions to answer if she did it later.

The town had changed since the start of the war, and especially so since her last visit. She noted the new gaps in the terraced houses, the increased damage to the shops in the High Street, and the ugly expansion of the sprawling industrial estate where there had once been fields and little cottages beside the dairy. The Camden Road school was gone, along with the block of flats that had once overshadowed the playground, and as she drove across the junction to Beach View Terrace, she noted the new bomb site on the corner of Camden Road, the tarpaulin covering damaged roofs, the scars of bullets in walls and the blasted remains of the house at the end of Peggy's cul-de-sac. That had not been a bomb but a gas explosion, and Dolly shivered at the thought of how close Peggy and her family had come to being killed.

Parking the car, she switched off the engine, checked her appearance in the mirror and retouched her lipstick. The house was so familiar, and so dear, and she was eager to be inside in the warmth and love that Peggy had imbued into every nook and cranny. There were almost twenty years between them, but they were friends and confidantes, and the age difference didn't matter one jot to either of them.

The heavy rap on the window startled her and she drew hastily back from the grinning face looming in at her – until she realised who it was. Opening the door she almost fell into his arms. 'Ron, you old devil, you half scared me to death,' she scolded, giving him an enormous hug before the smell of him made her stagger back. 'What the hell have you been doing, Ron? You stink like a fish market.'

'Ach, you didn't use to be so fussy,' he teased, his eyebrows wriggling above his bright blue eyes. 'I've got a fish or two in me pocket, that's all.' He pulled out a string of very fine sea trout from his poacher's coat and dangled them under her nose. 'Frank and I know a quiet corner of beach where we can get the boat out,' he murmured with a wink. 'But you keep that to yourself, wee girl, or I'll be in terrible trouble with Peggy, so I will.'

'Your secret's safe with me,' she said and laughed. 'Although you'll have to give her some explanation as to where they came from.'

'Fred the Fish is a good pal, so he is. He'll back me up.'

She regarded him fondly, noting the wild hair and brows, the weathered face and bright blue eyes. He was still a handsome man, despite his apparent reluctance to make the best of himself. 'Yes, I seem to remember the pair of you forever getting up to mischief when you were boys. It seems nothing much has changed.'

He grinned down at her. 'To be sure 'tis a wonder to see you looking so well, Dolly, but if it's Pauline you're after, she'll be home with Frank.'

'Actually, I've come to see Peggy,' she said. 'There's something I need to talk to her about – so if you could make yourself scarce for a bit, I would be grateful.'

His expression was suddenly sober. 'It's not about our little Danuta, is it? Nothing bad's happened to her?'

'Nothing like that,' she assured him firmly. 'I'm staying in touch with what's happening over there, and she's fine – really.'

'Well, that's good to hear. That wee girl has more courage than both of us, Dolly, and there are times when I wish with all me heart that I didn't recommend her to you.'

Dolly nodded, her thoughts flying to Danuta, who was now known as Marie-Claire. She was at this moment hiding with a cell of partisans in France, preparing for the destruction of a series of enemy gun emplacements on the coast. Communication had been erratic of late, but all seemed to be going to plan.

She reached into the car for her handbag and basket of gifts, locked the door and then tucked her hand into the crook of his arm, suddenly noticing the absence of his ever-present dog. 'I see Harvey's deserted you for the delights of Peggy's kitchen. Shall we join him?'

'Aye, but we'll go by way of the back door seeing as you're family.'

'How is Pauline, Ron? Her letters are much more cheerful these days, but I still worry about her.'

'She's doing well now Frank's back home, and of course she comes here for the night when he's out on fire-watch and such. She still frets over Brendon, but that's only natural.' He paused at the back gate and looked down at her thoughtfully. 'He's away from London just now. Did you know?'

Dolly shook her head, even though she'd already heard from Carol that he was in Devon. 'Where's he been sent, do you think?'

'He wouldn't say, but I'm guessing he's down in Devon helping the Americans with their rehearsals for the beach landings in France.'

'How on earth did you know about that?' she gasped.

He grinned and tapped his nose. 'You'd be surprised, Dolly Cardew.'

She smiled. 'Actually, I don't think I would, you old rogue. You always were the sharpest knife in the box, even as a boy.'

'To be sure you're not so blunt yourself. Now away with you into the warm for a wee dram of the good whiskey I managed to find the other day.'

Peggy heard the scullery door bang and was on her feet in an instant. She yanked open the kitchen door and in the spill of light from the kitchen focused on the large figure lurking at the bottom of the stone steps. 'Ronan Reilly, you'd better have a damned good excuse for disappearing all day,' she said crossly. 'Get yourself up here and sort out this leak.'

'Ach, to be sure, Peggy, that's no way to speak in front of visitors,' he rumbled, climbing the steps until he filled the doorway.

'Doris went half an hour ago,' she replied, still furious with him. 'Where on earth have you been?' She caught the whiff of fish, and glared at him. 'I hope you haven't been poaching on Lord Cliffe's estate again,' she said darkly.

Ron eased from the doorway to reveal a grinning Dolly. 'Don't be too hard on him, Peggy,' she said. 'Those fish are quite legal.'

'Dolly,' she gasped in delight, her arms open wide to embrace her as all thoughts of poaching and leaking pipes were dismissed. 'Oh, Dolly, what a wonderful surprise!'

'You see, I told you we had a visitor,' said Ron, taking the trout out of his pocket and slapping them onto a plate which he quickly put in the larder out of the reach of a very interested Queenie.

Peggy studied Dolly affectionately. 'I don't know how you manage to do it, but you look as if you've stepped out of a fashion magazine.' She gave her another hug and then drew her further into the kitchen. 'Cordelia's having a bit of a rest and Daisy's with Rita and Ivy upstairs, so we can have a jolly good gossip without being disturbed,' she said, hoisting the large tin kettle onto the hob.

Ron placed the Irish whiskey bottle and three glasses on the table. 'That'll keep the cold out better than tea,' he said, pouring generous measures.

'Where did that come from?' asked Peggy suspiciously.

'Ireland,' he replied tersely, raising his glass in a toast. '*Slainte*.'

Peggy sipped the warming drink and caught Dolly's eye above the glass. 'As you can see, things haven't changed around here,' she said dryly.

'I'll be up to the attic then,' said Ron, having drained his glass. 'Better that than having to listen to gossiping women. There's only so much a man can stand, especially when the moving shrapnel is the very divil.'

Dolly giggled as he stomped off with Harvey. 'I see what you mean, and I admire you for putting up with it. He always was a law unto himself.'

Peggy watched as Dolly took off her hat and coat to reveal tailored trousers, silk shirt and a mohair sweater.

Her only jewellery was a string of pearls, a watch and discreet gold studs in her ears. She looked elegant and sophisticated and, at first glance, at least ten years younger than she really was, yet on closer inspection, Peggy realised that her friend was tired and troubled. She didn't comment, knowing Dolly would tell her in her own time what was bothering her.

Dolly placed the basket on the table, chattering all the while about Bournemouth and the fun she was having with the old trouts at the WI as she took out pots of jam, packets of sugar and white flour, a box of sweet biscuits and two wedges of cheese. There was an exquisite party dress for Daisy, a cashmere scarf for Cordelia, and butter-soft leather gloves for Peggy. 'I'm sorry it's not much, but Bournemouth doesn't have a Harrods,' she said blithely.

'It's more than generous,' said Peggy, clapping her hands in delight. 'But I'll have to hide the biscuits, sugar and cheese from Ron or it will disappear before you can blink.' She bustled about putting the foodstuff in her larder, and then gave her another hug. 'When did you arrive? Pauline never said you were here.'

'I haven't seen her yet,' Dolly admitted. 'It was you I needed to talk to first.'

Peggy reached for the whiskey bottle, suspecting that Dolly had once more become embroiled in some love affair that had turned sour and needed to get it off her chest. But then that was the nature of their friendship, for they could talk to one another about anything and everything in the sure and safe knowledge that their confidences would go no further.

'Then why don't we have a fag and another tot of this while you tell me what's on your mind?'

Dolly lit both cigarettes, and after a sip of whiskey, she gave an anguished sigh. 'Felix has turned up again.'

Peggy felt a stab of unease. She knew all about Felix and the disastrous affair, for Dolly had confided in her many years ago. 'Felix is in Bournemouth?' she gasped. 'But why – what for?'

Dolly shook her head. 'Not in Bournemouth, Peg, but in Devon.' She took a drink of whiskey. 'As to why he's there, I'm sure you can work it out for yourself with all the rumours flying around.' Her smile was grim. 'It's hardly the best-kept secret.'

Peggy stared at her, her thoughts in a whirl over the rumoured invasion plans, and the requisition by the army of Carol's village. 'Devon – as in Carol's Slapton?' At Dolly's nod, she reached for her hand. 'Oh, Dolly. That must have been such a shock. What did you do?'

As Dolly told her what had happened between them in Devon, Peggy could see that her friend was edgy, and for once, unsure of herself.

'I made him promise to keep our affair secret from everyone – especially Carol – and despite everything that's happened since, I do believe he will keep that promise.' Dolly's hand was unsteady as she flicked her cigarette ash into the ashtray.

'And then – then . . . He turned up at a party I was attending on Christmas Day. I don't know how he knew I would be there, but it was clear he'd made a point of getting an invitation and was in no mood to leave before he'd said all he'd come to say.'

Peggy leaned towards her, her hand on her arm. 'And what was that?'

Dolly lifted her chin and looked back at her tearfully. 'He refused to accept that I no longer loved him – and he was right, I love him as much today as I did all those years ago – but I couldn't let him know that.' She took a shuddering breath, clearly fighting to keep her emotions under control. 'I denied it, of course, but then he kissed me, and I could no longer pretend.'

'But—'

'I know what you're going to say, Peggy, and believe me, I was fully aware of what dangerous waters I was flailing in. Starting up the affair again would be utter madness even though every fibre of my being was screaming for him, and it took a huge amount of will power to push him away and try to reason with him.'

She paused to sip at the whiskey. 'And then he did something that shook me to the core.'

Peggy held her breath, her gaze fixed intently on her tearful friend as her imagination flew in all directions. 'What did he do?' she managed in the ensuing silence.

'He asked me to marry him,' Dolly replied, her voice breaking. 'But of course it's too late – much too late. Impossible to even contemplate after all the lies I've told, and the secrets I've kept. I had to turn him down – reject him as harshly as I could bear so he would no longer pursue me.' She dipped her chin, her voice barely above a whisper. 'He was terribly hurt, and angrier than I've ever seen him – but I'm fairly sure he finally accepted it was over and there would be no turning back.'

Peggy dug out a clean handkerchief from her apron pocket as Dolly burst into tears. She waited for her to settle down, her soft heart going out to her troubled friend whose life had lurched from one disaster to another. She knew how hard it must have been for her to reject the man she'd always adored – but also knew the reason behind it.

Dolly gathered her wits and poured them both another nip of whiskey. 'I must look an absolute fright,' she said brokenly. 'But I do feel better for letting all that out after holding on to it for so long.' She gave Peggy a watery smile. 'Thanks for being such a kind, understanding friend, my dear. You must think I'm an utter fool.'

'Certainly never a fool,' Peggy murmured, 'just a woman in love trying to do the right thing, and Lord knows, you've listened to my woes about Jim and Ron often enough over the years.' She gave a little sigh, stubbed out her cigarette and took Dolly's hand. 'But it might not be too late for you and Felix,' she said gently. 'Not if you were really brave and told him the truth.'

'You know that isn't possible, Peggy,' she replied sadly. 'There would be too many repercussions that will ultimately destroy everything I hold most dear. It's better this way.'

Peggy hesitated before saying what was in her heart, for this was a delicate situation, and Dolly was clearly at the end of her tether. 'Better for whom?' she asked quietly.

'For everyone,' replied Dolly firmly.

Peggy persevered. 'But what if those secrets come

out? Don't the people they involve deserve to know the truth so they can make up their own minds about how to deal with them?'

Dolly took a shallow breath. 'I can't, really I can't. I couldn't bear the hurt that would cause; the mistrust, the loss of love and respect. You might think I'm tough and brave and unafraid to face the world head on, but under all this powder and paint, I'm just a craven coward who has to live with the utter mess I've made of everything.'

She squeezed Peggy's fingers. 'I lived a lie because the man I loved proved to be married, and refused to file for a divorce. Now he's free to propose all my chickens have come home to roost – and I must accept that and move on.'

'Secrets have a horrible way of coming to the surface, Dolly,' said Peggy urgently. 'Please reconsider before it's too late.'

'I've thought of nothing else since Christmas Day,' she replied, 'but it's helped enormously to talk to you about it.' She smiled affectionately. 'I've made the most awful shambles of everything, and really can't see a way out of it – but I'll think about it some more, I promise.'

She took a deep breath and made a sterling effort to regain her usual calm. 'Now, I want to hear how you are, how you're coping, and all about Jim's adventures in India, and what that scallywag Ron has been up to.'

Peggy accepted there would be no more talk of Felix today even though the issue had been far from resolved. However, she knew Dolly had merely wanted someone she could trust to talk things over with, and would deal with any fallout in her own way. She didn't envy her, for Peggy could see only trouble ahead.

Having replenished their glasses, Peggy gradually revealed her fears for Jim and her son-in-law, Martin, and the loneliness she felt as a mother parted from her children. And as they talked she felt the weight of her cares lift from her shoulders, which led to her hesitantly discussing the germ of an idea that had been slowly growing these past weeks.

It would be a radical step in a new direction for Peggy, and goodness only knew how Jim and Ron would react, but finding a proper job outside Beach View would solve her money problems and give her a new outlook on life.

'I think it's a brilliant idea,' said Dolly enthusiastically. 'But how on earth will you cope with all you have to do here? And then of course you have Daisy to consider.'

'If Solly Goldman agrees to take me on there's a crèche at the factory where Daisy would be looked after during my shifts.' She lowered her voice and leaned towards Dolly. 'This idea is still very tenuous, Dolly, and I have to think about it a bit more before going to see Solly, so you will keep it to yourself, won't you?'

'Of course I will, you silly goose,' said Dolly affectionately. 'And if you do decide to go for it and you have any trouble from Ron, let me know. I'll soon spike his guns, you'll see.' She glanced up at the clock, surprised at how quickly the time had passed. 'I must go,

Peg. Driving down that track to Tamarisk Bay is awkward enough in daylight, but once it's dark, it's a nightmare.'

'You will pop in again, won't you?' Peggy said after they'd embraced. 'It's so rare we see you, and I've missed you.'

'This is only a flying visit, but I promise to try. Take care of yourself, Peggy, and let me know how things go with the job.'

Peggy followed her out and stood on the doorstep as she drove away. It had been lovely to have Dolly to confide in, for there was no one else really. Cordelia would only fret over her, the girls had their own concerns, and Doris would probably say she was being over-dramatic and completely veto the idea of her going out to work in a factory.

She closed the front door and experienced a little squirm of fearful excitement at the daring thought of actually going out to work, learning new skills, making new friends – and, more importantly, earning her own money. She had little doubt it would prove to be a challenge, but having talked it over with Dolly, the idea had blossomed, and if she could find the courage to carry it through, then she'd at last feel she was doing something important towards the war effort.

30

Devon

It was now March, and with the full dress rehearsal looming, Felix was a worried man. It was clear that the troops were still ill prepared, the different services seemingly unable to work as one cohesive unit. Despite the passionate support of Brendon Reilly to his argument, the brass hats had refused to listen to their concerns about the men's inability to swim, and their ignorance over how to use the life jackets correctly. It seemed that as the exercise was meant to look, feel and smell like the real thing, the men on the LSTs and troop carriers had to experience seasickness, sodden, heavy clothing and clumsy life jackets – the last of which negated the need for swimming lessons as far as the brass was concerned.

Felix stood on the hill above Blackpool Sands in the freezing-cold wind, and watched through his powerful binoculars as yet another rehearsal ended in chaos, with tanks becoming bogged down in the sand and shingle, jeeps making hard work of getting up the beach, and men flailing about in the rough seas because some of the troop carriers hadn't advanced far enough into shore, and were now wallowing dangerously close to the other craft.

'God help you all when the navy starts shelling the beach, and the bombers begin their assaults,' he muttered with a shiver of apprehension.

He didn't want to watch any longer, but couldn't look away from the mayhem which now stretched from one end of the bay to the other in the dwindling light. The infrastructure for the landings was all there in the dummy enemy positions and concrete pillboxes manned by the artillery battalion, but the thirty-man assault teams landing from the troop carriers and LSTs were weighed down with mortars, machine guns, bazookas and flame-throwers, and making heavy weather of getting up the beach. He could only hope that coming under live fire would wipe away the complacency that had infected them all, and make them move their asses quicker.

Operation Tiger would take place over a week at the end of April, culminating in a full rehearsal under live bombardment from the navy, the artillery battalions on shore, and the air force. The idea was to amass landing craft in the Channel from Plymouth and Brixham, then stage a beachhead landing at Slapton, just as they would in June on the beaches codenamed Utah and Omaha on the Cherbourg peninsula. The troops and equipment would embark on the same ships, and for the most part, from the same ports from which they would later leave for France.

Felix turned his back on it all and climbed into the jeep beside Herbert. 'I need a drink,' he said morosely.

'It's all a bit of a pig's ear, isn't it, sir?' he replied sympathetically, firing up the engine. 'I'm glad I'm not going to play much part in it.'

'It's an almighty balls-up,' Felix growled. 'And if things don't improve soon, heads will roll. I can only imagine what Ike would say if he could see what was going on here – but thank God he's occupied elsewhere.'

Herbert steered the jeep over the rough terrain until they reached what passed as a main road in this county of winding country lanes. 'Back to your billet for that drink, sir? Or did you have somewhere else in mind?'

Felix noted the sly glance that accompanied this question, and decided the time had come to explain. 'Mrs Porter is the daughter of a long-standing and very dear acquaintance,' he said evenly. 'And as I'm in the neighbourhood, it's only right that I should spend some time with her.' He looked at his driver sternly. 'Do you have a problem with that, soldier?'

'Not at all, sir,' he replied cheerfully. 'The Welcome Inn's a nice, friendly little pub, and Mrs Claxton does keep a good pint.'

Felix smiled for the first time in hours. 'I guess the company of young Ida is quite a draw as well,' he teased. He saw the younger man redden. 'Just watch out there, Herby,' he advised. 'Ida strikes me as a bit of a wild one.'

Herbert grinned. 'That's why I like her, sir.'

Felix chuckled, remembering his own youthful days in the army when he'd enjoyed the company of girls like Ida until he'd bowed to his father's pressure and married his commanding officer's daughter, Olivia. She'd turned out to be wild beneath that demure facade – but it was a wildness that had led to her destruction, and, ultimately, the end of their marriage.

Preferring not to dwell on that dark memory, he turned his mind to the report he'd have to write later tonight. It wouldn't be easy to compose, for his concerns over the wisdom of these badly conceived rehearsals were legion. Yet write it he must, and if it gave those fossils in London a kick up the ass and made them see what was really going on down here, it might actually do some good.

He caught the delicious aroma of frying onions and grilled steak through the open window as they approached one of the sprawling camps, and his stomach rumbled. 'Pull in here and we'll have some chow first,' he said. 'It's been a long day, and we could both do with something before we drown our sorrows.'

Herbert grinned as he drove the jeep into the camp and came to a halt outside the commanding officers' canteen. 'I'll see you in an hour, sir,' he said, saluting before he hurried off to the junior officers' mess, eager for a meal that didn't consist of bully beef and over-boiled vegetables.

Felix ploughed through a T-bone steak and a mound of fried onions and potatoes, followed by apple pie and cream. Sated, he enjoyed a cup of rich, aromatic coffee, then checked his watch and went outside to find Herbert drawing up in the jeep.

'I said I'd meet Mrs Porter at seven,' he said as he climbed in next to him, 'so you'd better put your foot down, Herby. We don't want to keep the lady waiting.'

Herbert stifled a burp as he sent the jeep careering over the field and out through the sentry barriers. 'If I go on eating this well, I won't fit into my uniform,' he said. 'Not that I'm complaining. That cook certainly knows what he's doing. I've never tasted steak like it.'

'It's prime beef brought over from the States,' said Felix proudly. 'Born and raised on some of the finest grazing in the world, you won't taste better. Enjoy it while you can, son, because once all this is over you'll be back to British army rations.'

Herbert chuckled. 'I'll bear that in mind, General.'

It was Carol's turn to have a bath in the farmhouse this evening, for there was no hot water in the barn unless they heated up kettles on the primus, and with the restrictions, it meant that they'd been limited to two baths a week each, using less than four inches of water. She hated not bathing every day, and the awful feeling that the strip-wash she had each morning wasn't really enough to keep her clean.

She reluctantly climbed out of the cooling water and swathed herself in a towel while she scrubbed the bath clean of the scum that rimmed the water mark Millicent had painted on the porcelain. It was disgusting, but there was nothing she could do about it, and at least she felt clean enough this evening not to have to worry that she might be less than fragrant when she met up with Felix, who was always impeccably groomed.

Rubbing her hair dry, she stood close to the heavy iron radiator which blasted out welcome heat. Felix was an enigma, for although he appeared to be open and friendly, he'd said very little about his home life, and not even mentioned Dolly during their trips to the cinema, his favourite bistro, or the evenings in the pub. She'd been forced to come to the conclusion that he must be waiting for her to open that particular conversation – and as enough time had elapsed to further sharpen her curiosity, she'd decided to broach the subject of her mother that evening.

She quickly dressed in her one pair of smart trousers, and pulled on a knitted twinset of jumper and cardigan over her vest and a cotton blouse. It would be a freezing walk over the hill to the pub, and as she had yet to fully recover from a heavy cold and hacking cough, she didn't want to risk catching a chill. All the girls were coughing, spluttering and feverish after they'd been working long hours out in all weathers, and like them, Carol was impatient for spring to put in an appearance.

Brushing out her damp hair, she fixed the pearl studs her mother had given her for her twenty-first birthday into her earlobes, added a dusting of face powder, a dash of lipstick and a smidgen of mascara to her lashes. Ida's rather sharp jibe about being underdressed had struck home, and she'd taken to smartening up and wearing a bit of make-up when she went out – which had become quite a regular thing over the past two months. She eyed her reflection, nodded approval and pulled on her wellington boots, overcoat and scarf in preparation for leaving the warm bathroom for the bleak stable yard.

Ida looked her up and down and grinned. 'It's good to see you making the effort,' she said. 'Your general will approve.'

'He's not *my* general,' Carol replied, weary at having to repeat herself yet again. 'He's a friend of my mother's.'

'Well, he certainly seems to like your company,' Ida persisted, dabbing at her blocked-up nose. 'You've been out with 'im often enough.'

'Drop it, Ida,' Carol snapped. 'He's a family friend and wise advisor – in fact he's begun to fill the gap in my life that my father would have filled if he'd lived – so just shut up for once, and keep your dirty thoughts to yourself.'

A deathly silence fell as the girls stared at her in surprise, and Ida went scarlet. 'Blimey, gel,' she muttered. 'There ain't no need to blow yer top.'

Carol felt a little ashamed of her outburst. It was unlike her to lose her temper, but Ida had really gone too far this time, and all the snide remarks had to be nipped in the bud. She finished drying her hair, dabbed the last of her favourite scent on her neck and wrists, and clipped the lead to Nipper's collar.

'I'm meeting him and Betty at seven,' she said into the awkward silence. 'Are you lot coming, or shall I go on my own?'

'Nah, you're all right, mate,' rasped Maisie, with a hand to her sore throat. 'Me and the others don't feel too chipper and thought we'd stay in tonight and dose ourselves up on hot toddies.' She held up the remains of Brendon's rum.

Carol didn't feel overly bright herself and would have preferred to be tucked up in bed with a hot water bottle and rum toddy, but she'd made the arrangement a week ago, and as there was no way of contacting them, she couldn't let them down. She wrapped her scarf more firmly round her neck, pulled the woollen hat down over her ears and headed for the door. 'Enjoy the rum, and I'll see you later.'

'Tell Herby I'll meet him at the weekend,' said Ida before sneezing repeatedly into her handkerchief. 'And see if you can get the general to put 'is 'and on some more rum or whisky. This cold ain't gettin' no better.'

'I'll do my best.' Carol closed the door and set off with Nipper pulling hard on the lead in his eagerness to sniff every blade of grass along the way.

The pub was lovely and warm, and still quite empty but for a group of British military police and GIs sitting in the corner, and Felix waiting for her in his usual place by the window. 'Hello, Felix,' she said breathlessly. 'Sorry I'm late, but Nipper slipped his collar and I had the devil's own job to catch him.'

His face lit up with a smile and he leapt to his feet to help her with her coat and scarf, and make a fuss of Nipper. 'You look frozen,' he said. 'Why don't we move closer to the fire?'

'That would be nice. The others aren't coming tonight,' she added. 'They're still down with horrible colds.'

He made sure she and Nipper were settled by the roaring fire and went to the bar for her usual cider and then changed his mind. 'I don't suppose you've any whisky under the counter, Mrs Claxton? Only Mrs Porter's had a long walk, and she's still getting over her cold.'

'Well now, General,' she said in her West Country burr, 'seeing as it's you, I do happen to have a drop. It'll cost you, mind.'

Felix paid over the odds for the two tots of whisky, made a mental note to get some from the PX the next time, and carried them back to Carol. 'They're both for you,' he said, sitting down to his usual cider. 'You still look a little under the weather, if you don't mind me saying.'

She was a bit put out after she'd made such an effort to look her best, but she said nothing and sipped the lovely whisky, which went down like silk and warmed her still rather tender throat. 'I'm surprised Betty hasn't come down from her rooms yet. She's usually so prompt.'

'She was with me earlier, but then some guy came in and they both went upstairs. By the look of him he wasn't best pleased to see us sitting together, but he didn't give me the chance to explain before he bundled her away.'

Carol felt a stab of alarm. 'What did this man look like?'

'Tall, tow-headed, about thirty, and dressed like all the farmers round here. I think she called him Ken, but I couldn't swear to it.'

'Oh, lawks. I hope he's not here to cause trouble.' At Felix's enquiring look, she quickly explained: 'He's the chap she was seeing before the eviction – and before Brendon came on the scene. If word's got out about Brendon . . .' She set down her glass. 'I think I'd better go up and make sure she's all right.'

'It's probably best to leave them to it. Interfering in matters of the heart only leads to more trouble.'

Carol knew he was right and reluctantly sat back in her chair, but she was still uneasy. Ken was a big man, with an unreliable temperament – and if he'd heard about Brendon, then there was no telling what he might do.

The chatter and laughter continued around them as some of the land girls from the nearby farm came in accompanied by a group of GIs. A young military policeman started to play the piano, but it seemed no one was in the mood for a song tonight, so he continued to quietly coax some lovely melodies out of the battered old instrument, oblivious to the conversations going on around him.

Then, above the noise, Carol heard the unmistakable sound of a man's angry voice. Alert and fearful, she got to her feet and hushed the piano player. Others had heard it too, and as it continued at an even greater volume, everyone fell silent, their attention fixed on the staircase which led to the landlady's private rooms.

Mrs Claxton opened the flap in the bar just as there was the sound of a sharp slap and a yelp of pain. 'Right, that's it,' she said, squeezing her bulk through the gap and advancing on the stairs. 'I'll have no truck with that sort of going on.'

Felix stopped her, his expression grim. 'I'll go.'

Another cry came from the top of the stairs, and before Felix and Carol could reach her, Betty came tumbling down to land at their feet with a bone-jarring thud. Ken hurtled after her, vaulted over Felix and Carol, who were bending to see to Betty, and made for the door.

'Don't let him get away,' yelled Mrs Claxton above Nipper's excited yapping and the land girls' cries of horror.

There was a surge towards the door, and within minutes, Ken was hauled back into the bar having somehow gained two black eyes and a split lip along the way. Mrs Claxton used the military policemen's handcuffs to secure him firmly to a heavy chair, and ordered the grim-faced men to keep an eye on him.

'I didn't mean to hurt her,' he whined. 'She slipped.'

Mrs Claxton glared at him and sniffed her disdain. 'I'm telephoning the police,' she snapped.

'You'd better call the ambulance first,' said Felix as he and Carol knelt by the still, pale little figure lying at an awkward angle at the bottom of the stairs.

'You'll be lucky,' said Mrs Claxton. 'The nearest ambulance station is on the other side of the restriction zone, and it will take hours to get here.'

'Then I'll ring the American hospital, and get them to fetch her.' He left Carol with Betty and strode to the telephone on the wall behind the bar.

'That won't do you no good, neither,' Mrs Claxton muttered. 'That there hospital is for American personnel only – not the likes of us civilians.'

'We'll see about that,' he said grimly as he drummed his fingers and waited impatiently for someone to answer at the other end. 'This is General Addington,' he said the moment he got through. 'I have an emergency at the Welcome Inn in Beeson and require an ambulance and medic immediately.'

He cut off the woman's questions. 'She's a civilian, and I'm a three-star general. You will obey my order, or be on immediate charge. Is that clear?' He listened some more and then replaced the receiver. 'They'll be here in ten minutes,' he announced into the stunned silence.

Carol didn't dare touch Betty in case she'd damaged her neck or spine in the fall, but she held her hand, feeling utterly helpless and terrified at how ashen she was.

'Poor lamb,' said Mrs Claxton, covering Betty in the blanket she'd whipped off the old settle by the fire. 'I hope that brute gets put away for a very long time for what he's done.'

Carol barely glanced at Ken, who was still whining and protesting his innocence as Mrs Claxton called the police station and the men formed a daunting phalanx around him. 'I want to go with her to the hospital, Felix,' she said. 'She'll be so frightened and confused when she wakes up, and I can't bear the thought of her being alone.'

'I'm pretty sure I can arrange it. These three stars mean something, and I usually get my way.' He lifted Betty's limp hand and checked her pulse. 'Rapid, but quite faint,' he murmured, 'and she's very cold. Do you have more blankets, Mrs Claxton?'

With a nod, the plump woman thudded up the stairs and returned with two more blankets and a pillow.

'Not the pillow,' said Felix. 'We don't want to move her head until we know her spine is intact.'

A sob of distress escaped from Carol as she held Betty's hand and silently urged the ambulance to get a move on.

'It's okay, honey,' soothed Felix. 'I know you're frightened for her, but she'll get the very best medical care at our hospital.'

The minutes seemed to drag by, but at last they heard the urgent peal of the ambulance bell and within seconds there was a doctor rushing through the door followed by two army nurses.

Carol and Felix stood back and a tense silence fell in the bar as the doctor made his examination. 'She'll need X-rays,' he drawled eventually. 'But there doesn't appear to be any damage to her spine. We'll get her back to base where I can examine her more fully.'

'Mrs Porter and I will accompany you,' said Felix, his tone brooking no argument.

Betty was carefully lifted onto a stretcher by the nurses and was being carried out to the ambulance just as Constable Betts arrived with a colleague in his police van to cart Ken away to a prison cell in Kingsbridge.

Carol was about to follow the medics when she remembered she had Nipper to consider. Turning to Herbert, she handed him the leash. 'Could you take him back to the farm for me? Tell the girls what's happened, and warn them I probably won't be coming back tonight.'

He nodded and then glanced at Felix. 'Will you be needing the car again, sir?'

'I doubt it,' he said briskly. 'See to the dog and go off duty.'

Carol climbed into the ambulance beside the driver, with Felix crammed in alongside her. The doors slammed and within seconds they were roaring into the night at breakneck speed, just as a massed flight of Allied bombers flew overhead, their wings all but skimming the hills, the heavy-bellied roar of their engines making conversation impossible.

Carol sat tensely between the two men as the ambulance raced along the lanes which had been filled in to hedgerow height to accommodate the heavy machinery and weapons the Americans had brought in. She couldn't tell what was happening in the back with Betty, and could only pray that she'd come to no serious harm. The thought of the wining, craven Ken made her clench her fists, and although she wasn't usually of a violent nature, she wanted to spit in his blackened eyes and beat him to a pulp.

They arrived in the vast paved area surrounding the hospital and were greeted by nurses and doctors racing towards them as they screeched to a halt. Felix handed her down as Betty was stretchered onto a gurney and rushed through the doors. She was still out cold and looked very small and vulnerable beneath that pile of blankets.

Carol and Felix were ordered to wait in a side room while she was being examined. Although the chairs looked comfortable and it was a pleasant room, neither of them could relax, but spent the ensuing long minutes pacing the floor.

At the arrival of the doctor, they both came to a fearful halt. 'She's come round, but is suffering from concussion,' he said in his Southern drawl. 'There are compound fractures to her right leg and arm, and her shoulder is dislocated.'

'But she will be all right, won't she?' asked Carol tearfully.

'There's no reason why she shouldn't recover. But it would help if we could get her medical records. Y'all don't happen to know who her doctor is?'

'It's Brian Ferguson, who's been moved out to Swannaton,' Carol replied. 'But why do you need her records? What else do you think might be wrong with her?'

'Well, ma'am, I'm just concerned there might be underlying problems connected to the polio. I'll be keeping her in to reset the fractures and monitor the progress of the concussion, so y'all might as well go home.'

'I'm staying,' said Carol firmly.

'So am I,' said Felix.

The doctor eyed the stars on Felix's epaulettes and gave a sigh. 'There's fresh coffee and doughnuts through that other door to keep y'all going, but it could be a long night.'

31

Once the doctor had left, Felix went to find the coffee while Carol continued to pace fretfully back and forth. Betty was the sweetest, most gentle of girls, and for Ken to have attacked her like that . . . She had no words to describe her feelings, but knew that if ever she saw him again, she'd punch him on the nose.

Felix returned and she gratefully wrapped her hands around the steaming mug and breathed in the fragrant aroma of freshly ground coffee beans. 'Your lot don't stint on the luxuries, do you?' she said with a wan smile. 'I can't remember the last time I had real coffee.'

'The American army marches on good coffee and nutritious food these days,' he replied, settling into one of the comfortable chairs beside her. 'It was a mite different during the first war when the supplies couldn't get through, and those that did were riddled with weevils and mould.'

'My sister's father-in-law tells the same story, so it was obviously the same for all the troops, not just the Americans.'

She deliberately turned her thoughts away from what might be happening to Betty beyond that closed door. 'Thank you for making it possible for Betty to be admitted here so quickly,' she said. 'I dread to think how long we would have had to wait for the other ambulance.'

'It was the very least I could do,' he murmured. 'Betty's a sweet girl, and she didn't deserve what that brute did to her.'

Carol decided the time had come for some straight talking, for if nothing else, it would take her mind off Betty's plight and perhaps clear the air between them. 'We've been friends for a while now, and yet you never talk about your home, your family, or your army career – and although I've come to like you very much, Felix, I feel I don't really know you at all.'

He returned her gaze. 'The same could be said of you,' he replied softly. 'I know about your tragic loss, but nothing of your family, or your life before you came to Devon.'

This was the opening she wanted, and despite her concern over Betty, she knew she had to grab it. 'I was born in December 1915, in a small seaside town on the south coast, close to a place called Cliffehaven,' she began. 'My mother's name is Dorothy Cardew, but she prefers to be called Dolly.' She watched him carefully for any reaction, which disappointingly didn't come.

'She's been wonderful to me and my older sister, Pauline, and we accepted long ago that she wasn't cut out to be like other mothers.'

'How so?'

Carol blew on the hot coffee before taking a cautious sip. 'She's not at all domesticated, and is far too inquisitive and adventurous to be stuck at home; but when she does return from her latest exploit, she's the most loving, sweetest mother any girl could want, and we both adore her.'

'Growing up without her around must have been hard for you and your sister,' he murmured.

'Not at all. Our grandparents were marvellous, giving us all we could ever need in the way of love, guidance and time.'

'But what about your father? Why wasn't he there to take care of you both?'

Carol smiled. 'Pauline and I are actually half-sisters. Pauline's father married Mother, but didn't stick around for long after she was born – and mine was killed in an accident before Mother had the chance to tell him she was expecting me.' She gave a small shrug. 'Pauline and I don't know much about either of them, which is a bit frustrating at times, but as it upsets Mother to talk about her past, we've just had to accept the way things are, and get on with our lives.'

Felix lit a cigar and sat back in the chair. 'I recall you saying that your family's complicated,' he drawled. 'And I'm guessing Pauline is a good deal older than you to have had a son of your age.'

Carol nodded. 'There are fifteen years between us, and Brendon is five years younger than me. His size makes him appear older,' she said distractedly. 'I'll have to find some way of telling him what's happened to Betty before he hears it through the gossip-mill.'

'I happen to know he's over in Dartmouth this evening, catching up with some naval buddies. Morning will be soon enough, and I'll make sure I'm at his billet to tell him the minute he gets back.'

'He'll be furious,' Carol muttered. 'I hope they keep Ken locked up, because I dread to think what Brendon might do to him.'

Felix smiled at that. 'You can be quite fierce, can't you?'

She blushed and looked away. 'Only when someone I love gets hurt.' She took a faltering breath. 'When David was killed and I lost my baby, I wanted to strike out, raging against the unfairness of it all, but I soon learned that anger isn't the solution and doesn't help to heal. Not when others in our family have suffered their own tragedies because of this war.'

She gave a soft sigh. 'But there are times when I feel very alone,' she admitted, 'and wish my family were nearby – and that my father was still alive. I like to think of him as being strong and protective – the sort of father who could somehow fill the awful void left by David and my baby.' She smiled and blinked away her tears. 'It's silly to think like that, I know, but in the darkest moments it does help.'

He gravely nodded his understanding. 'You mentioned other tragedies,' he prompted gently.

Carol told him about her two nephews, and how her sister had never really come to terms with their loss, which made Brendon the focus of his mother's almost smothering attention. 'I can't blame her,' she said. 'I'd feel the same way – but I know Brendon finds it very hard to cope with.'

Silence fell between them and all Felix could hear was the ticking clock and the distant sounds of the vast hospital as he puffed on his cigar. He wanted to take this brave young woman in his arms and comfort her, for he could understand the loneliness and pain she tried so hard to overcome. But it wouldn't be at all appropriate, so he awkwardly patted her hand. It didn't feel right to continue questioning her about her childhood, the dead father and clearly wayward mother; but there were still so many things he needed to learn before he allowed his burgeoning suspicions to take real form.

Dolly was an enigma, that was for sure – flirty, gay and passionate one minute; secretive and cool the next – with a private life that was chaotic and filled with drama. And yet her daughters clearly loved her, so she must have done something right.

He contemplated the discreet enquiries he'd made about what she'd been doing coming out of that building with Sir Hugh. He'd learnt nothing – which only confirmed his suspicions that she was working with the secret services.

Did Carol and Pauline know about her other life in London? He didn't think so, for Carol had mentioned she'd retired as an interpreter and was now living in Bournemouth, and Dolly would have had to sign the Official Secrets Act which bound her to a lifetime of silence.

He smothered a deep sigh as he remembered their passionate kiss on Christmas Day. He'd known instantly that the flame was still there, that she loved and wanted him as much as ever – and in his delight, he'd gotten carried away, begging her to marry him, certain she would now accept.

Her cold, adamant rejection had stunned him – but running that little scene repeatedly through his head in the long, pain-filled hours that had followed, he'd come to realise there was a deeper reason behind that rejection than a lack of love, or fear that he'd let her down again. Dolly was keeping something from him – something which had put wariness in her eyes and given her the strength to ignore her feelings and push him away.

He glanced up at the clock, surprised that only an hour had passed since the attack on Betty. 'Would you like some more coffee?'

Carol shook her head, placing the empty mug on the low table next to the plate of untouched doughnuts. 'Now I've told you a bit about myself, I'd appreciate a few straight answers to all the questions I have,' she replied firmly.

Felix's pulse rate picked up. 'That sounds ominous,' he said lightly.

'I don't mean it to,' she said, 'but we've been dodging around things, and I think it's time you were honest with me.' She held his gaze. 'You already knew Dolly before you came down here, didn't you?'

He nodded warily.

'Then why haven't you said anything these past weeks when you couldn't have failed to realise I was her daughter?'

He chewed on his cigar, trapped into silence by the vow he'd made to Dolly.

Her gaze seemed to penetrate to his core. 'Were you lovers?'

Felix tried desperately to think how to answer her.

'We met in London in 1913,' he admitted. 'I'm sorry, Carol, but I promised your mother I would say nothing of what happened between us, and I have no intention of breaking that promise.'

'That's fine,' she said calmly. 'I'd already guessed how things were between you when I saw you both talking on my doorstep after Edith's funeral.' She leaned towards him. 'It ended badly, didn't it? Was it because she'd met my father and threw you over? He was an American too, you know.'

He somehow managed to hide his shock and the great tidal wave of doubt and disappointment that suddenly consumed him. 'No, I didn't know,' he said gruffly. 'What was his name? Perhaps we met.'

'He was Major Frederick Adams of the Intelligence Corps, and from the photograph I have, it appears he was very dashing. Mother told me he'd been orphaned at an early age, had no siblings and joined the army straight out of college. They met in London just as war was about to be declared and fell in love.' Carol gave a deep sigh. 'I rather think that was all she actually knew about him, for they weren't married, and I suspect he was just one of her flings.'

She looked at him keenly. 'Does the name sound familiar? Could you have met him?'

Felix made a sterling effort to steady his racing pulse and dismiss the clamouring thoughts that whirled in his head. He could see how much it mattered to her that he might have met the major, and he hated to disappoint her. 'I'm sorry, Carol. I have no recollection of the man, or the name,' he replied truthfully.

'That's all right,' she said on a sigh. 'It was just a faint hope anyway.'

Felix really did want to help, and it would be interesting to see what Adams looked like. 'Perhaps if you showed me his photograph it might stir some memory,' he said, 'but of course I can't promise it will.'

'I'll try and remember to bring it with me next time we meet,' she replied, glancing at the clock in impatience. 'How long does it take to fix a few bones and a dislocated shoulder?'

'I have no idea,' he murmured, studying her closely, seeing her mother in her eyes and in the dimple that appeared fleetingly in her creamy cheek. He wanted so badly to really talk to this girl about her father and Dolly – but the situation meant it was impossible.

'I suppose we were warned it was going to be a long night – but at least it will give us the chance to find out more about each other.' Her smile was fleeting. 'And don't worry, Felix, I'm not asking you to break any promises. I'm just interested in the man behind the uniform.'

Felix thought hard before he gave her a halting account of his childhood as an army brat, never staying long enough in one place to make real friends beyond the boundaries of the military camps, or catch up on his schooling, which had led him to enlisting straight out of college into the only life he knew.

He skimmed over the harsh facts of living with Olivia by telling her the marriage had not been happy, and that they'd spent the last twenty years of her life apart – whereas, in reality, it had become a nightmarish battle over her drinking and increasingly erratic behaviour which had culminated in her being admitted into a special clinic for the mentally disturbed.

'But something good came out of it, for we had a son,' he said proudly. 'Felix Addington Junior. A fine boy, who my mother helped to raise when my duties took me abroad. He was army too, but retired early to help me run my orange groves in California.'

She looked more disapproving than impressed. 'So, you were married when you met mother?'

'I'm not proud of the fact,' he admitted. 'I'm sorry, Carol, but I'm just an ordinary man with feet of clay who fell in love and had to live the rest of my life with the awful hurt I caused as a consequence.'

'I'm sorry too,' she said, taking his hand. 'I shouldn't have pried.'

He gently squeezed her fingers. 'You had every right to, but could we change the subject now?'

Carol nodded, but before either of them could think of anything else to say, the doctor returned.

'Miss Wellings has come through surgery, and will spend the next few days on one of our wards before she can be transferred to a civilian hospital,' he said. 'I'm a little concerned by her very low blood pressure and erratic heart rate, so I want to keep a close eye on her.'

'Can we see her?'

He shook his head. 'Not tonight, ma'am. Y'all go home and come back tomorrow afternoon when we should have a clearer idea of what's going on.'

'But she will pull through, won't she?' persisted Carol.

'Yes, ma'am, I have every hope that she will make a full recovery.' He saluted Felix, nodded to Carol and left the room.

'I'll see about commandeering us a ride home,' said Felix, relieved to be on the move again and free from any more of Carol's probing questions.

It was way past midnight as he helped her with her coat and they went out into the pitch black of the very early morning to find Herbert wrapped in his great-coat and asleep behind the wheel of the jeep.

'Thanks, Herby,' said Felix as the young man smoth-ered a yawn. 'You shouldn't have disregarded my orders, but I have to say, you're a life-saver.'

They drove in silence along the deserted lanes and past the sleeping camps until they reached the farm. Felix got out of the jeep and escorted Carol right to the door of her billet. 'I hope we can still be friends,' he said earnestly.

'Of course we can. And thank you for all you've done to help Betty. I'm sure it saved her life.'

He nodded and waited until she'd closed the door on him before returning to the jeep to tell Herby that Betty was expected to pull through, and to ask what had hap-pened to the thug who had put her in hospital.

'We all had to give statements, and then he was carted off,' said Herbert. 'He'll be up before the magis-trate later this morning and hopefully in a cell again by tonight to wait for a date in court. The copper said he'd need to speak to you and Mrs Porter as well.'

'Let's get back to base, Herby,' he said through a vast yawn. 'It's been one hell of a long day, and I need to get to Brendon's billet in less than five hours to inform him of what's been going on.'

Despite his weariness, Felix found it impossible to sleep, for his mind kept returning to the past and the two women he'd failed so badly. He'd done his best for Olivia, and he'd hated seeing her in that clinic, so heavily sedated that she'd barely recognised him. Hoping familiar surroundings and the sight of her little son might help her heal, he'd brought her home and paid for a series of private nurses to look after her.

But her fragile hold on reality was such that she'd taken no interest in anything and had spent her days lying in bed, gazing out of the window, her thoughts and feelings closed to everyone. When he'd been posted to London as adjutant to the American ambassador in June 1913, he'd regretfully re-admitted her into the clinic and sent his son to live with his parents in Nebraska.

As for Dolly, she'd become a beacon of light in those dark, dark days. He hadn't meant to fall in love with her, or make promises he knew he had no right to give, but Dolly was the woman he should have met and married years before – the woman who returned his passion and loved him without question, until he'd destroyed it all.

He'd known he had to tell her about Olivia and Felix Junior, but it had never seemed to be the right time, and as the months had rolled on it became harder still to confess. And then, on the second anniversary of their meeting, she'd said she no longer wanted to be his mistress and began to talk of commitment and marriage. She'd mentioned it lightly, but he'd seen the determination in her eyes, and had known the time to confess had arrived.

Felix pummelled the pillow and tried to find escape from the memories of what had happened when he'd told Dolly about Olivia and his son, and the impossibility of his situation which prevented any talk of divorce. The hurt and disbelief in her face haunted him, her cold withdrawal still chilling him as he remembered the lack of angry words, but the far more shaming look of utter contempt she'd shot him before she'd walked away, and out of his life without looking back.

He lay there staring into the past as dawn seeped round the blackout curtains, and the hundreds of Allied planes returned from their bombing mission to their West Country bases. It seemed Harris's campaign was in full flow, he thought distractedly before returning to tonight's revelations.

Had Dolly walked straight from him into the arms of Major Frederick Adams? She could very well have done, perhaps seeing it as an act of revenge, but knowing her as he did, he found the idea improbable – yet it was strange he was unfamiliar with the name, and that there had been no rumours of such a liaison. The circle he'd moved with in London had been close-knit, making it almost impossible to remain anonymous or keep secrets.

He twisted and turned restlessly and finally gave up on sleep when he realised Brendon would soon be returning to his billet. Yet, as he prepared for the day, his troubled thoughts continued to plague him. Dolly could certainly be accused of flightiness but she wasn't a tart, and he simply couldn't believe she'd thrown herself into another affair just to spite him. But then again, she had left London shortly after that awful exchange, and it was possible she'd met Adams elsewhere, which would explain why he'd never heard of him.

His earlier suspicion that Carol might be his daughter seemed faintly ridiculous in the light of what he now knew – but there were still too many anomalies for him to be totally convinced, and it would be interesting to see Carol's photograph of the mysterious Frederick Adams. There was really only one person who had all the answers; but she was probably in London and he was stuck down here for the foreseeable future. He would have to be patient until he could confront her, but in the meantime he'd contact a friend at the Pentagon with access to military personnel files, and find out just who Frederick Adams was, and where he'd been stationed in 1915.

32

Cliffehaven

March had proved to be a month of mixed fortunes and emotions for Peggy, and she rather hoped that this first April day heralded a time of calm in which she could catch her breath. She finished stacking the freshly ironed laundry, relishing the peace and quiet of a Saturday morning, and gazed out of the window, letting her thoughts drift back to the events of the past weeks which had both unsettled and delighted her.

Her one-time evacuee and ATA pilot Kitty Makepeace had arrived the night of the first Allied mass bombing raid over Germany, blooming in her pregnancy – although struggling a bit with the added weight on her prosthetic leg – and bubbling over with excitement. She and her brother's wife, Charlotte, had bought a cottage in Cliffehaven so they could be near their Wing Commander husbands, Roger and Freddy, while they awaited the birth of their babies. Peggy's delight in having them near tempered any initial disappointment that they wouldn't be moving into Beach View, for with Charlotte expecting twins, there would be three precious little babies to cuddle and spoil, as well as the chance to mother both girls.

Peggy's triumph at having overcome her nerves to secure a job as a sewing-machinist at Solly Goldman's uniform factory had been swiftly dashed by Ron telling her that Jim hadn't been in India since the previous October, but was now stationed somewhere in Burma. Stunned by the news and furious that the authorities had kept this from her for so long, she'd hung on to every word of the nightly newscasts until she realised the reports of the awful battles to oust the Japanese from Burma only increased her terror for Jim's safety. Knowing there was very little she could do about any of it, she'd determinedly swallowed her fears and knuckled down to sewing shirts at the factory, each stitch a silent prayer that the wearer would survive to come home.

There had been a bit of argy-bargy from Jim about her not asking his permission to get a job when she had home duties to be getting on with, but she'd fired a letter back telling him she was quite capable of making her own decisions without his permission, and to get on with winning the war while she saw to things at home. His reply had been contrite, no doubt because Ron, Anne, Cissy and everyone at Beach View had given her their wholehearted support in the matter, and had written to tell him so.

It was the condemnation by Doris that had really put the cat among the pigeons. Doris's evacuees worked in the same factory, and she was appalled by what she saw as her sister's further descent into the lowest of the lower orders. Her snobbish disapproval had led to an exchange of harsh words, revealing that she was once again in the thrall of Lady Chump-Chop, and cared only that Peggy's new career might taint her own standing in that self-satisfied clique. The fragile truce was broken, and now Doris refused to speak to her until she gave up the job.

Peggy was saddened by the falling-out, but had absolutely no intention of giving up the work she loved, or the new friends she'd made. Doris lived a very comfortable life and was incapable of understanding her need for independence, the chance to earn her own money and have a life outside Beach View – and as Daisy was very happy in the factory crèche under the supervision of Nanny Pringle, and Peggy was earning enough to pay Billy Wilmott to come in and do the house repairs, she felt quite justified in refusing to be bullied.

She gave a deep sigh as she carried the laundry upstairs to the airing cupboard, for despite her determination to make a better life for herself and her family, her new independence was restricted by this blasted war, and all the worry it incurred.

There was still no sign of the promised invasion into France, but at last the news offered a glimmer of hope. The campaign to destroy enemy arms dumps, factories, railways, airfields and industrial sites all over Germany, Belgium and France was continuing day and night, with over a thousand bombers attacking Frankfurt, Essen, Hannover, Nuremberg and Berlin. Every aircraft and pilot available was utilised, and the latest raid by several squadrons of Mosquitoes had pummelled targets in Hamburg, the Ruhr and the Rhineland.

Peggy's thoughts were constantly pulled into worrying about her son-in-law Martin, Rita's Matthew Champion, Kitty's husband, Roger, and Charlotte's Freddy, for the death toll amongst Bomber Command and their escorts of fighter planes was frighteningly high, and the pilots were under intolerable strain to remain alert despite their exhaustion and the loss of so many of their comrades.

Poor Martin was completely drained, brought low by the number of condolence letters he had to write; and the short leave he'd taken to go down to Somerset had not helped, for he'd imagined that Anne was getting far too friendly with the German POWs who were now working on the farm. This had led to him ordering Anne to bring the children home – which she'd very reluctantly agreed to do – but the tougher new travel restrictions meant that was no longer possible. Peggy was rather glad that Anne and the children hadn't had their lives disrupted, for she privately considered Martin's demands had been grossly unfair, but this latest blow was a terrible distraction for an already troubled man who needed to have all his wits about him.

And then there was Cissy, who'd experienced an anguished few days when her young American had been mistakenly reported as killed in action, and then mercifully found to be a prisoner of war. The fact that her daughter had kept her torment to herself worried Peggy, for it was unlike Cissy to remain silent, and she'd made her promise never to keep things from her again, no matter how awful they might be.

Peggy closed the airing cupboard door and glanced

into the bedroom shared by Fran and Sarah, which was as neat as a pin as usual, and then went to see if Ivy and Rita had, for once, managed to emulate such tidiness. They were a couple of imps, and rather more inclined to throw things under the bed or in the bottom of the wardrobe than put them away properly.

She felt a dart of loving exasperation as she eyed the unmade beds, the dirty cups and plates stacked in the corner, and the clothes and shoes littering almost every inch of the floor. She'd have to have yet another word with them, but with Ivy doing long shifts at the factory, and Rita busy at the fire station, she understood that they wanted to spend their leisure time having fun – not doing housework. And yet Fran and Sarah also worked long hours, so there really was no excuse, and she shouldn't let them get away with it.

Unable to bear the sight, however, she made the beds, folded the clothes away, opened the window to let the stale air out, and gathered up the dirty crockery to take downstairs, vowing that this would be the last time – just as she always did.

The house was quiet, with Fran, Ivy and Rita at work and Daisy spending the day at Gracie's so she could play with little Chloe, her new best friend from the crèche. Ron was out with Harvey somewhere, and Sarah had gone with Cordelia into town to change her library books. They would probably stop off at the Lilac Tearooms on the way home, so there would be time to put her feet up and re-read her letters before she had to think about what on earth she could rustle up in the way of lunch.

Peggy had just reached the kitchen when the

telephone rang. Dumping the crockery with a clatter on the table, she hurried to answer it, fearful as always it could be bad news.

'Pauline hasn't turned up for her shift,' barked Doris without even saying hello.

'I'm sure she must have a very good reason for not doing so,' replied Peggy, immediately worried that Pauline must be ill, for she loved her work with the WVS, and hadn't missed a shift since she'd started.

'I warned you she was unreliable,' stormed Doris. 'Lady Chumley is furious she's let us down when recruitment is so difficult now women prefer employment in factories – and none of this reflects well on me. You'll have to do something about it.'

'I don't see why,' said Peggy, stung by the barely veiled snipe at her own defection from the ranks of volunteers to her well-paid job.

'She's your sister-in-law and you introduced her to the WVS, so I think it's very much your responsibility. If this isn't resolved before noon, you'll have to come in yourself.'

'It's not convenient,' Peggy said flatly. 'My weekends are for the family now I'm working, and I'm not prepared to compromise on that, Doris. If you're so short-handed, why don't you and Lady Chump-Chop muck in for once? I'm sure neither of you has anything better to do.'

'Lady Chumley *cannot* be expected to pack comfort boxes or sort through old clothes,' gasped Doris in horror. 'And I have a very important meeting today with the leader of the council.'

'On a Saturday?' Peggy said in disbelief.

'These latest travel restrictions mean I'm unable to go to Anthony's for Easter,' Doris snapped. 'The meeting is to persuade him to get me a special travel warrant.'

'Good luck with that,' said Peggy. 'Those restrictions are for everyone, Doris. I doubt very much if he'll agree.'

'I'm not interested in your opinion, Margaret,' she said coldly. 'I need you to either get Pauline here, or come yourself.' With that, she disconnected the call.

Peggy slammed the receiver into its cradle and scrabbled in her apron pocket for her packet of Park Drive. Having lit a cigarette, she puffed on it furiously before marching into the kitchen to set about washing the dirty crockery with rather more vigour than was needed.

'Blast you, Doris,' she muttered crossly. 'I will not be bossed about, or give up my Saturday for you. And if you get that warrant, I'll be up to those council offices demanding an explanation.'

She dried her hands, finished the cigarette and looked at the clock. It was nearly ten, and Pauline should have been at the Town Hall over an hour ago. Something was wrong, and it was doing no good standing here swearing at Doris when she should be going over to Tamarisk Bay to check on Pauline.

She whipped off her headscarf and apron, reached for her coat, scarf and gloves, and shoved her feet into her sturdiest walking shoes. Tramping the hills between Cliffehaven and Tamarisk Bay was not her idea of fun, and the last time she'd done it she'd ended up puffing and blowing like an old steam engine. But a glance out of the window showed it was a bright, crisp day, and despite her concern over Pauline, she knew it would do her good to get some fresh air and walk off her bad temper.

She closed the basement door behind her, shivering in the long shadows cast by the house across the garden. Queenie looked down on her from a sheltered, sunny spot on the roof of Ron's shed. Wrapping her scarf more firmly about her neck, she pulled on her gloves and dug her hands into her coat pockets before setting off down the twitten that ran between the backs of the tall Victorian terraced houses.

The hill began gently enough, but as it became increasingly steep, Peggy felt the pull on her calf muscles, and a tightening in her chest. Her heart was hammering and she was gasping for breath before she'd reached halfway, and by the time she'd got to the top, she had to stop. Her legs felt like jelly, she couldn't breathe, and felt quite light-headed with all the exertion, but at least her bad mood had disappeared. How on earth Ron managed this twice a day she had no idea, but it was galling to have to admit that for all her running around after Daisy and everyone else, he was much fitter than she'd ever be.

She took her time waiting for her breathing to calm down and looked down on the town. She rarely came up here, but it was always interesting to see it laid out beneath her, sprawling up into the arc of hills, the barrage balloons above the factories gleaming silver in the sunlight, the smoke from the chimneys rising in the still, cold air as the townspeople took advantage of the lovely day to wrap up and stroll along the promenade.

Feeling ready to tackle the rest of the walk, which was fairly flat, she set off again, and soon saw the remains of the abandoned farmhouse and barn in the distance. They were a stark reminder of what the army did with requisitioned land and buildings, and she shuddered at the thought of what might be happening to Carol's village. Carol had written about her own fears, and although she hadn't gone into much detail, Peggy could well imagine the damage that could be caused by the influx of so many hundreds of men with their heavy and unwieldy machinery.

She paused and looked down beyond the vast Cliffe Estate to the farmland in the valley and the distant aerodrome with its runways, wooden huts, hangars and control tower. Martin and the others had probably been amongst the massive swarm of planes that had left at dawn, and somewhere down there was Cissy, anxiously awaiting their return. Peggy didn't envy her, for she was at the very heart of it all, and the increasing losses incurred on these raids were bound to be playing on her mind, stripping away her youth and natural vivacity and leaving her with memories that would probably never really fade.

Peggy gave a deep sigh and determinedly concentrated on the matter in hand. The only way in and out of Tamarisk Bay was either by boat or along a deeply rutted track which ran up the steep hill from the village road edging the boundary of Cliffe Estate, to peter out into a rough, narrow lane leading down to the tiny shingle cove and the row of fishermen's cottages that overlooked the sea.

Frank and Pauline's cottage was the only one still inhabited, for those of enlistment age had been called up, the elderly, the women and their children long since departed for safer billets away from what had become known as 'Bomb Alley', for this whole area was directly beneath the flight path of enemy bombers heading inland.

Where there had once been several fishing boats drawn up on the shingle, only Frank's now remained. It was the last of the small fleet once owned by Ron's family, for the larger vessels had been requisitioned by the navy to be used as mine sweepers, the rest beached and probably rotting beneath the cliffs for the duration.

As Peggy carefully picked her way down the rough lane, she could see how the cottages had deteriorated since being left empty and it saddened her, for she could remember how attractive they'd been before the start of the war. Now the walls were sagging, the wooden planking coming loose. The whitewash which had once gleamed was blistered and green with mould, and weeds sprouted from gutters and between dislodged roof tiles and rotting window frames. The tamarisk which had given the bay its name had gone wild, smothering the gardens and seeding itself in the most meagre drift of sand and earth to sprout new growth.

She was almost at the bottom of the lane when she heard the slam of a door and the sound of heavy footsteps crunching on the shingle. Rounding the corner of the cottage, she saw Frank stomping off towards his fishing boat which had been pulled up on the beach to escape the high spring tides. About to call out to him, she was forestalled by Pauline rushing out of the cottage and hurtling straight into her.

'Peggy,' she gasped, her eyelids reddened and swollen from tears. 'Oh, thank goodness you're here,' she babbled, frantically clutching at her. 'You've got to talk some sense into him.'

Startled, Peggy tried to calm her by putting her arm round her shoulder. 'Whatever's the matter, Pauline?'

'He's going off again,' she rasped, her voice rising with every word. 'Never mind leaving me all alone when I'm worried sick about Brendon. And I won't have it, Peggy. Do you hear?'

'Aye, that we can, Pauline, and I should think they heard you on the other side of the Channel as well,' growled Frank, plodding back to them with a face like thunder. 'There's no need for all this fuss. I shan't be gone for long.'

He reached out to her, but she slapped his hand away. 'You're selfish, that's what you are,' she snapped, glaring at him furiously. 'Selfish and stubborn, and so full of yourself you haven't even considered me. You've done your bit, and I need you here.'

She broke into a fresh wave of tears and clung to Peggy. 'You've got to tell him, Peg. He won't listen to me.'

Peggy held on to her and regarded the grim-faced

Frank. 'You both need to calm down,' she said firmly. 'I have no idea what either of you is talking about.'

They both began talking at once and Peggy knew she'd have to take matters in hand if she was to make sense of any of it. 'That's enough – both of you,' she shouted above their angry voices.

They fell into simmering silence.

'That's better. Now I need a cuppa after that long walk,' she said, purposefully steering Pauline through the door and indicating Frank should follow. 'And when you've both cooled down you can tell me – one at a time – what the heck this is all about.'

'He—'

'She—'

'I don't want to hear it,' snapped Peggy. 'Not until I've had that tea.'

Pauline sank into the sagging couch, buried her face in her hands and whimpered her distress as she rocked back and forth. Frank stood like a monolith beside the blazing range fire, his broad shoulders stiff with resolve despite his worried expression.

Peggy made the tea as Pauline's whimpers faded and a heavy silence descended, broken only by the sound of the waves on the shore and the occasional cry of a seagull. She placed the tray on the table and sat down. 'We'll drink this first,' she said, handing round the cups, 'and then we'll talk.'

She looked up at the big man whose head almost brushed the ceiling, his large presence seeming to fill the small, cluttered room. 'Sit down, Frank. You're looming as usual, and it's unsettling.'

Frank obediently perched on the edge of a kitchen chair, the cup looking tiny and delicate in his great weathered hands as he gloomily sipped the tea and shot wary glances at his wife, who was refusing to look at him.

Peggy saw him fidgeting and knew it wouldn't be long before he found it impossible to stay silent, so she wasn't surprised when moments later he pulled a leaflet from his pocket and slapped it on the table.

'That's the cause of it all,' he muttered.

'It's you that's the cause of it,' retorted Pauline, glaring at him.

'Ach, Pauline, love, don't take on so. It's only for a wee while and—'

'Hush, the pair of you,' said Peggy impatiently. She scanned the rather badly printed leaflet which had been sent out by the Ministry of Labour and National Service, calling for experienced sailors to man and service small vessels for short periods over the following six months to relieve naval personnel for war duty.

She finally placed the leaflet back on the table, understanding now why this row had erupted. 'How far have you gone with this, Frank?'

'I got permission to apply from the Home Guard and Civil Defence,' he replied. 'My application was accepted and I leave on Wednesday,' he added, almost defiantly.

'That's very short notice,' said Peggy. 'Why have you left it so late to tell anyone?

'It only arrived yesterday afternoon,' he replied

evenly, 'and I knew Pauline would be tired after her WVS shift, so I waited until this morning to tell her.'

Peggy guessed it had taken the night for Frank to pluck up the courage to tell Pauline, but she didn't labour the point. 'Where are you being sent – and for how long?'

'Where I'm going is between me and the Royal Navy,' he said. 'The most I'll be away is four weeks.' He turned to Pauline. 'I'll be back before you know it, love,' he said gently. 'But I can't sit about here doing a bit of fire-watching or messing about with the Home Guard when I have the skills to do something really worthwhile.'

'You've already done your bit in the army,' she snapped. 'I've been on my own for too long, and now with all this new worry over Brendon I need you here – not messing about with boats.'

Frank was about to reply when Peggy butted in. 'What's this about Brendon? What's happened?'

'He hasn't been home on leave since before Christmas,' said Pauline quickly, 'and apart from a few postcards and short notes, I've barely heard from him. And to make things worse, Mother said she hadn't been able to see him when she last went to London on one of her shopping trips.'

Peggy patted her arm. 'I'm sure there's nothing sinister about it all, Pauline. He's probably been refused leave for a while with everything that's going on, and it isn't as if he hasn't written, is it?'

'The postmarks are different.' Pauline said stubbornly, sniffing back her tears as she snatched a card from the mantelpiece and shoved it under Peggy's nose. 'See. It's not got RNR on it, just a series of numbers.' Her voice wavered. 'He's been sent back to sea to fight, I just know it,' she managed before bursting into tears again.

Peggy could understand Frank's impatience, for Pauline had clearly not inherited her mother's steel and was making rather more of this than was necessary. Nevertheless, she held her close and tried to coax her out of her tears. Then she caught the uncomfortable expression on Frank's face as he rose from the chair and began to prowl the room.

'Do you know anything about this, Frank?' she asked sharply. 'Did Brendon mention something on his last leave?'

He came to a halt, his gaze sliding away from Peggy's steady glare, his fists curling and uncurling at his sides.

'You do, don't you?' snapped Peggy, feeling Pauline stiffen and pull away from her embrace. 'Come on, Frank. Out with it.'

'He didn't say anything specific,' he replied, folding his meaty arms over his chest as if to form a barrier between himself and the two women. 'He just said all leave had been cancelled for the foreseeable future and that he was being sent somewhere he'd be of more use to the war effort than where he was . . .' He tailed off miserably, still unable to look at them.

'That means he's back on a destroyer, or a minesweeper,' gasped Pauline. 'Oh, my boy, my lovely boy,' she moaned.

Before either Peggy or Frank could reply, her mood changed like quicksilver. She jerked away from Peggy to stand and confront Frank, her eyes blazing with fury. 'How could you keep this from me? What sort of husband and father are you, Frank Reilly?' she shouted, pummelling his chest with her small fists.

Frank didn't flinch from the assault. 'Ach, to be sure, Pauline, love, I don't really know anything of what's going on. Please don't blame me for this – I'm not in charge of where he's sent, and we know he's all right because he's said so in his cards and letters.'

'We haven't heard from him for over a week, so we don't know anything of the sort,' she fired back, 'and now you're leaving me here on my own, dreading every ring on the doorbell.' She jabbed a finger towards his face. 'If anything happens to him while you're gone, I'll never forgive you. Never, ever, ever,' she shrilled.

Frank looked to Peggy for guidance, and she saw the awfulness of his situation clear in his drooping shoulders and sad eyes. 'That's unfair, Pauline,' she said firmly, coaxing her back to the couch, 'and you know it.'

Pauline sniffed and gave a reluctant nod. 'But he should still stay here. I need him in case . . . In case . . .' The hysterics were over and now the tears were rolling down her anguished face unheeded as her mind played over all the dreadful possibilities.

Frank knelt at her feet and took her hands, his expression full of love and concern. 'Please don't upset yourself like this, darlin', he murmured. 'Da asked him if he was going back to sea like before, and Brendon swore he wasn't, so there's no need to think the worst.'

'Do you promise that's the truth?' she begged, clutching at his shirt. 'You're not just saying that because it's what I need to hear?'

'I promise,' he replied, gently enfolding her hands in his. 'I talked it over with Da, and from the little Brendon said to him, he suspects he's helping the Yanks down in the West Country to prepare for the beach landings, and when the rehearsals are over, he'll be sent back to London.'

'So he won't be part of any real fighting?' Pauline's eyes were full of entreaty as she looked back at him.

'Not at all,' he soothed, settling on the couch beside her and gathering her into his arms. 'And I'm sorry, love, but I have to go, just for a little while.'

Pauline pushed against him in protest, but he held her even closer.

'You see, darlin', Brendon and me, we're doing the job we know best, and if it helps to bring this war even a second closer to an end, then it's our duty to play our part.'

'Oh, Frank, I'm sorry,' she sobbed, collapsing against his broad chest.

'I know, darlin',' he murmured into her hair. 'I know.'

Peggy crept out of the room, closed the door quietly behind her and walked slowly back up the track. Pauline would be all right for now, but once Frank had left she would need the comfort and love of family to see her through until his return. Peggy was fully prepared to take on the responsibility, but it was a great pity Dolly couldn't share the burden, for with the travel restrictions in place, Bournemouth might as well have been on the other side of the world.

She tramped across the windblown grass, going over everything that had been said during that upsetting exchange, then suddenly caught sight of Ron emerging from behind a gorse bush with Harvey dancing round him. Peggy decided the time had come for some straight talking – and this time, she vowed, she wouldn't be put off by his blarney.

He raised his bushy brows in surprise when he saw her walking determinedly towards him. 'It's not like you to be up here,' he said, shoving the net purses and dead rabbits into his poacher's coat pockets. 'There's nothing wrong at Tamarisk Bay, is there?'

'They're both fine for now,' she replied, and went on to describe what had happened. 'Did you know he'd signed up to this navy thing?' she asked flatly.

'We talked about it,' he admitted, 'and I did warn him that Pauline wouldn't take too kindly to the idea.' He took out his pipe and examined the tobacco in the bowl before reaching for his matches. 'So, he's off on Wednesday, is he?' he muttered.

'You didn't know?'

He spent some time getting the tobacco alight. 'To be sure he kept it to himself, so he did.'

'Just like you both kept Brendon's new posting to yourselves,' she said. 'And how come you're so certain he's down in Devon?'

Ron regarded her from beneath his brows. 'I'm as sure as I can be,' he muttered. 'Brendon couldn't tell me straight, but his silence confirmed my suspicions, and I've since heard things to back them up.' He waved his pipe at her. 'And that's all I'm saying on the matter, Peggy, girl, so don't waste your breath with any more questions.'

Peggy burned with frustration. 'What did you hear, and who from? If he's really down there, then why hasn't Carol written to tell us?'

'No one tells anyone anything these days,' he said moodily. 'There is a war on, you know.'

Peggy was about to reply that she was well aware of there being a war on but she was sick of being kept in the dark about things, when a rumbling filled the air. She stood with Ron and watched as several squadrons of Flying Fortresses and their fighter escort planes came thundering from across the Channel. The ground beneath them trembled, the down-draught bending the trees and making Peggy hold on to her hat.

Some were so shot up it was a miracle they were still airborne. The less damaged landed and quickly got out of the way as others hurtled in with their wheels still up, engines dead or dying, or with missing wings and shattered canopies, to belly-flop on the runway or go spinning off in a shower of sparks.

Even from this distance she could see the emergency services rushing to put out fires and rescue the pilots and their crews, and she cried out in distress and horror as a tattered Spitfire caught its drooping wing on the runway, somersaulted across the grass and exploded into a ball of flame.

Ron put his arm round her shoulder and firmly

turned her towards home as yet more bombers flew overhead. 'If we're to see an end to scenes like that, then we must stop asking questions and accept that our loved ones have to play their part,' he said close to her ear. 'Let's go home, Peggy, and be thankful that such men are defending us, for there are none braver.'

33

Devon

Felix took charge of the diplomatic bag which had just arrived by plane from London that morning, and waited until the soldier who'd delivered it left the room. He had mixed feelings about what the bag contained, for he'd yet to see Carol's photograph – she kept forgetting to bring it with her – and it had been four weeks since he'd contacted his friend at the Pentagon, and his reply might well be in with the other correspondence. Or there could be firm confirmation of exactly when Operation Overlord would take place.

The rehearsals in Slapton were finally beginning to take proper shape, but there were still areas of concern over the actual landings, which he knew made Eisenhower and Churchill reluctant to rush into cementing their plans. The original idea had been to make a two-pronged pincer attack, with a large force moving up from the south at the same time as the one in the north, but that had been scrapped once it was realised that because of the ongoing Pacific campaign, there were simply not enough ships to provide transport and cover for both invasions.

Felix knew there was a great deal riding on the

rehearsals in Slapton and the success of the invasion, for the memory of what had happened at Dunkirk where so many Canadians had lost their lives was still at the forefront of Churchill's mind – and neither he nor Eisenhower wanted Operation Overlord to turn into a similar disaster. Yet the ongoing delay was causing a great deal of tension amongst the service hierarchy, and although the date for the landings had been changed from 1st May to the 31st, it still wasn't written in stone.

Felix glanced out of the window. The weather had improved, but the forecast for Operation Tiger didn't bode well, with high tides, heavy seas and strong winds making any landing almost impossible. The long-range forecast covering the proposed date for Overlord was sketchy to say the least and, to make matters worse, there were concerns over the spring tides, the shortage of extra ships to defend the troops, and the lack of certainty about how successful the bombing raids on the gun batteries along the French coastline had been.

The men and women of the Resistance were doing a sterling job at sabotaging arms dumps, railway lines, communications and gun emplacements, yet there were still fleets of swift E-boats hidden all along the beaches, and enough enemy planes and U-boats to cause untold trouble to any invading force. It was a minor miracle that the Krauts hadn't cottoned on to what was happening down here, but the subterfuge of dummy airfields and service camps being built along the Kent and Sussex coast seemed to be working – drawing attention away from the west, making the enemy think any invasion would be coming from the east.

Felix emerged from his thoughts and opened the bag. He drew out a stack of heavily sealed envelopes marked 'Top Secret', most of which contained minutes of meetings held in London relating to the Devon operation. There were a few private letters from home, which he set aside to read later, and one that bore a very important seal which could not be ignored.

Felix slit it open and unfolded the single sheet of good-quality notepaper. It informed him that two VIPs and selected guests would be arriving in Slapton in three days' time at 14:00 hours to raise morale and inspect the troops.

The identity of these visitors made him gasp. 'Goddammit,' he muttered. 'That's all I need.' He strode out of his office to find his adjutant lounging back with his feet on the desk while he smoked a cigarette.

'On your feet, soldier,' he roared, making the man jump to attention and drop his cigarette on the floor. 'Put that out,' he snapped, 'and then round up the commanders of each and every unit – including the MPs, the medics, marines and Limeys. They are to be here within the hour.'

The man looked at him aghast whilst extinguishing the cigarette beneath his boot. 'But they're spread over miles,' he protested.

'That's what jeeps are for, soldier. Now scat.'

The man scuttled off and Felix glanced at his watch before reaching for the telephone on the desk. He'd planned to meet Carol this afternoon when she collected Betty from the cottage hospital, but the imminent arrival of two such revered visitors, with all the attendant hullaballoo, would make that impossible. He dialled a direct number and had to wait only seconds for Sergeant Cornwallis to pick up.

'Herby, I need you to check that Carol and Betty make it to the farm okay. I've had to call an emergency meeting of heads of staff, which will probably take up the rest of the day. Tell Carol that Lieutenant Reilly and I will try to get to see them both this evening, but it's unlikely.'

'Yes, sir.'

'You're to return here immediately for the briefing as you're the senior British MP. You have an hour.'

He cut off his reply by slamming down the receiver and returned to his office to read through the letter again and draft some sort of schedule for the visit. Hopefully there would be no expectation of any sort of display and he could get away with an inspection of the troops and a short tour of one of the bigger camps, followed by a top-rate afternoon tea – which would mean alerting the senior chef.

Felix regarded his scrawled notes and had second thoughts. Experience had taught him that he shouldn't assume anything, so he'd better make more detailed plans. He'd get men and landing craft prepared to do a dummy run up the beach and across the Ley under fire, with a couple of blasts from the big guns above Torcross to make things more dramatic. He'd have to use the marines, he decided, for at least they wouldn't throw up if the sea got rough, and knew how to swim should the landing craft have to anchor in deep water.

He scribbled more copious notes, and when he was satisfied he'd covered everything he leaned back in the chair and lit a cigar, his mind still testing the plans for any holes. His gaze fell on one of the private letters he'd set aside to read later. It wasn't from a member of his family but he recognised the handwriting, and despite all the other urgent duties he had today, he tore it open.

It was from his friend at the Pentagon, and took less than a minute to read. Coming to the end, he crumpled it in frustration. It hadn't really solved anything.

34

Bletchley Park

Dolly was well wrapped against the chill wind as she sat at the back of the large house in the pleasant sunshine drinking a cup of tea and smoking a cigarette while she watched the fun and games on the lawn. Some new recruits were being put through their paces by the hand-to-hand combat instructor, while another group dressed in gym shorts and vests were suffering the agonies of a brutal fitness class under the watchful eye of a bellowing sergeant major.

Dolly was glad she didn't have to go through such torture, and having tired of the sight of so much expended effort, let her gaze travel along the broad terrace to the small knots of men and women who'd come out from their various huts to get some fresh air and eat their lunch. She recognised only a few, for she rarely had anything to do with the decoders, boffins or engineers, and worked mainly in a classroom at the front of the main house. With a nod of recognition to one of the secretaries, she turned her attention to the house itself.

It was a rambling, over-egged pudding of a place – the sort of house designed by a committee that'd chucked everything at it, with red brick vying against white paint, domes, towers, lacy wrought-iron work, and tall chimneys. The park itself was still quite grand with its avenue of lime trees, but previous owners had sold off parcels of land, so there were just a few sheep grazing in the handful of fields, the old farm buildings turned into workshops alongside the new wooden huts which housed those working for the SOE.

Dolly stubbed out her cigarette and stared into the distance, her thoughts returning yet again to the dilemma of what to do about Felix. He might be many things, but she really couldn't believe he'd break his promise – and why should he? Her absolute rejection of his proposal was surely enough to guarantee his silence, and with all that was going on down in Devon he was extremely unlikely to bump into Carol. There was no reason for him to suspect a hidden motive behind her rejection, yet she was not so naïve as to ignore the fact that he was a clever man with a questioning mind, and that if Carol's natural curiosity brought them together, it wouldn't take long for the truth to come out.

She sipped the last of her tea and opened her handbag. Once she'd repaired her lipstick and added a dab of powder to her nose, she snapped the compact shut and eyed the letters that Hugh had sent on to her from London. Carol hadn't mentioned Felix at all, which either meant she hadn't seen him, or that she was keeping any contact with him to herself.

The earlier of Carol's two letters had been heavily censored, but knowing what she did, Dolly could tell she'd witnessed several of the early rehearsals down in Lyme Bay from the hills above the farm, and now all the speculation was focused on an imminent invasion into France. The second letter had been full of news about Betty's steady recovery, Nipper's growing reputation as King Rat-Catcher, and Pauline's rather hysterical letters about Frank planning to go off again, while she was also terrified for Brendon's safety. Despite Brendon being so reluctant for his mother to know where he was, Carol had realised it wouldn't be fair to her sister to keep her in the dark, so had replied, telling her he was in Devon – even though she feared she'd probably broken some official secrets act.

Dolly closed her handbag on the letters and thought fretfully about her eldest daughter. Pauline had always been melodramatic, even as a child, and she could remember the temper tantrums and extravagant tears when she'd thought she was being treated unfairly. Unfortunately, it seemed she hadn't changed.

Dolly knew she shouldn't feel such impatience with her, for the girl had gone through enough already, but she really did wish she'd pull herself together and realise the world didn't revolve around her; that the war meant men had to leave, and women were expected to knuckle down and get on with things without making a song and dance about it.

Poor Peggy would no doubt have to take the brunt of it all, and Dolly felt a deep stab of guilt at this, for Peggy had her own family to worry about, and Jim being involved in the brutal Burma campaign was of far more concern than Brendon messing about with boats down in Devon.

She found she'd tensed her shoulders and clenched

her fists, and made a concerted effort to quell her irritation. She'd write a stiff letter to Pauline, she decided, and try to get through to Peggy on the telephone tonight to find out how she was coping.

Dolly gave a deep sigh as her thoughts drifted to Pauline's father. He'd been working as a car salesman in a high-end London showroom when they'd met, and he'd swept her off her feet with his charm, his smile, the fancy clothes and the even smarter cars he drove about in. She'd been sixteen to his twenty and had fallen for it all, but when he'd lost the job shortly after their hasty wedding, his true character had been revealed. The reality of a cold-water room in a tenement and a crying baby had caused tensions between them, and the charm had quickly dropped away into dark moods and angry outbursts which threatened to become violent. It had soon proved too much for both of them, and she'd returned from her typing job one day to find him gone. There'd been no note of explanation, and with some sense of relief, she'd known she'd never see him again.

Dolly had kept tabs on him over the years, for she suspected that one day Pauline might try and find him. She rather hoped she didn't, for Paul Cardew had achieved very little in life, and was now forced to exist on charity in a Christian hostel, his liver rotted by alcohol – hardly the best role model for a young woman of frail temperament.

'Mrs Cardew?'

Dolly snapped from her thoughts and looked up at the young girl. It was Jane Fuller from the code room. 'Yes, dear? What is it?'

'This came through from Nightingale.'

Dolly frowned, and her pulse quickened as she took the slip of paper, for Marie-Claire wasn't due to report in until the weekend. The decoded message was short and to the point. '*Compromised within – moving on. Next transm . . .*'

'That's all there was,' said Jane worriedly. 'Do you think she was discovered before she'd finished?'

Dolly bit her lip. 'It's possible,' she admitted, 'but there could be a hundred other reasons if she's been compromised.' She gathered up her handbag and cigarettes. 'Thanks for bringing this straight to me, Jane. Don't send any reply. It might put her in further danger if the SS have got her.'

'I do hope she's all right,' said Jane, her blue eyes troubled. 'She seemed such a lovely girl – and so terribly brave.'

'I didn't realise you knew her,' said Dolly tightly.

'We only met a few times. I can't really say I *knew* her as such – she never gave anything away about her life before coming here – but we got along very well, and I liked her.'

'Do you always pick up her transmissions?'

Jane nodded, her short fair hair gleaming in the sunlight. 'I recognise her touch, and it was me who sent her new code over with Blackbird. She'd had the last one for too long, and I was worried someone might break it.'

'Keep an eye out for anything slightly off if she transmits again,' Dolly warned. 'The SS could be forcing her to send fake messages.'

'I do realise that, Mrs Cardew. It's happened before with other agents.'

Dolly nodded and hurried away into the house before the girl noticed the impact that unfinished message had had on her. Jane and Marie-Claire – Danuta – had never met before coming to Bletchley, despite the fact they'd both once lived at Beach View at different times, and Jane's sister Sarah was still there. Dolly had hoped to keep them apart, for friendships made between agents and code handlers had a nasty way of ending in tragedy – but it seemed the girls had met, if only briefly, and she could only hope Jane's work wouldn't be affected by what could turn out to be a tragic situation.

She ran up the three flights of stairs to her bedroom, and went straight to the telephone. Shrugging off her coat, she dialled directly to Hugh's London office and waited impatiently for the call to be connected. It was a secure line, but one was never too sure how secure, so she'd have to be careful what she said.

'Hugh,' she said the moment he answered. 'The Nightingale's song has been interrupted. It seems there's a cuckoo in her nest. I need you to investigate.'

'I'll do my best,' he replied smoothly. 'But it could take time. Where is she now?'

'I don't know,' said Dolly fretfully. 'She has simply flown her nest.'

'Then all we can do is wait for her to contact us.'

'There is a bird leaving the coop tonight. Should I ask them to investigate?'

'No – and don't send them to the same nest either.

We've lost too many already, and can't risk another.' He gave a sigh. 'I know you worry about her, Dolly, but she has to take her chances along with the rest. If she's able, she'll sing again.'

'I'll cancel tonight's arrangements and reschedule,' said Dolly shakily. 'Please do what you can, Hugh. I really don't want to lose her.'

'Dolly, I've already said I will, but as you very well know, there are no guarantees.'

She heard the click of a lighter and the sharp intake of cigarette smoke at the other end. 'Thanks anyway,' she said. 'I'll get on to changing the orders here.'

'Before you go, there is something I need to discuss with you,' he said. 'In fact, I was on the point of telephoning you about it. You're not going to like what I have to say, but in light of current events, and the depths of your involvement, I think it will do you good to get away.'

'I'm not going anywhere until I hear from Nightingale.'

'I'm very much afraid you'll have to,' he said firmly. 'This particular order is non-negotiable, and comes from on high.'

Dolly gripped the receiver. 'You're not about to dismiss me, are you?' she asked warily.

'Don't be silly, dear,' he drawled. 'You're far too valuable. But you do need to put your house in order, Dolly, which is why I have agreed to you going down to Carol's hamlet.'

'What on earth for? And what do you mean by "putting my house in order"?' she demanded.

'This business with the American has gone far enough and needs to be resolved,' he replied evenly. 'Your mind hasn't been fully focused on your work, and this order from above gives you the perfect opportunity to clear the air once and for all.'

'I don't know what you're talking about,' she retorted.

'I've made certain enquiries, Dolly, and I know far more than you think.' He paused to draw on his cigarette. 'Rather propitiously, an eminent group of your colleagues is leaving London tomorrow morning to attend a demonstration, and you've been invited to accompany them. It was felt by our esteemed leader that a feminine presence would brighten things up.'

'I'm not prepared to be his token female – I'm worth more than that,' she snapped. 'And just by being there, my security status will be breached. You can't do this, Hugh. It's too dangerous.'

'It will not be compromised – all attendees have the highest security clearance.'

Dolly remembered Carol's letter describing how everyone at the farm had made a daily trek up the hill to watch the rehearsals on the beach. 'There are at least two members of my family in the vicinity – not everyone who might recognise me will have such clearance.'

There was a moment of silence. 'In that case, I would advise you wear one of your splendid hats.'

'Don't be flippant,' she snapped. 'I'm not prepared to risk jeopardising everything on a bit of straw and net. I refuse the invitation, Hugh. I'm not going.'

'It's not that kind of invitation,' he retorted. 'You'll follow orders, Dolly, or there will be consequences.'

She flinched at the unusual sharpness of his tone. 'I'm not a child to be bullied, Hugh,' she said tightly. 'How dare you threaten me like this?'

He gave a sigh. 'I'm sorry,' he said, 'but those orders don't come from me – I'm just the lowly messenger. Try to see this as a chance to put things right so you can return refreshed and ready to do what you do best. I'll arrange for you to stay nearby after the demonstration, and put a car at your disposal. That way, you'll be free to come and go as you please.'

'I really don't like the sound of any of it, Hugh,' she said fretfully.

'It won't be easy, I know, but I've always thought of you as a courageous woman, and believe you still are. Don't disappoint me, Dolly.'

Dolly heard the click as the call was disconnected, and she stared at the buzzing receiver for a long moment before returning it to its cradle. She was furious with Hugh for prying into her private life and using this order from on high to interfere, and could only guess who'd issued the order – but knew she had no option but to obey it.

'Damn the man,' she muttered crossly. 'Damn, damn, damn them all.'

The anger died as a wash of dread swept through her at the thought of having to face Felix, and the daunting prospect of the ensuing fallout that might leave her bereft of both her daughter and the man she loved. The thought galvanised her into action. She snatched up her coat, stuffed her cigarettes in her pocket and ran down the stairs, her heels clattering on the bare wood.

The wind was colder now the sun had begun to sink behind the surrounding trees, and she shivered as she headed for the main office to reschedule this evening's flight, see if there had been any further communication from Marie-Claire, and prepare for the long journey back to London.

But it wasn't the brisk wind that chilled her; it was the thought that her past had finally caught up with her. The gossamer strands of that web of lies were in tatters, and now there was no escape.

35

Devon

Carol and the three girls stood back with Millicent
Burnley to admire their handiwork. The little-used
boxroom between the farmhouse kitchen and bathroom had been transformed and now looked twice the
size and very welcoming.

Where there had once been piles of boxes, suitcases,
mouldering farming magazines and assorted bits of
furniture cluttering up the space, there were now
freshly whitewashed walls, a scrubbed and varnished
floor, pretty floral curtains to match the counterpane
on the single bed, and a brightly coloured rug Pru had
made by using a crochet hook to pull strips of unwanted
material through the threads of a potato sack.

Carol had lent a dressing table and padded stool,
and Ida had come back from the farmers' market one
day with a chest of drawers loaded into the wagon,
which she'd set about cleaning and painting until it
looked as good as new. Millicent had sewn the curtains
and bedspread, and not to be outdone, Maisie had
painted a surprisingly good series of little water-
colours depicting the farm and its surroundings, which
now took pride of place on one wall. Mrs Claxton had

commandeered an army jeep and a young GI to bring Betty's belongings over, and had spent some time folding her clothes away and sorting all her books into alphabetical order on the small bookcase she'd taken from Betty's room at the pub.

'We've all done a splendid job,' said Carol. 'And Betty will love it. I can't thank you enough for offering her the room, Millicent.'

Millicent tried not to look too pleased with herself but didn't quite manage it. 'Mrs Claxton and I agreed she couldn't be doin' with'm stairs at the pub. It's no bother 'aving'm here until she can manage on her own again.'

Carol smiled, for although Millicent had saved the day, she'd also be receiving payment from the government for Betty's board and lodgings – but it was a bit uncharitable to think like that. She patted Millicent's arm. 'It's time I went to fetch her. Anyone want to come with me?'

'They'm got work to do,' muttered Millicent. 'No time fer gadding about.' She regarded Carol with some warmth as the others went moodily back to cleaning out the chicken run and pigsty. 'You'm be careful driving. Yanks think'm own the roads.'

'I'll be careful,' Carol assured her. She checked that the precious photograph of her father was tucked away carefully in her handbag so she could finally show it to Felix, then grabbed her coat and hurried off, with Nipper scampering eagerly at her heels.

Nipper loved going out in the car, and as Carol drove away from the farm, he stood on the passenger seat with his front paws on the dashboard, mesmerised by everything he saw, his tail going like a metronome.

Carol smiled at his antics, for she too enjoyed these trips. It was an absolute joy to be driving again after her own car had been garaged for the duration, for Betty's little motor was quite nifty in comparison. It had also made life so much easier once Betty had been transferred to the cottage hospital, which was stuck out miles from the nearest station or bus stop.

There had been a very real worry that she wouldn't be allowed to use it, since it had a special licence for a disabled driver, which also provided extra petrol coupons. And if permission had been refused it would have meant not seeing Betty again until she was discharged. Carol had discussed the problem with Jack Burnley and, to her enormous relief, he had proved his mettle by using his status as local councillor to get a short-term licence to cover Carol until Betty was fit to drive again. It was proof, once more, that even the most unlikely people stepped up to the mark when they were really needed.

The cottage hospital was a pretty, sprawling bungalow set amid a large, well-tended garden which sloped gently down towards a lake shaded by willows where swans glided regally amongst the bustling moorhens and ducks. Carol drove through the open gate and along the curving gravel driveway to park next to Felix's jeep.

She left Nipper in the car and walked out of the bright sunlight into the sudden gloom of the reception hall. It took a moment for her eyes to adjust, but she soon found her way to Betty's room, which was at the back of the building and afforded a spectacular view of the lake.

Betty was dressed and sitting in a wheelchair, her suitcase on the floor beside her, while Sergeant Cornwallis fidgeted on the window seat. He leapt to his feet as Carol entered. 'I'm sorry, Mrs Porter, but I can't stay long. There's a flap on at HQ, and I have to get back there.'

'I don't suppose you can tell us what it's all about?' asked Carol, having kissed a smiling Betty and noted how well she was looking despite the sling and plaster casts.

'Sorry. I have no idea what's going on as yet. But General Addington sends his apologies and will visit you both as soon as he can.'

Carol opened her handbag and pulled out the envelope. 'I've been meaning to give him this for weeks,' she said hesitantly. 'Could you pass it on to him for me?'

Herbert nodded and Carol reluctantly handed it over. 'You will take great care of it, won't you? Only it's the only photograph I have, and it's very precious.'

He tucked it firmly into an inside tunic pocket, promising to guard it with his life, then surreptitiously glanced at his watch.

'If there's a flap then it must be important, so we'd better not make you late, Sergeant,' Betty said in her best brisk school teacher's tone. 'Come on, Carol. I've said all my goodbyes and signed their papers – now I want to get out of this stifling room and breathe fresh air.'

Herbert took charge of the wheelchair while Carol carried the case. As they emerged into the crisp air and bright sunshine, Betty closed her eyes and breathed deeply. 'What absolute bliss this is after being cooped up for most of the day,' she murmured.

They reached the car and Carol opened the door. Nipper promptly tumbled out to explore the undergrowth beneath the nearby hedgerow. 'I'll round him up in a minute,' she muttered. 'Let's get you in and settled first.'

'I'm utterly useless, I'm afraid,' Betty fretted. 'What with one leg and arm in plaster and a calliper on what passes as my good one, I can't hop, even with this blessed walking stick.'

Herbert reached down and gently plucked her from the wheelchair to settle her into the passenger seat.

Betty giggled and adjusted her sling. 'Well, there are some compensations for being crippled after all.' She grinned up at Herbert. 'You'd be my knight in shining armour if I didn't think it might put Brendon's nose out of joint. Thank you, Sergeant, you're very kind.'

She and Carol exchanged amused glances as Herbert went scarlet, but managed to keep straight faces while he handed Betty her walking stick, folded up the chair and tried to squeeze it into the boot.

It stuck out too far whichever way he tried and, unable to fasten the boot, he fetched a length of rope from the jeep and lashed it around the handle and through the rear bumper. He gave the rope a good tug to check it would hold.

'That should do it,' he said, 'but it might be wise to

steer clear of any big bumps in the road.' He frowned. 'Perhaps it would be better if I took the wheelchair in the jeep,' he murmured, glancing again at his watch.

'It'll be fine where it is,' Carol replied. 'Thank you for your help, Herbert, now you must get on. Please tell the general that we'll see him once the flap is over.'

He saluted, then climbed swiftly into the jeep and drove away, the tyres sending up spatters of gravel to leave deep ruts in the once pristine driveway.

'Well done on finally remembering that photograph,' said Betty. 'Let's hope Felix does recognise him and can tell you more about him.'

'It's a faint hope, Betty. I'm not expecting anything from it.' Carol went off to round up Nipper.

'Perhaps they're bringing things to a head down in the bay,' Betty suggested once Carol had returned to the car. 'It's been fairly obvious that each rehearsal was leading to something big, which could explain why neither Felix nor Brendon could come today.'

'If it is, we'll soon know about it,' said Carol, steering the car through the gateway and heading back towards Beeson. 'There'll be enough guns and booms going off to alert everyone from Dorset to Land's End. I'm just amazed Jerry hasn't yet realised what's going on down here.'

'They're probably too busy dodging our bombers to take any interest in what we're up to,' said Betty. 'I just hope that if this is the final rehearsal, Brendon won't immediately be sent back to London. I've got rather used to seeing him about the place.'

'I'm sure that even if he is, he'll stay in regular touch.' Carol knew just how smitten Brendon was with Betty.

'Do you really think so?'

Carol smiled. 'Oh, yes, I'm certain of it.'

Betty's homecoming had been greeted with great delight, and once the milking was over and they'd spent a long time chatting over their supper, Carol helped her friend prepare for bed.

'I'm sorry to be such a nuisance,' Betty said once she was in her nightdress. 'It'll be easier all round once the district nurse comes in to do this sort of thing.'

'I really don't mind,' Carol assured her as she plumped up the pillow beneath her plastered leg and eased a woolly sock over her exposed toes. 'Now, are you sure you've got everything?'

Betty laughed. 'There's a glass of water, a lamp, my book and Millicent's little bell to ring if I need anything in the night – though I doubt I'll have the nerve to disturb her. She's still quite fierce, isn't she?'

'She wants us to think she is, but I suspect that under that belligerent exterior beats a warm heart.' Carol squeezed her hand. 'Sleep well, Betty. It's lovely to have you back.'

Betty's grasp on Carol's hand tightened. 'I know you've all avoided talking about Ken,' she said quietly, 'but I'd like to hear what happened to him.'

Carol hesitated, but at Betty's encouraging nod, she could no longer hold back. 'He was found guilty of serious assault and sentenced to five years' hard labour. Normally, he would have gone to prison, but as he's of enlistment age and perfectly fit to serve his country instead of hiding behind his reserved occupation as a farmer, he's been put into the army, where he'll probably stay until the war's over.'

'Thank you, Carol. I realise you all kept quiet because you thought it might upset me, but I needed to know.' She gave a little sigh. 'There's been no word from his family, but I suppose they blame me for what happened.'

'It was *not* your fault,' said Carol firmly.

Betty smiled. 'I know. Goodnight, Carol. See you in the morning.'

It was now past ten o'clock and the kitchen was deserted, so Carol quietly shut the front door behind her and hurried across the cobbles to the barn.

'She's all tucked up and cosy,' she said to the other girls who were still preparing for bed. 'It's just a shame Brendon couldn't call in, but I suppose if there's a flap on we won't see much of any of them for a while.'

'I wonder what it is,' said Maisie, who was plaiting her long hair.

'Probably something and nothing as usual,' replied Ida, climbing into bed with a hot water bottle and a copy of the *Picture Post*. 'I wish I'd been there to see Herbert this afternoon. I'd've got him to tell me what's what, and that's a fact.'

'He said he didn't know anything,' said Carol, 'and I believed him, so no amount of flirting could have made you any the wiser.'

The knock on the barn door made them all jump and Nipper immediately rushed towards it, barking furiously.

'Who the bloody hell's that?' hissed Pru, clutching the bedclothes to her chin.

'How the bleeding 'eck should I know?' snapped Ida, throwing back the bedclothes and stomping barefoot to the door as Carol snatched up Nipper. 'Who's there and what d'yer want?' she shouted.

'It's me – Herbert.'

Ida flung the door open and dragged him inside. 'You gave us a right fright. What you doin' 'ere?'

'I can't tell you, but these might help you find out,' he replied, opening a kitbag and tipping out five pairs of army-issue binoculars onto the couch. 'Be on the top field before two the day after tomorrow. I can't guarantee anything, but you should see enough to make your day.'

'See what?' demanded Carol.

'It's the big final rehearsal, ain't it?' breathed Ida, her eyes bright with excitement.

Herbert grinned as he shook his head. 'It's something much bigger than that.' He put his arm round her waist and drew her against him. 'But you've got to keep that pretty trap shut, Ida, or I'll be stripped of my rank and thrown in the glasshouse.'

'Blimey,' she breathed. 'It must be the King.'

'The King?' the others chorused.

'Do I have your promise to keep this to yourselves?' he asked earnestly. 'I've broken all the rules by coming here with those, and the general will have my guts for garters if he finds out.'

'We solemnly swear not to tell a soul,' said Carol, looking at each girl in turn for their agreement. 'But can't you give us just a tiny clue as to what we'll see?'

'Sorry. It's top secret.' He gave Ida a peck on the cheek. 'See you at the pub tomorrow night, all being well.'

Carol and the three girls stood in silence as his hurrying footsteps faded. Then they looked at each other and all began to speak at once, speculating on what they might see through those binoculars, and how on earth they could find a way of getting Betty up to that field without raising Jack and Millicent's suspicions. It was a long time before any of them got to sleep.

36

On the Way to Devon

Frank had finally managed to secure a seat on the packed troop train when a mass of servicemen alighted at Southampton. As the train panted its way along the tracks in the darkness, he closed his eyes and tried to snatch some sleep. The windows had been boarded over because of the blackout, so there was nothing to see, and the single light bulb dangling from the carriage ceiling was so weak it was impossible to read the newspaper his father had thrust at him just before his train pulled out of the station.

He'd left Cliffehaven at six this morning and now it was almost midnight, and he was tired and hungry, having snatched only a cup of tea and a sandwich from the WVS wagon at the last stop, which he'd guessed by the number of sailors getting off was Southampton. But sleep wouldn't come, for the memory of Pauline's sterling effort to hold back her tears, smile and wish him well haunted him still.

Her eyes and ashen face had spoken of her inner struggle to put on such a show, and he'd been riddled with guilt – to the point where he'd almost jumped off the train before it had left Cliffehaven. Yet he'd come to his senses. He was no deserter, and if he turned his back on his duty, he'd never again be able to hold his head high. Pauline would be all right. She had Peggy and Da to look after her for the short time he'd be away, and he'd make sure he sent her lots of letters to keep her reassured that he was alive and well.

As the train rattled and chuffed through the night, the rhythm of the wheels and the gentle roll of the carriage finally soothed his troubled spirits. His travel warrant said he was heading for Salcombe, and as he'd had no idea where that was he'd gone to the library to consult an atlas. Learning it was in Devon, he'd felt a stab of hope that Da was right about Brendon being down there, and that there might be a chance to see him.

Frank smiled inwardly at the naïve hope, for Devon looked like a big county and it was against the odds that they should be anywhere near each other. But hope stayed with him as sleep finally claimed him.

It was barely dawn when the train pulled into Salcombe station. Frank felt stiff and sluggish as he adjusted his Home Guard uniform jacket, pulled his kitbag from the overhead rack and slung it over his shoulder. His mouth tasted foul, and his stomach felt as if it was sticking to his backbone he was so hungry.

He joined the crush of servicemen that poured onto the platform, and looked around for the exit. His orders were to go outside where there would be a jeep waiting to take him to his billet and then on to the dockside workshops. Hitching the kitbag more firmly over his shoulder, he weaved through the milling crowd and finally found his way outside, where he was met by the very welcome sight of another WVS wagon, and the alluring aroma of frying onions.

A quick glance round at the vast numbers of servicemen still pouring out of the station, and the complaining gurgle of his stomach made up his mind. It wouldn't take long to get something to eat and drink.

The cheerful woman behind the counter was just handing him a sausage and onion sandwich and cup of tea when someone tapped him on the shoulder, making him jump.

'Gotcha!'

He whirled round, the hot tea scalding his hand. 'Brendon? Brendon, you young divil,' he roared in delight, trying to embrace him and not drop his breakfast. 'To be sure you caught me good and proper, but me stomach thinks me throat's been cut, and I didn't think it'd matter if I was a bit late.'

'Then it's a good thing it's me picking you up and not Sergeant Major Bright,' said Brendon. 'He's a stickler for punctuality.'

'But how did you know I was coming?' Frank asked through a mouthful of sandwich.

'I was in the workshop a couple of days ago checking over a minor repair to an LST, and the engineer in charge mentioned that there was another volunteer expected today by the name of Frank Reilly. He asked if he was a relation, and as I was curious to find out if it was you, I asked Bright if I could come in his stead.'

'Well, now you know,' said Frank, 'and as your grandad would say, to be sure you're a grand sight, so you are.' He grinned and hastily finished his breakfast, then wiped his fingers clean on his handkerchief and returned the cup to the wagon. 'Shall we make tracks? I don't want to be too late on my first day.'

'There's not much danger of that,' said Brendon as they headed for the American jeep parked at the kerb. 'You're not due to start until tomorrow, and I've somewhere very special to take you before then.'

'Oh, aye? Where's that? Some nice pub you've found, is it?' Frank slung his kitbag into the back of the jeep and settled into the passenger seat.

'You'll find out soon enough,' Brendon replied, switching on the engine. He turned to look at his father with a broad grin. 'What the hell are you doing here, Dad? Aren't you a bit long in the tooth for all this?'

'That's enough cheek from you,' he retorted, giving his son a light punch on the arm. 'There might be snow on the roof, my lad, but there's fire in me belly still – and it would be a waste of a lifetime's experience not to use the skills I have.'

'What did Mum make of it?'

'She didn't like it, but she understands why I'm here.' He regarded his son evenly. 'It wouldn't hurt to write to her more often,' he said. 'You know how she gets ideas in her head.'

Brendon nodded and drove out of the station forecourt.

Slapton

Dolly had dressed very carefully for the long, tedious journey in a lightweight lavender tweed skirt and jacket, silk blouse and the most robust shoes she possessed, which were a rather lovely pair of low-heeled black pumps. She'd chosen tweed because it didn't crease, and after a great deal of trying on and agonising over her collection of hats, had picked out the black one with the netting she could pull down almost to her nose.

It had started out as an uncomfortable journey, for her five companions were stuffy old boffins from Bletchley, who took no notice of her as they discussed weighty scientific matters in a language she barely understood. But things had improved when they'd stopped for lunch, and she'd asked the SOE driver, Susan Matthews, if she'd mind awfully if she sat up front with her.

She'd proved to be a lovely chatty girl, and after the overnight stop at a rather pleasant hotel, they continued to gossip until they drew nearer to the vast American camps. Dolly nervously checked her appearance in her compact mirror then carefully drew the delicate veil over her eyes. Her hands weren't as steady as she'd have liked, and her stomach was churning at the thought that within minutes she'd have to meet Felix, and the charade would begin.

Susan drove the car towards the barrier where armed GIs checked their identification papers and then saluted as they passed through. 'I say,' she murmured, 'that's quite a welcoming party.'

Dolly felt like a rabbit caught in Ron's lamplight as she saw Felix standing with other officers in a long line. A military band was playing, flags were fluttering in the stiff breeze, and the troops were standing ramrod stiff as the car drew to a dignified halt and they saluted. She pulled her astrakhan coat over her shoulders and gripped her handbag as Susan opened the door for the boffins and an American naval commander helped her out.

'Delighted to meet you, Mrs Cardew,' he said. 'I'm Commander Moon. May I introduce you and your colleagues to the officers of Operation Tiger?'

Dolly nodded, unable to reply as Felix stared at her in stony surprise, and watched her shake hands as she went down the line. She finally reached him and didn't dare meet his eye as the commander introduced them. 'Delighted to make your acquaintance, General Addington,' she managed.

'It's a pleasure, ma'am,' he replied solemnly.

Their hands touched fleetingly and moments later she was being led away towards a large marquee which had been decorated with Allied flags and furnished with plush chairs, a bar and a table groaning with food. She took a glass of white wine from a steward, but didn't dare drink it, for Felix was advancing on her.

'What are you doing here?' he rasped.

'I was invited.'

'By whom?'

'One of your most illustrious guests,' she replied. 'Look, Felix, this wasn't my idea, and believe me, I'd rather be anywhere else. But once this is all over we need to have a serious talk.'

'You've got that right,' he snapped. 'But it can't be here.' He gave a short sigh of exasperation. 'Goddammit, Dolly, you do pick your moments, don't you?'

Her lips twitched with a smile. 'Haven't I always?'

His expression remained grim. 'Where are you staying tonight?'

'At the King George just outside Dartmouth. I'll wait for you in room twenty-eight.'

He was about to reply when they all heard the sound of a light aircraft approaching, and without another word, he walked away to get everyone gathered for the welcoming party.

37

Coombe Farm

The girls had managed to get through a whole day and a night without letting slip their secret plans, although Carol had of course told Betty, knowing she'd keep mum. The special day dawned bright and clear, and they'd got through their morning's work without any sign of Jack or his wife, for he'd gone off to market very early, and Millicent was ensconced with Betty in her kitchen to do her weekly baking.

Carol and the others were just congratulating themselves that Herbert's late visit had gone unnoticed, when Jack returned and came plodding over to them, his expression boding trouble.

'What were'm racket t'other night?' he asked, eyeing the girls suspiciously as they shooed the reluctant cows out of their field and into another.

'Nipper spotted a rat,' said Carol quickly. 'Sorry if he disturbed you.'

He grunted. 'Thought'm heard a jeep by the gate.' His glare encompassed them all and they instantly looked away. 'There'm be no hanky-panky on my watch,' he growled. 'Or you'm out on thy ear.'

'I can assure you, Jack,' said Carol to forestall Ida's

angry retort, 'that none of us would dream of committing hanky-panky on your farm – or anywhere else, for that matter. You must have been mistaken.'

She smiled at him and closed the gate on the last cow. 'What do you want us to do after lunch, Jack?' She crossed her fingers behind her back. 'I thought the top field looked as if it needed weeding before we put the other cows in there. I could have sworn I saw ragwort yesterday.'

'I'll check'm out,' he muttered before stomping off.

Carol exchanged worried glances with the others and kept her fingers crossed as he headed for the steep field that overlooked the sweep of bay and sprawling army camps. They could only hope he found something he didn't like the look of, for if not, they'd have to find some other way of getting up there this afternoon.

'Let's have lunch and see how Betty's got on this morning,' she said, leading the way down to the farmhouse.

'That were quick thinking about Nipper,' muttered Pru. 'There's nothing wrong with the old so-and-so's hearing, is there?' She grimaced. 'It were a good thing 'e didn't come outside to see what it were all about. We'd've caught it, and no mistake.'

They were greeted by the delicious smell of baking bread and thick vegetable soup. Betty was flushed from the warmth of the range fire, and she shot a surreptitious wink at Carol as they joined the elderly farmhands at the table and tucked in.

'The nurse told me this morning that the plaster casts will be off next week,' she said. 'After that it's just a case of strengthening the muscles.'

'That's marvellous news,' said Carol. 'But you mustn't rush things and try to do too much.'

'I need to get back to work before the school board send someone to replace me,' Betty said fretfully. 'I've already missed most of this term, and although Miss Jones is putting a brave face on things, I can tell she's not happy about coping with so many children on her own.'

'Fresh air and sunshine will soon have you'm right,' said Millicent. 'You'm not to be fretting over that dry old stick. She'm quite capable of 'andling a bunch of small children.'

'What a brilliant idea, Millicent,' said Carol. 'We could take Betty out this afternoon.'

'And where do you'm think you be going? There be work to do on the top field,' rumbled Jack, glaring at her from beneath his brows. 'That ragwort be everywhere.'

'The four of us can easily get her up there, and she can sit in her wheelchair and look at the sea while we work,' said Carol. 'The salt air will do her no end of good.'

'It be a fair trek,' replied Jack, turning his attention to his soup and bread. 'Best if I carry'm up there, while you bring the chair.'

This really wasn't what she wanted, but Jack was being so helpful, she could hardly refuse his offer. 'That's very kind of you,' she murmured, setting her empty bowl to one side. 'Come on, Betty, let's get you ready.'

Carol wheeled her friend out of the kitchen and into her bedroom, closing the door firmly behind them as they stifled their giggles. She glanced at the bedside clock. 'We haven't much time, it's after one already,' she whispered.

Betty wriggled her good arm into the sleeve of her thick coat. 'Goodness, what an adventure this is. I wonder what's happening down there. Do you think we'll see Brendon and Felix?'

'I doubt those binoculars are that strong,' said Carol, bundling her up as best she could in woolly hat, scarf, overcoat and blankets, 'but you never know. Now, try and keep a straight face – this is just a jaunt to get you some fresh air, remember.'

She wheeled the chair back into the kitchen to find it deserted by everyone but Jack, and could only surmise that the other girls had gone to fetch the binoculars. 'Here we are,' she said gaily, 'all ready for our trip.'

Jack rose to his feet and effortlessly lifted Betty into his arms as Nipper yapped and ran in circles, confused by this odd behaviour. He carried her outside, where Millicent was waiting with the girls in her gumboots, overcoat and woolly hat.

'Thought I'd come too,' she said. 'Hurry up, Jack. Can't be standing about all day.'

Carol and the girls shared puzzled looks and hurried after her, with Jack striding out beside them, and Nipper racing ahead. It was most unusual for Millicent to be out in the fields, and none of them knew what to say. They took it in turns to carry the wheelchair, and despite being inured to steep climbs, they were all out of breath by the time they reached the top.

Ida dumped the heavy wheelchair down so it faced

the magnificent view of the bay, and after a bit of a struggle, managed to get it open and stable. 'There,' she said. 'Blindin' view, ain't it, Betty?'

Jack gently lowered Betty into the chair and Millicent fussed about, making sure the blankets covered her bare toes and that she was comfortable.

'Thank you very much,' said Carol. 'We can get on with the weeding now if you want to get back to other things.'

'What you'm say, Millicent?' asked Jack. 'You'm want to go back and miss all the fun down by there?' He turned and winked at the girls.

'You knew all along,' gasped Carol. 'But why didn't you say?'

He grinned. 'You'm having too much fun to spoil it,' he replied. 'I knowed there be something up when I heard the jeep t'other night and dog barkin'. Waited for young Herbert at the gate and made him spill the beans.'

He turned at the sound of an approaching light plane and drew two pairs of binoculars from his coat pocket. 'Better get your'n out if you'm don't want to miss'm.'

The binoculars were distributed from the bulging pockets and Carol helped Betty adjust the sights, made sure she had a firm hold of the binoculars in her good hand, and then saw to her own. They stood in a line either side of the wheelchair and followed the path of the incoming plane, which landed by the American hospital, and therefore out of sight.

They could see that the two Royal Navy warships had come closer into the bay to keep watch, the crew lined on their decks, and three LSTs were anchored just offshore, the large bay doors opened just enough to show they were loaded with medium and half-track tanks and heavily armed personnel. There were several ranks of soldiers lining the concrete apron and the banks of the Ley, and they could hear the distant sound of a military band striking up. Whoever this important person was, they'd certainly chosen the right day, for there was a bright sun, clear blue skies and a crisp edge to the wind which gently ruffled the sparkling sea.

After an agonisingly long wait they saw a shining black staff car lead a convoy of similar limousines slowly along the approach to the road between the Ley and the beach, the roof on the leading car folded back so the passengers could be seen. The rotund figure smoking a fat cigar was unmistakable.

'Crikey,' breathed Pru. 'That's Winnie, ain't it? But who's the tall bloke next to 'im?

'General Eisenhower,' said Carol excitedly. 'And look who's sitting behind them. It's Felix.'

'That's my 'Erbert driving,' shouted Ida as the car came to a halt and he stepped out smartly to open the door and salute both great men. 'Lawks, don't 'e look 'andsome?'

'My mum will never believe it,' gasped Maisie. 'I seen Churchill – and look, he's even smoking one of 'is famous cigars and doin' his "V for victory" sign.'

Churchill and Eisenhower were joined by a retinue of men in overcoats and bowler hats as they went along the ranks of soldiers. The men in the LSTs stood to attention, and whistles and hooters went off on the warships.

'There's Brendon, look, on the corvette,' said Betty excitedly. 'Oh, my word, I feel so proud I want to cry.'

Carol turned her binoculars from the world leaders to focus quickly on Brendon, her heart swelling with pride at how marvellous he looked as he stood beside his commander on the bow and saluted.

About to turn back to the inspection parade, she saw a face that looked strangely familiar. Thinking her eyes must be playing tricks, she adjusted the sights, and he came sharply into focus. 'Good grief,' she gasped. 'I don't believe it.'

'What is it?' demanded Ida, who was getting over-excited. 'What you seen?'

'It's Brendon's dad,' she breathed, still unable to absorb what she was seeing. But there was no mistake, for there he was, bold as brass amid the ranks of sailors in his Home Guard uniform, his stance erect, his salute firm. 'What's he doing here, and how the heck did Brendon wangle that?'

'Reckon it pays to have friends in high places,' muttered Jack. 'That there general pulled strings, I'll be bound.'

Carol realised that was what must have happened, but it still didn't explain why Frank was down here in the first place. She thought of her rather highly strung sister, and could only hope that Peggy was on hand to deal with the fallout from Frank's actions, for he'd clearly gone through with his threat to volunteer for something, and that wouldn't have gone down well with Pauline.

The two great men finished inspecting the troops,

saluted the men in the LSTs and were driven back towards Blackpool Cove. The distance was too great to really see much, but it looked as if some sort of viewing platform had been erected on the hillside over there. Flags were fluttering and there was more saluting as the cars drew to a halt and the passengers alighted to climb the steps and sit beneath a striped awning.

'I'm surprised you weren't invited to meet them, Jack,' said Carol.

'Sir John Daw and the Mayor be down there somewhere,' he growled. 'The likes o' me didn't get a sniff.'

Millicent gave a grimace, patted his shoulder in sympathy and continued to watch the goings-on down on the beach as Nipper went off to explore new scents.

A cannon went off with a loud boom, signalling an instant bustle down on the shore. The LSTs edged nearer to the beach, and the men and tanks poured onto the shingle as more guns sounded from Torpoint and machine-gun fire came from the hills beyond the Ley. The heavily armed marines fired back, racing to get the pontoons across the Ley so they could storm the 'enemy' dug in on the other side.

Carol and the others flinched at the cacophony, their eyes glued to the binoculars so they didn't miss any of the action. The booms and bangs continued for about fifteen minutes, the marines captured the 'enemy' and then everyone stood to attention as the band struck up the national anthems of Britain and America, and both flags were raised with great ceremony.

The convoy of cars left the viewing area and

disappeared amid the sea of tents and huts at the centre of the biggest camp. The troops along the foreshore and in the foxholes quickly dispersed, and while the corvette and the destroyer slowly returned to their watch further out to sea, the three LSTs withdrew and headed back towards Salcombe.

Jack lowered his binoculars. 'Them nobs'll be eating and drinking now,' he said gloomily. 'Better get on with clearing this field.'

The girls gave deep sighs, for the excitement was over and it was back to work as usual, but they'd hear a lot more about it in the pub tonight, and have something very special to write about in their letters home – if the censors allowed it.

38

The King George Inn

The King George was a sixteenth-century coaching inn, with heavy, dark beams, lath and plaster walls and floors which seemed to dip in every direction. Dolly's room overlooked the garden and was furnished with a four-poster bed, heavy chests of drawers and a wardrobe big enough to hide an army. The beams and heavy wooden furniture deepened the gloom, for the diamond-paned windows had been heavily taped, and very little light came in, which made it feel claustrophobic.

Dolly felt quite sick with anxiety as she paced back and forth, the ancient floorboards protesting beneath her feet, and waited for the knock on the door. The whole day had been a trial, for she'd had to smile and talk and pretend she was enjoying herself while being constantly aware that Felix was nearby, and someone might recognise her and blow her cover. She'd pleaded a headache and stayed in the car during the troop inspection on the seafront, and had quickly found a seat at the very back of the viewing platform.

She had no idea when Felix would come, for no doubt there were things he had to see to following Churchill and Eisenhower's visit, but she did wish he'd hurry up. The stress of waiting for what she suspected would be an unpleasant and painful meeting was exhausting, and she just wanted it to be over.

The light rap on the door stilled her, and with a racing pulse and dry mouth, she ran her hands down her skirt, then went to answer it. He filled the doorway, as handsome as ever, but with no warmth in his eyes and tension evident in his jaw.

'Thank you for coming,' she said, stepping aside to let him in. When he made no reply, she asked nervously if he'd like a drink.

He shook his head. 'I gave my driver the night off, and I need a clear head to tackle those lanes.' He dropped his peaked hat onto the bed and glanced round the room. 'The SOE certainly look after their operatives well,' he observed quietly. 'I'm amazed they could find a room at all now the whole south coast is flooded with troops.'

Dolly decided she needed to keep a clear head as well – although she could have murdered a gin and tonic – so she sat on one of the plush chairs to light a cigarette. 'I trust you'll keep that knowledge to yourself, Felix, otherwise my work will be in jeopardy.'

He regarded her coldly and remained standing. 'Your secret's safe with me, and has been since I learned of your involvement some months ago.'

'You knew?' she gasped. 'But how?'

'It doesn't matter how,' he said dismissively. His expression gave away nothing of his thoughts. 'Why did you come? What made you risk everything by turning up where you could be recognised?'

'I had no choice,' she replied. 'It was the sort of invitation that couldn't be turned down. Now I have a question for you – what is Frank doing here?'

'He's filling in as a volunteer mechanic at the maintenance sheds over in Mill Bay. Brendon got permission from his commander to have him on board the *Azalea* for the afternoon. He's probably back at the workshops by now.'

'You do realise that Carol and the others at Coombe Farm are watching your every move on that beach, don't you?' she asked.

'Of course – and they're probably not the only ones. I've seen the glint of binoculars from all over the hills – but with exercises this large, it's impossible to keep them completely secret.' He coolly held her gaze. 'Let's get down to brass tacks, Dolly. I don't have all night.'

His animosity was tangible, and Dolly was chilled by it. She stubbed out her cigarette and tightly locked her fingers in her lap, determined to finish what she'd started.

'I have something to tell you,' she said, 'but before I do, I want you to know that what I did was not out of spite, but because I could see no other way out.'

She dared to glance up at him, but his expression remained stony as his blue eyes turned arctic and he continued to stand there in rigid silence.

Dolly looked away, unable to withstand the coldness in him. 'Do you remember that day back in the spring of 1915 when I suggested we should get married?'

He nodded.

She dipped her chin, her fingers nervously plucking

at her skirt. 'I'd been so full of wonderful plans that day – had worked out what I'd do and say and even imagined how you would react. In short, I was in a haze of love, happiness and excitement.'

He didn't respond, and she finally found the courage to meet his gaze. 'And then you confessed you had a wife and because of her illness you couldn't get a divorce. My happiness fell away, my hopes and dreams were shattered, and I suddenly saw everything in a whole different, blinding light that stripped away the heady gloss of our romance and left only the tawdry reality behind.'

'It was never tawdry,' he said gruffly. 'I loved you, truly loved you.'

'But not enough to be honest with me right from the start,' she replied. 'If you had, things might have been very different, and we wouldn't be having this painful inquest today.'

Those cold blue eyes seemed to pierce her to the core. 'And just how honest have you been? Did you never lie, or keep secrets from me?'

Dolly swallowed nervously, her gaze trapped by his, unable to escape. 'Yes, I had a secret,' she admitted softly, 'which was why I had to turn down your proposal at Christmas.'

'Just the one secret? Surely there were more?'

She frowned at his scathing tone. 'I don't know what you mean,' she stammered.

'Oh, I think you do,' he replied coldly. 'But I'd like to hear what this solitary secret was, and why you deem it so important to actually confess it.'

An icy foreboding made Dolly shiver. The tension between them was almost at breaking point and she could barely think straight. She dragged her gaze from him and lit another cigarette with trembling fingers. 'You can choose to think what you will, Felix, but I've kept only one secret,' she managed.

He remained silent, and Dolly willed herself to keep her thoughts clear and unhampered by his lowering presence. 'That day you confessed to having a wife and child broke my heart. I was filled with such joy that it felt as if the sun was glowing inside me – but it wasn't the sun, Felix. It was our precious baby.'

She looked up at him, hoping to see some sort of reaction, but he regarded her with almost a blank indifference.

'Why didn't you tell me then instead of now?'

His lack of emotion rattled her. 'I would have thought that was obvious,' she replied sharply. 'You were tied to a sick woman you couldn't divorce, and you made it plain we had no future together.'

There was still no reaction from him and she took a shallow breath, determined to make him see that she'd done what she'd thought was best. 'I wasn't prepared to carry on being your mistress, and I certainly didn't want a part-time father for my baby who'd only take an interest out of a sense of duty. You'd have gone back to the States and soon forgotten about us, so it was better to end it there and then. What you didn't know wouldn't hurt any of us.'

'You should have told me and let me decide what sort of a father I might have been to Carol.' His features looked as if they'd been carved in stone. 'That's if I actually was her father.'

'But of course you were,' she protested, at last getting to her feet. 'You were my love, the only man I ever really wanted. I was never, ever unfaithful to you.'

Felix drew a brown envelope from his pocket, opened it and pulled out a photograph. 'Who's this man?'

Dolly gasped as she recognised the photograph she'd given to Carol all those years ago. 'You've discussed this with Carol?' she managed.

'Indeed I have,' he replied coldly, 'and it was most interesting to hear what she had to say.' He held out the photograph. 'You haven't answered my question, Dolly.

'It's Frederick Adams,' she said, 'but I can explain—'

'I'm sure you can,' he replied tucking the photograph away again. 'And I'd be most interested to hear what your devious imagination can come up with, but I happen to know that the man in the photograph is not Frederick Adams.'

Dolly stared at him in confusion. 'Of course it is,' she stammered. 'He—'

'It's Sir Hugh Cuthbertson, former attaché to the British ambassador in Paris, career diplomat, and now the head of MI5, and your boss. I made enquiries and it seems you've known each other for many years and are extremely close. Did you have an affair with him? Are you protecting his good name by giving him an alias?'

'Don't be ridiculous,' she snapped. 'He's not in the least bit inclined that way.'

'I know,' he said evenly. 'So why pretend he's Frederick Adams – and Carol's father?'

Dolly's mind and emotions were in such turmoil she couldn't answer him.

'Who *was* Major Frederick Adams? Was he the man you ran to when you left me? Could he be Carol's father?'

His words hit like machine-gun fire and she flinched. 'It was a name I plucked out of the air,' she stammered. 'He wasn't real.'

'And you have the gall to accuse *me* of being a liar,' he said scornfully. He pulled a cigar case out of his jacket pocket and went to stand by the window, taking his time to cut and pierce the cigar before lighting it.

Dolly saw the tension in his shoulders and the slight tremor in his hand as he put his lighter back in his pocket. 'I had to tell Carol something,' she said tremulously, 'and I thought that if I gave her that photograph of Hugh and told her he'd died, she'd be satisfied and would stop asking questions.'

'Did you do the same to Pauline? Was that all lies too?'

'No,' she said firmly. 'I told Pauline the unvarnished truth about her father, and she has our wedding photograph as well as the divorce papers. If she wants to find him, I won't encourage it, but she's a grown woman, and must make her own decisions.'

Felix carried on smoking his cigar. 'Carol has a right to the truth as well,' he said gruffly.

'This has all come about because you broke your promise to me and couldn't resist talking about us to Carol,' she snapped.

He whirled round to face her, the colour heightened

in his face. 'No, Dolly. This is because you told lie upon lie, and refused to discuss anything with either of your daughters. Carol yearns to know more about her father, but was always mindful that you got *upset* when questioned about your past.' He pushed past her and began to prowl the room.

'Which is hardly surprising,' he continued, 'when you consider just how tangled that web of lies must have become over the years. But she trusted me enough to ask if I knew Adams because we were both in the American army, so I contacted a buddy of mine back in the States to look up the military records for that time.'

He turned to face her. 'There were no records for a Major Frederick Adams of the Intelligence Corps, but there were two men of the same name serving at that time, and both of them had been in London that spring.'

Dolly felt the blood drain from her face. 'It's coincidence,' she stammered. 'I swear to you, Felix, I knew neither of them, and was never unfaithful to you.' To her chagrin, she felt the prick of tears and quickly blinked them away. 'I loved you, only you, and I swear on all I hold precious that you are Carol's father.'

He took a deep breath and let it out on a sigh. 'Yes, I know I am. I'd worked it out a while ago. The story about Adams knocked me off balance until I saw that photograph of Hugh, realised those soldiers were mere boys just out of school, and knew I'd been right all along.'

'Then why . . . ?'

His expression darkened as he looked down at her. 'You said earlier that what Carol and I didn't know wouldn't hurt us. But it has – deeply. You need to understand how much damage your lies have caused – how they've aroused suspicions and doubts, poisoned everything and shattered trust – and once that's gone, there's nothing left to salvage.'

'I didn't mean to cause you and Carol such hurt,' she said tearfully. 'But I wasn't the only one at fault.'

His expression held not a shred of compassion. 'I fully admit the shameful part I played in all this, for I should have been straight with you right from the start – and for that, I'm truly sorry. But Carol needs a father in her life after being denied one for so long, and she deserves to know the truth. Are you going to tell her – or shall I?'

'I will,' she replied tremulously.

'Tell her she can come and see me any time she wants. I'll warn the guardhouse. But don't take too long about it, Dolly – I'm running out of patience.' With that, he jammed the cigar in the corner of his mouth, snatched his hat from the bed, and in two long strides was out the door.

Dolly closed her eyes, the chill of his departure making her tremble. She'd never seen him so angry, or so determined to cause her hurt, and realised suddenly that he'd been mirroring her rejection of his proposal back in London. There would be no coming back from this – it was truly over – and tomorrow she'd have to face Carol.

Felix climbed into the jeep and drove quickly through the broad arch which had once accommodated horse-drawn coaches. The dark streets beyond were bustling with soldiers and sailors making the most of their night off duty. His anger had died, and he was left feeling empty and ashamed for what he'd done to Dolly tonight.

He weaved through the drunken sailors and screeching girls that staggered across the road from pub to pub, and headed out of town to the utter blackness of the countryside. But as the noise of the town faded and the blanket of stillness enfolded him, he was overwhelmed with sadness. He pulled into a farm entrance and switched off the engine.

Looking up at the endless galaxy of stars, and out over the stretch of empty land where a pale moon gilded the tops of the hedgerows, he was made aware of how small and insignificant he was in the scheme of things. It was like sailing his boat, alone at the helm with the bow slicing through the dark waters, the moon and stars his only guide. He'd always felt at one with the night and the sea, but now a sense of isolation filled him and he knew that this awful loneliness would remain with him for the rest of his life. They'd lost each other, and there could be no going back.

He threw the cigar butt in the road and saw the sparks fly as it hit the ground and rolled away. He watched the small glow slowly die, and when it was gone, he remained sitting there, staring at nothing in particular as his thoughts plagued him.

What if Carol didn't want him for a father – or worse still, couldn't forgive either of them for what they'd done? It wasn't entirely Dolly's fault they were in such a mess, and he suspected she'd been punished enough. Perhaps all was not lost, he decided. Carol was a sensible and understanding girl, and she might come round to the idea of having him as a father – or at least a father figure – and the idea of having a daughter made him smile. If that happened, then surely he and Dolly could find a way to forgive each other, and then, at some distant time, perhaps they could rekindle the sparks that were still between them.

On that happier thought, he switched on the engine and sent the jeep roaring down the hill on the way back to his billet at the old manor house.

39

Burma

Jim folded Peggy's letter and carefully tucked it away in his backpack, along with all the other letters and photographs from home. This latest batch had taken three weeks to reach him, and with everything that had happened over the past month, he'd almost forgotten about the documentary film that had been made whilst he and Ernie had been on short leave. It felt strange to think about it now, as if it had happened to someone else in another lifetime, for his reality had become the humid jungle, with its strange noises and ever-present sense of lurking danger.

He remembered how he'd rehearsed what to say that morning, but when the time had come he'd been tongue-tied and embarrassed when faced with the camera, and was fairly certain he'd made a complete ass of himself. But at least he'd told everyone at home that he loved and missed them, and could show them he was fit and well. Peggy had written to say how handsome he'd looked and how much she missed him – and that even Harvey had rushed up to the screen wagging his tail and barking in recognition – so maybe it had allayed some of her fears for him, and he was glad of that.

He closed his eyes and tried to relax in the short time he had before preparing to leave this jungle camp. Every muscle ached after having spent the last two days clearing a runway through the teak tree plantation for the C-47s which would take them over the great Irrawaddy River to Chowringhee, which was 150 miles behind Japanese lines.

'They'll be here in less than an hour if all goes to plan,' muttered Ernie, getting to his feet. 'We'd better get ready.'

Jim saw that the other men were already moving about the camp in the flickering shadows of the many small fires that had been lit for warmth and to brew tea. He stripped off his sweat-stained vest, pants and filthy khaki shorts, and dunked himself in the nearby river before he began to dress for the expected enemy encounter they would face at the end of their journey.

He donned clean underpants and vest, two pairs of thick socks knitted by Peggy, green cotton trousers held down at the ankle by short puttees, a khaki flannel shirt worn outside his trousers, and nailed boots. He hung the silk panic map of Burma and a pair of binoculars round his neck, and attached a water bottle, ammunition and compass to his webbing. On his left hip was slung a small canvas pouch containing basic field-dressings, two condoms which would come in useful as waterproof wrapping for his watch, compass, cigarettes and matches when crossing a river; and on his right hip he buckled a wickedly sharp hunting knife in a leather sheath which he'd won in a game of poker back in Chittagong.

He settled his slouch hat at a rakish angle on his head, his carbine over his shoulder, and hoisted up the large backpack which contained five days' worth of K-rations, one half of a lightweight green blanket – two men, one half each – a groundsheet, two more pairs of Pauline's socks, toothbrush and paste, mepacrine tablets to fight an attack of malaria, shaving kit, hand towel, nail scissors, iodine pencil, plimsolls, an American field jacket, a small bottle of rum, his dirty clothing, and his precious letters and photographs from home.

He felt strong, alert and fit for action as he eased the strap of the carbine loose from the backpack so it was immediately to hand, and lit a cigarette. Wingate was a commander he trusted and greatly admired, the men around him totally focused on the job ahead of them as they formed into groups with the mules, jeeps, supplies and trucks to be loaded onto the planes which would soon land on the jungle airstrip.

There was silence as they waited in the darkness and looked skyward through the widely scattered trees that soared high above them, the tension rising with every passing minute – for surely the Japanese must know by now what was going on here.

'Here they come,' muttered Ernie as the distant throb of the C-47s became audible.

It was a sound Jim and the others had heard many times over the past months and it had become instantly recognisable. He watched the black wings sweep over the moon, which was a day away from being full, and saw the red glow of the engines as the cones of their headlights lit up the heavily guarded jungle airstrip. If the Japs were about, this was the moment they would attack. He stamped out his cigarette and fingered the carbine's trigger, alert for any sign of movement within the blackness of the surrounding plantation.

The C-47s were from the RAF and the USAAF, and they swarmed in to park on the extra-wide runway. Once the mules, vehicles and supplies had been loaded, the groups of men assigned to each plane swiftly followed them, and within minutes the planes took off again, two by two.

'Aircraft B-18 – load!' shouted the plane master.

Jim and Ernie marched to the checkpoint behind their senior officer, who had to shout above the noise of the engines to make himself heard. The backdraught kicked up great swirls of dust and debris and Jim had to screw up his eyes against it and hold on to his hat before it was tossed away and lost forever.

They climbed the ramp into the body of the plane and were met by the sight of the large rear ends of three mules which had been jammed in tight across the forward half of the cabin, their noses against the forward bulkhead and cockpit door.

The animals' heads had been tightly fastened to a strong bamboo pole which had been anchored to bolts in the reinforced steel floor, with an extra-thick pole running under their behinds which pushed them forward, giving them very little room to move or buck. Their saddles and loads had been stacked on the floor, and straw had been spread beneath their hooves to stop them slipping, but with the plane tilting sharply down from front to rear, this was not wholly successful.

Jim and Ernie sat down with their backpacks between their knees as the flight lieutenant in command of the aircraft peered through the twitching ears of one of the mules and exchanged a thumbs-up with the platoon commander before slamming the cockpit door with a purposeful clang which made the mules shift and twitch their ears in alarm.

The cabin lights went out, the engines changed pitch and throbbed earnestly as the pilot taxied with increasing speed for take-off. The mules brayed in fear, showing their enormous teeth as they threw up their heads, fought against their restraints and tried to kick out. The pilot opened the throttle and the plane surged forward and lifted into the air.

Three men were quickly sent to act as buffers against the mules' backsides while the muleteer readied his carbine in case the animals broke free. But as the airfield lights sank from sight and disappeared into the night, the tail of the plane rose until the floor levelled out and the mules slowly calmed down.

'It'll be fun and games again when we land,' said Jim. 'Those poor wee beasts will be all but looking over the pilot's shoulder and giving him advice when the nose drops.'

Ernie grunted, closed his eyes and was snoring within seconds. Jim was constantly amazed at his friend's ability to do that at the drop of a hat, for try as hard as he might, sleep eluded him on flights like this – and there had been many over the past months – some of them quite stomach-churning.

After an hour the plane's nose dipped, the mules pressed against their keeper, and Jim and the others hoisted their backpacks on again in readiness for landing. He looked out of the window and saw the moon shining on a mile-wide river that ran through black, featureless jungle, and guessed this must be the mighty Irrawaddy.

He nudged Ernie awake, helped him with his pack and they both peered out of the window for their first sight of Chowringhee. Ten minutes later they saw the lights glittering along the rectangular landing strip, much brighter than any they'd seen in the Calcutta street after which this makeshift landing-place had been named.

Two cones of bright headlights advanced slowly at the far end of the runway before turning, whilst others shone out into the jungle, or across the strip. A plane passed directly below them, pale points of fire shimmering from the exhausts as another circled above, with yet another above that.

The pilot eased back on the throttle, and with a heave and a lift the undercarriage came down. There was another heave as the wing-flaps opened, and then they descended swiftly, landing with two soft bumps on the runway which had been finished only the day before. The usual jungle trees flashed by as the earth raced in a blur beneath them until the plane lost speed and the tail began to sag.

Another group of men were sent quickly to push

against the rumps of the mules, which were once again fighting their restraints, as the plane taxied to a halt and then the bay doors were flung open. Long ramps were hastily brought to unload the mules, and once they were clear, Jim and the men jumped down and were ordered off the airstrip away from the lights and the growling engines into the cover of the surrounding jungle.

Guards were organised and patrols were sent out to search for fresh water, but for the rest it was a chance to eat, relax and swap tall tales. As always, the gossip was rife amongst the men. There had been no real disasters, though it was said that a USAAF plane had turned too quickly on the ground, chopping off a section of tail from an RAF plane that was already parked. The USAAF officer in charge of the flying ops was now said to be using the cockpit of his own plane as a control tower.

'Ach, to be sure this tastes all right,' said Jim appreciatively, tucking into one of his packets of K-ration, 'but what I wouldn't give for Peg's steak and kidney pudding right now. Set me up good and proper, so it would.'

Ernie grunted and tucked into his own rations while swarms of huge red ants scurried about over them on their busy way – strangely not at all interested in biting them, or stealing their food. 'I wonder how long we'll be stuck here,' Ernie said eventually.

Jim shrugged. 'For as long as it takes to get everyone here.' He pulled his half of blanket around him and lay with his head resting on his backpack to watch the planes coming in. One landed and took off every three minutes by his reckoning, each plane being allowed twenty-four minutes on the ground to unload, turn around, refuel and take off again. It was certainly a tightly run, efficient operation, and it was amazing that the Japs hadn't caught wind of it.

As he watched them cruise overhead like shoals of glistening, ghostly fish, Jim was finally lulled to sleep by the sound of their droning – yet was subliminally alert for the sound of enemy aircraft engines.

It was close to dawn on the third day when the final plane had unloaded its cargo and taken off. The American air commando in charge climbed down from his makeshift control tower and was joined by two others as they went to inspect the abandoned RAF plane with the chunk hacked out of its tail.

Jim, who'd been stuck on guard duty since midnight, shifted a bit nearer to listen in to the conversation, and was startled to hear one of them speculate that it could probably still fly despite the damage. They talked it over for a bit and then one of them said that he was willing to give it a go.

Jim watched in admiration as the RAF plane climbed away in a wide turn to be followed by the American C-47. With a wry smile, he wondered how long it would take after landing at Hailakandi before the RAF insignia was replaced by the USAF star and diagonal white stripes proclaiming that she now belonged to no 1 air commando.

The shout of his commanding officer snapped him

from his thoughts and he raced back to hear the orders of the day. They had two weeks to make the 130-mile march to a rendezvous point, but before they could reach that, they had the mighty Irrawaddy to cross.

It was now bright daylight, the heat and humidity rising by the minute. They'd been marching in battle formation for about an hour, the flank scouts on their right following the path of the river, the forty heavily laden mules and their keepers keeping pace at the rear.

They were marching through a plantation of small teak trees interspersed with others that were also small, but unfamiliar. They were slender, giving no shade or cover, and some were gaunt, grey skeletons that had been girdled and killed for felling by the Burmese loggers. The terrain was mercifully flat, but covered with the huge, curled leaves of the recently fallen trees over a layer of the powdery compost left over the years. These fresher leaves crackled alarmingly beneath their heavy boots, and every man was alert to a possible ambush, for surely they could be heard for miles.

And then, at a signal, the long column came to an abrupt halt and hit the ground. They could now hear the drone of swiftly approaching aircraft and knew instantly they were not friendly. Carbines, machine guns and Brens were readied, sights aimed towards the sound.

'What stinking luck to be caught so early on,' breathed Jim into the leafy detritus as the huge column watched the nine Zeroes pass overhead at about 5,000 feet, the low sun shining on the red circle of Japan that was painted on the underside of their wings.

'They'll turn and come down at us out of the sun,' replied Ernie, clutching his Thompson sub-machine gun. 'But I'm ready for the bastards,' he snarled.

Jim did a rapid calculation in his head. Nine Zeroes equalled fifty-four machine guns – but they could shoot back, and with such skilled and battle-hardened men in their ranks, the odds were just about even if their luck held.

The Zeroes peeled off and dived out of sight. The distant roar of machine-gun fire was carried faintly to them through the jungle to be followed by the boom, crash and thud of exploding bombs.

Jim, Ernie and the rest of the column lay there on the leaf-strewn ground in great puzzlement as the onslaught in the distance continued for about five minutes – and then they realised what had happened, and began to chuckle in glee.

Gliders had brought in bulldozers to improve the airstrip for the mass fly-in. Some of these light aircraft had suffered the usual mishaps of missing their target, smashing themselves in the jungle or landing too heavily. They'd been abandoned, some clearly still laden with petrol cans for fuelling the bulldozers, and these were what the Japs had spotted rather than the column of men in the jungle, and were now proceeding to give these derelict wrecks hell.

Jim and the others rested on their elbows to watch pillars of oily black smoke rise to the east of the column's position, and the Zeroes – no doubt congratulating themselves on a successful mission – went back into formation and returned to base unaware of the watching men beneath them.

Jim and Ernie grinned at one another as they dusted themselves down, got back into line and resumed the march. They'd survived to fight another day, but for how much longer would their luck hold?

40

Cliffehaven

Peggy had just finished her long shift at the uniform factory, and was now steering the pushchair through the April twilight towards home. She listened to Daisy's happy prattling about her little friend Chloe and her day at the crèche, but her mind was really on Pauline, and the difficult conversation that could no longer be avoided if the harmony of Beach View was to be safeguarded.

Peggy had promised Frank she'd keep an eye on Pauline while he was away, but she hadn't reckoned on her moving into Beach View for the duration of his absence. It was proving very difficult to withstand her moody silences, the sudden fits of bad temper, the tears, and her habit of disappearing upstairs every night straight after tea and not coming down again until morning.

Things had come to a head the previous evening when she'd snapped at Ivy for not being sympathetic. This had led to Ivy telling her she was a miserable, moany old cow, and they were all fed up with her, before slamming out of the house. Rita had defended Ivy and followed her out, and then Cordelia had told Pauline rather sharply to pull herself together and stop enjoying her misery, which elicited tears from Pauline and her storming upstairs to her room. It couldn't go on, for Peggy hated discord, and she was determined to put things right, no matter how tricky it became.

The kitchen was warm and welcoming, the lovely smell of vegetable stew and dumplings making her mouth water in anticipation. Sarah was setting the table as Fran stirred the stew and checked on the potatoes, closely watched by Queenie from her shelf above the sink. Cordelia was berating Ron over the mess he'd left in his bedroom, while Rita and Ivy were giggling over some article in the *Picture Post*. Harvey lay snoozing at Pauline's feet as she smoked a cigarette and stared into space, unaware of his presence.

Peggy waited until tea was over and she'd settled Daisy for the night before going upstairs to find Pauline and have things out with her. Opening the door without bothering to knock, she wasn't surprised to find her curled on the bed, her face almost buried in the pillow as she wept.

Peggy tamped down on the surge of irritation, and went to sit beside her to take her hand. 'This has to stop, Pauline,' she said firmly. 'If you carry on, you'll make yourself ill, and that won't help anyone – least of all Frank and Brendon.'

Pauline sniffed, dabbed her eyes and slowly sat up. 'You don't understand the torturous worry I'm going through,' she said mournfully. 'Frank wrote to say he and Brendon are in the same place, but he didn't say where, or what they were involved in – and I just know they're in danger.'

'You don't know anything of the sort,' said Peggy briskly. 'At least they're together, and as Frank is a volunteer over a certain age, they'll still be in England – not out in Burma fighting the Japs, like my Jim.' Her tone sharpened. 'And don't you *dare* suggest that I don't know what worry is, Pauline. I live with it day in and day out.'

'You haven't lost two sons,' she said, mopping her eyes.

'And I thank God for that every day – but that is not the issue here. You've got to stop looking back, Pauline, and consider how your behaviour is affecting the son and husband who are still alive.'

Pauline stared at her accusingly through tear-filled eyes. 'They love me and understand my awful suffering, which is more than you do.'

'I tell you what, Pauline,' Peggy said evenly, 'if you weren't so wrapped up in your misery, you just might see the damage you're actually doing to them.' She grasped her hands again. 'It's got to the stage where Brendon is almost afraid to come home in case you get upset and make him feel even guiltier at having survived when his brothers didn't. Can you even begin to imagine what that must feel like?'

Pauline's eyes widened in shock.

'And poor Frank has had to shoulder his grief alone because you turned your back on him and refused to let him reach out to you. Now he's doing his best for his country, and instead of making him feel guilty, you should be telling him how proud you are.'

Pauline remained silent, her gaze sliding away.

Peggy quelled her rising anger and steadied her

tone. 'You know I'm speaking the truth, Pauline, so pull yourself together, and face the fact that there's a war on. Men leave, and the future is uncertain for all of us; but while those men are fighting for our freedom we women have a duty to find the strength to hold things together until it's won. If we don't, then we dishonour the sacrifices made by your sons and all the others who gave their lives.'

Pauline dipped her chin. 'Mum said something like that in her last letter,' she muttered. 'But what does she know? She doesn't stick around long enough to find out how I'm really feeling.'

'Now you're just being childish,' snapped Peggy. 'Dolly would be here in an instant if she thought she was really needed, but she knows you're surrounded by people who care about you. But I warn you, Pauline, there's only so much sympathy to go round when they have their own worries, and if you don't buck up, you'll find yourself very much alone – and I don't think that's what you want at all.'

She regarded the bowed head and the fingers pulling at the sodden handkerchief, and felt a stab of guilt for being so harsh. But if she was to get the message through to Pauline, this was not the time for sympathy and soft words – but a hefty dose of reality.

'Carol isn't wringing her hands and feeling sorry for herself,' she continued. 'She might have lost her husband and baby, and been evicted from her home, but she's knuckled down to doing her bit on that farm without complaining. Yes, it's tough, and life can be cruel, but if we want to see an end to this bloody war, then that's what we all have to do. Weeping and wailing and being miserable cuts no ice with any of us – and frankly we've all had enough of it.'

Pauline swung her legs off the bed. 'If that's how you feel, then I'll go,' she snapped. 'Ivy and the others have made it very plain that I'm not welcome here.'

Peggy grabbed her shoulders and gave her a shake. 'Wake up, Pauline, and ask yourself why they feel that way,' she said crossly. 'You do nothing but moan and feel sorry for yourself – it's no wonder Ivy snapped at you last night. You need to sort yourself out. All this misery isn't healthy and it's starting to affect everyone.'

Pauline burst into tears and collapsed into Peggy's arms. 'I didn't realise Brendon felt that way,' she sobbed. 'Or that I'd shut Frank out when he most needed me.' She took a trembling breath. 'Oh, Peggy, how could I not have seen – what have I done?'

Peggy held her close and tenderly stroked her hair, the anger swept away. 'You were simply lost in your grief, holding it so tightly inside you that it made you blind to everything else,' she said quietly. 'But now you know, you can put things right between you – and that will, in turn, make you feel very much better.'

Pauline eased away from the embrace, her reddened eyes full of hope. 'Do you believe that, Peggy? It's not too late for them to forgive me?'

'It's never too late for forgiveness, Pauline, especially between people who love one another.'

She reddened and dipped her chin again. 'I've behaved very badly, haven't I? It's no wonder everyone here wants to see the back of me.'

'It has been difficult,' said Peggy evenly, 'but I'm sure that once you show them you're doing your best to make amends, they'll come round. They're good people, Pauline, and always willing to open their hearts. They know what you've been through, and understand how hard that must have been for you – but Sarah's separated from her family and worried sick about her fiancé and father; Rita's terrified for Matthew; Ivy barely survived the bomb at the armament factory and is still having nightmares; and Fran has to witness the most awful things at the hospital. Poor Cordelia puts up a brave front, but I know she feels deeply for all of them, and is saddened by the way this blessed war has stripped them of the joys of their youth. So you see, you're not alone, Pauline. We all have our sorrows.'

Pauline dried her eyes and straightened her shoulders. 'Thanks for making me see how things really are. I know it couldn't have been easy for you, but it's what I needed.' She gave a wan smile. 'I'll write to Frank and Brendon tonight, and after my shift with the WVS tomorrow, I think I'll go home and start on the spring cleaning. Frank will appreciate having a nice fresh home to come back to.'

'You don't have to go,' said Peggy.

'I know, but it's time to stand on my own two feet and get on with all the things I've let slide.' She gave Peggy a hug. 'I'm so glad I have you, Peggy.'

Peggy returned the hug. 'I'll always be here if you need someone to talk to.' She pulled gently back from the embrace and smiled. 'Let's go downstairs and listen to *ITMA* on the wireless, while I make us all a nice cup of tea.'

Pauline looked hesitant, and Peggy pulled her to her feet. 'The first step is always the hardest, but I'm with you all the way. Come on, love. They won't bite.'

It was a week later and Peggy was near the end of her shift at Goldman's. She finished sewing the bell-bottom trousers, cut the thread and added them to the neat pile next to her machine. She hadn't had a cigarette since her lunch break, for there were strict rules about not smoking on the factory floor, and she felt the need for one now, along with a reviving cuppa.

She nodded and smiled at the girl who came to fetch the finished garments, then stretched her back and eased her stiff shoulders before gathering up her coat and bag and heading over to where her friend Gracie Armitage was in charge of the cutting tables.

Gracie was a decade younger than Peggy, but the moment they'd met on the promenade they'd become friends, for their little girls were about the same age, Gracie's husband was in the RAF and the two women shared the burden of worry over their men and the struggle to make ends meet in these austere times of rationing and uncertainty.

'Shall we grab a cuppa in the canteen before we fetch the girls from the nursery?' Peggy suggested.

Gracie set aside her lethally sharp shears and took off her overall and headscarf. 'That sounds like a very good idea. With all this lint floating about, my mouth's as dry as a desert.'

The canteen was busy during shift changes, and the many voices echoed in the large, featureless annexe with its concrete floor, tin roof, bare walls and metal furniture. They fetched their tea from the counter and found a table in a corner where they could catch up after not seeing one another for a week.

'I'm glad the night shifts are over,' said Gracie once they'd both lit cigarettes. 'It's almost impossible to sleep during the day, especially with Chloe being at her liveliest. I've told Solly I won't do it again – though I'll certainly miss the extra money.'

Peggy thought it was a bit of a liberty of Solly to have asked her to come in on the night shifts when he knew she was in sole charge of a lively three-year-old who could not be left in the factory crèche for twenty-four hours a day over a whole week. But an emergency order had come in from the army, Gracie's deputy had refused point-blank to change her duty roster, and as Gracie was the senior cutter, she'd had little choice. Peggy had felt very guilty at not being able to help with Chloe, but as her own shifts were during the day, it had simply not been possible.

'Did you see them all taking off from Cliffe early this morning?' she asked, after she'd commiserated with Gracie.

'I certainly heard them. The racket they were making was enough to wake the dead, and Chloe was in a thoroughly bad mood during breakfast. I dread to think how she's been with Nanny Pringle.'

Peggy chuckled. 'Nanny Pringle is quite capable of dealing with tantrums, so I wouldn't worry.'

She eagerly returned to the spectacular events of that early morning. 'It was a tremendous show, bigger than ever,' she said, 'and made me feel so proud that I thought my heart would burst out of my chest.' She smiled at her own foolishness. 'The others came out to watch on the front doorstep and thought I'd lost my marbles, because I was jumping up and down and waving fit to beat the band. But they were a magnificent sight, Gracie, and I just couldn't help it.'

'I know, and I agree, it does make you burst with pride when they fly over in such huge numbers. But I always wonder if Clive is up there with them, and that sort of takes the shine off it.'

'Have you heard from him lately?' Peggy asked, at once concerned.

Gracie nodded. 'I got a letter yesterday, but it sounds as if he's exhausted, poor lamb. This endless bombing campaign and lack of leave is taking its toll on all of them.'

Peggy swallowed a sigh. 'I know. Martin's at the end of his tether, as are Freddy, Roger and Rita's young Matthew. Cissy's already had a scare over her Randolph, who's now a POW, and Rita, Kitty and Charlotte are trying to put a brave face on things. But it's a terrible worry with so many of them not coming back from these raids.'

'That's not something I can bear to think about,' said Gracie. 'If I did, I'd go quite mad with worry.' She sipped her tea, and then changed the subject. 'Did the dreadful Doris get her travel pass?'

Peggy clenched her teeth. 'Yes, she damned well

did. How, I have no idea, but I suspect a bribe was involved – that councillor's known for being bent, and when I bumped into him the other day I let him know what I thought of him. It's so unfair when Anne and the children were refused permission to travel home. It would have bucked up Martin's spirits no end to have her here.'

Gracie gave a little shrug. 'No doubt it would, but I got the feeling Anne was being pressured into it from what you've told me, and that doesn't make for a happy homecoming.'

'I agree,' said Peggy, 'and although she was only trying to do the right thing by Martin, I'm actually relieved she had no choice but to stay where she is. She's safer there now Jerry's bombing us again – and if this invasion into France ever comes off, it will probably get worse.'

They chattered some more about Anne, Gracie's father and brothers who were all serving in one force or another, and the worry this brought her poor mother, who'd thrown herself into charity work to keep her mind busy on other things. 'We all have to find our own way of coping, I suppose,' said Gracie. 'By the way, how are you getting on with Pauline? Is she still as miserable as a wet weekend?'

Peggy grimaced. 'Her moods were affecting everyone, and there was enough tension in the house without her adding to it – so I had a stiff word with her last week.' She gave a little sigh. 'I was a bit harsh with her, to be honest, but she needed telling a few home truths – which of course she didn't like – but it seems to have done the trick. She's making a real effort to muck in when she stays overnight, and has begun to spring-clean her house in preparation for Frank's return. I didn't like reading her the riot act, but sometimes it's the only way to get through to someone.'

Gracie's hazel eyes warmed with affection. 'I can't imagine you getting cross, Peggy. You always seem so calm and gentle.'

Peggy grinned. 'Appearances can be deceptive, Gracie. You should see me when Doris winds me up.' She looked at her watch. 'I'd better get home. Daisy will be tired and Fran is cooking tea again tonight, so I mustn't be late.'

They picked up their little girls from the crèche, said goodnight with a swift hug, and went their separate ways – Gracie to her small flat behind the recreation ground, and Peggy to the peace and harmony that had been restored at Beach View.

41

Devon

Carol hadn't seen Felix, Brendon or Frank since Churchill's visit, and Herbert had only managed to get to the Welcome Inn for a couple of hours at the weekend to see Ida and return Carol's precious photograph before he'd had to return to duty. There had been no backlash over the stolen binoculars, so they'd decided to keep them until the rehearsals came to an end and then sneak them back somehow.

It had been easy to see that the rehearsals were accelerating towards something very big, which looked as if it was imminent by all the activity that had been going on along the bay, and over the past week it had become a regular thing to trek up to the top of the hill once all their early chores were done. This Friday morning was no exception.

Carol stayed with Betty as the others went on ahead with Nipper, for although the plaster casts had been removed ten days before, Betty's leg muscles were still quite weak, and this was the first time she'd attempted the steep climb.

'Are you sure you don't want some help?' Carol asked anxiously.

'I'm fine, really,' Betty panted, pausing to lean on her walking stick and catch her breath. 'Please don't fuss, Carol. I need to do this on my own.'

'I'm just worried you're doing too much. The nurse said—'

'I know what she said,' Betty broke in, 'but she doesn't have a classful of children and a harassed headmistress waiting for her. The new term's starting in four days' time and I have to be fit and ready for it if I want to keep my job.'

Carol walked alongside her as she struggled to go the last few yards. She admired her tenacity, but there were times when Betty could be too stubborn for her own good, and she only had to stumble or fall and she'd back in the wheelchair again.

'There,' said Betty triumphantly some minutes later. 'I told you I could do it.'

Nipper yapped and ran round her excitedly as the girls enthusiastically applauded. They helped her to lie down on the blanket they'd brought, and once she was settled, they turned eagerly back to the view along the bay where the morning's rehearsal was in full swing.

There were six extra LSTs and more Motor Gun Boats and Motor Torpedo Boats involved now, while the two Royal Navy destroyers and the corvette kept watch out at sea. There was a lot going on down there, with mines being laid on different sections of the beach, including a wide arc to the side of the evacuated Royal Sands Hotel, and a high barrier of barbed wire closing off and protecting Torcross village.

LSTs were coming ashore at Blackpool Cove to off-load fuel, supplies and heavy equipment, and the engineers were refining and improving the speed with which they could build the pontoon bridge over the Ley to the fields beneath Slapton village. Ships sailed in from Dartmouth, Salcombe and Portland Bill loaded with men and machinery as the artillery divisions secured the beachhead which was under fire from the batteries of guns in the hills and on the cliffs at Torpoint.

The five girls lay on their stomachs and watched it all through the binoculars until Jack appeared, looking very much out of sorts. 'You'm got work to do,' he grumbled. 'There be no time to be watching Yank shenanigans.'

'Just a few minutes more,' pleaded Betty. 'I've taken ages to get up here, and look, something different is happening down there today.'

Jack shielded his eyes from the low sun and peered down to the bay where the LSTs were loading the machinery back up again, and scores of GIs were being driven away in trucks. 'They'm be pulling out,' he muttered.

'It certainly looks like it,' said Carol. 'Do you think all the rehearsing is over and that this is the start of the actual invasion, Jack?'

He shrugged. 'Maybe,' he said grudgingly, watching the LSTs, MTBs and MGBs load up with men and machinery and pull away to head round Torpoint.

They all turned and watched them until they'd gone out of sight around Start Point.

'There are more trucks and jeeps leaving the camps down there,' said Ida, 'and they've taken down most of the flags too.' She grinned at Maisie and gave her a nudge. 'I reckon we'll have front row seats up 'ere for the invasion if we can get the cows milked before it's light. What you say, Jack?'

'I reckon it'll be quite a show if it really is an invasion,' Jack agreed. 'I'll get the missus to pack up breakfast so we don't miss nothing.'

As the last ship disappeared from view and the beach became deserted, the girls went down the hill, chattering with excitement over what they might see tomorrow – and how lucky they were to have an unobstructed view of the entire bay.

Felix had been invited to sit in on the meeting of the officers commanding the various battalions taking part in the week of increasingly larger rehearsals which would culminate over the next two days into a full-scale operation. He stood to return their salutes, and when the door closed behind them, he paced the room, his thoughts focused on the schedule that was about to unfold.

Operation Tiger involved 30,000 men, and the past six days had been spent marshalling troops and practising embarkation onto the landing craft. These landing craft were timed to leave port at different times and would begin deploying men from the 4th and 29th Infantry, 82nd Airborne, and 188th Field Artillery with their equipment through a mine-swept channel onto Slapton Sands. The first assault wave was due on the beach at 7:30 the following morning. The live barrage from the navy, and the men posing as enemy defenders on shore, would begin fifty minutes earlier while they were still at sea.

At midnight on the same day, a follow-up convoy of Landing Ships, Tanks would leave Dartmouth and Plymouth to assemble off Start Point. It would be escorted by the Royal Navy ships, HMS *Azalea* and *Scimitar*, while the lumbering HMS *Saladin* would remain in port unless there was an emergency. The LSTs would carry engineers, combat truck support, signalmen, medics and more infantry, as well as amphibious trucks, jeeps and heavy engineering equipment, fuel, ammunition and medical supplies – all to be landed from dawn in Blackpool Cove at the eastern end of the bay.

Convoy T4 would consist of eight LSTs, one of which would be towing the two pontoon causeways to bridge the Ley. They would proceed in a straight line at six knots with 700 yards' interval between ships, and manoeuvre in a wide loop off Lyme Bay for the same amount of time it would take them to cross the Channel to France before deploying to shore. This was to get the men used to being below decks during a long sea voyage.

The bulk of Operation Tiger's protection was many miles south of Lyme Bay, and had been in place throughout the rehearsals to safeguard against enemy attack and the reported presence of E-boats patrolling near Cherbourg. It consisted of the cruiser, USS *Augusta*, the new O-class destroyers, HMS *Onslow* and *Obedient*, as well as the Tribal-class destroyer, HMS *Ashanti*, with a covering force of Motor Torpedo Boats and two more LSTs. Radio communication from these ships to shore HQ would be maintained throughout.

Everything was timed to ensure a cohesive, smooth operation, but Felix and the other officers had repeatedly gone over the plans looking for flaws. They'd finally come to the conclusion that nothing could be guaranteed – especially during a wartime amphibious landing which had historically always proved difficult, if not impossible – but if the manure hit the fan, the troops and their naval escorts were hopefully experienced enough now to handle it.

Felix stared out of the window at the camps, which were virtually deserted now that most of the men had been sent to their action stations. The commanders wanted authenticity, and the exercise under sustained fire would certainly give the troops a real sense of what they might expect on the other side of the Channel, for up to now, the shooting had been sporadic and light, using dummy bullets.

He reached for the notes he'd made during the meeting, and found the list of the ten officers who had the highest level of security and an in-depth knowledge of Operation Overlord's invasion plans. Committing their names and where they would be during the exercise to memory, he tore the notes into shreds, dropped them in an ashtray and set fire to them.

He waited until they were ash, and then glanced at his watch. It was almost seven o'clock, giving him plenty of time to get some chow and a good few hours of sleep before he drove up to the hills above Blackpool Bay to watch the operation in the comfort of his staff car.

He strode out of the building and headed for Herbert Cornwallis, who was standing by the jeep, gazing out to the calm bay where the dying sun dazzled points of light on the water that gently rolled onto the sand and gravel of the beach.

'It looks peaceful, doesn't it, sir?' he said, watching the gulls drift overhead.

'It'll be a different story tomorrow morning, Herby,' Felix replied, climbing into the jeep. 'So you'd better find some earplugs.' He settled into the seat, wrapping his greatcoat about him against the chill. 'Do you have any messages for me?'

'None, sir. Were you expecting something?'

Felix shook his head and hid his puzzlement. 'Get me back to the billet, son. I've a feeling it's going to be a very long, cold night.'

As the young military policeman drove past the numerous deserted camps and headed for the old manor house, Felix thought about the day to come with mixed emotions. Everything was set for a successful rehearsal, but no matter how thorough the plans were, things could still go wrong – and he could only pray that the harsh lessons of what had happened to the Canadian troops at Dieppe had been learnt.

Determined not to dwell on things he really had no control over, he switched his thoughts to Dolly. He'd heard nothing from her since that confrontation, and Carol hadn't come up to the camp, so he had no idea whether Dolly had spoken to her or not. He didn't even know if Dolly was still at the King George, for he'd been too occupied here to go and find out. If she'd broken her promise to talk to Carol then it would be up to him to break the news, and that really wasn't something he was looking forward to. Having to face a tearful, bewildered young woman with such a stark truth would be far more difficult than anything else he'd done, and he was furious to think that Dolly might have walked away and left him to clear up her mess.

The narrow, winding lanes were empty now of the heavy machinery which had scarred or demolished the flint walls and left deep tracks in the once pristine fields. Eventually the jeep slithered to a halt outside the front door of the manor, and Felix climbed out. 'I don't need you or the jeep again tonight, Herby, so take the evening off until you have to report to your post.'

'Thank you, sir. I would like to see my girl before the show tomorrow. Is there any message I can give Mrs Porter?'

'Just send my regards and tell her I'll see her when I can – and Herby, tomorrow's exercise is *not* to be discussed with civilians, is that clear?'

'My lips are sealed, sir.'

Felix made no comment, for he knew very well that Herbert had provided Carol and the others with those binoculars he'd seen glinting from the top of the hill. 'It's probably too late for secrecy, anyway,' he conceded. 'The civilians seem to know as much as we do, and have no doubt guessed that something big is in the air now the camps are empty.'

Felix regarded the younger man with some affection, for he reminded him a little of his son at that age, and he'd proven to be likeable, sharp-thinking and dependable. 'Tomorrow's a big day for all of us, son. Where will you be posted? In one of the foxholes?'

'No, thank goodness – I find them claustrophobic. I shall be down at the Royal Sands Hotel to give covering overhead fire.'

Felix nodded and smiled. 'You should be safe enough there. Just don't stand on any of those darned mines.'

'The field's well marked, sir. The hotel itself is clear.'

'Good luck, Herby. I'll see you after the show.' He returned the younger man's salute and went indoors to see what the cook had prepared for the evening meal.

Coombe Farm

Carol and the others were about to prepare for an early night, in the expectation of rising well before dawn to finish the milking. It was exciting to think that they would be at the forefront of an historic occasion that might finally bring this war to an end, and they doubted they'd be able to get to sleep at all.

The sound of a jeep pulling up outside the barn had Ida racing for the door, and as Herbert came in, she threw herself into his arms. Carol and the others exchanged amused and slightly embarrassed glances as the pair went into a clinch, and Nipper sat whining at their feet in puzzlement.

Ida finally withdrew from the embrace. 'It ain't that I'm not pleased to see yer,' she said breathlessly, 'but ain't you supposed to be somewhere else like all the rest?'

'I've only got three hours before I have to be back at my post, so I thought we might go for a bit of a drive into Kingsbridge.'

'I'll get me coat.' She hurried to pull on another sweater over her trousers, jam her feet into boots and drag on coat, hat and scarf.

'The general said he'd visit as soon as he can,' Herbert told Carol. 'He's a bit busy, as you may have noticed.'

'It's all very thrilling, isn't it?' Carol said delightedly. 'Just think, Herbert, this could really be the beginning of the end, and you'll be playing a part in it.'

Herbert was about to reply when Ida grabbed his arm. 'There,' she breathed. 'All ready for that draughty old jeep.'

He put his arm round her waist and smiled. 'You've got me to keep you warm,' he murmured against her cheek. 'Come on, let's get out of here.'

The door slammed behind them and the girls looked at one another and broke into giggles. 'I reckon none of us will sleep tonight, so why don't we go to the pub?' said Maisie.

Agreeing this was a very good idea, there was a bustle as they prepared for the chill weather outside. Once Carol had fastened the leash to Nipper's collar, they set off with Betty arm in arm between them, a shielded torch lighting the way to prevent her from falling down a rabbit scraping or tripping over a tree root.

The pub was unusually quiet, with just a few

farmhands and land girls sitting in desultory knots about the room. 'Blimey,' muttered Pru with a grimace. 'It's like it were before the Yanks turned up.'

'We're certainly going to miss them when they do leave,' said Carol, shrugging off her coat. 'I've just got enough to get a round in. Cider as usual?'

Having tied Nipper's leash to the leg of a chair, she nodded greetings to everyone and headed for the bar to order the drinks. 'It's quiet in here tonight, Mrs Claxton.'

'Aye, that it is. You mark my words, Carol, there's something afoot. I can feel it in me water.' She poured the cider into glasses and put them on a tray. 'But it's good to see Betty up and about again. I've missed having her about the place.'

'I think she's planning on coming back to you before the start of term, if that's all right, Mrs Claxton. You do still have her room free, don't you?'

The older woman nodded. 'She's already said she would, and she knows she's always welcome here.'

42

Mill Bay, Devon

Frank wiped his hands on the oily cloth and walked back into the Nissen hut workshop to sign off the repairs he'd done to the LST. There was definitely something in the air, for the slipway and bay were rapidly being cleared of serviceable craft and there was a buzz of excitement around the place. He knew from gossip that the rehearsals had been going on in Lyme Bay for some time, but there had been more urgency recently in getting the landing ships seaworthy, and the rumours were growing by the minute that tonight might actually see the start of the long-awaited invasion into France.

He went back outside to rid himself, not only of the smell and taste of petrol and oil fumes, but of the sense of unease that had been plaguing him all day. He couldn't put a finger on what bothered him, and nothing had presented itself to give him any sign that his misgivings were based in reality, yet the feeling persisted.

He stood by the slipway where the larger boats were being taken out of the water on a huge wheeled trestle and guided up on a steel rail so they could be worked on by the small army of volunteer engineers like himself. The sergeant in charge was already ordering the men to get the LST back in the water, and as Frank watched, the American boat slid down, and within minutes the crew had her out into the bay and heading down the estuary to the sea. She'd be going to either Dartmouth or Plymouth to be loaded with small-track tanks, men and supplies, just as they'd all been doing over the past week.

He lit a cigarette and regarded the crescent bay where a few houses clung to the side of the wooded hill. It possessed little of the drama of Cliffehaven's white cliffs and jagged headlands, but had its own, softer beauty in the sandy beaches and hidden coves to be found beyond the headland where the estuary opened out. The light was different too, putting everything into sharp focus, enhancing the verdant green of the surrounding hills and the blue of the water, and now, as the sun slowly sank, it diffused everything in a golden, hazy glow. The sight eased his troubled thoughts and he gave a small sigh of pleasure.

'Idling on the job, Da?'

Frank smiled in delight and gave his son a hug. 'Where did you spring from?'

'I've got three hours before I have to be back in Brixham, so I thought I'd come and see what you've been up to.' Brendon gazed out to the water where a group of smaller landing craft were assembling. 'It's a lovely place, isn't it? Shame there's a war on to spoil the serenity.'

'I'd like to bring your mother here for a proper summer holiday once it's all over,' said Frank.

'She'd like that,' said Brendon softly. 'And I'm glad she's feeling so much better about things. I have to admit her letter made me quite tearful, but knowing she understands what we've both been through has helped no end.'

Frank nodded. 'I agree, and we can thank Peggy for making her see. It couldn't have been easy for her.' He turned to look at his son, his expression solemn as the unnamed dread came once more to the surface. 'Is tonight the start of the big one, Brendon? Will you be off to France?'

'As far as I know it's only a full dress rehearsal. Those in charge tell us very little, even the general, but I suspect we'll be warned beforehand if it is to be the real thing.'

Frank breathed more easily. 'I don't suppose you could wangle me a place on board with you?'

Brendon shook his head. 'Sorry, Da. Naval personnel only from now on. I was pushing my luck by asking my commander's permission last time.' His dark blue eyes sparkled. 'But if you want to see what we're up to, I might be able to sort something out. It would mean getting you a pass or transfer somehow, which might be tricky, but I'm sure I can think up a good excuse.'

Frank perked up. 'Aye, I'd like that, as long as it doesn't make trouble for you.'

Brendon grinned. 'Get your things together while I speak to the sergeant. I borrowed a sporty little car, so it won't take long to get there, and we can talk on the way.'

Frank watched his son stride off, so tall and straight and full of life that his heart ached with love and pride – and a sudden overwhelming fear. He shook it off determinedly and went to collect his bag. He didn't believe in omens; the talk of invasion had merely spooked him. It was just a rehearsal. Nothing would go wrong, and when it was all over he'd tell Brendon how close he'd come to thinking he could see into the future – and they'd have a good laugh about it.

Carol and the other girls were just finishing their last round of drinks when the heavy curtain over the door was swept aside to let in a blast of cold air, swiftly followed by Brendon and Frank.

Brendon rushed to Betty, while Carol leapt to her feet and flew into Frank's arms. 'It's so lovely to see you,' she breathed, disentangling herself from Frank's bear hug. 'But what are you both doing here?'

He quickly explained Brendon's plan for him to watch the exercise from Coombe Farm's top field. 'To be sure I don't know how he managed it,' he said, his gaze full of pride as he watched his son talking to the landlady, 'but I've got a forty-eight-hour transfer to Brixham – only Brixham aren't actually aware of it.'

'But where will you stay? It's too late to disturb Jack and Millicent, and you can't possibly share our billet.'

'It's all arranged,' said a beaming Brendon. 'He's staying here.' He clamped his arm around a glowing Betty. 'I think this calls for a drink, don't you? Just the one, mind. I have to report for duty in an hour.'

43

The George Inn

Dolly had suffered a week of absolute hell, tormented by her thoughts and trying to work out a way of telling her daughter about Felix without causing her too much pain. She'd gone for long walks, sat in cafés drinking cups of tea she didn't want, and had even driven out towards Beeson twice, determined to get it over with, but losing her nerve at the last minute.

She'd thought about booking a room at the Welcome Inn in the hope it might make her focus more clearly on what she had to do, but for the first time in her life, she'd chickened out. 'Come on, Dolly,' she muttered. 'Do buck up and phone the wretched woman before you lose your nerve again.'

Finishing her glass of sherry, she went downstairs to use the public telephone that was in an ornately decorated wooden booth by the reception desk. Dialling the number, she put a coin in the slot and waited with her finger hovering over button A for when it was answered.

'I'm sorry, caller, but that number is temporarily out of order. Please try later,' said the girl at the other end.

'But this is an emergency,' protested Dolly.

'Everything's an emergency these days.' She disconnected the call.

Dolly angrily replaced the receiver, reclaimed her coin and then changed her mind. Dialling Hugh's private line, she tapped her fingernails on the metal box in impatience.

'Has the Nightingale been heard?' she asked before he'd finished saying hello.

'She sang from a different tree. All is well, and she has a new nest.'

The relief was enormous. 'Oh, thank God,' she breathed. 'Do you know where?'

'I really couldn't say,' he replied carefully. 'Are things resolved your end?'

'Not quite.'

'Then get on with it, Dolly. You're needed here.' He disconnected the call.

Dolly ground her teeth, furious to be cut off for the second time – and doubly furious that Hugh was ordering her about like a schoolgirl. She took a deep breath, then realised that of course he was cross with her – everyone seemed to be at the moment – and it was time to stop dithering and get on with doing what she'd come for.

She went to the reception desk. 'I shall be leaving tomorrow morning,' she said to the elderly man in charge. 'Please make up my bill and send it to my room.'

'Your bill is already covered, Mrs Cardew,' he replied rather snootily. 'A gentleman from London telephoned before your arrival.'

She saw the look in his eye and the curl of his lip, but

didn't put him straight. She had quite enough to contend with without dirty-minded hotel workers. Going up the stairs, she started to pack her small bag, her thoughts on Carol and how on earth she was going to admit that she'd lied to her all her life. She could only hope Carol would forgive her, and that because she'd obviously come to trust Felix enough to talk about her private life, she would accept him as her father. But whichever way she looked at it, it was a mess, and if she didn't tell her soon, Felix would – and that was the last thing she wanted. It was her mess, so it was up to her to sort it out before it became a total disaster.

Coombe Farm

The milking and morning chores had been completed in record time despite their late night, and the girls hurried into the kitchen to help carry chairs, blankets and baskets of food up the hill. Carol had warned Millicent that Frank would be coming, and so she'd added more bread, cheese and small vegetable pasties to the basket.

Emerging from the farmhouse, they saw the giant figure of Frank striding towards them, and Carol waited for him as the others waved and began the steep climb. He took the heavy basket from her, patted an over-excited Nipper and they set off in the wake of the others.

'Did Brendon give you any hints of what we might see today?' asked Carol.

'It's just another rehearsal,' he replied. Seeing her crestfallen expression he smiled. 'But it's going to be big, with everything thrown at it, so it should be quite a show.'

'Hey! Hold on a minute! Wait for me!'

They turned in shock to see a rather dishevelled Dolly attempting to follow them up the uneven ground in her high heels. 'What on earth are you doing here, Mum?' called Carol.

'I'll tell you later,' she called back, struggling to keep her balance.

'Take those shoes off, woman,' roared Frank through his laughter. 'The cows won't mind.'

Dolly glared at him, then eyed the curious cows which were slowly advancing on her, took off her shoes and ran. She was out of breath by the time she'd reached them, and they were both startled by her untidy hair, gaunt face and the dark shadows under her eyes.

'Are you all right, Mum?' gasped Carol, still unable to get over seeing her so unexpectedly. 'You look as if you haven't slept for a week.'

'It's a long story,' she panted with a grim expression. 'I'll tell you later.'

'Come on then. We don't want to miss anything,' said Frank. 'Would you be wanting a hand there, Dolly?' he teased. 'You seem a bit out of condition.'

'That's enough cheek from you, Frank Reilly,' she retorted, swiping away his hand before setting off again. 'What are you doing here, anyway? And why are we climbing this blasted, impossible hill in the middle of the night?'

'It's seven o'clock, Mum; hardly the middle of the night,' protested Carol, who'd been up before four. 'And we're going up here to watch the big rehearsal down in the bay.'

'Whatever for?'

'Brendon will be taking part at some point, and Ida's young chap, Herby, will be too. As we've been watching the build-up to it over the past week, we didn't want to miss the finale.'

They finished the climb in silence, and once Frank had been introduced to Jack, Millicent and Ida, they set up the chairs, wrapped themselves in the rugs and opened the picnic basket.

'What be happen to you'm?' asked a wide-eyed Millicent, eyeing Dolly askance from head to foot. 'Looks like you'm been through a hedge backwards.'

Dolly took a restorative breath and let it out on a sigh. 'My friend lent me a car, and unfortunately, it wasn't all that reliable on steep hills. It got slower and slower, and almost stalled when I tried to change it down to a lower gear, so I stopped and pulled on the handbrake.' She gave the ghost of a smile. 'It didn't hold and the damned car rolled backwards, straight into a hedge, the rear wheels stuck in a ditch. Hence my appearance,' she said with a flourish. 'I spent ages trying to push it out, and in the end a very nice chap stopped and helped, otherwise I'd still be there.'

'Honestly, Mum, you're not safe to be on the road.'

'It wasn't my fault this time,' she said stoutly. 'Though what my friend will say when he sees the state of the car, I don't know. As for the state I'm in . . .'

She regarded her reflection in her compact mirror and gave a theatrical shudder.

Carol realised she was playing to her audience, but could tell that something was worrying her other than the damage to the car. She watched her repair her make-up and tidy her hair, curious as to what had brought her here. 'You clearly didn't come down to watch the rehearsals, Mum, so why are you here – and more to the point, how did you get around the civilian travel ban?'

Dolly was clearly in a better mood now she'd fixed her make-up, for she smiled brightly and patted Carol's cheek. 'I wanted to make sure you were all right, darling. As to the ban, I have a friend who sees to inconvenient little things like that.' She brought the subject to a halt by turning to Frank. 'What time is the fun supposed to begin?'

'Brendon didn't say, but I got the impression it could be quite soon,' said Frank.

Dolly lit a cigarette, regarded the binoculars everyone had slung round their necks and scrabbled in her large handbag. 'Oh, good, I didn't forget them,' she said, drawing out a velvet bag which contained a pair of dainty opera glasses.

Carol burst out laughing and gave her a hug as the other girls giggled, Jack smirked, and Millicent looked po-faced. 'You are utterly priceless, and as daft as a brush, but I do love you, Mum.'

Dolly hugged her back and frowned. 'I love you too, darling, but I don't see what's so funny,' she said in bewilderment. 'All my friends carry them because they're so useful.'

There was really no answer to that, so they swallowed their giggles and concentrated their binoculars on the sweep of the bay, and the line of ships just visible on the far horizon.

44

Above Blackpool Cove

Felix had slept surprisingly well considering all the things that were on his mind. He'd eaten a hearty breakfast, and driven out to the hills above the cove just after dawn to discover that five other senior non-combatant retired officers were there to oversee the operation. He'd have preferred to monitor the events alone, but he parked the car neatly in line with the others and got out to exchange salutes and pleasantries before taking a bit of a walk to stretch his legs and get some fresh air.

The entire beachhead had been transformed over the last week, with defences built up by the engineers, rolls of barbed wire, gun emplacements and dummy pillboxes to emulate what the men would find on Utah beach. The few barrage balloons above the exercise area floated high from their anchoring cables and moved gently in the light breeze like benign silver whales. It looked as if the weather would hold, for the sky was quite clear, and the sea was calm. However, he knew how swiftly things could change down here, and he'd been fooled before by a sudden squall of wind and blinding rain that had churned up the seas.

He checked his watch. There was just over half an hour to go before the barrage was due to begin, and some time after that he'd get sight of the first wave of landing craft coming around Start Point.

Raising his powerful binoculars to check that the artillery men were properly deployed on shore and in the gun emplacements above Torcross village, he slowly panned across the line of pillboxes to the high barbed-wire fencing that was supposed to protect the village from the naval bombardment and deter landings – and then up to the clifftop guns.

Satisfied, he then turned his attention to the Royal Sands Hotel, which had already been badly damaged by shellfire during the recent rehearsals, and actually managed to pick out the knot of armed military police-men passing the time of day with men from the Royal Engineers. He continued to scan the Ley, the foxholes and new fortifications in the hills where men playing the part of the enemy defenders were waiting by their guns for the signal to open fire.

He gave a sigh of relief. It was a good start, for it looked as if everyone was where they should be. 'And long may it last,' he muttered, turning his attention out to sea where the naval destroyers had drawn closer to shore in preparation for the bombardment.

Then, unable to resist the temptation, he raised the glasses to the hill above Coombe Farm and adjusted the sights. There was quite a gathering up there, and he gave a wry smile as he slowly panned along the line of rather blurred figures, for they really shouldn't have been there. He recognised the five girls and Brendon's father; assumed the older couple were the farmer and his wife, and then froze as the unmistakable figure of Dolly came into view.

He looked away, trying to dismiss all thoughts on whether Dolly had spoken to Carol, and what her reaction might have been. He would no doubt find out soon enough – for right now he had far more important things to occupy him, and he needed to concentrate.

As the time approached for the naval bombardment he was joined by the others, who stood rigidly to attention, their field glasses scanning the bay and the destroyers lying at anchor close by.

'I say, old chap, what time do you make it?' asked a whiskery old British colonel. 'Shouldn't the barrage have started by now?'

Felix quickly checked his watch. 'You're right, sir. They're late.' He felt a stab of alarm. 'And look, the first wave of landing craft is just rounding Start Point.'

Six sets of binoculars were quickly focused on the Royal Navy destroyers – and then back to the beach. The silence was deafening.

'What the dickens is going on?' demanded a portly brigadier. 'Why are the guns not firing?'

No one could answer him, for they weren't in communication with Naval HQ in Plymouth, or anyone else for that matter.

'Damned bad show, if you ask me,' muttered the old colonel into his flowing moustache. 'If the army had been in charge things would have gone to plan.'

They watched in puzzled silence as the large fleet of flat-bottomed landing craft approached the shore to be met by a smattering of half-hearted gunfire, which quickly died. The heavily armed men clambered out the moment the boats scraped against the shingle, and ran up the beach, doubled over beneath their huge backpacks, to take cover where they could find it.

As yet more craft arrived unhindered by gunfire or naval bombardment the foreshore became covered by infantrymen and engineers crawling like crabs towards the Ley in preparation for the inland assault that would come once the beachhead had been secured.

Felix glanced at his watch again. Almost an hour had passed since the bombardment should have started – and now the second wave of landing craft was slowly emerging from around Start Point. What the blazes was going on at Plymouth HQ? Had there been an incident out at sea? Or had Admiral Moon decided to cancel the bombardment altogether?

He was about to put his theories to the bluff old colonel when all hell broke loose.

Three RAF Typhoons screamed overhead and dived towards the inland 'safe' targets, letting loose their under-wing rockets before going into a steep, arcing climb for a second run. The deep booms of naval gunfire filled the air, and the men on shore took this as their signal to open fire, while others were still approaching in the shallow landing craft.

But the firing was so wild, Felix felt the zing of a bullet pass by his ear, and although the troops on shore had been given dummy bullets, all six men dropped instantly to the ground to continue their observance on their bellies.

The Typhoons raced back, letting off more rockets before swiftly leaving the area as buildings and farmland exploded into dust from the shells coming from the destroyers. Bullets were flying on all sides, men were scuttling for any shelter they could find, and the landing ships were bobbing about on the water like corks as the naval onslaught turned the calm sea into a maelstrom.

The men aboard the ships kept their heads down as the skippers wrestled to get them ashore, and once they were in shallow water, they scrambled out and tried to wade in. But the sea was churning, waves swelling and breaking over them with every blast from the ships, throwing the men off balance, their ungainly packs, heavy weapons and sodden uniforms weighing them down so they were forced to crawl ashore.

And then two more light bombers arrived, letting loose their deadly cargo over targets on the beach and further inland. The explosions rocked the ground, blistering the air with deafening blasts as the naval guns continued their heavy shelling.

Felix and his elderly companions ducked and covered their heads as the nearby Manor House Hotel took a direct hit, showering them in debris and dust, the wind of the explosion threatening to blow them off the hill.

Two more explosions followed in quick succession, and then the bombers roared away, their task over for the day. The naval bombardment fell silent – as did the guns on shore – and Felix dared to lift his head. What he saw sent a chill right through him.

The Royal Sands Hotel was just a pile of burning rubble, and where the beach had once reached its boundary there was now a massive bomb crater. Surely no one could have survived that? But there was movement down there, so perhaps, by some miracle, young Herby was okay.

He scanned the area with his binoculars. Fires were blazing from hill targets, men were lying on the beach as if afraid to move, while others struggled to reach the beach from the still turbulent sea.

And yet, among all the chaos, landing craft were still coming in.

Felix knew that the landings would take the rest of the day and all through the night, for once the beachhead was secure, the supplies, fuel and equipment for the men would be offloaded at Landcombe Cove, which lay between Blackpool Sands and Strete. Convoy T4 would leave harbour after midnight tonight to deliver their cargoes tomorrow morning so the push inland could go ahead to complete Operation Tiger – and then in early May there would be a final exercise, code-named Fabius, which would be carried out over six days. He could only pray it would go better than today's fiasco.

He felt quite sick as he looked down at the beach where the old hotel had once been, for now the medics were attending – stretchers were being carried away to the line of waiting ambulances – and the men he'd thought frozen in fear on the beach were still there, but now covered in blankets to await the same swift transfer.

'I'm going down there,' he said.

The brigadier stopped him by grasping his arm. 'You have no clearance to be on the exercise ground.'

'Clearance be damned,' he said, wrenching away from him and running to his car.

He realised he'd actually do no good down there, so drove at speed without a thought for his own safety, and within minutes was screeching to a halt outside the crowded hospital assembly area. There were five ambulances, three jeeps and four trucks – the latter bearing the walking wounded who were immediately assessed by the nurses before being helped into the hospital by the comrades who'd brought them.

Felix gave each man a word of encouragement and then waited on tenterhooks until the doctors had finished examining the men in the ambulances. There seemed to be a lot of them, and by the look on the doctors' faces, the news wasn't good, and as the blankets were drawn over them, his greatest fear was borne out.

'I'm sorry, sir,' said a young American nurse, 'you can't be here.'

'I'm looking for Sergeant Cornwallis of the Military Police,' he said firmly. 'He's my driver, and I need to know he's all right.'

She was about to reply when one of the doctors climbed out of the ambulance and grimly shook his head. Felix's heart thudded and an overwhelming feeling of dread chilled his blood. 'Herby Cornwallis?' he asked gruffly.

'I'm sorry, General. He didn't make it.'

'Can I see him?'

'If you wish, but I warn you, it's not pretty.'

Felix had been in enough battles to know how ugly death could be, so he nodded his thanks, climbed into the ambulance and firmly shut the door.

He drew back the blanket, looked at the devastation caused by those shells and cradled what remained of Herbert Cornwallis gently into his arms.

'It's okay, son,' he said softly. 'I've got you now, so you rest easy.'

45

Coombe Farm

Nipper had shot off with his tail between his legs at the first bang, no doubt seeking shelter from all the noise under someone's bed. Carol had gripped Dolly and Betty's hands as the bombardment had begun, flinching at every boom and bang, gasping in horror as the rockets and bombs tore the heart out of the hills and the beach she loved.

None of them had spoken while the flotilla of landing craft struggled to get to the beach, the men fighting their way through the churning water as the carnage unfolded around them – and then still more boats had come into the bay and the gunfire had rung out, machine guns hammered and shells exploded.

Ida, Maisie and Pru clung to one another, perhaps reliving the London Blitz which had wiped out their homes and killed so many of their friends, while Millicent hid her face in Jack's shoulder, unable to watch as yet more troops arrived in their landing craft.

Frank's expression was grim, his great frame unflinching even when two bombs went off almost simultaneously on the beach below them. He went to Betty who was trembling and tearful and tried to reassure her that Brendon was in Plymouth – that his part in the rehearsal was quite straightforward and safe, and wouldn't take place until early the next morning.

Carol doubted he knew that for certain, and she wondered if his words of comfort were as much for himself as for Betty.

The bombardment came to a sudden end as the fighter bombers flew away and the shooting petered out on the beach. They left a deafening silence behind them.

Dolly's hand had been like ice in Carol's grip. Now her face was ashen as she borrowed Carol's binoculars and looked through them to the distant headland above Blackpool Cove where they'd all seen the blurred figures earlier.

Dolly breathed a trembling sigh of relief. 'I've seen enough,' she said quietly, handing back the binoculars.

'I think we all have,' said Jack, helping Millicent to her feet. 'If there's to be more of the same tomorrow, I'll take'm leaf out of Nipper's book and stay at home.'

Dolly looked at Carol. 'I'll go back and get settled in the pub. Perhaps, this evening, you could come over and join me?'

Carol regarded her thoughtfully and then nodded. 'I'll come straight after supper, and then you can tell me what's bothering you.'

'Oh dear, am I that easy to read?' Dolly plastered on a smile. 'We'll talk later. I can't think straight after all that terrible noise.'

Pru and Maisie had rushed off straight after supper to help Jack and Millicent with the calving while Ida was taking her turn in the bathroom. Carol was washing dishes and tidying the kitchen when she heard the sound of a jeep pulling into the yard.

'Tell Herby I won't be much longer,' yelled Ida from the bathroom.

Carol grinned and went to answer the door. 'Oh, hello, Felix,' she said in surprise. 'We all thought it was Herbert coming courting.' She looked out towards the jeep and frowned when she noticed it was empty.

'This isn't a social call, Carol,' said Felix, his expression sombre. 'Is Ida here?'

Carol's heart began to thud. 'She's in the ... It's not ... Please, Felix, tell me it's not Herbert.'

The sorrow was stark in his eyes. 'I lost five young men today, Carol. Now I need to talk with Ida.'

'Where is he then?' demanded Ida, emerging from the bathroom, dressed and made up to the nines. 'Don't tell me you left him outs—' She fell silent as she looked from Carol to Felix, her smile crumpling, the muscles working in her face as tears filled her eyes. 'Not my Herby,' she whispered, shaking her head. 'No, not Herby.'

Carol hurried to put her arm about her shoulder as Felix stood awkwardly before them, hat under his arm, his features stony. 'What happened, Felix?' she demanded.

'I regret to inform you, Ida, that Herbert passed away in the line of duty this morning. I will inform his mother personally, but thought it was right to tell you before you heard from loose talk.'

Ida collapsed into a kitchen chair with a howl of distress, buried her face in her hands and sobbed. 'My Herby,' she wailed. 'My lovely Herby. I can't bear it.'

'What went wrong, Felix?' asked Carol.

'I don't know, but I aim to find out,' he replied grimly. He gently put a hand on Ida's shoulder. 'I'm sorry, honey,' he said softly. 'He was a fine young man, and I know he was very fond of you. I hope you can take some comfort from that.'

Ida shrugged off his hand and looked up at him, her face streaked with make-up and tears, her eyes filled with rage. 'I loved 'im, and now 'e's gorn – and you done it – you and the bloody army and navy and them bastards in charge. It were just supposed to be a rehearsal,' she ended in a screech. 'A bloody rehearsal!'

Carol grabbed her before she could attack Felix, and held her tightly as the storm of tears continued. 'You'd better go,' she said to him. 'I'll manage here.'

'Where are the others?'

'Betty's moved back into the pub and the others are busy with the calving. They won't be back for a while. But you could go to the pub and warn Mother I won't make it over there tonight.'

'I didn't realise she was here,' he replied coolly. 'But of course I'll tell her. Do you want her to come and be with you?'

Carol shook her head. 'Tell her I'll see her tomorrow.'

46

Cliffehaven

Beach View was in mourning, and Peggy felt utterly helpless as she lay in the darkness unable to sleep because of the disturbing and painful images that were flashing through her mind. Matthew Champion was dead – all that youthful exuberance and sweet nature gone in an instant as his plane had been shot down.

Peggy shuddered, for she'd witnessed the dog fights over the Channel and seen planes bursting into flames and plummeting to earth – it was a horrendous way to die, and she could only pray that Matthew had known nothing about it.

Poor little Rita was devastated, and although Peggy yearned to comfort her, she'd gone upstairs to mourn alone. And then there was her Anne's Martin, Kitty's Roger and Charlotte's Freddy – all listed as missing in action. The only glimmer of hope to cling to was that parachutes had been reported in each case. But had they survived? How badly injured might they be? Would anyone find them in time and give them proper medical care?

She turned restlessly on the pillow, her thoughts

going to Owlet Farm in Somerset where Anne would have received the news by now – and to the tiny cottage in Briar Lane where Kitty and Charlotte were faced with the possibility that their unborn babies might never know their fathers. Peggy could barely imagine the pain and fear they would all be going through, and for poor little Kitty it would be doubly hard – for not only might she lose her husband, Roger, but also her beloved brother, Freddy.

Peggy's only solace was that the girls had each other to bear the awful burden, while her Anne had Aunt Vi and young Sally; but what of Anne's little girls – would they lose the father they'd only just got to know? The thought was too much to cope with, and she buried her face in the pillow as the hot tears came.

She felt so alone, yearning for Jim's arms around her, his soft, lilting voice soothing away her fears as she heard the steady beat of his heart against her ear. But he was on the other side of the world, fighting the Japs – and the realisation that the next knock on the door could be for her made her curl up, the pillow stuffed over her mouth to stifle the wracking sobs that might wake Daisy.

The soft tap on the door was followed by the pad of bare feet, and the dip of the mattress as Rita climbed in beside her. Peggy determinedly swallowed her tears and tenderly drew the motherless, heartbroken girl into her loving arms to give her comfort and the assurance that her grief was shared and she didn't have to mourn alone.

Yet, as Peggy cradled the sobbing girl, she stared

into the darkness, aware that the long hours of waiting for any news of the others had only just begun.

Coombe Farm

They'd all been woken by the sound of the big guns at two in the morning, and had come to the conclusion the rehearsal must be continuing out at sea. As it was a pitch-black night, there would be nothing to see but flashes of gunfire on the horizon, and because they'd witnessed more than enough the previous morning, and it would only upset Ida even more, they'd vetoed the idea of rushing up there to watch and tried to get back to sleep.

Carol had lain awake, fretting over why her mother had turned up so unexpectedly, refusing to reveal what was worrying her before she'd returned to the pub. If something had happened to Pauline or anyone at Beach View, surely she would have said – so what on earth had brought her down here?

She became aware of Ida moving restlessly about in her bed as the distant booms and bangs continued. The poor girl was distraught, and Carol knew just how she felt, for that initial shock was a body blow, and it would take time and many tears to come to terms with her loss. But at least she was surrounded by her friends, and Jack and Millicent had been very kind when they'd all returned from the byres to discover what had happened. It was at times like these that people pulled together, and Carol knew from experience that the unity went a long way to help in the process of healing.

She pulled the blanket over her shoulders and shivered as a particularly loud bombardment echoed through the silence. Brendon would be out at sea tonight, and she could picture Betty alone in her room at the pub, probably awake and just as worried, having witnessed the debacle on the beach that morning. Carol shivered, for she knew from the experience of waiting to hear if David had survived the latest battle that it was these waiting hours that were the hardest to bear.

The Welcome Inn

Dolly had woken at two in the morning, and in the darkness she heard the faint sound of heavy gunfire which seemed to be coming from the Channel. Knowing that her grandson was out there tonight, she shivered with apprehension. These manoeuvres might be rehearsals for the real thing, but something had gone terribly wrong the previous morning for boys to have been killed, and she dreaded to think what disasters might lie ahead.

It had been a shock to see Felix striding into the pub earlier that evening, his expression grim, his words terse as he'd told her what had happened. Her first instinct had been to go to the farm, but Felix had been adamant she should wait until tomorrow. He'd left as soon as he'd passed on the news about young Herbert, clearly not in the mood for pleasantries, or even curious as to whether she'd spoken to Carol – and so she'd gone straight to bed, her dreams troubled by the sound of gunfire and images of young men lying too still on a beach.

Restless and unable to settle to anything, she dressed and then paced the small bedroom, impatient for the dawn. Her troubled thoughts veered from the conversation she must have with Carol to her worry over Marie-Claire, then on to what might be happening to Brendon out at sea – and finally to Felix.

He would no doubt be blaming himself for what had happened on the beach that morning even though he was merely an observer, and had therefore taken no part in the planning and execution of the exercise. But she'd seen from his expression earlier that the loss of his young men had hit him hard, and that he would demand to know how things had gone so very wrong.

Dolly stubbed out her cigarette in the overflowing ashtray and went to lean out of the open window in an attempt to clear her head. The world was in chaos, the future for all of them hanging in the balance, and at the mercy of the commanders in charge who were proving as ineffectual and disorganised as the ones during the last shout.

She gave a deep sigh and reached for yet another cigarette as the distant gunfire echoed through the stillness. The waiting hours before dawn were always the longest.

47

Convoy T-4, HMS *Azalea*

Radio silence was the order of the night, for it was vital
the Germans didn't get wind of the convoy, or the reason it was in the Channel. Brendon stood on the bridge
of the corvette as his commanding officer, Lieutenant
Commander George Carlow Geddes RNR, followed
the convoy of eight heavily laden American LSTs
through manoeuvres in Lyme Bay. It was after one in
the morning and bitterly cold; visibility was non-
existent in the darkness of a moonless night, but the
water was reasonably calm, and Geddes was a highly
decorated and experienced commander who'd seen
action on this corvette in the North Atlantic: the *Azalea*
and her crew were in safe hands.

The convoy was strung out in a line at 700-yard inter-
vals, moving at a steady six knots as the ships executed
the wide, looping route out into the Channel before they
turned back towards the landing point at Slapton Sands.
This manoeuvre was to get the men below the decks of
the American LSTs used to being at sea for the length of
time it would take them to get to France for the actual
invasion, but Brendon shared Geddes's concern that
they'd be sitting ducks if Jerry spotted them.

He looked through his binoculars, scanning the black Channel waters where the cruiser USS *Augusta* and the three British destroyers formed a line of defence ninety miles off the French coast, accompanied tonight by a flotilla of British Coastal Service MGBs and MTBs, along with two more LSTs. There had been reported sighting of the swift E-boats patrolling the Channel off Cherbourg during the week, and it was vital that the Germans didn't suspect what was happening in Lyme Bay.

Geddes seemed to read his mind. 'There was an enemy spotter plane sighted two days ago, and with all the American radio traffic coming out of Lyme Bay, it's highly likely Jerry's picked up that something's going on there. It's a damned nuisance HMS *Scimitar* was holed while in port and ordered to stay there. We could have done with the added protection.'

'The *Saladin* should be on her way by now,' said Brendon, still scanning the Channel.

Geddes grunted. 'For all the good she'll be. It takes her half a day to turn round, and four knots is about all she can make without falling to pieces. She's held together by rust, and it would be a kindness to break her up.'

It was now two in the morning and they were west of Tor Bay and steaming NNW for their final approach to Slapton Sands.

The radio suddenly crackled into life, and a calm English voice said, 'Nine enemy torpedo boats spotted north of defence screen. Advancing at thirty-six knots. Scatter. Scatter.'

Geddes called for battle stations, and shouted down

to the engine room for full steam as he began a sharp turn in order to get his powerful guns facing the oncoming enemy.

Brendon braced himself as he turned his binoculars on the LSTs still strung out in front of them. 'Why aren't they scattering? They must have received that—' His words were cut off by a massive explosion.

LST-507 had been hit amidships by two torpedoes and was on fire, the flames quickly becoming an inferno as they reached the full fuel tanks in the many jeeps and trucks that were chained topside on the deck. The lifeboats were burning, so the men abandoned ship by diving into the freezing water or scrambling down the cargo net that had been dropped over the side. Within minutes the raging blaze reached the storage containers of petrol and boxes of ammunition stored below deck, and the ship exploded, broke up and sank.

The *Azalea*'s guns opened fire as the convoy finally – and swiftly – broke formation. But the enemy boats were painted the same black as the night and the water, and were invisible.

LST-531 blew up, and as Brendon watched in horror, it sank so quickly there was no chance anyone had survived.

The sky was lit up with red tracers and bright magnesium flares as the convoy's guns continued to boom. Fires were quickly extinguished; lifeboats, landing craft and cargo nets were lowered to try and rescue the floundering men in the water.

In the utter chaos the LSTs lost their bearings, while the swift and deadly E-boats hunted their prey in pairs, firing indiscriminately, their torpedoes slicing through the water towards ships, landing craft, lifeboats and helpless men. LST-498 fired on LST-511 in the confusion, while LST-58 was hampered by the two pontoon causeways she was towing. Screaming men leapt from their burning ships to plunge into the water that was now alight from the spilled oil and petrol.

LST-289 was hit by a torpedo, and as the crew raced to put out the fires, she slowly turned away in an effort to limp back to port, the lifeboats jammed in their rusty hawsers as cargo nets were slung over the side to pick up survivors.

Brendon and the other officers had gone on deck to back up the ship's guns by shooting at the enemy they could hear but couldn't see, and they all breathed a sigh of relief as the welcome bulk of HMS *Onslow* loomed out of the darkness, all guns blazing.

The E-boats put up a thick screen of black smoke and used their speed and agility to make their escape. The booming guns eventually fell silent, and now the night was filled with the sound of men pleading for help.

Geddes ordered the lifeboats to be lowered and gave Brendon permission to leave the bridge to organise a rescue party from the deck.

Brendon checked his life jacket was fastened correctly and went back outside to the pitiful sound of the desperate men crying out in the water. As the lifeboats were swiftly launched, he got the remaining crew to form two chains down the cargo net, with others waiting topside to carry the survivors inside, and then clambered down until the water reached his waist.

Desperate cries came to him out of the darkness as hands reached out, clawing at him, threatening to pull him into the water now churning from the wakes of the ships.

Brendon and the crew worked swiftly, for the sea was freezing, the men exhausted, injured and smeared in oil. But as time went on the cries for help faded, and all they could see were the hundreds of bodies, most of which were soldiers with their heads deep in the water, their feet in the air, top-heavy from their packs because they hadn't worn their life jackets correctly.

The lifeboats returned with a few injured survivors, while Brendon and the others pulled in as many bodies as they could. But the task was hopeless. The number of dead was overwhelming.

And then Brendon saw something pale moving in the gathering light of dawn and thought he heard a cry for help. He ordered the crew to be silent, peered into the half-light and listened hard, praying he'd hear the cry again.

When it came it was youthful and faint, the boy too far away and too weak to swim towards the *Azalea*. Brendon took off his boots and swam out to him awkwardly, for the life jacket made movement difficult, and the freezing water had already cramped his muscles from the waist down.

He found the boy clinging to a piece of wood, his life jacket the only thing that had kept him afloat. 'It's okay, wee wain,' he said, grasping the life jacket and turning him on his back. 'You're safe now.'

He spat out the oil-infused saltwater and crabbed

back towards the *Azalea*, the youth resting against his chest, so limp that Brendon feared he'd lost him. But as willing hands lifted him away, he opened his eyes and smiled before passing out again.

Brendon didn't know how the lad had survived for so long, for he was freezing after just a few minutes, his body seizing up to the point where he could barely hold on to the netting. But as he struggled to cling to the rope, the crew dragged him out of the water and lifted him onto the deck, where he was immediately stripped of his sodden uniform and bundled into a blanket before being taken inside.

Brendon was shivering so badly he couldn't hold the cup of tea that had been thrust into his hands without spilling it. His hands and feet were white and numb, and as he tried to smoke a cigarette, all he could taste was engine oil. 'How's the wee boy?' he asked the harassed medic through chattering teeth.

'He's lucky; he'll make it,' he replied. He jerked a thumb at the many rows of bodies which had been respectfully covered by tarpaulin on the outside deck. 'Which is more than can be said for those poor souls.'

The man regarded Brendon through his spectacles. 'What the devil just happened out here?'

'Hell happened,' shivered Brendon. 'And I aim to find out who was responsible.'

The medic grunted. 'Good luck with that,' he said. 'The top brass will cover it up, you'll see. Something like this isn't good for morale.'

Brendon regarded the bodies on the deck and thought of all the others still in the water. 'Bugger morale,' he muttered. 'The families of all those men need to know why they died.'

Slapton Sands

Felix was having the same thought as he watched the extensively damaged LST-289 limp past on her way to Dartmouth to offload her dead and wounded. Almost her entire rear end had been blasted and buckled, and it was a miracle she was still afloat. It was barely dawn, and he paused in his gruesome task of hauling in the bodies to look helplessly out at the hundreds more that were slowly being washed ashore.

The surviving LSTs and landing craft were coming in as planned, but along with the supplies and vehicles, they brought in more bodies to be laid upon the beach until the sand was all but hidden by them. Ambulances and trucks flooded onto the causeway as stretcher bearers, nurses and doctors rushed to clear away the evidence of the night's tragedy – no doubt under instruction from the commanders whose incompetence had caused it.

Felix continued to help the infantrymen and engineers pull the dead men and boys out of the water. There were too many boys – youngsters who'd not been given the chance to grow old; whose lives had been snatched away through sheer carelessness and bad judgement.

He was seething with anger, trembling with it as he gently laid yet another kid on the sand. He could have wept. But tears wouldn't bring them back or solve anything, and he knew he had to find the strength to accept that he'd played a part in this carnage by not being more forceful about those life jackets. But he would demand answers from those commanders and ensure that mistakes like this would never happen again.

48

Coombe Farm

Unable to get back to sleep, Carol had clambered out of bed to get dressed and tiptoe out of the barn with Nipper. It was almost four in the morning and the guns had been silent for over an hour, and as she went out into the hazy light of early dawn, she caught the stench of cordite and burning oil in the air, and quickened her pace.

Arriving at the brow of the hill, she was startled to find Frank, Dolly and Betty standing there, transfixed by something down on the beach. 'What is it?' she asked in dread.

Their faces were ashen, their eyes dull with shock and horror, and Dolly reached out to her. 'Don't look, darling. It's too distressing.'

'Brendon? Has something happened to Brendon?'

'No, thank God,' breathed Betty. 'Or at least it appears he's all right. That's his ship off Portland Bill, and it looks to be in one piece.'

Carol ignored her mother's staying hand and went to look for herself – and immediately wished she hadn't. With a cry of distress she saw the bodies float-ing in the water and covering the sand – saw the ambulances, the stretchers, the dazed and bewildered troops milling about as more ships came in carrying the dead and injured. And in the middle of it all she saw Felix. At this distance, she couldn't see his face, but she could only imagine how he must be feeling as he watched another body being covered by a blanket and stretchered away.

'Dear God,' she breathed, the tears streaming down her face as images of David lying dead on the desert sands of Africa flashed through her mind. 'How could this have happened?'

'We don't know,' said Frank, 'and no doubt we never will. The brass won't want something like this getting out, even if it was a surprise enemy attack.'

'Do you think that's what it could have been?' Carol asked. 'Is there any way you can find out, Frank? Would Brendon confide in you, do you think?'

'I doubt it, Carol. Whatever happened, he'll be ordered to keep his mouth shut – and I suggest none of us speak about this again, because we've seen something we shouldn't have, and could be arrested.'

'But they can't hide something like this,' Carol protested tearfully. 'There are so many dead, and I just know that Felix will not let this be hushed up.'

'He's been an army man and obeyed orders all his life,' said Dolly, her eyes bright with unshed tears. 'And with something like this . . .' She turned to Carol. 'Felix is a good man with a deep sense of honour. He'll tell the brass what he thinks of them if this slaughter was their fault. But in the end his will be one voice, and if Churchill and Ike order complete news blackout he'll have no choice but to remain silent.'

Carol turned her back on the carnage, trembling with the horror of it all. The war had finally come to Slapton, and the stark brutality of it was something she'd never forget.

'I need to get to Brixham to make sure Brendon's all right,' said Frank. 'Can I borrow your car, Dolly?'

She nodded, her attention focused on Carol. 'The keys are in the ignition, but watch out for that broken handbrake,' she replied distractedly.

'Can I come with you, Frank?' pleaded Betty tearfully.

'I'm sorry, wee girl, but you won't be allowed through without an army pass.' He put his arm round her shoulders. 'But I'll come straight back and tell you about Brendon, I promise.'

As Frank and Betty headed down the hill, Dolly embraced Carol. 'I'm so sorry you had to witness that,' she murmured. 'I do hope it hasn't upset you too much and brought things back.'

Carol dried her tears and tried to find some sort of calm to distil those images still in her head. 'I hope David had someone to care for him the way Felix so obviously cares about those boys,' she managed. 'It's awful to think he might have died alone.'

'I'm sure his fellow officers were with him and took just as much care as Felix has.' Dolly lovingly cupped her cheek, and wiped away Carol's tears with gentle fingers. 'You've come to like Felix, haven't you?'

Carol regarded her warily and then nodded. 'I didn't tell you because I thought it might upset you, but yes, we've become friends.' She flicked back her fair hair as it was blown by the wind across her face. 'As you say, he's a good man, and I find him easy to talk to and confide in.'

'And what did you talk about?' asked Dolly, drawing her slowly down the hill as the other two disappeared from view.

Carol frowned, puzzled by her mother's questions, and reluctant to reveal just how close she and Felix had become over the past months.

'You can tell me, Carol,' Dolly said. 'I know you've become friends.'

Carol had no idea how she knew that, but it was a relief not to have to keep it a secret any more. She told her about Betty's run-in with Ken and the night they'd spent in the hospital. 'We talked about a lot of things that night,' she finished.

'I suppose he told you that he and I had once been very close,' said Dolly.

'He didn't say anything much about your relationship, but then he didn't have to. I'd guessed a long time ago that you'd been lovers,' said Carol. 'But what I still don't understand is why you were so determined not to talk about him. It's clear he still loves you and you love him – so why did you turn your back on him?'

'Our affair didn't end well,' said Dolly, taking her hand.

'Yes, he did tell me about his wife and son – and I can understand why you broke things off.' She regarded her mother thoughtfully. 'He regrets hurting you, and fully admits he should have been honest with you right from the start – but he's on his own now, and if you still feel so strongly about each other, why can't you forgive him?'

Dolly sank onto a patch of grass and hugged her knees. 'I forgave him years ago,' she admitted quietly. 'The person I can't forgive is myself.'

Carol frowned and sat next to her. 'Why, what did you do?'

'I walked away without telling him something he had a right to know,' Dolly said softly, 'and I've spent the following years living a lie.'

Carol sat very still, her gaze fixed intently on her mother, the niggles of previous, half-dismissed doubts rising swiftly. 'What didn't you tell him?' she asked evenly.

Dolly lifted her chin and met Carol's gaze without flinching. 'I didn't tell him I was expecting you,' she said.

Carol reeled from the blow and stared at her mother in horror. 'You were having an affair with my father at the same time as Felix, and didn't think to mention you were pregnant by him?'

'No, no, you've got it all wrong,' said Dolly, grabbing her hands. 'I was faithful to Felix, and you're his daughter.'

Carol snatched her hands away. 'Then who is Major Frederick Adams?'

As Dolly haltingly explained everything, Carol looked at her and wondered how she could have lied to her so well and so consistently for the past twenty-nine years. It was no wonder she'd refused to talk about her past.

Dolly finally came to the end of her unedifying tale. 'Please forgive me, darling. I only did it because I thought it was for the best.'

'Best for whom, Mother? You've robbed me and Felix of the years in which we could have got to know one another and become proper father and daughter. You've lied and lied and lied – even to the point of giving me a picture of some man you know, pretending he was my father so that I'd stop asking questions you clearly had no intention of answering. And now you want me to *forgive* you.'

She stood up, the anger so great she was trembling. 'Did you lie to Pauline too? Did you pluck the name Paul Cardew out of the air because her real father is out there somewhere, ignorant of her existence?'

Dolly scrambled to her feet. 'No, Carol, no! I told Pauline the truth, I swear it.'

'Then it's a great shame you didn't have the decency to be truthful to me,' Carol said coldly. 'I adored and trusted you. I'd have understood and forgiven you. But not now.' She took a quavering breath. 'Did Grandma and Grandpa know?'

Dolly shook her head and reached for Carol's hand. 'I'm so sorry, Carol. Please don't be angry with me.'

'Angry?' she snapped, slapping away her hand. 'I'm so furious I can barely look at you.' She balled her fists. 'Have you admitted to Felix you lied to him?'

'Yes, I've spoken to Felix,' Dolly admitted. 'He isn't happy with me either.'

'Are you *really* that surprised?' Carol stormed. 'Just go home, Mother. You've done enough damage for one

day, and frankly, I could do with you not being anywhere near me at the moment.' She turned on her heel
and almost ran down the rest of the hill, the little dog
chasing at her heels.

Dolly went back up the hill, blinded by tears, her
heart and soul crushed and aching with such intensity
she could barely breathe. She folded her arms tightly
about her waist as she watched Felix help to clear the
beach of the last few bodies.

'What have I done to you both?' she whispered. 'Can
either of you ever forgive me?'

It was as if Felix had heard her, for he raised his head
and seemed to look right into her eyes before he turned
back and helped carry the final stretcher to the
ambulance.

Dolly sank into the grass, heedless of the mud that
was ruining her slacks, and wept for all that she'd lost.

49

Devon

An urgent signal from Eisenhower's HQ in Portsmouth had come through within hours of the carnage, ordering all personnel – military, civilian, naval and medical – not to discuss, mention or question the events, under severe threat of court martial. There was to be an immediate and complete news blackout to keep the disaster from the enemy, for it was imperative they never learned how close they'd come to wrecking all the plans for the D-Day landings.

Felix had sat in on the hastily arranged meeting of the commanding officers, in which blame and counter-blame had flown back and forth, until it was realised that the ten men who knew every detail of the classified plans for Operation Overlord had gone missing.

Officers were hastily sent to Portland to check the dog tags of the dead who'd been taken there prior to being temporarily interred in a World War I US military cemetery at Blackwood. Navy divers searched the seabed for the one hundred men who were still unaccounted for, and when it was discovered that all ten had perished and not been taken prisoner by the raiders as first thought, the relief was short-lived, for

749 men had needlessly lost their lives during the last twenty-four hours, and this shameful loss covered no one in glory – least of all the American Admiral Moon, who'd been the overall commander of Operation Tiger.

Felix listened in growing horror as the reasons behind the debacle became all too clear. The first fatal error had been for the order to put back both the landings and bombardment by one hour, as some of the thirty landing craft were not yet in position to leave port. Tragically, not everyone got the message, and the landings coincided with the bombardment, killing Sergeant Herbert Cornwallis and four others.

The chain of disasters that saw the sinking of two LSTs and the heavy loss of life following that night's E-boat attack began when HMS *Scimitar* had been holed and kept in port. No one had thought to tell the commander, so the *Saladin* wasn't called in to back up the *Azalea* as further protection for the convoy until it was far too late.

But the most devastating revelation came when it was discovered that, due to a careless typing error, the American LSTs were on a different radio frequency to the *Azalea* and the British Navy HQ ashore. Ignorant of the situation, the commander of the *Azalea* had assumed the LSTs had heard the warning of incoming enemy, and the order to scatter – and when the captains of the LSTs sent out urgent pleas for help, the radio stations along the coast had no knowledge of the secret exercise, and thought they were an enemy hoax. It was only because an alert radio operator heard the words 'T-4' that the naval command were quickly informed that Operation Tiger was in trouble and sent help in the form of HMS *Onslow*.

To compound this incompetence, the MGBs of the British Coastal Services had seen the flashes of battle while on patrol, but were not ordered to intercept or investigate, so remained unaware of the unfolding disaster nearby. Likewise, the British Fighter Direction tender had sailed out of Portland to provide radar and communications cover, but received a signal to 'make port all haste', which she did.

The cause of so many deaths was attributed to drowning and hypothermia, although several men had succumbed to terrible injuries, mainly from burns caused by the thousands of gallons of unnecessary fuel that had been carried on the ships for the exercise.

During the following week of intense discussion, it was decided that things would have to be improved if further disasters were to be avoided. Radio frequencies were to be standardised; better training on the correct wearing of life jackets for landing troops was to begin immediately; all lifeboats were to be checked and overhauled; only the necessary amount of fuel was to be carried on the LSTs; and additional small craft would accompany the fleet on D-Day to help pick up floating survivors.

Felix felt a certain sense of justification about the order to train the men in life-jacket usage, but the despair that he'd not been listened to before it was too late over-rode any other emotion. He left the meeting and walked back to his billet, needing the clean air and brisk exercise to clear his head and rid himself of the terrible things he'd witnessed, but the images remained, the dead boys' faces haunting him day and night.

Finally returning to his billet, he sat at his desk and wondered how many more would lose their lives on the beaches of Utah, Omaha, Gold, Juno and Sword. He'd been a soldier all his adult life, had fought in the 'war to end all wars', and now, just over two decades later, the world's youth was again being sacrificed.

It was the sheer incompetence and lack of common sense that ate away at him – and the fact that he was unable to trust that the commanding officers would in fact follow the directives so recently laid down. Yet he felt helpless to do anything about it. He might have donned the uniform again and have the stars pinned on his breast pocket, but they meant nothing in the scheme of things, for he was simply background scenery – an observer – without a real voice.

He sat back and lit a cigar, his gaze fixed on a distant point beyond the rolling fields, his mind conjuring up images of the orange and lemon groves of home and the blue Pacific cleaving beneath the keel of his sailing boat as the sun shone down and the white sails swelled with the salty wind. He gave a deep sigh of longing, for he wanted to be back there; to take Carol far from these war-torn shores where death and destruction hung like a pall over everything. But his orders from the Pentagon meant he must stay until Exercise Fabius was completed in May – and he had yet to even talk to Carol.

He'd received a terse telegram from Dolly confirming that Carol knew he was her father, and although he'd written a long letter to the girl, explaining why he was unable to see her until all the meetings were over, there had been no word back, and it worried him.

It couldn't have been easy for Carol to come to terms with what her mother had done, and having heard from Brendon that Dolly had left Beeson in a hurry, he could only surmise that things hadn't gone well. But why hadn't Carol written back – was she angry with him too, or was the thought of him being her father too difficult to accept?

He stubbed out his cigar. There was only one way to find out, and that was to go to Beeson as soon as his duties permitted, and talk to her.

Coombe Farm

Carol had packed the photograph of Hugh Cuthbertson away, and with it the fantasy of Frederick Adams. She had confided in Betty but said nothing to the others over the past ten days, for she was ashamed of how she'd reacted, and had been forcefully reminded that there were far worse things to worry about.

Poor Ida was struggling to come to terms with losing Herbert, and although she'd thrown herself into her work, she spent most nights sobbing into her pillow. The scenes on the beach that awful morning still haunted Carol, bringing back the pain of her own loss, and the disturbing letters from Pauline and Peggy had simply underlined the horrors of this war, making her put things into proper perspective.

It didn't matter a jot who her father was when Martin and his men had been posted as missing in action, with no clue as to whether they were still alive or not – and she could well imagine what Peggy's Anne must be going through. Her predicament seemed ridiculously trivial when boys were being killed on beaches; husbands, brothers, sons and lovers were shot from the skies; and small children and unborn babies were left fatherless.

It was now May and the lighter evenings encouraged her to take Nipper for long walks after the day's work was over, and she usually dropped in to the pub to see Betty before returning to the farm. The Welcome Inn was much quieter now, for although no one dared speak about it, the events on Slapton beach had sobered the GIs who came in fewer numbers as the new exercise began and the actual date for the invasion loomed.

She pushed through the heavy blackout curtain and closed the door behind her, noting immediately that Brendon was sitting in a huddle with Betty in the corner of the bar. 'It's so lovely to see you,' she said in delighted relief as she hugged him. 'We didn't think you'd get leave until this latest exercise was over.'

'*Azalea* developed engine problems so she's in dock, and I get an evening ashore,' he replied with a broad smile.

As Brendon went off to buy her a glass of cider, Carol leaned towards Betty. 'I'm sorry to intrude when you have so little time together,' she murmured. 'I'll just have this drink and leave you to it.'

'Don't be daft,' Betty replied. 'Brendon was saying

earlier that he hasn't seen you in a while.' She regarded her affectionately. 'You seem more like your old self again. Have you heard from Dolly?'

'She's written twice, just short notes telling me she's sorry, and I wrote back yesterday, saying I was sorry too. I shouldn't have spoken to her like that, she really didn't deserve it. As for Felix, he sent me a lovely letter, but as I'm really not sure what to say to him, I haven't replied.'

'He'll think you're rejecting him,' said Betty, 'and that would be a shame after you've become so friendly. Perhaps you should just send a note acknowledging his letter, and telling him you need time to absorb everything before you meet again.'

Carol nodded, and then looked up at Brendon who'd returned with her drink. 'Have you got any news about Martin and the other pilots?'

'I managed to get through to Beach View this morning, and they're all on tenterhooks. Grandad Ron says Martin and another younger pilot were being led to safety by someone from the resistance, but were then caught by the Germans.' He leaned closer, his voice barely above a whisper. 'Jerry's usually very good at reporting back on men they've captured, with details of which POW camp they've been sent to – but there hasn't been a peep out of them, and that is very strange.'

Carol rubbed her face with her hands. 'The worry's never-ending, isn't it?' she sighed. 'Poor Anne must be going through hell.'

'I suspect Grandad Ron is on the case. You know what he's like. He's bound to know someone who might have inside information.' Brendon grinned and patted Nipper, who was sitting at his feet. 'He's like this wee terrier, for once he gets his teeth into something he doesn't let go.'

Carol smiled as the little dog put his front paws on Brendon's knee to encourage more fuss. 'Life's so much simpler for a dog, isn't it?' she sighed. 'I think I'll come back as one next time.' She took a long, welcome drink of cider, vaguely aware of the door opening and closing behind her.

'It looks like you've got a visitor,' hissed Betty.

Carol turned to find Felix standing by the door. She smiled tentatively and it encouraged him to approach. 'Hello, everyone,' he said. 'I thought I might find you here.'

Brendon got swiftly to his feet and saluted. 'Will you join us, sir?'

'Thank you, but I'd like a private word with Carol, if she wouldn't mind.'

It was the first time Carol had seen Felix look unsure of himself, and his diffidence warmed her to him all over again. 'We can go over there,' she said indicating another table.

'Why don't you use my room?' said Betty. 'You'll be private there.'

Felix looked at Carol, who nodded. 'Thanks, Betty, it's appreciated.'

Carol left Nipper with Brendon and led the way up the narrow staircase to Betty's room, which also served as her study. Opening the door she found it was as neat as a pin, the desk beneath the window piled high with exercise books. And yet the intimacy of the bed taking up most of the room made her feel uncomfortable, and she saw it was having the same effect on Felix, who was standing awkwardly by the door.

'There's not much room in here, is there?' she said lightly to cover her nervousness. 'So why don't you sit by the desk, and I'll perch on the bed.'

They sat in an awkward silence as the bedside clock ticked away the time.

'I'm sorry,' they both said in unison, and the awkwardness melted away as they chuckled.

'You have nothing to be sorry about,' said Carol. 'You were as much in the dark as I was, but I was wrong not to reply to your sweet letter. Thank you for that – it did make me feel better about things.'

'I'm glad you've been so accepting, Carol. All of this must have come as a terrible shock to you.'

'It did, and yet it didn't,' she replied. She smiled at his quizzical look. 'You see, I'd begun to have my suspicions after that awful night in the hospital, and I suspect you were already thinking along the same lines.'

He nodded. 'It had occurred to me, but the mention of Major Adams threw me for a while. What led you down the same path?'

'Mother refused to talk about you, and was being so secretive about your relationship, even going so far as to make you promise to say nothing to me about it. I couldn't work out why she'd go to such lengths, unless she was hiding something from both of us. That idea took hold, and I began to question everything.'

'Including Major Adams?'

'He'd always been a shadowy figure, and Mother told me nothing about him, really – which suddenly seemed odd, considering she'd been so open with Pauline about her father. It hadn't bothered me much before, but as I examined things more closely, that lack of openness began to niggle.'

She took a deep breath and let it out on a sigh. 'Realisation didn't come as a blinding flash or anything quite so dramatic; it was more a slow dawning that there could only be one answer.' She bowed her head. 'I didn't want to believe it, because it would have meant she'd lied to me all my life, so I pushed the thought away, telling myself that I was imagining things.'

'You weren't alone, honey. I felt the same,' he said dolefully. 'And when Dolly finally confessed she'd kept you from me your whole life, I'm afraid I didn't react too well.'

'Neither did I,' said Carol softly. 'In fact I told her I couldn't stand the sight of her and she should go home.' She shot him an embarrassed smile. 'I have written since to apologise, but I am still cross with her.'

'Me too. She stole the time we could have had getting to know one another, and although I was in no position to be a proper father to you, I would have done all I could to make sure you knew that I hadn't abandoned you.' He gave a wistful smile. 'We're both hurt and angry right now, but Dolly acted in haste, not stopping to think of the consequences. She didn't know that fate would bring us together, and I think we can forgive her, don't you?'

'Yes, she's easy to forgive because we love her.' Carol regarded him evenly. 'And, despite everything, you *do* still love her, don't you, Felix?

'She's in my heart and will stay there always,' he admitted softly. He reached for Carol's hand. 'I want you to know I'm proud to have such a daughter as you, Carol. You're a fine, intelligent, beautiful young woman who has shown compassion and understanding throughout, and I would be honoured if you'd let me be a part of your life.'

Carol smiled through the gathering tears. 'You already are,' she replied. 'And I'm so very glad we've found one another.'

He pulled her to her feet, swept her into his arms and against his heart, knowing he would cherish her until his last breath, for she was a part of him and Dolly, born through a love that would never die.

EPILOGUE

Bletchley Park looked lovely in the early June sunshine, and as Dolly emerged from the decoding room, her heart was lighter than it had been for weeks. Marie-Claire had tracked down the missing pilots and by some miracle had managed to persuade an officer of the Luftwaffe to get them transferred from Buchenwald to Stalag 111. She was now in a safe house back in Paris, and would be coming home within a matter of days.

Dolly couldn't help but smile as she took her usual table on the broad terrace. It had been a wonderful day, and for the first time since this war had begun, she felt hopeful. Operation Overlord was due to take place in a matter of hours now the weather had changed for the better, and if all went as planned, it could be the beginning of the end.

She lit a cigarette and glanced at the letters that had arrived over the past weeks, each one so precious, she'd carried them with her ever since. Carol had forgiven her, and was expecting to return to her cottage around Christmastime when the ordnance had been cleared. Once the war was over, she planned to rent both cottages out and travel to America, where she would stay for a while with Felix and get to know his son and extended family.

Dolly sighed with pleasure. Felix and Carol were getting on so well that he'd stayed longer than planned so he could be with her. She smiled at the thought of him living at the Welcome Inn and trekking each day to the farm to help with the milking, planting and early harvesting. But going by the photograph Carol had sent it was doing him good, for he looked fit and tanned, and both of them were smiling so happily that she felt a pang of deep remorse for having kept them apart for so long.

She found the letter Felix had sent shortly after he and Carol had begun to pick up the threads which would bind them ever closer, and read it again, her heart filled with love and hope.

My darling, darling girl,

I'm not one for flowery speeches, but I need you to know that I love you, have always loved you, and when this war is over, I hope we can begin again, and give our daughter the family she so deserves. I shall be returning to the States soon, but I dream that one day you will do me the honour of becoming my wife – but that is for the future, when the world is once more at peace. For now I am content just to know that my love is returned, and that our daughter knows that too. I enclose a lovely song written for the American soldiers and sailors during the First World War. The words express all that I feel.

With my love, Felix

Dolly's heart was full and tears blurred her eyes as she read the beautiful words on the accompanying slip of paper, for they encompassed all that was in her heart and promised them all a bright, beautiful future.

When the great red dawn is shining,
When the waiting hours are past,
When the tears of night are ended
And I see the day at last, I shall come
Down the road of sunshine,
To a heart that is fond and true,
When the great red dawn is shining,
Back to home, back to love, and you.

THE END

Dear Readers,

I'm sure you've noticed that I have gone back in time from the previous book, *Until You Come Home*, and I do hope this hasn't spoilt your enjoyment. The story of what happened at Slapton Sands in Devon was one I've wanted to write since I began the Cliffehaven series, but as the dates clashed with what happened to the characters, it meant there had to be two books, the storylines running parallel. This wasn't an easy project, and at times I was tearing my hair out, and wishing I'd done things the other way around, but when a story hooks a writer, it's impossible to ignore it, and as so much happened during those months in 1943/44, I felt I had to tell all of it!

The war is slowly coming to an end, but there are still many stories to write about Peggy and Jim's extended family, and I hope you continue to enjoy them. I've come to love the family at Beach View, and although they still have many trials and triumphs ahead of them, I'm sure they'll face them all with humour and fortitude.

I wish you all well,

Ellie x

Did you love *The Waiting Hours*?

Look out for the next Cliffehaven novel

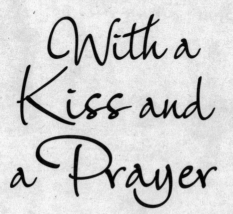

ELLIE DEAN

Pre-order now in paperback and ebook

Out 25 January 2018

Lose yourself in the

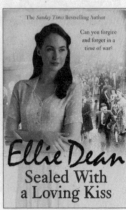

Find Love.

world of Cliffehaven . . .

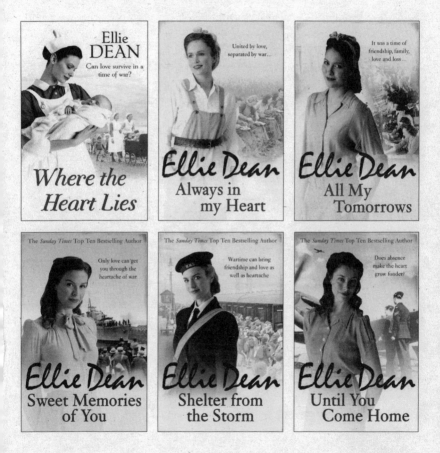

Ellie DEAN
Can love survive in a time of war?

Where the Heart Lies

United by love, separated by war...

Ellie Dean
Always in my Heart

It was a time of friendship, family, love and loss...

Ellie Dean
All My Tomorrows

The *Sunday Times* Top Ten Bestselling Author

Only love can get you through the heartache of war

Ellie Dean
Sweet Memories of You

The *Sunday Times* Top Ten Bestselling Author

Wartime can bring friendship and love as well as heartache

Ellie Dean
Shelter from the Storm

The *Sunday Times* Top Ten Bestselling Author

Does absence make the heart grow fonder?

Ellie Dean
Until You Come Home

Find Hope.